Third Party

A novel of the 1992 Presidential Election

By Jay Beck

Published by Mindstir Media, LLC
45 Lafayette Rd | Suite 181| North Hampton, NH 03862 | USA
1.800.767.0531 | www.mindstirmedia.com

Printed in the United States of America
ISBN-13: 979-8-9856345-3-2

Other Novels by Jay Beck

Treasure Hunt

Panama's Rusty Lock

Casting Stones

Island in the Storm

MINDSTIR MEDIA

Third Party - Chapters

Preface – Berlin

Part 1 - Third Party Takes Shape

Part 2 - Just Another Day at the Office

Part 3 – Crunch time

Part 4 – Told Ya So

Afterword

Main Characters

BARTOW INDUSTRIES

William Bartow	Candidate for President
Bernice Bartow	Bartow's Wife
George Lewis	Campaign Manager
Safta Kleg	Press Secretary
Sally Crockett	Director of Volunteers
John Burchmeyer	Director of Security
Peter Newman	Comptroller, Bartow's Son-in-law
Reid Field	Administrative Director
Susan Kaufman	Deputy Director - Issues
Admiral Jeff Duncan	Temporary Vice-Presidential Candidate

REPUBLICAN CONSULTANTS

Ralph Collins	Deputy Campaign Manager
Benny Weinstein	COO Campaign Operative for Collins
Don Rizzo	Campaign Veteran
Blane Harper	Campaign Scheduler
Frank Press	Media Consultant
Chappy Knight	Media Consultant

DEMOCRATIC CONSULTANTS

Mark Young	Deputy Campaign Manager
Vicki DuVall	Issues Director, Wife of Mark Young
Ben Menendez	Field Manager
Missy Winston	Deputy Press Secretary
Letty DuVall	Vicki's Sister

Foreword

This is the third and final historical novel where a political consultant, Mark Young, is the lead character. It is an insider's look at a U.S. presidential campaign from 1992. The book tracks that campaign year and is faithful to many of the events, situations, and plans I observed while working for the third-party candidate, Ross Perot. I did use many names of real people involved in the 1992 presidential campaign as characters to add realism to the story, but used creative license and did not intend to ascribe motives, speech or actions to any persons living or deceased. Other fictional characters were created, and the reader should not assume they were based on actual persons or events.

Although this novel looks at the intrigue inside of the 1992 political campaign, the key historical elements are:

1.Before this election, most viable candidates for president worked their way through local and state government positions to the federal level. They were creatures of the political parties. For the first time, in 1992, a billionaire with no previous elective experience ran for President of the United States.

2.Ross Perot was not only the most viable third-party candidacy in U.S. history, he was also the only candidate ever to hire teams of both Democrats and Republicans to run his campaign.

3.1992 was the last time that candidates accepted the federal government matching funds to pay for the general election campaign. Both the Democratic and Republican candidates were provided funding from a small portion of federal taxes and limited the candidates to a fixed amount, which in 1992 was about $50 million each.

4.It was also the last presidential campaign where the U.S. debt and deficits were given any serious consideration. In the previous twelve years, deficit spending had become the way the government largely financed its excesses. Since 1980, balancing the budget became more of a political campaign talking point and not a realistic aspiration. At the time of this story, from the founding of the U.S.A. in 1776 until 1980, the total U.S. debt was under $1 trillion. When President Reagan left office eight years later, it was $2.9 trillion. When President Bush left four years after that, our national debt was $4.4 trillion. By that time, we were off to the races with higher and higher annual deficits adding to the debt and heading toward an eventual financial disaster.

With gratitude

I am indebted to friends who gave me helpful advice and editing suggestions for this book.

Tim Kraft is one of the best field organizers ever, and it has been a privilege to work with him over the years. I also appreciate his friendship.

Roz Thomas has been my best friend for longer than either of us will admit and has provided thoughtful suggestions and editing skills to all of my writing.

I briefly discussed the deficit and debt aspects of this story with Roy Lassiter, business associate, CPA, and manager extraordinaire, as well as Jim McIntyre, the former OMB Director under President Carter. I also spoke to Herky Harris, a savvy businessman with a history of success in financial management. Any mistakes in this book describing the deficit and debt occurred when I did not listen to them or follow their advice.

Thanks to Alyssa DuVall for her wonderful artistic design help in the cover design and other graphics.

All three of the books about political campaigns were based on my experiences, and the reason I had those opportunities was because my friend, Hamilton Jordan, allowed me to come along for the ride on an adventure that led to my career. It is an honor and a debt that can never be repaid. Hamilton brought me into the sphere of Jimmy Carter, where I was exposed to countless people gifted in intelligence, humor, ability, and the passion to make the world a better place. That world gave me proximity to the superior minds that guided most of my life and filled it with interesting friends and associates.

Preface - Berlin

Determined young men carrying sledgehammers walked the streets on a cold November night. Arriving at the brick and concrete barrier, the motley crowd took turns banging away in the blind belief that whatever they could change by its destruction would be better than what they had. It was slow going. The imposing structure was solidly built, tall and thick with rebar. Those waiting in line cheered on the others and drank cheap champagne as young women danced to loud music in the streets, with mugs of beer sloshing back and forth. As they watched the graffiti gradually disappear in chunks, they were all amazed that nobody was being shot.

Many of them were enthusiastic students not used to the heavy hammers, and they swung wildly with little effect. Yet they hoped to become instant celebrities by reshaping tyranny along with the crumbling structure into a reunified homeland. Excited, cheering young men and women stood above them on the wall, swaying suggestively back and forth, keeping time like a human metronome as the steel hammers did their work. Sturdier men wearing the scruffier jackets of laborers took their turn using industrial goggles and heavy gloves for protection from the flying sharp-edged rocks.

Progress was made through the night and into the next day as more chunks fell and smaller bits disappeared into pockets for souvenirs. Whole sections fell. Some in the crowd became tired of dangling their legs or waving defiantly for the cameras and slipped down to look for a bathroom or another drink. Still, the sharp bangs penetrated the cheers and rock music as the protesters kept at it, working to bring down the massive symbol of hate and division. Mark Young could smell alcohol and piss everywhere.

His ears hurt from the raucous cracks and steady gong-wave, pulsing noise, and he had developed a splitting head-ache. He winced as he huddled his six-foot two-inch frame across the narrow street in the fall air, absorbing this monumental event and overarching symbolism. The international press swarmed to get the best shots of the most photogenic of the protesters, the girls on the top of the wall swaying and leaking the promise of their passion to the young men showing off.

Over to his left he saw Bruce, his tough-love, manipulative mentor in the CIA, nursing a beer with a cigarette on the side of a nearby building protected from the camera's view by the edge of the alley entrance. Though hunkered in a frumpy posture, his eyes rotated back and forth like radar following years of tradecraft.

Mark noticed that as Bruce's career advanced in the agency, he had become more aware of his appearance and wore better clothes, tailored to his lumpy shape. He also had found more flattering eyeglasses, and could it be that someone was grooming his unruly hair? Was this the influence of a girlfriend? Mark wondered what kind of woman could stomach him for a long period of time.

Despite Bruce's marginal improvements in his appearance, he was one of those middle-aged men who had gained a gut that would never leave him no matter the diet he tried. He was an eternally dumpy and unattractive man, which for a field agent was not a bad quality to have, because visually above all else, he was not memorable.

He could see thinning in the mop of Bruce's hair and then quickly searched his weary reflection in a window for similar signs. Nope. So far so good. He was still a fairly fit for a man who had passed 40 and who women still noticed despite the fact he was very happily married to Vicki DuVall, who managed a team of researchers back in Washington on Capitol Hill.

Two days before, Mark had gotten the call to drop whatever he was doing and join Bruce in the center of Germany. Mark was to observe the changes in Berlin and write a memo on the impact it would have on U.S. and world politics. At first, he wondered how Bruce knew something was going to happen, then he figured, oh yeah, this was Bruce and he likely had a hand in it. No doubt elsewhere, here today, there were other CIA annalists doing the same thing perhaps with a different angle on the event, but this was the job they had assigned to him.

He turned away from the window back to his notes and wrote, 'the Berlin Wall began to crumble along with the Soviet Union on Thursday, November 9, 1989. The world changed that day.'

Part 1 – Third Party

Volunteer Room - Bartow for President

A little over two years after he had documented the fall of the Berlin wall, Mark Young entered the enormous Bartow for President volunteer room to find Sally Crockett efficiently managing an operation that involved 200 volunteers working the phones. She looked up, smiling, "Morning, Mark! You ready for me to put you to work?" Something about Mark's serious face caused Sally to come up short. "Woah. What's wrong? You look don't look so good."

Mark thought of many days he had watched her use her boundless enthusiasm to organize and motivate this incredible throng of volunteers. "Morning, Sal. I've just had a long night. Look…" He pointed to a large TV in the corner. "Do you think you can find any more of those around? There's going to be a press conference in a little while that I think all the volunteers will want to see."

"Sure. We can rig something up. What's it about?"

Mark needed to keep the message private until the candidate was ready to make his statement. "I can't go into any details, but it's important. When it starts, you need to get everyone here in front of a TV."

Sally's eyes squinted with a worried look. "Well, is there

anything wrong?"

Mark, not meeting her glance, said, "You know how things have a way of changing around here when we all least expect it."

Sally nodded, a little brighter. "You got that right. We'll have the TVs ready. Come see me later."

As he turned quickly to leave, he said softly, "You bet."

Press Announcement

In the campaign press office, a banner had been placed behind the podium with rows of "Bartow for President" logos across the cloth as a TV backdrop. The media filed in, set up cameras, and took their seats while speculating in a roaring buzz about what was going on. One of the reporters standing in front of the podium was speaking into the camera. "We're at the campaign headquarters of Bill Bartow, third-party candidate for president, who recently has taken the lead over the Democrats and Republicans in national polling. It also has been rumored that he is about to make a gigantic media buy amid potential changes in the campaign staffing. We can only speculate that is what today's press conference is about."

Just before 10:00 a.m., William Bartow, independent candidate for President of the United States; Safta Kleg, his press secretary; George Lewis, his campaign manager; and John Burchmeyer, chief of security, entered. All the television lights were turned on and everyone blinked to adjust their vision.

As the other campaign staff lined up on one wall, the short, trim Bartow strolled up to the podium and gripped it firmly with a hand on each side.

By himself in front of the banner, Bartow looked even more compressed than normal, which was accentuated by his trademark thin-lapelled dark suit and black tie. Although he looked weary, he began without any preamble. "Good morning. I've got an announcement to make, but first let me say that for the past few months I've had the privilege of traveling this great country of ours and visiting with some of the most wonderful people on the earth. Their patriotism and enthusiasm have been a source of inspiration to me, and my family and we just think the world of them for their help." Briefly, he paused and massaged the edges of the podium with his hands.

There was a slight rumbling in the press corps as they whispered to each other.

Everyone in the volunteer room was gathered in front the large TVs placed around the room. In the background, the phones were ringing, unanswered. Many of the volunteers looked a little uncertain as Bartow's voice continued from the TV.

He glanced to the left and right before continuing. "Now you all know I got into this thing because there was no one else to step forward. What I did not know at the start was the effect the campaign might have on my family." He took a deep breath. "Now, I don't mind what people might say about me or what rumors or stories they might make up. I know that's the looney tunes that you folks in the press are used to and that's fine. I'm willing to put up with all that." He stopped and sniffed.

Bartow continued, "What has happened in the past few weeks is… that there has been an increase in some of the dirty tricks and mud-wrestling coming from the other campaigns... and that's just the kind of story you folks in the media love to report, whether it is true or not. Well, now all those folks have started to come after my family. They have started telling lies and making calls at night with threats and saying they are going to do this and that." He waved one of his hands then regripped the podium.

In the volunteer room, some of the women were starting to cry. A few of the men were now sitting down and looking worried, then bewildered then frightened.

Some of the press in the room looked like they wanted to ask a question about what he was saying and started to raise their hands.

Bartow continued, ignoring the unrest of the press corps before him, "Now I'm gonna ask you folks today for once to have the decency to let me finish what I'm trying to say and not interrupt me."

At the edge of the room, George Lewis and Safta Kleg were looking sad and pained. Burchmeyer, standing next to them, was surveying the room as if there were potential terrorists in the crowd he needed to spot.

Bartow continued, "I know that's hard for you, but just for today try to use the manners your mama taught you. Now, as much as I love this country, I love my family more. If those folks doing all these dirty tricks just want to fight me, I'm here. I'm not hard to find. But they insist on taking the fight to my wife and my kids. I'm not going to stand for that." He rocked back and then continued, "Now, I'm worried more and more that my candidacy will split up the votes three ways and throw this election into the House of Representatives for them to decide who will become President. I don't think that is fair to the voters and I think it is a bad way to decide who will lead our country. As much as I want to continue this campaign, I'm going to stop it today. That does not mean I won't keep speaking out when I feel it's right to do so. But I'm not going to put my good family through this meatgrinder any longer, and that's pretty much all I have to say."

As Bartow turned to leave the room, the press corps collectively jumped out of their seats and moved toward the podium, shouting questions. Several security people immediately rushed forward to form a wall in front of Bartow as Burchmeyer led him toward the exit. The press corps continued to howl at him as he left the room.

George Lewis pushed off the wall and ran after him down the corridor leading from press room to catch up with Bartow before he reached the vehicles waiting at the service entrance. "Bill! Bill! Wait up!"

Bartow stopped, turned to face Lewis, and said, "Glad that's over. Come on over to my office later and we'll talk."

"But, Bill, we've got all the campaign staff and everyone assembled in the volunteer room. They'll want to hear from you, and they need to see you."

Bartow flinched and his eyes hardened. "They don't need to see me. I've done all of this I'm going to do for today. You go talk to them."

Lewis panicked and reached out to touch Bartow on his sleeve. "But, Bill, they were here for you. They believe in you.

You can't just walk out on them."

Bartow, now with anger in his rising voice, said, "I never walked out on anything in my life. I did this for my family. You just heard me. I don't owe anybody anything. Play them the tape. I need to be with my family right now and that's where I'm going."

Bartow turned, jerked away from Lewis, and walked with the security detail towards the door leading outside to his car.

Lewis was now red-faced. "Are you just going to... My God! Those poor people."

The motorcade of Bartow and his security roared out of parking garage past handheld TV cameras and people running after the vehicles. John Burchmeyer's stern face could be seen reflected in the window glass looking for threats in the crowd.

In the volunteer room, groups of people were in shock, and many wept. The phones were still ringing. Sally Crockett sat looking out at the cavernous room, ashen-faced. The door opened and George Lewis; Reid Field, chief administrative officer; Mark Young, co-campaign advisor; and Ben Menendez, head of the field operations, entered, all with extremely long faces. Missy Wilson, deputy press secretary, had set up a microphone and speaker near Sally Crockett's desk. Lewis looked over at the microphone and slowly walked up to it. Field, Young, and Menendez shuffled off to the side.

As Lewis gathered his thoughts, he looked over the crowd slowly. "What happened today... is difficult for us all... the people here in this room are winners. Mr.... Mr. Bartow had to leave... and asked me to..." Lewis looked down and his shoulders began to shake. Sally Crockett rose, walked over, and gave him a hug. She moved past him and positioned herself behind the microphone as he stepped back next to the wall, fighting to regain his composure.

She glanced around the enormous room for a moment before speaking. "What George wanted to say is how much everyone involved has appreciated all of you and the thousands and, I guess, millions of volunteers across the country who have given so much to this effort. We have all spent many long hours for many long days here together working to make our country better. No one will forget what you have done. You have been the backbone of the movement. We're all just sorry that it did not work out."

One of the volunteers in the back of the room shouted, "We ain't done yet!"

There were cheers from the others.

Now another volunteer shouted, "This ain't over. We'll be back."

In the front of the room, members of the management team stood silently with George Lewis and Sally, who were now standing next to each other. Sally was biting her lip. Another volunteer shouted, "We think you're great. We're ready to set things straight any time."

One shouted, "Yeah. The problems that brought us here have not gone away."

There were loud cheers.

Another shouted, "We're gonna fight on."

There were bigger cheers.

Radio Star

Six months before Bartow's announcement, Mark Young was listening as the smug voice of the radio personality bullied his listeners with rapid-fire overconfidence on his mid-day talk radio program. "What is wrong with America anymore?" As he paused to let that sink in, the sound of the creaky chair could be heard rocking back and forth, made unstable by his massive stomach.

With perfect timing, he leaned into the microphone and continued, "We're running up on the 1992 presidential election with a bunch of losers. Doesn't anyone in politics have any cojones? We've got a bunch of idiots ruining the Democrats AND the Republicans." There was a slight pause to the sound of ruffling papers. "The Democrats have got themselves led by a corn-pone doofus and the Republicans a silk-stocking namby-pamby. You have heard me say for the past three years that we need to stay tough and strong and not even think of letting any third-rate, Third World, third choice, wishy washy wusses get elected dogcatcher. Can I get a 'Yes, sir' out there?" He leaned over to check the lines to see how many were already lit. His staff screened them carefully and only allowed fawning fans or inarticulate callers who had the gall to disagree and who he could humiliate and crush over whatever subject was at hand.

He quickly turned back to the microphone. "I've been hoping. No! I've been holding out hope that there would be a massive rebound. I've been holding out a prayer that the president could pull this thing out, but it doesn't look like that's gonna happen, and I have my career to think about. My God!" The sound of a newspaper rattled. "Did you see what happened last week? We've got a Republican president... a Republican who is so removed from reality he can't even use the scanner to check out of a grocery store. What's the world coming to?"

There was the sound of a breath expelled in disgust. "Jeez. You folks out there would not listen to me unless I continued to tell you the unfiltered truth, and I'm about the only one who gives it to you straight and filled with prophecy. Let me tell you, the mood of this country is not where I am right now. So, my friends and listeners, I've decided that I'm the one that's gonna have to change it. I have accepted the challenge to have the courage to make a change, and I'm ready to lead the charge. I am here today to tell you that, and listen up, folks... I may be the only one who understands the mood of the majority of the people in this country.

"We've got the liberals spending money we don't have, on things we don't need, in places we've never heard of. We've got conservatives, CONSERVATIVES, my God, racking up deficit spending like they don't know any better. They both are doing the same thing, wrecking the economy of our government and our country. What are we gonna do?!

"If they let me in there with a chainsaw and a weed eater, I'd get Congress and the White House straightened out in a day. Just LOOK at these news headlines." There was the again the sound of a newspaper rattling.

"Public 'Fed Up' with Washington."

"What happened to our leadership?"

"Polls say... Independent movement is growing!"

"Public rally in Kansas City draws three hundred protesters to complain about our government!"

"Somebody do something, please."

"Self-organized independents meet through notice from an email string."

"Well, my friends, I'm not sure what an email string is. I'm only interested if that is wrapped around a stripper. But something is going on and let's hope the public in America is finally about to rise up and kick some government ass. You heard it here first. Can I get a 'Yes sir'?"

Mark Young shook his head as he turned down the radio. He was driving home from dropping off a memo at CIA headquarters in Langley, Virginia. He thought that occasionally it was amusing to hear the theatrics of feigned outrage by the new crop of rabble-rousing radio celebrities, popular more for their entertainment value than any news importance or political acumen. This one specialized in bullying his listeners to agree with him about anything he said or they would be seen as naïve to the realities of current politics and the world at large.

Mark was worried how these loud voices were becoming more influential in political circles, like so much TV wrestling. He wondered if voters actually considered issues or ideas when supporting any political position. The revelry and fantasy of these talking heads was forming public opinion much more than any facts or research. Much of what they said was total fabrication.

There was a change in the air. Maybe that should be the subject of his next memo. There was a public attraction toward these quirky, simplistic, and untried diversions. It was as though the unknown theories of hucksters held more promise than the plodding and predictable news organizations with proven investigation and analysis. The public was asking for somebody else out there to 'fix this thing.' People were choosing sizzle and instant gratification for leaders over the old, comfortable politicians. Before, leaders had been selected for stability, decorum, and a reasoned process, but that system was getting shaky. Like the massive ego of the radio guy said, "What are ya gonna do?"

Oh well, that was not his job. He had a part-time consulting arrangement with the CIA to write memos about international and domestic politics. He was not sure they were ever read, but the extra money was a benefit to him, his wife Vicki, and their young daughter, Olivia, and it provided the basis of a trust for the child's college fund. Vicki had pared back her job as a researcher and information manger on Capitol Hill several years ago to be with their daughter after their marriage and only returned to the Hill, where she was still in great demand, part-time over the last two years.

During the same time, Mark had begun his CIA indoctrination and trained in southeast Virginia at the marshy lowland

9,000-acre Camp Peary near Williamsburg, also known as the Farm. There his old proficiency at weapons from hunting during his South Georgia childhood and time in Vietnam paid off with high marks in the firearms course and proficiency in hand-to-hand. He also trained in the growing field of computers, communications, new technology, and other spy-related stuff, which he reckoned he'd never use. So far, his main task had been to analyze foreign campaigns and election situations and handicap the outcomes of political conflicts. There were hits and misses, and he had been amazed to learn how many people had similar roles as part-time consultants to the agency.

He was surprised that his analysis of foreign governments oftentimes reflected U.S. domestic politics as well. He had thought that the FBI handled the U.S. mainland and that the CIA was offshore. It's true there was overlap, but it seemed Bruce, his boss at the agency, was actually interested in how international trends might influence the inclinations of domestic presidential candidates and ranking members of key Congressional committees. Mark often wondered what they did with the information he gave them.

Several years before, Mark had met the unlikable CIA agent, Bruce, during an election campaign in Panama. He had reconnected with the same agent when he was involved in a political campaign in Greece. At that time, unusual circumstances resulted in the defection of a top Soviet Embassy official and the theft by the CIA of an extremely valuable Greek sculpture that previously had been unknown.

His income as a political consultant had been increasing for statewide races so with that compensation and his CIA supplement, he could now back off from the rapid pace of work he had endured for over 20 years. Now he could pick his shots. The new work environment enabled him to spend more time at home with Vicki and Livy. He realized there was no compensation that could match coming home to have Livy jump up in his lap, lean into his chest, and look up to tell him what she had been doing that day.

A few years earlier, he had worked for his friend, Angus

Whelan, in a several exciting international campaigns and he continued to see his old friend occasionally, but he was relieved not to be flying off to some distant country to help him with yet another campaign. That part of his life had been fascinating, but now it was time to stay home.

Though her work commitment was part-time, Vicki was actually a key person in the Congressional Research Service of the Library of Congress. They had a comfortable family income and both felt personal and professional satisfaction. Fortunately, whenever they were overwhelmed with work, Vicki's sister, Letty DuVall, recently divorced and living nearby in Bethesda, Maryland, loved to babysit her niece whenever the opportunity rose. She was fun and competent, bright and interested in everything, even though a hesitance in Letty's hazel eyes revealed the appearance of someone who had known too much loss. Having her as part of their family was a benefit to them all.

Bartow Announces

That night, Mark turned on CNN to watch Larry King hosting his talk show behind thick glasses and wearing his trademark wide suspenders over a dark blue shirt and floral tie. As Mark settled down, he moved several magazines and an old newspaper off the couch and noticed that a brochure for the expensive Montessori private primary school had once again found its way to the top of the pile.

King's visitor tonight was an eccentric billionaire from Georgia named William Bartow, who filled the screen with his close-cropped head, plain face, and pinched shoulders as he began to talk in a folksy, twangy voice. "So, it's like this, if that crowd in Washington can't get their heads screwed on straight and figure out how to run this great country with the respect it deserves, then someone else should step in and give them a hand."

As Bartow was speaking, Larry King, smiling at his guest, listened to his producer through the earpiece. "The lines are already lit up. He's got an opinion on everything and doesn't mind sharing it. People love that. No telling what he'll say next. Push him!"

King leaned forward on his elbow and nodded warmly to his familiar guest. He knew just how much he needed to lead Bartow to get the response he desired. "Gosh, Bill, who'd you have in mind?"

Bartow, still playing his role as a semi-celebrity commentator known for giving off-the-cuff remarks, sat back stiffly in his narrow-lapelled dark suit and thin black tie. He appeared to be someone unaccustomed to the polish and verve of television commentators, which validated his authenticity. "Well, there are any number of capable people out there, but if one of them doesn't step forward, some people have talked to me about giving it a shot."

King, now seeing ratings gold by creating real news and not just rehashing tired suppositions, smiled softly, squinted, and affected a puzzled look as though he was unsure of what William Bartow meant. He cocked his head. "I'm not sure what you just said. You're telling me right here, right now, on this show, tonight… that you are considering a run for the presidency of the United States?"

Bartow made a slight jerk with his shoulders, as though he had never thought of the idea before that moment. He leaned back slightly, apparently taken aback by King's suggestion, then shrugged. "Well, here's as good a place as any, and I'm only saying that if these folks we have running now don't come to their senses and see what this endless partisan bickering is doing to our country, and if no one else steps forward, and if the people want me to run, then I guess there is no way in good conscience not to get on out there."

King, thinking quickly of how he could milk this admission into promotional spots for his program and make it onto other networks' news, decided to draw out this conversation as much as he dared. "Well, Bill Bartow, self-made man and billionaire from Atlanta, Georgia, what would it really take, bottom line now, to ensure that you were going to get into the race?"

Bartow, still sounding as thought he was making his comments up as he went along, mused, "Larry, if one million people from across this great nation of ours call my office in Atlanta by the end of this month and ask me to run or sign a petition asking me to run, I'm in."

King, now legitimately gushing with this career-making television coup, smiled broadly, leaned back in his chair, and said, "This is just great news. We've got to take a break now, and when we come back, we'll have the number on the screen for you to call if you want this very successful man to run for president. We'll be taking your phone calls right here in the studio with none other than Bill Bartow himself."

Mark thought to himself, *The guy is a ratings magnet. The media are going to be fighting to have him on TV, and if for no other reason, that free exposure will make him viable.*

Bernice Bartow

William Bartow's security dropped him at his enormous house just off Tuxedo Drive in the Buckhead section of Atlanta near the Governor's mansion. As he stepped from the limo, he paused to look back over the expansive lawn sloping down through manicured shrubs banked with pine straw and fertilized flower beds to the street below. He felt nervous for the first time since he had left the CNN studio. Looking through the window, he could see that his wife of almost forty years, Bernice, was waiting up for him, sitting with the effortless grandeur of the super-rich.

As he entered the den lined with stained, oak-paneled walls, Bernice sat down her crystal glass with a clunk onto the mahogany table, turned her head slightly at an angle, and with her calm but strong demeanor asked, "What did you just do tonight?"

Bartow stopped dead still for a moment, before continuing to sit down opposite her in one of the handmade wingback chairs by the massive cast-stone fireplace. "Well, it was sort of a spur-of-the-moment thing. I… I got caught up in the energy of the program and it felt… I don't know… I felt sort of compelled to say what I did." Bernice leaned forward to speak and Bartow continued before she had a chance. "I've been training for this all my life. I know I can do it."

She closed her dark blue eyes demonstratively then opened them to give him the look he always dreaded. "Won't this invade your family's privacy? Isn't this something you should have talked to me, to us about?"

Bartow squirmed as he adjusted himself, sliding back in the chair, his feet now just touching the floor. "Yeah. You're right. I should have, but it just happened. I'll make sure this doesn't bother you and the kids. I'll…"

"Bill, you just told everyone in America, in the world, that you were going to run for President of the United States. You let that creepy nerd bait you."

"Wasn't like that. We're buddies, kind of. He's trying to help me. He respects me. Look, I know that I'm smarter and a better manager than either Bush or Clinton. I—"

Bernice stood suddenly, cutting him off. "You should have discussed it with the family. WE needed to be prepared for this. And, Bill, being smart or a good manager is not what gets someone elected president. You've worked hard all your life in an area where you know what you are doing. You're the best at real estate management there is. You have built a great team to support you. This political thing is…" She took a deep breath. "You've never gotten into anything like this before. NOW you are suddenly wanting to start at the top?"

Playing catch-up, Bartow sputtered, "I'll get George Lewis to help and we can hire the nuts and bolts people." He pointed through the beveled glass window. "The people out there like me. They want me to help them straighten this country out."

Bernice sighed and shook her head. "You owed us a warning. Just promise me that the campaign thing will not hurt our family. I've always supported you and will again in this... thing. Just don't let it invade us."

As Mark had predicted, the media exploded with Bartow's announcement. Reporting on a legitimate third-party candidate who was quirky on camera would churn the news programs, and that would give a shot to the ratings. Bartow's office was besieged with media calls for interviews, as well as requests for him to run. People wanted to know who he was, what he stood for, and what he planned to do. Bartow and his office reeled from the onslaught. Bill Bartow did not have a clue what to do about any of it.

Volunteers

Outside a strip mall in Akron, Ohio, near the Discount Dollar Store, two collapsible six-foot tables were manned by people with folding metal chairs behind handmade signs reading Bartow Speaks my Language and Sign up for Bartow taped to the front surface edges. Behind them on the broad walkway between the parking lot and the store entrances, others paraded up and down, directing the surprised shoppers to the tables where they were encouraged to sign petitions being offered on several clipboards.

One volunteer worker had already made silkscreen T-shirts overnight to advertise their cause. Messages on the shirts of the workers read: Take back America, Stand up for Bartow, and Run Bartow Run.

A self-appointed leader gave orders to several others who appeared eager to help. "Take those extra T-shirts to the folks over on West Market Street. And tell them to make sure you can read everyone's name, phone number, and address on those sign-up lists."

He turned to another woman and said, "Dorothy, can you come back on Saturday? We're going to go to the big mall over near the intersection with I-76."

"Yeah. You bet. We're serious. I've got my kids helping." She continued toward her car.

The man shouted after her, "Send a fax to tell the others to come." He turned to a shopper who was approaching the table. "Hey, you look like a smart lady. Would you like to sign up to have a fresh face and a new party in American politics?"

As the activity swirled, a local TV crew jumped out of a van to record what was going on. After observing for a few minutes, a reporter edged to the side of the man who seemed to be in charge. She waited for a truck to pass then turned to face the camera, making sure she was in the camera frame, and asked, "So, can you tell us what you are doing and who you are working for?" Then she turned to hold the microphone closer to the man, after making sure she would continue to be seen on camera while he answered.

In the background by the entrance to the store, volunteers were continuing to get shoppers to sign the petition. Several people waved Bartow T-shirts or held up handmade posters towards the camera. The man wearing a slightly puzzled look spoke questioningly to the pretty lady holding a microphone in his face. "Didn't you see William Bartow on the Larry King TV show? We're working for the American people to help him get elected president." He turned away from her to hand over more forms to one of the volunteers who were signing up people on the petition.

The reporter, first checking again to see that she and the man were in the frame together and trying to give context and deeper meaning to her interview, tapped him on the shoulder and turned him to face her again. She looked past him at the tables, chairs, people carrying signs, and then back to him again now, expecting an answer that would explain the piece to her news director. She asked with a big smile, "What is it exactly you people are trying to do here?"

The man stared back at her. Then he said, "Lady, we're getting names on a petition to get Bill Bartow's name on the ballot. People are doing this everywhere. That's what you have to do to run as an independent." Then, with confusion on his face, he added, "Don't you know that?"

G.H.W. Bush

Except for a few top advisors in hushed backroom meetings, there was a big secret inside the White House in January of 1992. George Herbert Walker Bush was not sure he wanted to run for re-election. Bush had put in his time, paid his dues, and, as Ronald Reagan's vice president, was next in line to run for president as a Republican. He had won in the 1988 general election over a weak candidate, and yeah, they had whipped Saddam Hussein only a year ago, but now the economy was tanking. He was taking hits from the Democrats and even those from the far right in his own party. It was a hard job.

George Bush was basically a nice man. He had been embarrassed by the elements of racism in his campaign's 1988 commercials, and his wife Barbara did not enjoy life in the White House spotlight. He was, however, besieged by a collection of Republican consultants, officeholders, and even some in his own family to suck it up and make the effort. Too many people had too much to lose.

The Southern sparkler that had run the campaign to elect President Bush in 1988, Lee Atwater, had died recently of a brain tumor. Without his now-deceased first-among-equals to guide the effort, the 1992 campaign was taking shape as an embarrassment of riches with a cluster of managers. With his status as an incumbent president running for re-election came wads of money and tons of advice. The campaign struggled to jam all the cooks into the kitchen. The gaggle of second-tier egos contriving for excuses to get into the room for the big meetings were never fully placated.

The flashy, gilded effort was led by the blue blood Robert Adam Mosbacher, Sr., who had the title of campaign chairman. Other roles were sought for the abundance of talent that lined up early, ready and more than willing to work to keep the presidency in Republican hands. Frederic V. Malek, veteran of managing Republican conventions and OMB, as well as being known earlier for ferreting out the 'too influential' Jews in the Labor Department for Richard Nixon, was named as campaign manager. Malek's job was to keep the trains running on time. Veteran pollster Robert M. Teeter was the chief political strategist. Mary Matalin, wife of the man running the Clinton campaign, was the token woman and political director for Bush and was tasked with running the day-to-day campaign activities. Veteran political manager and par excellence government official, James A. Baker, III, kibitzed on the side and helped in fundraising. President Bush's rough-edged oldest son, George W. Bush, was at the campaign without a well-defined role, but his aggressive demeanor and unfiltered access to the candidate put him in most key meetings.

Down the list, among the other Republican operatives elbowing for room, was Charles Black, who was named senior campaign adviser. He was the person channeling the spirit of Atwater as a southern strategist and tasked with putting a sharp edge into the campaign. Black represented not the blue-blood, white-shoe mainstream Republicans most comfortable with Bush, but the increasingly vocal far right wing. He was senior partner at a lobbying firm that represented the interests of many shady offshore clients. Black knew he could call on two of his partners, Paul Manafort and Roger Stone, to handle the backdoor dealings for him in the campaign. His junior partners had cut their teeth in the Young Republican politics of the late '70s and early '80s. Atwater had been a partner in his firm and all of the Bush people hoped the amiable Charlie Black had the ability to revitalize the campaign and add the magic and passion of his former colleague.

William Jefferson Clinton

James Carville, just arrived back in his Washington, D.C., office from Little Rock, was anxious to see the latest polling results. He sat with his feet crossed on the corner of his desk, squinting at the numbers comparing his democratic candidate, the former governor of Arkansas, William Jefferson Clinton, with President Bush. Now the pollsters were adding the public opinion results from the upstart Bill Bartow from Georgia. The quirky newcomer had suddenly announced a third-party run on a TV program and already millions of people claimed him as their favorite. The SOB had never held office and did not even have a campaign! He was unknown and yet all these people were telling the pollsters they wanted him to be their president. It was nuts.

Carville had assumed that a wealthy, successful business-man with a history of pro-military activities would pull support from the Republicans and be a benefit to a moderate Southern Democrat. He understood that Bartow's popularity was because no one knew anything about the guy and just assumed that he was somebody they could like. This poll, however, showed an almost equal theft of backers from both his guy and President Bush. The billionaire whacko also pulled from the independents and undecideds. Damn.

Bartow was sure to screw up and tank once he was forced to take some real positions, or his unscripted mouth got his foot stuck in it, but for now, he was unexpected trouble. Clinton needed to show steady progress, which would be more prob-lematic with this oddball in the race. He'd recommend to Clin-ton that he should ignore this Bartow guy for now and hope the novice politician would self-destruct. In the interim, he'd get some new opposition research going. It was not enough that he had to contend with the Republicans and his own candidate's unhealthy impulses, now this third-party nut ball was making it all the harder to figure out what to do.

Before Bartow, he had hoped that the growing group of disaffected independents would see his guy as the place to go instead of a silk-stocking dilettante with a summer home in Kennebunkport, Maine.

Just damn.

You would think that after growing up in Louisiana, and being involved in Southern politics, he'd have heard more about Bartow when he ran Zell Miller's campaign for Georgia governor in 1990. But in that campaign, Bill Bartow was just some rich contributor with a quirky affection for the military, not that those sentiments weren't common in Georgia. This guy had to be some kind of a crackpot to think he could just step into a presidential race, and as a third-party candidate, no less. He had no infrastructure. He called George Stephanopoulos to start some research on Bartow, to find his weaknesses. The rich guy simply had to have some.

Runaway Train

John Burchmeyer was a former airborne ranger with one job: to protect William Bartow. He was not a big man, but he had a sharp-edged, trim, lean body and no-nonsense eyes that commanded attention. Just after midnight, he checked with the security guard on his new digital Motorola International 3200 portable shoe-sized phone to ensure the cleaning crews were out of the building.

It was just him and the boss entering the underground parking of the Bartow Plaza building in his large SUV with the tinted windows. He used his special magnetic key pass to access the newly established campaign offices on the ground floor of the expansive concourse. They left the main lights off and found their way using the luminous glow from the outside streetlights plus a few security lights near the elevators and stairs.

Although it was still early in the campaign, he was amazed at the job the Bartow administrative staff had done throughout the massive lobby to create an open office configuration with rows of well over a hundred folding tables and chairs. Nobody was better at this stuff than Bartow Industries. The desk surfaces of the volunteers were already becoming crowded with personal photos, in and out files, and coffee cups with their names on them or messages like "World's Best Dad." He looked at the expansive ceiling, high above, ghost-like in the dark with the light from the street outside diminishing as it filtered up several floors into a hazy, brooding heaven. Their footfalls echoed in the empty industrial cathedral.

Walking beside Burchmeyer, William Bartow ambled uneasily, noting all the changes. Years ago, he'd ordered elaborate decorations to make this a jaw-dropping place to inspire anyone bringing prospective business deals through the rotating doors. Before the recent change, there had been large trees, a giant sculpture, and a well-appointed common area shining in tasteful metallic and leather lounge furniture. Now, the shambles of its appearance unsettled him.

The place now had a warehouse look of commonplace humanity and the smell of stale coffee. All that he had built over the many years of carefully grooming his public persona had been swept away and replaced with this glorified call center staffed by strangers he had not vetted, saying things about him he had not approved.

A shock came over him that the junky desks and accoutrement of the great unwashed had become his public face. It was such a complete antithesis of how he had planned and carefully grown his career that he should be represented by this communal, tasteless circus. As he walked through the lobby, he could see lists of names and phone numbers, pads of notes, all of it so far removed from who he was. His career and reputation were at risk here in the hands of strangers. These people were now working diligently to make him bit by bit into something new, something foreign to the person he had worked so hard to become, something middling and humdrum. This public thing was not who he was or had ever intended to be.

Then he noticed there were phones ringing all over the office—here, then there, then over there. Who could have been calling at this time of night? Did they not know the time here in Georgia? What could those people be doing with their lives to want to call a political campaign in the middle of the night? No one was answering, but after a few rings, the phones would stop and others start. He imagined an enormous answering machine filling with these random callers asking God knows what—and a chill came over him as he stared at the chaos.

From this mess an idea was taking root about how his achievements gave him the capability to solve all of the nation's problems, and that made all these faceless people respect him. Yes, this had somehow become his reward after many years of building up his company by his own hands with little help and support. Yes, it was about his coming out ahead on all those deals where he got the best of everyone and made them grovel or acquiesce to his demands. His success was coming home.

The phones continued to ring.

But this muddle? What was this place? What was the purpose of this space all about—with the phones ringing and all those blackboards and charts on easels along the sides of the room with names and flowcharts and organizational charts? Over by the far wall, there were maps of the entire United States and then various state maps. What the hell did all this clutter mean? Did anyone know what was going on here? He felt very uncomfortable to have turned his life over to this chaos. The mess here did not look like success.

This lobby, his lobby was now a place of ghosts and spirits that were taking away his soul and his fortune, and he had no control over what was happening or how to stop it or to control it. He had to do something to grab control of this runaway train before it was too late… but what?

Bartow was determined the next day to find a way to run his own show. A plan formed in his mind about what he must do. He knew that he always must be in charge. He could never let anyone see he was not the person in control, and to do that he could never be wrong, never admit any mistake. He needed a direct method to let people know what he thought. If he said something, or gave an order, then those other people down the campaign organization chart would parrot what he said and follow his lead. Maybe television could help him to do that.

Most importantly, he needed to say what he thought. Those pollster people, speechwriters, issue annalists—they all just made up bullshit. He'd contributed to other campaigns where he'd seen campaign managers and outside consultants make candidates into stick-figure puppets. That was not going to happen to him.

The rest of this campaign business would have to react to him and follow what he wanted, then whatever else they did would not matter. They could do whatever they did to get the votes and run the campaign mechanics in the back room. He would decide what the product was, lay out its specs, and course correct for quality control. He would run the boardroom.

They could be the manufacturers, advertisers, and distributors. That approach would work.

Third Party

Campaign Manager

George Lewis, one of Atlanta, Georgia's most successful lawyers, finished turning over the growing firm's remaining business to one of his partners. Although they handled a variety of legal issues for a number of clients, the firm's anchor was Bartow Industries. They got the job twenty-five years ago when the dynamic William Bartow was just emerging from being a successful local real estate developer to become the owner of a vast empire of national business interests. The law firm rode the wave with him as he bought and sold companies with abandon, usually with an upward trajectory of income and profits.

Over time, the firm expanded through various legal negotiations into the areas of business, environment, labor, bankruptcy, tax, real estate, and litigation, and their bottom line grew much larger over the years. They were experts at contracts.

The firm had also become proficient in representing Mr. Bartow in litigation, as conflicts were inevitable in the atmosphere of real estate deals, high finance, and moving around large companies—taking parts off here and adding them there. Lewis had seen plenty of compromises and unpleasant situations, but he had adapted to the aggression needed to be successful for his family and everyone in the firm who depended on him. Bartow had made the firm a success and had made George Lewis into a celebrity lawyer.

He protected them all from the Bill Bartow no one would ever wish to know. Sometimes the restructuring involved gutting the company's assets, selling off the parts, firing hordes of employees, and securing the remaining cash in Bartow Industries' growing portfolio of liquid interests.

Over time, Lewis and Bartow came to know each other quite well because many of these deals resulted in long and contentious meetings—battles, actually—negotiating the finer points of creating a fortune. Some referred to George Lewis as Bartow's adopted son, although they had always retained a professional demeanor with a thin wall of propriety between them, as well as mutual respect.

As Lewis became a smooth and polished lawyer, he learned to read Bartow's moods in difficult circumstances and knew his anger and the lethal focus he could apply to win a contest where money was at stake. He had covered for Bartow in unpleasant and even repulsive situations. He protected him from financial and moral harm through well-timed roadblocks thrown in front of opponents at unexpected moments that usually guaranteed their acquiescence. His legal footwork had made Lewis over $100 million while helping Bartow's net worth exceed several billion.

Lewis shielded his family from Bartow's rough edges. He did what he had to do to sustain their wealth and comfort, particularly for his wife, who cared for their autistic son. His son's affliction prevented the family from partaking in many of the social interactions enjoyed by others in their economic class.

Although Bill and Bernice could be demanding, they understood close relationships and were generous in their support of George and his family. Bartow showed loyalty where the families of his associates were concerned.

When Bartow impulsively threw his hat into the ring to run for President of the United States, one of his first calls was to George Lewis to ask him to manage the campaign. Lewis had supervised a campaign for the governor of Georgia 10 years ago and continued to be active in the state's Republican party. However, he felt woefully unqualified to take on a presidential campaign for a third party.

At the same time, he felt compelled to agree to Bartow's request. His fortune and that of the flamboyant billionaire were inextricably linked, and he had witnessed Bartow's vindictiveness when he did not get his way. He was hooked, and he wondered what soul-twisting things he might have to do for Bartow this time. So, after discussing the situation in a cautionary weekend with his family, he began calling friends around the country to recruit campaign talent for the first third-party candidate in U.S. history with a realistic chance of winning.

The Berlin Report

Bruce angrily pushed away the newspapers and files scattered on his desk in his Langley, Virginia, office. He was frustrated with the political environment. His bosses at the CIA wanted certainty, and he did not know what to say when they asked, "What the hell is going on with the U.S. election?"

Who would have thought a rich business guy, a third-party loose cannon with a wild demeanor and squeaky voice, could have captured the imagination of what… something like over 10% of the U.S. electorate? The American public were becoming more unpredictable every day. Forty percent had yet to make a choice.

Then he remembered a report that Mark Young had written two years earlier about the consequences of the Berlin Wall coming down. Mark had blamed the Soviet collapse on the philosophical ineptitude of communism and the inability of the moribund Soviet organizational system to be productive, plus a lack of money to fund any of its ideas or buy the loyalty in marginal countries, as they had done in the past.

But there was something else in the summary he was half remembering now. He pulled the report from the files for another read. He perused the document as Marks's characteristic non-governmental language jumped about from one idea to the other. Bruce flipped over to the conclusion section.

United States Domestic Political Implications After the Fall of the Berlin Wall

Executive Summary

The Berlin wall fell on top of the polite predictability of American domestic politics.

For over 40 years, patriotism has been defined by who was more vehemently against communism. Since World War II, all successful presidential candidates needed to have a military record or have been in the forefront of anti-communism—the one area where both the Democrats and Republicans agreed.

Fear of the Soviet Union has been the common focus that bound us to a stable political nationalism. Although it has not completely collapsed, it's leaning over with one foot in the air and the other on a banana peel. Now who or what will replace it as our convenient external villain?

Without a stalwart Soviet menace, how will Congress and the executive branch justify unlimited funding for excessive defense spending? Will we now actually examine the viability of proposed weapons systems? Will congressional representatives stop asking Congress for more military bases for their districts?

What will the defense contractors do to attract support of those elected officials if they can't spread construction projects all over the country into every key congressional district? Now how will our politicians show off their macho? How will our left and right pull together in a crisis if there is no mutual enemy to hate?

The Center

It is a distinct possibility that without the Soviet Union as an existential threat, Democrats and Republicans will become polarized on the end fringes of the left and right where often the loudest voice in the room will carry the day. Policy needs may be replaced by puppy love for glamorous candidates.

Politics may become mud wrestling to guarantee a large television audience. Simple messages will diminish facts. Truth will be a casualty. The electorate will divide into smug camps of the like-minded. People will wish to reinforce what they already believe, even if it involves the addition of fantasy.

Currently, our elections are usually determined by those undecideds sitting in between the extremes of liberal and conservative. The radicals in both traditional parties could become more popular, galvanizing the left and right and pushing moderates toward the center. Moderates from both parties will feel alienated. The tug-of-war for those undecideds will be what future elections will be about.

However, that assumes there will only be two choices. Could this environment create an inclination among registered voters to split their votes roughly into thirds, of liberal, conservative, and moderate? An undefined, amorphous, and welcoming center might emerge to challenge both opposite ends. That would put elections even more up in the air.

A politician running a centrist campaign could draw support from both sides of the U.S. political spectrum. This grouchy, disaffected center of independents could make up the third leg of a political stool. Think third party.

A third-party candidate with charisma and money could pull from the disaffected voters on both the left and right and cobble together a winning 35% or even greater. This hypothesis increases the potential for charlatans and posers to become candidates on either end of the political spectrum.

In the past, U.S. politics with a common external enemy maintained the semblance of collegiality. Now, the techniques for deceit and treachery we have known in foreign intrigue could become a part of our political system. Cold war psychological weapons may now be unrestrained to discredit, trick, cheat, and lie on our shores.

Politicians will find it's easier to get people to hate and fear an idea rather than to love its opposite. The work ethic present in the daily grind of politically honest labor could be replaced by the itch for a lottery. Competitive politicians will sell tickets to watch things sizzle.

End

He put the memo down.

What if Mark was right? He leaned back in his chair and wondered. Would that development be good or bad for him?

Then he pulled the research file on Bartow and remembered that he had been very supportive of the families of veterans, even quietly and out of the media spotlight, which meant he was sincere. A few years ago, they set up a family foundation and had awarded a Soldier of the Year prize for valor both in the field and at home doing charity work or helping other soldiers. That would play well if it were publicized like it would be in a campaign.

He was relatively unknown outside business circles, and he had the money to create an attractive image of himself. He was not controlled by any institution, and that meant he was ill-informed about America's international interests. That also meant he was perhaps easily influenced and unpredictable. This guy was a threat to the status quo and needed closer watching. A plan to get involved began to form in Bruce's mind.

Mark Young

Mark Young, now 43 years old, had become a well-known domestic and international political consultant. He sat at his computer credenza, where he had been typing on his word processor, and squinted to read what he had written earlier on the small, dim screen. The phone started to ring, and he looked around his home office at the scattered clothes magazines and newspapers in piles. His eyes landed on CNN murmuring softly in background with the volume low. His wife, Vicky, called for him to pick up the phone as she was getting their six-year-old daughter dressed for a trip to the National Zoo. Mark fully muted the TV and picked up the phone to hear, "This is the White House operator, please stand by for Mr. Walter Wallace."

Wallace's booming voice, deepened from his early years as a military officer drilling groups of soldiers on a parade ground, said, "Hello, Mark. You'll never believe who just called to check you out." He was surprised to hear from Walter, whose duties on the National Security Council staff kept him rather busy.

Mark smiled, remembering the big, gregarious Wallace, whom he had met after he returned from Vietnam but before he left the military. "No. I probably wouldn't. Check me out for what?"

"You met George Lewis a couple years ago when you were working on the Senate race in Georgia. He's the guy who is the lawyer for William Bartow."

Mark did remember. "Yeah. He was a nice guy. But he's a Republican, isn't he? What would he want with me?"

"Hey. Don't knock us Republicans. Anyway, he read the piece you wrote for *Campaigns and Elections* about the opening for a third party this year and he wanted to know if you really were dissatisfied enough with my boss, President Bush, and that guy from Arkansas, to consider working for an independent."

"Well, it would depend on who it was. Like I said in the article, the time is right for a fresh face that could challenge both political parties. As you know, I've mostly worked for Democrats. Although, right now, I think both parties are bankrupt. Both are becoming captive to the extremes on either end of the political spectrum."

"Mark, you can save the speech, and no offense taken, although I think my guy is doing just fine. We did kick Saddam's ass and saved Kuwait, as you may remember. We're gonna get re-elected. No sweat. Well, what do you think about William Bartow?"

"I think he's rich, like in the multibillion range. He seems to be right wing and patriotic. He must have some skills and ability to have built up those businesses, and I remember reading somewhere he has been generous in helping others. I saw him on Larry King, but if he's really serious about running... God! I don't know. Does the guy know what he would be getting into? What does he stand for? You know, all that."

"Well, Lewis wanted to see if you would consider coming to Atlanta to talk about... all that."

"Sure, I'm for anything that can shake up what we have now."

"Aren't you originally from Georgia?"

"Yes."

"So, you know this guy?"

"Nah. Never met him. I've been gone a long time, and I think his only involvement with politics has been to write a check."

"Well, you'll probably be hearing from Lewis or one of his associates. Anyway, I've delivered the message, so it would be a conflict of interest for me to have anything more to do with whatever you decide. Although I'm not political, you may end up working against my boss, and we could end up on opposite sides in the next election. By the way, don't ever forget, we won the damn Gulf War. Don't push your luck. I'm making this call for old times' sake."

"Thanks for the call. Say hello to whatever friends I have left over there."

Mark hung up as Vicki was entering the room with their daughter, Olivia, who he and Vicki called Livy. The precocious six-year-old was dressed in a design ensemble of her own creation that consisted of colorful stripped leggings, a bright-colored plaid skirt, checkered sweater, and multi-colored, although mostly pink, scarf wrapped several times around her neck, and a large, puffy hat. She paraded in front of Mark as he choked down a laugh that, to the sensitive Livy, would have implied criticism or disapproval. He nodded at his daughter and said, "Looking sharp." Then he spoke to his wife. "Hey, Vick. You'll never guess what that was about."

Not to be denied a prominent place in the attention of the household, Livy, ignoring his comment to Vicki, cautioned, "Dad, you're not ready for the zoo?"

"Almost, Muffin, I had to take a call from an old friend of your mother's and mine. I'm getting ready. You will need a warm coat; it's cold and windy out today."

Vicki said, "Tell me on the way. We've got to get there before they feed the pandas. And you are not to buy Livy any more of those dolls. The floor of her closet is already littered in black and white bears. Let's go."

Mark made a boohoo face to Livy as he rubbed his fists next to his eyes. She ducked, then tilted her head back to look at him, and smiled back conspiratorially with the look she used when something was their secret. He watched as his wife smoothly gathered the necessary clothing and toys to take with them.

Vicki moved with authority and grace, as she and their daughter worked in sync. Because of her energy and fitness, he could tell she would not add much weight as she aged, and the beginnings of lines at the edges of her stunning face only added to its character. He wondered if he would ever fully understand women. He was so grateful he had not lost her during his last foreign political venture in Greece.

Watching them together, he remembered there had been an event at his high school called Twerp Season. For a week, in a role reversal, the girls ruled and asked the boys to go on dates or to a big dance. He found it intimidating and worried that he would not be asked out. Worse still, that the girl he was interested in would show her real interests by asking out someone else. Conversely, he might be invited by someone he did not wish to go with and then face the potential of hurting her feelings. That... or having an awkward time and risk being ridiculed by his peers. Could that be what young girls felt like all the time? Duh! The thought made him nervous for his six-year-old's future.

Over at the White House NSC office, Walter Wallace thought for a minute, rocking back and forth in his swivel chair, and then placed a call on his secure line to let Bruce over at the CIA know that he had delivered the message in such a way that Bruce's manipulative fingerprints were nowhere to be seen.

Black, Manafort, Stone

Paul Manafort watched the petite blonde woman rush from the pouring rain and enter the back of the taxi next to him. She expelled a breath from the exertion as she leaned back and collapsed her umbrella. He slid his handmade Italian shoes to the side as the rainwater pooled onto the rubber floor mat. When she was settled, Manafort instructed the driver to take them to Dulles for the international flight. He wondered to himself why the president was not interested in a more attractive woman. Well, that was above his pay grade. Next to him the woman finished getting settled and gave him a quick, short, sweet smile.

He handed her the bundle of documents. "Here is your ticket. You will be met when you arrive in Paris. There will be a very comfortable apartment for you near the embassy. It's already stocked with food and other essentials. In addition to a job at the embassy, a bank account will be set up for you at the Banque Nationale de Paris. They call it BNP and there is a branch near your apartment. There are papers in here to access that account."

She took the package with eyes now reflecting pain and disappointment, then turned toward the street and watched out the window as they cruised along Georgetown Pike. As she crunched the paper with a tight squeeze, she said to the rain, "I just wish I didn't have to leave like this. It's just so...so..."

Manafort worked to infuse concern in his voice. "I know what you mean. But... you know those Democrats have their dirty-tricks people and there is a huge risk they would try to make something... something that was not needed. We must keep everyone safe so they can't make anything out of it. You can come back as soon as it's done." Manafort now turned and looked out the other window, wishing the long drive to Dulles was over. This was the first task in service to the ripe plum that had landed in their laps, and although he was anxious to get back to the office, he would continue to handle this small job quietly and carefully.

Later he returned to the tony suite of one of Washington's top Republican political consulting firms he managed with his partners, Charlie Black and Roger Stone. As Manafort entered Charlie Black's office, he announced, "Okay, Jennifer Fitzgerald is on her way to Europe."

Stone grinned and said, "You think the Clinton folks will smell a rat—fair game and all?"

Manafort grimaced. "I doubt it. None of it is really fair. It's only when you look at a hound dog like Clinton or Kennedy and compare them to discreet people like Reagan, Bush, or even Johnson, that you understand the difference."

Black slapped his hand down on his knees. "At any rate, we need to be prepared to build backfires." Looking at Manafort, he continued, "Get our press people at the campaign to play up the family stuff. We can't take any chances in being compared to Clinton on sex. We've gotta make that what he's known for. Just to be safe, get our people in Arkansas to locate every big-haired woman he's ever had a drink with. We gotta find those who need money and will talk to the press. Roger, you stay on that."

As the senior partner, Black liked giving directions. He cupped his hands behind his head and swiveled back and forth in his chair. "Okay, guys, listen up. We've now got this nut case, Bartow, jumping into the race as an independent. It's too early to tell if he is just a flash in the pan, but he's got a lot of money and a big ego. Could be a problem for Bush. We're gonna need to get into the trenches and gut this doofus and his campaign before he starts to make our guy look bad. Rumor is that they are going to get some advisors from both Democrats and Republicans. Whoever the Republicans are, we've got to get a hook in them and drill some holes in their boat. Any ideas?"

Roger Stone shrugged, but Paul Manafort leaned in. Although there were only three senior partners, he needed to assert his place. "It might be Ralph Collins. He's already gotten a call about a meeting with one of the Bartow lawyers. If it's Ralph, he'll try to bring in a bunch of other guys to actually do the work. He's got this little team he's worked with in the past. Benny Weinstein, Don Rizzo, and some others."

Charlie Black smirked. "Don't know 'em. I know Ralph, of course, but he'd be crazy to cut his ties to the Republican Party. He'd never get another job."

Manafort let his charming smile radiate and leaned back in his chair. He was handsome, like a slightly dissipated version of the cabaret singer Robert Goulet. "Right. So, it's in his interest to maintain those ties in secret with a backdoor channel to allow him to return. I've worked with one of his guys in the past and if this happens, I can offer him and some of the others a kind of restitution as long as they keep me informed. I think he'll do it, but you've got to work through the Bush people to make sure the deal is solid. Find someone you can trust with those Bushies to keep it quiet, but who has the clout to bring them back into the tent afterwards with no penalties?"

Stone now chimed in. "That sounds good. We just can't let it get out. Some of those old-time Bush people are northeastern, Ivy League wimps."

Black nodded. "Yeah. The three of us don't say anything to anyone else. If it's not Ralph Collins, we need to network into whoever they do get. We can make it worth their while. I've got a person in mind to coordinate with the Bushies." He pointed at Roger Stone. "Roger, get some of your guys digging into Bartow and plug some people into his campaign. There's got to be some problems there. You and Paul are going to have to carry the water over there. I'm too busy liaising with all the regular campaign staff, state coordinators, and all the bullshit, endless meetings. Call some of those guys Atwater used to use. They were good at finding out dirt like we did with Dukakis. Give me a budget and we'll come up with a way to get the money paid where no fingerprints will be on it. Maybe make it offshore." Stone nodded eagerly as he leaned forward like a kid in the schoolyard, happy to be one of those picked early to be on the team.

Manafort spoke quickly before Stone had a chance. "I'll keep my ear to the ground and, assuming it's Collins, I'll cut the deal with my guy on his staff. I'll find out how many of them we have to take care of with get-out-of-jail-free cards, and let you know. It'll be manageable."

Black nodded at his protégées. "Good. Let's get this settled and we'll be the heroes after the dust has settled. Whatever the case, they're counting on us to fuck over Bartow, so let's be creative and look for more ways than one way to do it." He looked over at Stone. "Call Richard Viguerie. Get his direct-mail firm to rev up some critical letters on Bartow from the religious people and maybe... the gun people. Back him into a corner and accuse him of all... the usual stuff."

Stone frowned. "But what if Bartow is for all that stuff already?"

Black homed in. "That doesn't matter, Roger. We need to hit him with criticism now. Rock him back on his heels. Get that Schlafly woman on his case."

Stone frowned again. If there was one thing he hated, it was being taken for granted and not considered smart enough to be one of the players. "We're gonna need access to money to cover things off the books."

Manafort countered with a casual smile. "I've got a couple hundred thousand in an account already and we can get more if you run short."

For a moment there, sitting with his other two business partners, Stone really hated Paul Manafort.

Campaign Office

Inside a 20,000-square foot open space on the third-floor offices of Bartow, Inc., tables and chairs were being set up as fast as the Bartow workers could haul in the big rolling racks of office equipment. Technicians were busily installing phones and fax lines, which were emerging from an access space under the floor panels. Splitter cables reached like squid tentacles, providing lines for each phone sitting on each desk inside rows of five-foot-tall office partitions. In other sections of the area, full walls for discreet offices were being erected.

Bartow Industries had achieved uncommon success as an outsource business, an administrative arm for companies that did not want to be bothered by the details of office configuration and equipment. The people swarming through the open area tasked to reconfigure a section of the Bartow corporate offices for the campaign knew what they were doing.

Below, on the ground floor, they had begun in one corner of the expansive lobby and worked frantically toward the other end of the gigantic space setting up the tables, chairs, and phones. Across the cavernous space, a continuous queue of workers waited impatiently to fill the rows of desks stretched in endless waves across the massive floor.

Once seated, the volunteers began to take down information from the throng of calls that were overwhelming the 800-number released on the Larry King program. The technical people working for Bartow had devised a way to roll over the calls to new open lines once they were connected, but the calls were still backed up, lights on the phones blinking, while more spaces were being configured. Even though the volume on each phone was turned down, they had not devised a way as yet to quell the cacophony of telephone rings that began as each new line was secured. As soon as a worker finished writing the information to document the level of political support and hung up, the line would ring again. Someone had set up a row of folding tables with coffee, water, and doughnuts.

Off to the side, three men from Bartow Industries wearing white shirts, two with pocket protectors and thin black ties, watched the chaos with an equal mixture of amazement and admiration. They marveled at the discipline of the volunteers to wait their turn and then move quickly to fill in the space. These men were used to corporate clients making outrageous demands to expedite the job and then watch as the clerical workers meandered, talking with each other rather than jumping right into work.

Although these management engineers appreciated the calm and disciplined self-organizing taking place in the large room, they recognized an undertone of anarchy. No one was in charge. In front them were a bunch of ants drawn to sugar.

They listened to some of the conversations nearby but found that no directions had been given to the volunteers and no standards set for phone protocol. The conversations were like so much random noise. Many of these people were not used to wide-area telephone service or WATS lines of unlimited long distance.

The closest man was answering the latest ring. "Hi, this is Bill. Can I help you?"

Next to him a woman said, "Mr. Bartow's office... or place, what ya want?"

Another man next to her was saying, "Hi, do you want to join our group?"

The first man, evidently responding to a question from the person on the phone, said, "Yes, we are getting calls from everywhere. Where are you from? How's the weather there?"

Then the other man said, "I don't know how many... we need help here on the phones... they are going all day and night."

Another said, "For sure Bartow believes that. He would never betray our trust; he's the real deal."

Next, the woman was now saying, "Honey I don know if he's

chere or not. I ain't got the hang of this thing but I can sign you up if you're ready. Let me find me a pencil."

The organization professionals who had been with IBM for many years before coming to work for Bartow's organization cringed at hearing this unorganized babel. They prided themselves at being buttoned down to NASA standards, and this rabble representing their boss made them queasy. They whispered among themselves and made immediate plans to send a memo to Reid Field, Bartow's chief administrative person, strongly recommending that he put some organizational management over these volunteers, and soon.

Vicki

Before heading to Atlanta to talk to the Bartow people, Mark wanted to get a feel for the growing attraction of a Bartow candidacy first-hand. To balance his political instincts and give him another perspective, he asked Viki to join him for a Bartow rally in northern Virginia.

Recently she had taken on supervising a team of researchers at the Library of Congress. Like everyone else in Washington, she was intrigued by Bartow, and readily agreed in hopes of learning the cause of this sudden surge of support for a man few knew anything about. As she settled into the car, she smiled, then shook her head and tossed one of Livy's panda dolls into the back seat. Vicki had asked her sister, Letty, to take Livy for a visit to the Museum of Natural History to see the massive elephant with what Livy called the big front teeth while both she and Mark were attending the political rally.

As they drove across the Potomac into Virginia, Vicki realized this was the first time she and Mark had actually worked together. She did not want his experience and past success to overshadow her, so as they drove to the political rally, she reached to touch his arm gently and gave him her no-BS look as she said to him, "When we get there, let's split up. I don't want anyone to see me as your secretary. You do your research, and I'll do mine. We can compare notes later." They both agreed to recruit some of the people attending to come to a nearby Shoney's restaurant afterwards for an informal focus group on what they had observed.

As they walked toward the meeting in the Holiday Inn, Mark overheard one of the Washington, D.C., local network affiliates, standing with the motel sign showing over his shoulder, say, "Several hundred people have turned out this morning for a William Bartow organizational rally. I was told by one of the people responsible that they charged each person $20 to attend to cover the cost of renting the ballroom and used something called a fax blast that shared the invitation for the gathering to multiple addresses at the same time. We're going in now to hear what they have to say." Then the reporter looked over at the producer watching a video tape monitor and asked, "Did you get that?"

As Vicki peeled off to talk to some of the people standing together in small clusters outside the rally, Mark entered the large ballroom and walked slowly to blend into a group gathered just inside. As he looked around, he could see the room was full of people of all ages, races, and seemingly all economic incomes. He listened for a few minutes and then continued to circulate as the noise level grew louder, with more people gathering and talking among themselves. Some carried signs or wore Bartow T-shirts. Most had a pen and a notepad. It looked as though they had arrived for a large college seminar.

Near the back wall behind folding tables, people were selling posters and other materials containing all kinds of logos and slogans reflecting an independent but patriotic theme. They were mainly silk-screened and carried the Bartow name in a jumble of typefaces and colors. Some contained claims of policy positions that Mark had never heard the would-be candidate profess. They just assumed the candidate agreed with them.

Then an announcer tapped a microphone on the stage and began in a voice that rose in rhythm and volume with every word. "Good morning, everybody! We're here today to organize for a third-party presidency and save our nation." There was a thunderous applause, cheers, and stomping of feet.

The man waved his hands to quiet the outburst. "We would appreciate it if all you people in the back could find a seat. If you haven't yet signed a ballot petition, we have some on tables in the rear. We've also got forms to fill out so we can locate you as this organization takes shape. Today, we're going to hear from several people who have done political organizing before and others who need volunteers to help in northern Virginia counties. If we're going to conduct a presidential campaign, let's figure out how to do it correctly.

"After those speakers, we'll have an open microphone, and any of you who want to say anything will have the chance. We hope you will bear with us because none of us have ever undertaken anything like this before, but we believe we have right on our side and we believe with you good people and thousands, no millions, of us across this country, we can take our nation back and build a better future for our kids and grandkids."

There was more spontaneous cheering. The meeting continued for over two hours in an orderly way, showing respect for the various speakers. Although there was some discussion of policy positions, mostly it was a nuts-and-bolts primer on how to lay out a neighborhood for canvasing using lists of registered voters, how to get petitions signed, and the other basics of political organizing. Mark thought this was a very smart way to start and was amazed that the audience stayed interested and did not seem to get bored with these details that were certainly the less sexy aspects of politics.

Mark was impressed with the sense of commitment. An organizing meeting like this one took patience to attend, and these people were not shouting or promoting personal grievances. Instead, these political novices showed a motivation to learn how to make change from the bottom up. While Mark was absorbing the content of the meeting, Vicki had been moving through the crowd talking to select attendees. She invited them to join her and Mark after the rally at the nearby Shoney's and promised them a meal and $20 for their time.

Shoney's

After the meeting, Vicki and Mark crowded into a big round-ed-corner booth at Shoney's with the announcer and several others. Vicki made sure the people she recruited had not met each other before the rally. Over the meal of burgers, they asked Mark questions about politics and organizing. Then Mark moved aside the ketchup and other condiments and began the more structured purpose of the conversation. "So, everybody, I really want to know what got you into this campaign, and what you hope to gain from your time and effort?"

Two people said together at the same time, followed quickly by a third, "Nothing."

Then the man who had been the announcer spoke up. "Well, I'm not speaking for everyone here, but I think we all feel frustrated with the way things are in politics today and we've had it up to here." He waved his hand up by his neck.

One of the middle-aged white women spoke up. "We don't want anything for ourselves. We're just so tired of hearing the same promises and seeing the same waste and neglect and, excuse my French, but we're pissed off."

Then the black woman of about the same age spoke, nod-ding over at the white woman. "You're right. It doesn't matter what color or what party or where they are from, all politicians are alike. You can't believe what they say. Promises mean nothing. We are discriminated against by the Republicans and condescended to by the Democrats. We just want to be seen as people without first being seen as black people."

There were affirmative nods from others around the table.

She continued, "We're here and we've been giving up our time with our children and family since the Larry King show to work for a way to change all what's been going on. We've got to do something, 'cause we can't count on anybody else to do it for us."

One of the white men about forty years of age in a plaid shirt then spoke. "She's exactly right. We're all coming from all over the lot in terms of our political beliefs on issues and such, but we're willing to put all that aside and band together to make something happen."

Then an Hispanic man in a work shirt for a heating company that had 'Raoul' written on the front over his left shirt pocket spoke. "And it's not that we are looking for anything. We're doing this because someone has to, and if we don't, our children are not gonna to know the wonder of this place." He looked around, obviously talking about the country, not the restaurant.

Then the man who had been the announcer spoke again. "It's incredible, we're hooked up to people from all over the state and other states on email and the internet. Everybody feels like we do, and I don't know where they're all coming from, but every day there's more and more signing up."

Then the black woman spoke again. "And I don't know what an email is or the internet." She nodded over at the announcer. "And most of us have not been involved in politics before, 'cept maybe to vote, but let me tell you, we're here now and we're here to stay." The others nodded.

Vicki then leaned in and said, "How much of your time are you willing to put into this?" The consensus from the group appeared to be between 10 to 15 hours a week.

"What makes you think Bartow will be any different from other people in politics? What do you know about him?"

"He's not been there making the problems worse."

"He's a businessman and knows how to run things."

"He talks straight to you."

"He has always been strong for the military."

"He talks like a regular person, not this fuzzy way politicians talk."

"He'll get them straightened out over there in Washington."

"He'll stop the waste and stealing and get the money to people who need it."

Vicki began to go through a list of questions with the small group that enabled her to put together a profile of these Bartow supporters. Mark deferred to Vicki's knowledge gained from countless surveys with various congressional members, and she kept a profile of voter attitudes that was updated frequently of regional political interests cross-referenced for the philosophical left and right.

After the people left and Mark and Vicki were rehashing what they had heard, Vicki wrinkled her brow, digesting what she wanted to say before she began. "Our group was semi-informed—better than most, but there was far more passion in their ideas than in most voters. These people are motivated and will likely remain so unless the candidate disappoints them with some dramatic real-life failure. Even then, I'll bet they will give him some slack because their belief in his ability to fulfill their expectations is so strong. Their idea of his persona represents a balance of their dislikes as well as their likes." She hesitated and pursed her lips. "It's not because he actually has those beliefs himself, but they have attached their ideals to him, and the illusion is that Bartow represents a life preserver to these folks. They'll hang with him because they'd be losing faith not only in government but also in themselves if they lost it in him. Their passion reminds me of what you and I have talked about on why we got involved in politics. We're looking at personality cult stuff.

"Obviously, this group was superficial, but I've been doing this kind of thing for 10 years and I've never seen, or more importantly felt, such dissatisfaction that was more focused and channeled to make a difference. It's like this is a life choice for these folks. Today was not a bitch session. It was about motivation to change. It's like Bartow represents the last train out of town before the bad guys come in and start killing people.

"Maybe this just represents a significant block of alienated people who are 'mad as hell and aren't going to take it anymore,' but it feels like the intensity of the Vietnam protests. There may not be enough of them to elect Bartow, but this movement, for lack of a better term, will make him a significant player. And the amazing thing is that he doesn't seem to need any validation from anyone else. These people have put their hopes for America into an ideal of Bartow that is much stronger than any endorsement by an existing politician or organization. For them, Bartow is real. Mark, you've got yourself a candidate here."

Bartow Campaign Office

Inside the large volunteer room at the Bartow main campaign headquarters, a heavyset woman broke from the cue and half jogged across the lobby to take her place at the newly erected table where a phone awaited. The man who had been in line just before her was setting himself up to share the table space by organizing his pad, pen, and a pack of Post-it notes. In the area she had vacated, another person stepped up and impatiently eyed the room.

Nearby, George Lewis, campaign manager, and Reid Field, administrative director, looked over the ever-expanding array of volunteers handling phone calls flooding into the office. Lewis felt overwhelmed but was grateful that he had next to him the trim, balding Reid Field, known for his unfailing honesty and hatred of corruption. Reid was one of the many ex-military men Bartow hired to keep the flow of his business empire running smoothly. Field had recently moved to the campaign from consulting with the large office supply and administration outsourcing business which, with the computer data management firm, had been the foundation of Bartow's billion-dollar success.

Because of the noise, the two men stepped back into the adjacent hallway. Lewis looked hard at Reid, whom he had known well for over eight years. "You didn't get here any too soon. Call your number two, Sally Crockett. She needs to come over here and be the volunteer director and take charge of this mess. It's a circus in there. Cut the noise, set up personnel recordkeeping, training, and standardize the work. Script the calls."

Field nodded. "Got it. I'll get Sally down here after lunch and she'll whip these troops in line. I'll have a growth flow chart by close of business."

Lewis smiled. He knew Field loved a challenge and had handled logistics in the Marines, where he could move tons sup-plies over thousands of miles and have it all operational, with each element supporting the other so when the trigger-pullers arrived, they had everything they needed. "That's great to hear, Reid. We're trying to recruit some political pros to come down here to help us."

Field wondered aloud, "Really? Democrats or Republicans?"

"A little of both, actually."

"Huh, well, that's smart. Where you gonna get your political experts from?"

Lewis turned to head back to his office. "Already working on that. You'll see them soon enough."

Mark Comes to Visit

A taxi brought Mark from the Atlanta airport to a sprawling complex of buildings in the suburb of Buckhead. There he was met by one of the Bartow staff who was neat, bright, focused, dedicated, and clueless about political campaigns.

The man began an orientation as they walked through the entrance of the largest structure in the office park. "We're lucky. Mr. Bartow had a company move out of here only a couple of months ago and the space is available. Also, his office is right over there." He pointed to a nearby building behind a security fence. "Anyway, we put the people answering the phones in here, near where Mr. Lewis has an office and also some of the other Bartow support staff. Is this always what it's like when a campaign starts?"

As they continued through the door, Mark was impressed by the orderly construction and quality of the space. "To tell you the truth, I don't think there has ever been a campaign with this much potential. Most of the ones I've been with were in dumps. This place looks like what my mama would call 'high cotton'."

The man smiled. "Well, come on in. We'll get you signed in at the desk and they'll give you a temporary personal pass to allow you on the elevator and the campaign floor." They walked through the huge volunteer room and continued the tour. "They're getting almost 75,000 calls a day. We were tying up all lines in this part of town, so the phone company had to put in another big trunk line to handle it. We start getting calls about 6 a.m. and are going like this until one or two in the morning. We get calls from the West Coast and Hawaii at the strangest times. Anyway, they are running three shifts of volunteers just to handle phones now, and more are needed."

On the third floor, they moved to another door, where the man swiped a credit card-sized pass that allowed them to enter a long and rectangular cavernous space. During the walk, he explained the layout. "There is a master plan for all this. Mr. Bartow has a business that outsources administrative and building management. They came in here two days ago and have everything mapped out and ready to push the button to set it up." As they continued to move through sections of office space, for the fourth time he swiped a coded door and they entered into a fully furnished operations office buzzing with efficiency. "Well, here are the executive offices where Mr. Lewis has space. This was put in only about three days ago. That's Lucine, Mr. Lewis' secretary. She's very good."

Mark stopped to look about at the well-appointed, efficiently organized space. "This place is very impressive. The security is like the Pentagon."

"Yeah, these admin guys can really move when they need to, but they've never been involved in anything of this scale. Here, let me introduce you to Lucine; she'll take care of anything you need."

As he waited in the anteroom, he could hear part of an interview at a low volume with William Bartow from at television program that morning that was being replayed by the staff.

"...I'm just saying there is a lot of waste in Washington, DC. Those folks don't know how to manage a budget."

The interviewer, in a frustrated voice, replied, "I've heard you say that before, Mr. Bartow, but exactly where do you think they need to cut? Give me some specifics."

"Just look around! There's waste everywhere. Start at the top and work down. Those folks haven't had to meet a payroll. They don't know about inventory control. They haven't had to answer to the stockholders who are the American people."

Lucine smiled at Mark. "Mr. Lewis will see you now. Please go right in." She waved her arm to toward door.

Inside the comfortable office, George Lewis, the handsome, well-groomed campaign manager, shook Mark's hand and invited him to join a group of others who were already seated. "Come on in, Mark. I want you to meet some of the people you'll be working with." The three, all approaching middle age, were seated in chairs near Lewis' desk and each got up to shake hands as they were introduced.

Lewis smiled and said to the group, "Mark Young sent me the memo you've all seen with suggestions on how to organize the campaign structure. I would like you to meet Safta Kleg. She has been with Mr. Bartow for over 10 years and has handled his media inquiries. She'll be the press secretary."

"Great to meet you. You've got a tough job ahead."

Safta appeared to be a solid professional with her firm grip, well-coiffed hair, and an expensive suit. She smiled confidently. "Oh, I've found the press generally to be a nice group so far. Though too many of them are asking for Mr. Bartow's time for interviews."

Mark smiled back. "That'll get worse."

Lewis turned. "And this is Peter Newman. Peter has come over from Bartow Industries' accounting office to be the comptroller."

Newman looked more like a high school athletic coach than an accountant, 35, trim and fit. Mark nodded at him. "When you have time, I'd like to talk to you about some of the tricks of the Federal Election Commission."

Newman smiled confidently. "I'd appreciate that. The FEC is new to me. I've got all the instruction books on what I'm supposed to do, but setting priorities would be great. I hear they don't know what they're doing half the time."

Mark nodded. "Well, they're the government and not as efficient as you guys in the private sector, but they're authoritative about their jobs."

The earnest Peter Newman said, "It just seems like government never gives us a straight answer. I hope you can help us with that." Mark nodded.

Next, Lewis turned to the other person in the office. "And this is Reid Field, who is going to be our admin officer. He used to head that division for Mr. Bartow in the big company until he made too much money and is semi-retired as a consultant, but we've managed to persuade him to rejoin us for this fight."

Field was in his mid-fifties and had the trim and efficient

look of a former military officer. "Wouldn't miss it for the world. Mr. Bartow's been awfully good to me and my family, and if I can pay him back, I'm glad to do so. Besides, he'd be a better president than any of those other bozos."

Mark laughed. "I like your attitude."

Lewis continued to lead the discussion. "Well, we all wanted to welcome you and let you know how glad we are that you and the other professionals are going to join us." He nodded to the others. "Mark's coming on to be one of the co-campaign advisors, or maybe senior, or executive consultants… We haven't worked out the titles as yet. At any rate, he's had a lot of experience running campaigns."

Mark laughed. "Why don't you just call us advisors? We're hired hands and don't need our egos stroked."

Mark looked around and thought to himself that the atmosphere reminded him of the military where a no-nonsense culture demanded respect for hierarchy. These people seemed comfortable and secure about each other's roles. Although it had been 20 years since he had worked in a similar environment, it still felt comfortable.

He added, "You folks have done a great job to date. Better than most so-called professional politicians. I can't speak for Ralph Collins and the guys he's bringing here, but I believe he would agree that we are just here to help. We've all been around the block a few times and share the view that we need to do something to shake up the political system in this country. From what I've seen and heard, Mr. Bartow might just be the man to do that."

Lewis leaned forward. "Oh, Burchmeyer is not here. Mark, we'll need to introduce you to John Burchmeyer, the director of Mr. Bartow's security. And he's been with us just about eight years now. He's going to provide campaign security. You know, Mr. Bartow has just about decided not to have Secret Service."

Field partially confirmed this. "Yeah. John told me he couldn't join us because he was checking on one of the rallies and hiring some more staff."

Mark felt compelled to give his opinion on the Secret Service, who could be a real benefit to a campaign in more ways than just protecting the candidate. "I've read some press speculation about you not having Secret Service. There are pros and cons for having them, but I'm sure your guy has thought it over. They do have medical and communication skills and can coordinate with other law enforcement quickly and efficiently."

Lewis countered, "Well, actually, it's as much the decision of the old man as Burchmeyer. Our guys are good at protection, and Bill does not like the idea of having his entire life suddenly controlled by federal agents."

This was not a battle Mark wanted to fight. "Well, he's got a point there."

Safta Kleg, mulling over her job to sell Bartow to the media, asked, "We haven't yet been able to meet with Ralph Collins and the Republicans he's bringing on board. What do you think he and his team might recommend to improve our communications?"

Mark demurred, "I'd be reluctant to speculate on what Ralph and his people might say or do. I do believe we need to set up a system so our collective advice to George here,"—he motioned over to George Lewis—"can be analyzed, and then George can decide on how to use it for the benefit of the campaign. We might end up with a lot of cooks in the kitchen, but there should only be one head chef."

Newman nodded. "That's for sure."

Mark continued, "There are occasions when political movements can make history, and I believe we are living in one of those times. No one seems to trust the politicians in the two political parties who have been out there for the past number of years. They've been repeating the same things and doing nothing but fussing with each other." Heads nodded around the room. "I also believe voters are skeptical of the smooth and polished way many politicians talk and will be very receptive to a plain-spoken candidate. Mr. Bartow has the ability to articulate in a folksy and unusual way some of the frustrations people are feeling."

Field slapped his thigh. "That's just what I've been saying."

Mark continued, "Now, let me tell you who I plan to bring on to help us... with your approval. Ben Menendez is the best field manager in the business. He and I have worked together on several campaigns and he has a way of organizing and managing a field operation in the states down to the congressional district. He is good at what he does without having an ego that needs to be satisfied every five minutes. Egos among staff can be a big detriment to a campaign."

Field said, "We need that. We've got dozens of former young military officers here wanting to help. I don't know what to do with them."

Mark continued, "Missy Winston is someone I'm suggesting as the deputy press secretary to you, Safa. She's experienced in the nuts and bolts of how to manage the media and can anticipate what they might be asking and what their hidden agenda might be."

Safta smiled. "I'd welcome that kind of help."

"The last person I'm recommending is Vicki DuVall. She's been one of the top researchers on Capitol Hill in D.C. for 10 years. She will put together briefing documents and position papers that the media will need, as well as all the campaign staff. She can direct the speechwriters on how to define what we stand for."

George said, "Man, we can really use her."

Mark smiled. "That's good, because she's also my wife and we are a package deal. I'm not leaving my family and young daughter for several months to be in another campaign where I never get to see them."

Lewis nodded. "I like that. Family should come first. We'll find you a good house here in Atlanta where you all can be comfortable. Get with Reid Field here to go over salaries and benefits for everyone. You'll find us accommodating." Lewis looked at his watch. "We've got a staff meeting to plan for tomorrow. And, Reid, you've got a campaign to build."

The buttoned-down Reid answered confidently, "That won't be a problem."

As they were breaking up, Lewis pulled Mark to the side.

"Now that you are on board, I'd like you to go with me to a meeting next week. You may know that Admiral Jeff Duncan has agreed to lend his name to help us in the states where we are required to have both a president and vice president listed on the petitions to get on the ballot. I'd like you to meet him, and I may need a political professional with me to answer any complicated questions. He needs some reassurance about the campaign and how his role will work out. "

Mark agreed and was glad to be able to dive right into the action.

James Carville

Back in his Little Rock office, the lean, imposing James Carville put aside the daily news summary of editorials and columns written that morning, as well as the transcripts of the previous evening's news programs, and glanced intensely at the election map. He frowned and shook his bald head. All three candidates now could claim to be southerners. That was almost shocking, since the east and west coasts had been the mainstays of national politics for some time, with the exception of Jimmy Carter in 1976. It was unsettling. None of the three presidential candidates could solely claim to represent the region. He wished he could find some way his candidate, the handsome and articulate former governor of Arkansas, could be the legitimate Southern guy.

He wondered what that gaggle of prima donnas over at the Bush campaign were thinking. They had many resources going for them, including the White House as an anchor and a united Republican Party solidly behind them. They had everything except a good retail candidate. George Herbert Walker Bush was a résumé in search of a personality. He could not get past his patrician roots no matter how hard he tried. He always looked like he'd just stepped out of the door of his great-grandfather's palatial home in Kennebunkport, Maine—slate shingles, nor'easter weather gear, and white shoes at the "summer house" where polite gentility was "de rigueur."

Well, Carville thought, *those were not the symbols one needed to muscle into the presidency during the 1990s.* Bush was too nice. He was incapable of presenting himself as a tough guy or as a good ole boy. Voters wanted someone who could take charge. They wanted to balance the intellectual side of a candidate with a strong fist on the table who could eliminate their worries. Carville knew Republican voters were motivated by someone they could look up to, someone to fit the competent image they had of themselves. Bush lacked that.

Clinton's folksy ways, intelligence, youth, good looks, and drive were exactly the correct formula to move independent voters from the Reagan and Bush eras of old, out-of-touch fuddy-duddies to the Democrats. Clinton could sell genuineness. Hell, Clinton could sell anything.

Now, however, they had to deal with the weirdo from Georgia with the $4 billion. This squeaky-voiced, knotty-looking aw-shucks business guy trumped Clinton for genuineness. More importantly, he had the money to sell it. He had heard today that Mark Young was going to be getting involved in the Bartow effort. He'd met Young pitching candidates for business years ago when they were competing against each other to get the management contract for a governor's race. Young had the looks and a good record, but he was not aggressive enough. He was not too worried about him as the competition. Young was too polite to be in this business anyway.

However, he'd also heard that Bartow was going to get some Republican consultants from the small group of leftovers who had not been hired by Bush. Oh well, whoever those guys were, they'd be second stringers and would likely run a campaign by throwing money into negative ads. Well, before those guys with Bartow and the Bush campaign started in on Clinton's late-night proclivities, he needed to bank some positive image credentials so they could weather the storm that was sure to come. Mmmm... jogging for the cameras, eating cheeseburgers at McDonalds... that kind of stuff. He also needed to find some way to use Bartow to pull more votes from Bush than from Clinton. Maybe this third-party guy and his pro-military and pro-business BS could be used to drive a wedge into the moderate Republicans. That would make Bush look like a wimp. It was worth a try.

Vicki and Mark

Mark was on the couch reading a story to Olivia when Vicki came flying in from work, threw her briefcase on a chair, kissed Mark and Livy, then swept Mark's feet off the coffee table and sat down. "So, Mr. Deputy Campaign Manager, or whatever you are called, I thought you were done with this election stuff." She leaned down to her daughter, almost touching forehead to forehead. "Livy, angel, can you go play in your room for a few minutes? I need to talk to your daddy, and THEN I'm coming in there to play with you. Special girls time!"

Livy bounced away, bored with her father's reading and excited about playtime with her mother. Mark smiled as he watched her leave, then turned to Vicki. "This is really an opportunity of a lifetime. When in politics does anyone have a chance... well, there has never been an opportunity to actually have a chance to WIN with a third party. We really could change things here. I've never felt this excited about politics before."

Vicki smiled at his enthusiasm. "Those folks we met and talked with in northern Virginia were nice people and seemed very committed. I hope he deserves support from people like that. What's he like?"

Mark frowned. "I only met him for a few minutes. He's... like most people about politics. Lots of opinions and few facts. The opportunity, however, is enormous. They—"

Vicki leaned over and gave him one of her skeptical looks over the top of her glasses and down her nose. "Hold up. That sounds familiar to me. Very familiar. Mark, before you start a new campaign, you've always been this excited. Tell me about the candidate."

"Well, George took me to meet him... we didn't have too

much time to talk because he was in the middle of a merger deal or something."

"And?"

"When I asked him why he was running, he stumbled around and basically said what he didn't like. He said that he grew up poor. If he was president, he'd like to see that people were taken care of, have a job and food and good health. He said government had been incompetent and needed leadership and management, which is what all politicians say. He seemed adamant about not wasting money and did say we needed to balance the damn budget."

"Anybody there know what is involved in a campaign?"

"Bartow and those around him understand how to use print, radio, and TV to sell something tangible like a resort development or an office building. They don't understand politics, which involves selling the concept of how best to live in the world. They have no idea how to articulate all the issues and ideas into a message that defines a candidate. You know, the kind of stuff you do."

Vicki shook her head. "That is a lot to overcome in a few months."

"Well, he seems a lot more serious in person than he appears on TV. I think part of the TV stuff is just a good-ole-boy show. Even though he does have this folksy way of talking, I think he can learn to become a good candidate. His office is filled with patriotic memorabilia. Battle flags, documents, statues, all original stuff. I get the sense this really was a kid from a very modest background who made it big and actually loves American for it. His political innocence could just be our marketing leverage."

"Does he know what it will take out of him to do it?"

"No. None of them have a clue. George, maybe—you know, the campaign manager and an old friend of Bartow. He managed a race for governor a few years ago. But nothing like this. I think Bartow has to run as the unconventional guy he is. That's part of his charm. We can't manage him too much. He won't play well as slick. The honesty of all those people out there, like those we met in Virginia who are coming together for him, and the whole third-party thing, is the core vehicle of the message. We can't mess with that."

"What about the Republican guy they are bringing in to balance you... that guy Collins? What little I know about him always seemed a little gruff, but still pretty conventional to me. He's your typical Republican pol. He follows the polls. He has always had the money to do whatever he wanted, and he fires big guns. He is good with the press, and that will be a big plus. The media could kill us early, but they need this story. It's too good for ratings in an otherwise boring campaign season. They'll give us a free ride for a while, but Collins will spin them and give us time to build some kind of an organization, message, and platform."

"Can you two work together?"

"I don't see why not. We are having lunch tomorrow to go over a few things. We'll need to define some turf and just talk to each other often enough not to let pressures and old animosities build up. Lewis and the others are infatuated with his reputation. I think most of the Bartow people are Republicans. The opportunity is too big to be petty about different styles. He does seem like a guy I can work with, but he just can't stay away from the press, and he loves to be quoted and to be on camera. I'm sure that has helped his career, but I think sometimes he has done that at the expense of the candidate."

"Moth to a flame?"

"Well, that is how to get out the message and explain things. Still..."

"Okay then. What have you and Livy decided to cook for supper? I'm starved."

"We're gonna have my famous tuna noodle casserole. See, I've got the cans of mushroom soup, green beans, slivered almonds, onion rings, and tuna over there on the counter and the noodles ready to put in the pot to boil."

"That's the gunk you learned how to make in college,

right?"

"Well, yeah. However, first I've got something to run past you."

Vicki heard the suspicious tone in Mark's voice and gave him a questioning look. "So, what is it, mystery man?"

"Well, they're putting the campaign together from scratch. These people are very organized and good in business, but they don't have much in the way of government backgrounds. They need someone to head up the research and issues area. I told them a little about you and they seemed very interested."

"You WHAT?! Mark, I'm not a campaign person. I'm a book nerd. I—"

"Hold up there. In addition to being incredibly beautiful and over-the-top sexy, you are one of the most informed researchers on Capitol Hill. You know how to find out anything and write it up so average people can understand it. You know how to present the pros and cons for any subject under discussion. Where are they going to find someone as good as you? Plus, you can easily take off from what you are doing now. And… the most important thing is that we can be together in Atlanta for the campaign. We don't have to be apart, and that lets us be a family with Livy. You can get Letty to come down with us to be a nanny to Livy. I think she'd love to come. Their divorce is almost done, and she needs a change. She and Livy love each other. But the best part is we can all be together in a big house in Atlanta and… we'll both make a lot of money. We need to think about Livy's verrrrry expenssssive school to consider in the next few years. We'll have plenty to pay Letty a good salary and have a nice place to live. After this, we'll both have enough saved to get a good house here in D.C."

Vicki frowned. "I'm not a sellout. I don't care how much money the guy has. There needs to be a reason for me to like him and actually want to work for him. Other than balancing the budget, what does the campaign stand for?"

"You are making my point. That's why they need you… why I need you. We need to develop a compelling reason why this guy should be president. How many job offers do you get with that as the tag line?"

A look of recognition showed on Vicki's face as she realized Mark's plan actually sounded very attractive to her. She started to say something to him, but he continued his sales pitch. "You will have a staff and a nice office. You can select a place for us to live that's near the job so we will be near Livy if either of us needs to run home. I'm not going to do this campaign without you. We're not going to be separated again."

Vicki shook her head and smiled. "You know, you always start with the compliments when you have a difficult pitch to sell." She thought some more. "You're right, though; it makes sense to do it. The timing will be good. They need to get the issues defined soon because as far as I can tell, no one knows what this guy stands for, including Bartow himself."

"We've got to pull that out of him and make it understandable and politically acceptable. Be thinking about a list of questions we can ask to get the heart of the campaign beating."

Vicki, with a recognition she was already thinking about being in the campaign, declared, "Oh my. You've sucked me in."

Mark grinned. "Plus, they will get someone to help us find the right furnished house for a short-term lease. In anticipation of you wanting to join the campaign, I asked them to send over some housing options for you to look at tomorrow. And they'll be paying the rent so we can get something big and nice and with enough room for everyone. Also, they'll likely cover our costs to keep this place here until after the campaign, so we don't have to sell now. These people are super-efficient at administrative things. So, after the campaign is over, the end result is that we will get the new house here in D.C. you've been talking about almost constantly since we got married."

From the back room, Livy yelled, "Mom, you and Daddy have talked enough. It's time to play."

Vicki stood, gave him a stern look, then slowly smiled. "Don't you choke on the tuna noodle casserole. I don't want to lose the house." She left him to the cooking.

Third Party

Debate

After dinner that evening, Mark watched a televised debate between representatives of the Bush and Clinton campaigns. The handsome and confident moderator, who was a former political consultant, tried to maintain a tone of neutrality as he shuffled the papers in front of him. "We're here today on *What do You Really Think* with representatives from the George Bush and Bill Clinton campaigns to debate the economy. Before we start,"—he nodded left and right—"I think it's fair to say that President Bush believes the American economy is fundamentally sound and that free-market economics should be allowed to work. At the same time, he does not fully agree with Housing Secretary Jack Kemp and other supply-siders who never met a tax cut they didn't like."

He then turned to the Clinton representative. "On the other hand, the Governor of Arkansas, Bill Clinton, to quote James Carville... 'It's the economy, stupid' and he believes that our economy is in the tank. He's for more government tinkering, but at the same time is cautious about huge tax increases to fund new, giant government programs that some other Democrats want."

He restacked the papers in front of him. "Now... Let's hear... What do you really think?" He turned to the Bush representative. "President Bush claims that Americans are taxed too much. What's the alternative to raising taxes if we are ever going to balance the budget?"

The impeccably dressed man with his hands neatly folded in front of him nodded. "Thank you for that excellent question. We believe cutting government restrictions on business regulations and allowing free enterprise to work will create a bounty of wealth in this nation with a minimum of interference that will allow free trade to flourish." He stopped and made a pained face. "Governor Clinton, on the other hand… a promising, although quite inexperienced politician, wants to have a kind of social engineering based on some European model that would choke the free marketplace and overburden our society with a new batch of needless regulations. If he knew better, he'd see that he is proposing to take us on a very dangerous and irresponsible path of reckless spending."

The Clinton representative rolled her eyes and entered the fray. "As a governor who knows the problems and hopes of real working people, Bill Clinton wants to use the influence of government to improve people's lives. That involves managing energy conservation, better education, environmental protection, and better healthcare. He believes those initiatives will provide a strong foundation to our workforce that will invigorate the American worker." She then stopped and nodded at her opponent. "He does not believe in cutting programs like Social Security, job training, and environmental protection just to give more money to the fat cats that are supporting President Bush's campaign. You balance the budget by growing the economy, not cutting it."

The moderator took over. "So, reading these tea leaves, what I'm hearing is that neither candidate thinks the budget deficit is the real problem." He looked at the Bush campaign spokesperson and continued, "So, despite the tax increase President Bush agreed to as part of the budget deal, he'd rather keep taxes low than use them to bring down the deficit or even begin to look into the debt. He's not going to cut back on healthcare, welfare or means test Social Security to balance the budget; he's just going to talk about it."

Before giving the Bush representative a chance to answer, he turned to the Clinton representative. "And your candidate, Governor Clinton, wants to spend even money on more government programs rather than take on the deficit. That likely means we would move further and further away from ever balancing the budget."

He looked back and forth between them. "In fact, when you get past the campaign rhetoric, neither candidate is for any substantive change in the budget deficit or has a real plan to deal with the debt."

Mark smiled and thought to himself, *That's the campaign.*

Livy to Atlanta

Gap-toothed Livy ran to greet Mark when he got home the next day. Seeing her reminded Mark that they needed to plan a visit from the tooth fairy soon.

Livy pulled him into the den, where she showed him the colorful drawing she was working on of the Washington mall, with not only the Capitol building, and the Lincoln and Washington monuments, but with a facsimile of their imaginary house sporting a purple roof with two lollipop trees. She had drawn Mark, Vicki, and herself standing in the front of the house holding hands in a yard that took up half the space between the Capitol and the Washington monument.

As Vicki came in to join them, Mark was telling Livy how she got Mommy just right with her skinny legs and hair that stuck out all over Constitution Avenue. Vicki reminded him that her legs could still outrun his any day of the week.

Then, with a prearranged script, they told Livy how they were planning a big vacation to a wonderful place called Atlanta, where there was so much to do that would be loads of fun. Skeptical at first, Livy asked what those things were. Fortunately, Vicki had prepared a list of several kid-friendly activities that included the Six Flags amusement park, the Center for Puppetry Arts, the Atlanta Zoo, swim classes, boating, theater, and the large Piedmont Park. She emphasized that Aunt Letty would be coming with them and spending a lot of time with Livy.

Livy had a particular fondness for her aunt, who was forever coming up with arts and crafts projects and loved to take her to what she called "play days" in the Washington area. She planned to teach Livy how to cook while they were on this vacation, an activity that had intrigued Livy for the past year. Letty was available because of her divorce from a man who had become obsessed with his job title, self-importance, and his new secretary.

They explained to Livy that they would have a big, new house to live in while in Atlanta, plus some of Livy's friends might be able to visit her there. Livy smiled and said that it all sounded like a great adventure. She made sure that her raggedy toy dog, Fluffy, could come too. Fluffy had seen better days, and despite the loss of one of its eyes and several repairs along the seam of one leg that often served as its handle, it had been a constant companion for the past three years.

Now that Livy's questions were settled, they started to think about packing. Vicki had found an intern from Capitol Hill to housesit while they were gone. They only had to think about clothes and a few personal items.

That evening, Mark talked to Vicki about how much he was looking forward to the next week when he was going with George Lewis to talk to Admiral Jeff Duncan, a war hero who had been held captive by the North Vietnamese for seven years. The admiral retired from the U.S. Navy soon after his release from the North Vietnam prison, where he had often been beaten and tortured and still suffered constant pain and PTSD. Duncan was only lending his name as Bartow's vice-presidential running mate to help Bartow petition in several states to get on the ballot. Lewis had reminded Mark that Bartow had been very generous to the Vietnam POWs. After talking to Lewis, Mark discussed with Vicki his growing concern that the potential for confusion over the vice-presidential running mate and ballot access might just be one of many misunderstandings that could occur throughout the campaign.

From the back room, Livy yelled, "Mom, you and Daddy have talked enough. It's time to play."

Ralph Collins

The portly Ralph Collins, now past 60, had reached the point in his political consulting career where he knew he was not likely to climb higher, definitely did not want to drop lower, and was only in it for the money. He had been part of the national Republican brain trust for 30 years starting with presidential candidate Barry Goldwater, and had been involved with everyone of consequence since. He was big and gruff, heavy and balding... jowly. He had been the political director in the White House during a Republican administration and was tired of the boring and predictable governor and senate races that now came his way. He'd figured out every angle how to make money from a campaign and was getting to the stage of his life where early retirement was not out of the question.

All and all, he'd had a good run. He was glad that he had chosen the Young Republicans while in college because they were the pathway to the money boys. He had found it easy to rage against government spending, foreign aid, and the liberals' support for those welfare cheats. The campaigns he had run for the past 30 years had the same formulas, and the candidates could have been interchangeable, with good looks and the ability to recite what they were told to say, and vote how the donors asked. Voters often saw an attractive face on television spouting platitudes and thought, *that's who I want to represent me*. The other side of the aisle seemed much the same to Collins, and he wondered why voters never did any research in elections or read anything before they pulled the lever. Good thing they didn't, as it had made his career easier.

Collins felt he had found his greatest talent only recently as a television commentator. He had the look of a rumpled sage, not unlike his friend Lyn Nofziger, but less dumpy, less threatening, and more polished. He projected the supremely confident experienced warrior on camera, and as he aged, he had added glasses to promote a more intellectual look to his spin master profile. He had developed a hesitating way of answering television hosts that made it seem as though he was giving the subject some thought, when actually his answers were carefully planned in advance to make the points he wished to make no matter what questions were asked.

He would expose his opponents with pithy barbs in a discussion or polite debate and make them appear to be lightweight novices. Viewers would assume his opponents should never have dared to challenge such a knowledgeable expert. At the end, he would simply dismiss his unworthy sparring partners with a smirk. Collins realized early in his career that on television, the persona was as important as the discourse.

His girlfriend, a producer at NBC, said his talent was in delivering his wisdom in such a way that it left the audience with the impression that only he could have divined such an astute reply. She often called on him when she needed a Republican sage on a talk show and had coached him to growl his words as though they had to plow through rocks to come out, mulled by decades of sleeves-up, backroom battles that made them irrefutable. He relished winning arguments with confident style points.

Now that the George Bush campaign had signed up all the fancy blue bloods in the Republican Party, he had been left on the sidelines. He imagined all those egos in boardroom meetings and prolonged budget fights over their pet areas. That was a bad way to run a campaign.

When George Lewis had called from Atlanta about a third-party run, he thought, *Why not?* That guy Bartow was loaded, and it would be a good payday. Besides, it would be sweet to show all those elite sycophants crowded around Bush what he could do with a lot of money and an independent candidate. Why the hell not? He'd bring along some of the other second-tier Republicans he knew were out there pissed off about being left off the Bush bandwagon. Now that the economy was continuing to tank, this might be a sweet gig and safe place to be for the next few months. Steady paychecks were always a good thing to have.

Bruce

Bruce wiggled his feet in his new shoes. They'd need some breaking in. He wondered how he looked to the others in the office with his new clothes and more stylish glasses. He glanced down at his increasing paunch and wondered if his tailored wardrobe helped to hide it. Thanks to his success in Greece a few years ago, he was now a player in the intramural competition of the intelligence community. He was moving up in the agency and needed to think more about how he appeared during meetings. He looked in the bathroom mirror and brushed over some hair to cover the skin peeking through.

Back in his secure, windowless office inside the CIA building, he thought about how nicely the presidential campaign was shaping up. He had worked a backdoor invitation to Mark Young to join the Bartow campaign as the resident Democrat. Mark would never have taken the job if he had known it had been Bruce's idea. Now he had someone on the inside of the Bartow campaign he knew well and could anticipate how he would react.

On the other side, he had also found a way to check the Republican box by networking into the Ralph Collins' guys. It was in the interest of the CIA and the country to see that Bartow would be a suitable president. It definitely was not in the interest of the CIA or the country to have an uninformed loose cannon deciding about foreign policy.

Though Bartow seemed patriotic, he doubted the Atlanta billionaire knew much about how the international political world worked. He seemed like a chest-thumper, and those people usually just wanted to push other nations around and did not understand the importance of balance and subtlety in foreign policy or defense protocol. He assumed those Bartow Industries advisors only knew about closing a merger or getting a contract tweaked to their specifications. Bartow would require close observation. Loose cannons were never good.

Charlie Black

Charlie Black came back to his office after another interminable staff meeting at the Bush campaign headquarters. He was impatient to get back to his other clients. He stuck his head into the office of his partner, Paul Manafort, who waved him off with a finger to his lips because he had a live fish on the line from eastern Europe. He had convinced the chief of staff to the nation's premier to pay the firm of Black, Manafort, and Stone a retainer fee of $250,000 a month to provide guidance on the political mood in Washington and advice about how to handle any legislation that might affect the interest of that nation. Even though it was a mid-size client, he wanted to nail it down and get the money flowing before the demands of the U.S. campaign heated up. If they were lucky, it would be several months before the client would actually have any work to do over there.

As he walked away, Charlie Black mused at how good Manafort and Roger Stone were in meetings. They wore their expensive, handmade suits molded to their weightlifting physiques and carefully groomed hair, which presented confidence to the existing or potential clients. They also had an air of assurance and certainty, and they knew exactly when to drop in some Washington gossip to pique the interest of the client and show that they really did have the inside track. If the client was sometimes reluctant, they knew just the person in the U.S. Congress they could persuade to introduce a bill that would have catastrophic consequences for the naïve nation in question. Once hired, they could call up the same congressional person to kill it. Soon thereafter, they would make a significant donation to that person's campaign that would be paid back as expenses disguised as research to Black, Manafort, and Stone by the foolish nation.

As Charlie Black thought about Manafort and Stone, he

realized he needed to nudge them to get off their asses and start to find some more dirt on that yahoo Clinton and the thick-headed Bartow. Clinton was easy because he was so active and so vocal anyone could just hang out near him in a restaurant or a bar and pick up tons of juicy material. Bartow was more problematic. Once Collins and his guys were entrenched, he'd see what he could pry out of them. They might be in an opposing campaign, but they had to return to the Republican Party afterwards, and he could help open that door to them, for a price.

The word in the business community from those who had dealings with Bartow was that he was mercurial and had a temper. He was used to getting things his way and his people would jump to please him, which meant you could likely ruffle him if you upset his predictable life. He thought, *Well, Mr. Bartow, you'll find out that the one thing presidential campaigns definitely are not, is predictable.* He'd get them to dig into Bartow's family, as well as his business dealings. Anyone who had done as many deals as Bartow had to have lawsuits and must have pissed off scores of losers in those deals. Charlie Black was confident they'd find something good in the trash pile.

Next on his checklist was the necessity to have one or more of their people imbedded in the Bartow campaign. They'd need to get qualified people to look for job openings in the more trusted spots, as well as the volunteer areas. They required intel, and the sooner the better. He had handed that off to Roger Stone and walked down the hall to his office to check on the progress Stone had made.

Stone tossed his Gucci sunglasses onto the desk. "Yeah, Charlie. Got one started this week. She's an old friend of Atwater and has done this kind of thing before. Got her to come over to Atlanta from Columbia, South Carolina. May take her a little time to worm her way up in the organization, but she's aggressive. Working on two others."

Ralph Collins

Mark entered the executive offices of the Republican consultants hired to help the Bartow campaign. Whether both groups could pull together to create a winning middle ground remained to be seen. Mark noticed that Collins had made some extra demands for more spacious offices, and the Bartow organization had readily agreed to his request.

In the Republican consultants' area, there was a central space configured into four outer offices with a reception area and a secretarial pool in the center. The space had been created and furnished in two days by the amazing Bartow logistics team. Mark heard that the Republicans had arrived earlier that day, and he went to welcome them. As he walked in, he could overhear two of the secretaries talking to each other.

"The USA Today poll has us up two points since last week. At that rate, we're gonna be competitive in three weeks."

"Yeah, but we gotta run some real numbers. That early head-to-head stuff from the networks doesn't mean anything."

"I hope I didn't move all the way here from California for nothing."

The woman said, smiling at the other one, "That's not what I heard!"

The other woman leaned back and glared at her. "What are you trying to say? You think I got a better deal than you did?"

Then one turned to see Mark approaching and said in a louder voice than necessary to quiet the other, "Hello. How may I help you? I know it's noisy in here, but we're still getting set up."

"Hi. I'm Mark Young. I came to see Ralph and meet the guys."

Two other secretaries in the office stopped what they were doing to take a look at Mark.

"Oh, yes, Mr. Young, we've been expecting you." She buzzed the office and said over the speaker, "Mr. Collins, your meeting is here." Then she paused and nodded at Mark. "They're all in there. Go ahead."

Mark smiled at the woman. "Thank you." And then he nodded at the others in the office. "Ladies."

As he entered, Ralph Collins, the veteran Republican consultant, called out to him, "Mark! Good to see you again. I believe you've met Benny Weinstein." He nodded to his right and pointed to a chair across from Weinstein. "Over there is Don Rizzo from California."

Mark nodded to Weinstein and said, "Big win in the Colorado Senate Race." Weinstein waved back but did not attempt to get up.

Mark said, "Nice to meet you. I've heard of all of you, and I believe I felt the sting of some of your work in Virginia about four years ago."

Rizzo smiled. "Oh, yeah." He spoke with a false confidence and condescension. "The governor's race. At least you won. Hope there's no hard feelings." Mark remembered that Rizzo had worked for Richard Viguerie's direct-mail operation and later for California Senator and then Governor Pete Wilson. He recalled hearing of some recent voter fraud controversy involving Rizzo not long before he turned up here. Rizzo might be sleazy, but he had a reputation of being competent.

Mark forced a smile, remembering the tactics in Virginia, which he felt crossed over a line of decency. "New day. New candidate. I'm glad I don't have to work against any of you guys this time." Mark sat down on the edge of a credenza. "Well, I just dropped by to say hello. My understanding," he said, turning to and talking to Collins, "is that you are going to handle the printed voter contact, scheduling, paid media, and polling and that my group will work on messaging, field operations, issues, and some of the administrative and internal campaign operations, but we'd kibitz on the free media together."

Collins nodded. "That's right. That's what I've told these guys." He pointed around the room. "Everyone seems to have their separate operations already started."

Mark mused, "We haven't exactly worked together before, and I just wanted to say that if you think my team needs any advice, we're open to it. We're all here to win. Whatever has happened in past campaigns where we may have been on opposite sides... well, I hope it won't affect how we work together here."

Collins nodded at Mark. "You can count on it. Same here. If your guys see any place we can improve, let us know."

Rizzo smirked as he thumbed through the *Atlanta Constitution*. "Mark, have you noticed all these Bartow Industries people around? They seem to want to get into everything. What are we going to do with all these yo-yos?" Rizzo, still looking at the paper, continued, "I think we ought to just ignore them. Freeze 'em out."

Weinstien then said, "No. No. You got to put them to sleep. Just be nice to them and defer everything. They'll find something else to do and forget about you." Mark looked over at Weinstein and noticed his right shoe was built up more than an inch from the other. Just enough to be noticeable. Not much of a handicap, but enough to have made a difference as a kid in sports and in dating. Weinstein would have had to wear those special shoes, learn to hide his feelings of insecurity, and work extra hard to rise to the level he was at today. To avoid ridicule in the macho, competitive world of Young Republicans, that inch or two would have moved him into the cerebral realm of books and planning and using his brain to manipulate others.

All of it made him calculating and dangerous.

Rizzo now looked up from the paper and said in an almost angry tone, "Yeah. But, Mark, have you met that admin guy, Reid Field? He wants to know everything about what we're doing. I'm not going to let some third-rate clerk look over my shoulder. I know what I'm doing. I just need the space to do it. Wait. Holy shit!" He scanned the paper more closely. "It says here the FDA is telling everyone we should stop using silicone for breast implants. Sell your stock in strip clubs now! The damn government is meddling everywhere."

Collins growled, "Put the paper down and focus on your job."

Mark was used to a frat-house atmosphere in campaigns but did not want to get drawn into a conversation that trashed their hosts right off the bat. Remembering his offshore campaign activities, he looked around and wondered if there was an audiotaping system in the offices. He said, "I think Reid's just going to make the trains run on time and deliver the mail." He smiled over at Rizzo. "He probably can help us there unless you want to do it."

Rizzo sat up, looking a little offended and not used to being contradicted, and said, "Hey, you know what I mean."

Collins now stepped in. "Of course he does, Don. Leave Reid to Mark. Be polite to these guys. Okay?"

Rizzo nodded. "You got it, boss."

Mark replied, "Guys, I look forward to getting to know you all better, but I can see you were in the middle of something, and I've also got things to do. I'll see you all at the morning staff meeting."

Weinstein puffed, "Going to meetings is all the Bartow people do so they can find out what's happening... which, in their case, is nothing, since they don't have a clue about a campaign."

Collins, now exerting more authority, said, "Settle down, would you? We've got to work with these people, including the Bartow staff, at least for part of the time, and we can do it better if you are not pissing them off. Anyway, we need to get control of this campaign and quick. We've got to get a budget settled and get some media started. We can't waste any time. Don't you agree, Mark?"

"I'd say you're right, Ralph. However, these people and Bill Bartow have gotten the attention of the whole United States. They've got volunteers out the ass and put themselves into double digits in the polls without our help. They're not polished campaigners, but I believe they have something to offer, and they are a lot closer to the candidate than any of us."

Rizzo objected, "Yeah. But Mark, you've been here before.

The brother-in-law and the local Kiwanis Club get a candidate to some pissant place in the polls, but we've got to come in and take control if the guy is gonna be able to make it over the top. This bunch don't know what's gonna hit 'em."

Mark nodded. "You're absolutely right about not knowing what's gonna hit them. But I believe we can help them understand some of what's going on, and I believe we need them right now more than they need us."

Weinstein, now looking perplexed, asked, "Where the hell do you get that?" Weinstein had his hair razor-cut to perfection, outlining his head in a clean edge and leaving just enough hair to comb it in a part over to one side. It was a look that tried to command respect by its sharpness. Mark remembered an article about his bitter divorce recently from the daughter of an Ohio industrialist. The article gave Weinstein's background as having worked at the Heritage Foundation following several years on the staffs of Ronald Reagan and Barry Goldwater.

Mark tried to give Weinstein a warm smile. "In other campaigns, guys like us are usually brought in because a congressman wants to be a senator, or an attorney general wants to be a governor. Sometimes it's a businessman who wants to take the first step, but here we have a guy who has never held office trying for number one?"

From across the coffee table, Rizzo frowned. "But what's your point?"

Mark moved to sit closer on the arm of a nearby couch, leaned back, and folded his arms. "Guys, we don't know Bill Bartow. We know he's got over $4 billion. We know he's moving up in the national polls right out of the box. We know there's a jillion wackos out there selling T-shirts on every street corner in the country. We know there's an opportunity here. But Bill Bartow is not our friend. We haven't worked with him for twenty years. He's not used to all the drama that happens to someone when they run for office. We don't know what Bartow or any of these people will do when they start blasting him as a baby killer or being against gun rights or for the death penalty or corruption in his business practices. We don't know how he will react when a peroxide-haired lady holds a press conference a week before the election to declare she is having his baby."

Weinstein threw out a hand disgustedly. "Aww. Gimme a break. That's bullshit and you know it."

Mark looked at him. "I know it, but will they?" He pointed toward the door leading to the other offices. "Will Bartow? The point is that I don't know how Bartow or any one of these people will act or react to any situation. Neither do you. But..." He pointed again at the door. "...they do. Or at least those people on the Bartow staff have a better idea how he might react. There are people here who know how to make a better argument to Bartow when it comes time to make tough decisions about the campaign. Like budgets. Like media. Maybe we can make the right pitch, but those people on his staff will know how to make whatever proposal we have sound better to Bartow. We may need their help to sell it."

Collins got up and walked over to Mark in a move of solidarity and put his hand on Mark's shoulder to indicate the meeting was ending. "Mark has a point. I guess that's the Democrats' equality-for-the-people bullshit talking." Everyone laughed. "But at least for here and for now, what he said makes sense to me."

Rizzo began to protest, "Yeah, but tha—"

Collins dropped his hand from Mark's shoulder and quickly replied, "AND, I think for now we need to cut the Bartow people some slack. There are a lot of decisions for the candidate to make. We may need all the help we can get so they are made in our favor. So, let's not PISS OFF THE LOCALS. Are you okay with that, Don?"

Rizzo popped a sarcastic salute. "Yeo. Captain."

Almost Caught

The attractive young woman had been noticed by several of the young former military officers when she went to visit the crowded area where they were working. She had been flirting for two weeks now with a just-released army captain and begged him to show her where he worked. Her pouts and the short skirt she wore had worked to get him to check her into the inner sanctum because she did not have the proper clearance on her pass. As she oohed and aahed over him and the other officers, she was careful to shoot photos with her small camera when no one was looking. After chatting with some of his friends, sitting on the desk with her legs crossed, someone said they needed to get back to work and she had to return to the volunteer office. She said she would show herself out and gave them an exit walk to remember.

Well... before she left, she did make some detours in the massive third-floor operations area of the campaign. She had her story ready that it was so easy for a girl from the volunteer office to get lost here where all the major work was being done. Then the security people began to make their rounds and looked at her harder than she had wished.

Still, it had been a good day's work. She had gotten photos of the area where all the military officers were working. Got the maps on the wall, photos of some lists on the desk, and the nearby offices. She had seen a place where they were building a windowless room in an otherwise open-floor place. Something like a closed box. She had the floor plans.

Now those security guys were after her, all muscle in their blazer jackets and suspicious faces. She had ducked in this storage room and was squatting behind a spare copier and a pallet of paper. God! If they found her like this she'd be cooked for sure. No excuse.

She heard the talking and footsteps. Oh my God. She squinched herself down and held her breath as the door opened and the light came on. Moments passed. Then the light went off and the door closed. She waited until there was almost no noise and the muscles in her legs were aching. She rose slowly, rubbed her legs, and, using her small pen light, grabbed some filing folders. She left the storage room as though she had just ducked in for some supplies and walked directly back toward the elevator, head down, nerves shot.

Issues

As Mark entered Vicki's office, he was proud to see how fast she had settled in as the Bartow issues director. He passed the neat, slightly crowded exterior area outside of her office that was buzzing with young staffers who would do the actual research. Half were law school graduates that Vicki had brought with her from Capitol Hill in Washington, and half from prestigious law firms in Atlanta. She was in her private office with the business-like Susan Kaufman, her deputy director, who was in her mid-forties, heavyset, and going gray. Susan worked in the legal department of George Lewis' law firm representing Bartow Industries and was his inside person for the campaign's policy positions.

It was Vicki's meeting and she set a professional tone. "Good to see you. Have a seat. You know Susan." She immediately started the meeting. "This job is a lot crazier than some of the committee work I've done in D.C. I've had 10 people going over everything he has ever said or written to find out his positions and stake out inconsistencies. Susan is familiar with much of his past, and we've been careful to make sure we aren't vulnerable to flip flops."

Mark and Vicki both felt they should be deferential to the Bartow staff until they knew them better. He looked over at Susan, who said, "Sounds about right."

Vicki continued to talk but had a slightly pained expression on her face. "Well, the good news is there aren't many inconsistencies that matter. The other good news is that, because he is not a public figure, he hasn't taken too many positions on controversial issues. But… that's also the bad news in a way."

Mark said, "Meaning?"

Vicki looked over at Susan. "Well, you jump in here anytime, Susan."

She said, "Okay, but you're right so far."

Vicki sighed. "Well, we have no idea where he stands on many campaign positions needed to form a platform or to debate or to write speeches or just about anything else. And…" She looked over at Susan.

Susan finished her thought. "… Er, Mr. Bartow has not had the time to sit down with us to give us his views on what he feels about many of these areas. I sat over at his office the other day and grabbed him going out and he told me to come up with some options."

Mark looked over at Vicki, who winced in acknowledgment, then back to Susan, who looked slightly embarrassed. "Did you go to George Lewis with this? He's the campaign manager and knows that we need this information."

Vicki nodded. "Yes. He is going to talk to him about these positions, but George has a really long list of other items to go over with Mr. Bartow, and I'm not sure when we will get a definitive answer. As you're aware, there are many areas to cover in defining a campaign's platform, and we're running out of time to do them justice."

Mark turned to Susan. "Susan, any ideas? Is there anyone else who can solve this problem other than George?"

Susan made a forced smile, put her hands between her knees, and leaned forward when she spoke. "Not really. Mr. Bartow will listen to him, but most of his existing staff are here more to carry out his directives rather than to offer objective analysis or quiz him on what he thinks."

Vicki held up several sheets of paper. "We sent a request over to his office in writing which asks for definition of about 20 of the most important areas, but neither Susan nor I believe he will respond."

Susan gave another forced smile. "He doesn't really work that way."

Mark bowed his head and made a note. "Well, I'll put it on the next staff meeting as a priority issue to discuss with Lewis. I'll also talk to him separately. I'll also ask Collins and see if he or any of his guys have any ideas." Mark sighed. "In the interim, we know some of Bartow's ideas on economics, how he runs his companies, the things he has said publicly about the management style of the Democrats and Republicans and the mess our economy is in, and the debt. Start there. Define opposition positions which reflect who we are: an outsider, third-party campaign. We have got to shake things up.

"Consider what's in the news. The Europeans have signed the Maastricht Treaty to join together in a quasigovernmental collective called the European Union. That has huge implications, as does the treaty the U.S., Canada, and Mexico are about to reach called NAFTA. The U.S. has been involved with the UN convention discussing climate change. It's just a fact, and it's only going to get worse if we do nothing. South Africa has voted to end apartheid. Just a few weeks ago, Chicago had this huge flood downtown. There are several major cities also under similar threat with their old infrastructure.

"There's a lot to consider about what's going on in the world just by reading the newspaper, and we need positions for Mr. Bartow on them. Try to be creative and think inside his head. Let him tell us when we're wrong."

Susan raised her eyelids. "Oh, he will."

Mark said, "Good! At least that's something. Some of those weenies in Washington wouldn't raise their hand if the staff was driving them off a cliff. There's a mood out there now. You can feel it in the volunteer room and at the rallies. Let's take the tough positions on balancing the budget and cutting costs and caring for people and citizen activism in local communities—charity stuff.

"But we really need to define some foreign-policy positions. Likely it is safer at this point just to tuck in where the other candidates are, but we need to know if he has radically different ideas in any area. That could give our opposition something to attack us on. Also, if other heads of state did not like where he was on some foreign-policy area, the media would make a big deal out of it." Mark thought for a moment. "However, I think mainly we need to run on the economics. Because he's a businessman, people will expect him to have well-thought-out economic positions. Some of that on the deficit may be controversial, but it also needs to be said and will help separate Bartow from our opponents.

"Republicans are branded as the champions of tax cuts. That's irresponsible because taxes are how we pay the government's bills. Democrats have been branded as big spenders. Somewhat unjustified, but it has stuck. Think about it. In the economics of an average household, both are the extremes. Families have to balance their budgets, pay their bills, and try not go into debt. We can't get caught up in the normal clutter. Whatever our economic theme is, it must fit into almost every other issue. We've got to stand for something, and the something has to cut through the bullshit. It's got to be in the middle of everything, easy to understand, make sense as practical, and give us some flexibility to negotiate on the back end."

Vicki leaned forward. "You mean all that stuff everyone's been saying for years in the think tanks but were afraid to put out as legislation?"

"Exactly. Well, not all of it. Everyone knows this country is going to hell if we don't start to balance the budget and stop runaway spending. Everyone knows we have to means test the growth of entitlement spending. Everyone also knows we have to cut the defense spending. Everyone knows way too much of the money for the social programs gets scrapped off in the pipeline, and everyone knows there are far too many tax breaks. Congress is owned by the special interests and will never be responsible or agree on priorities, like what to support and what to cut. We need to shake things up. There is actually plenty of fat in the budget for pet projects and all kinds of things lobbyists have stuck in there over many years. We may need to consider an across-the-board cut, with some stop gaps for specific critical areas. Let's recommend we do it all."

Susan frowned. "Wouldn't that be risky? I mean, the economists..."

Mark shook his head. "Their arguments for adding to our deficit financing and debt are irrational because we are not in a crisis like a depression or war. We're doing it because the money fulfills a desire and pleases people politically. Left and right—both are wrong.

"As a third party, we need to show something different. Let's make it something better. Remember when Bush was running against Reagan? He called the idea of increasing spending and cutting taxes at the same time Voodoo Economics. He was right."

Susan continued, "Still so risky."

Mark came back more quickly that he intended. "Yeah. Like the Monopoly money we're throwing at our economy now to make everyone feel good politically is not—"

Vicki cut him off. "We'd have to try to manage the recession turning off the faucet would cause."

Mark replied, "Yes. It would have to be done in a slow and steady shutdown to avoid wrecking the economy."

Vicki said, "Now rather than later."

Susan rolled her eyes. "I'm not sure it's possible to 'manage' a recession."

Vicki now became more animated, and a darker color came into her face. "Yes, it is. We move more tax breaks into a social safety net to balance and cover the cuts. That'll fit Bartow and his family's millions given to charity and work in education."

Susan now perked up. "Lord, yes. They wrote the book on getting others to match the funds from their donations and getting communities involved with local problems."

Mark smiled as well. "That's what I see out there. That's what's in the eyes of those volunteers. They want a change in spending and cuts to management waste."

Susan got more enthusiastic. "We've got people all over the place who will support that and will come out for the positions he's taken to help people through his charities."

Vicki said loudly, "My God! If we ever could get people to understand the disaster our deficit is in. Do you know we're headed towards spending as much on paying interest on the debt as we spend on protecting the national defense boundaries of the United States?"

Mark pointed at her. "That's a line to go to the speech department."

Susan leaned forward. "We can do this."

Vicki leaned back now. "Well, now we've got something to work on. Thanks, Mark. I knew there was a reason I married you."

Mark slapped his knees as an indication that the meeting was ending. "You folks know what to do. My job is to think how some of this will play out. I believe in the absence of any strong opinions of the candidate, we ought to stay true to what needs to be done and what our supporters already believe. Once we define their beliefs,"—he looked over at Susan—"that may actually convince him to recognize them as his beliefs. I think those crowds of people are the story here. I've never seen such enthusiasm or such togetherness. These folks are willing to put aside strongly held ideas on some of the hot button issues for the sake of this campaign. Any time you're not sure, listen to them, you know, not too closely, and not literally, but listen to their spirit. That's what we are selling. If you run across a subject we don't know what to do with, look at what Clinton and Bush think and chart a path between them."

Vicki nodded. "So, this is a campaign like no other and we are in uncharted waters."

Susan got up and straightened her dress, smoothing it down in the back. "Well, I don't know about you guys, but I've got to go to work."

As Susan walked out the door, Mark said, "Me too. See you soon, Susan."

Then Vicki leaned forward on her elbows. "Okay, tell me, what kind of a chance do you think we have?"

Mark looked at her evenly. "The polls now are giving us every break. As soon as we take any positions, we'll begin to lose support."

Vicki looked at the door where Susan had left. "So this is risky."

"Yeah, but it's correct both from a financial point of view and a political one. It's how you save this country and, conversely, not being responsible is how other nations in history have fallen into ruin. It's an argument that will make sense to most people."

Vicki smirked. "I thought most people just wanted government to give them the toys."

Mark smiled. "If we can force the other candidates to stake out what they really believe, we can define the debate on our terms. That only works because no one knows what Bartow believes. Everyone is interested, and since we have their attention, we would be crazy not to use that as a weapon."

"Will he go along?"

"Vic, I'm beginning to think that no one knows. That thing about him not giving Susan the time of day bothers me."

"Well, at least it would be something to see all these guys talk about reality for once, even though it is a scary thing to contemplate."

"Let's see where this gets us. Be thinking of some of the foreign policy positions that Bush and Clinton are showing in their position papers. Track to that until we hear differently. By the way, how's Letty?"

"I talked her just before you got here. She's taking Livy to the zoo later today. She's great to have with us and fun to be around." Vicki added, "Still, let's set up a schedule so that at least one of us can get off this job at a reasonable hour and be home to be with our daughter for some quality time and give Letty some relief before Livy goes to bed each night."

"Yes. Let's talk after lunch each day to see how our schedules are going." Mark stood. "See ya later."

"Where are you off to in such a hurry?"

"Got to go on a short trip with George Lewis, and the car is waiting to take us to the airport. Be back tonight."

"Safe travels."

VP Candidate

Admiral Duncan walked with a noticeable limp and a list to one side. He held on to the edge of the chair as he slowly let himself down. Behind the discomfort was a kind, grandfatherly face steeped in the manners of etiquette acquired in the strategy rooms of military diplomacy.

After the pleasantries, Lewis explained the need to get Bartow on the ballot and the tight timetable of the campaign. He carefully defined the rules that put the Bartow campaign on most state ballots and emphasized the requirement to have both a president and a vice president listed together. As they sat, Duncan listened calmly as Lewis gradually compressed the telescope of his presentation to get to the point. Then Lewis leaned forward earnestly toward the admiral. "Please, Jeff, Bill needs you on this."

Mark was immediately shocked that he was at a sales meeting and the agreement with Admiral Duncan was not set in stone. At the campaign offices, everyone talked as though it was a done deal. Mark now understood that George Lewis had invited him to see Admiral Jeff Duncan because having another Vietnam veteran in the room would make Lewis' mission more palatable, and that made Mark feel like a prop.

Duncan spoke with a soft voice and an unsure cadence. "George, you know how much I appreciate all that Bill Bartow has done for Vietnam POWs and our military on active duty and other veterans for many years. He may be the biggest private sector backer we have, but, George, I'm no politician. I'm in pain all the time from what they did to me over seven years in that cage. I'm no public speaker. I'm a fighter pilot… at least I used to be. Now I can't even climb into a cockpit."

Lewis leaned forward, one hand clasped over each knee. "No one appreciates how much you have given to this country more than Bill Bartow. That's the reason he gave you that big dinner years ago when you got out of the hospital. But, Admiral, this is just so we can get on the ballot in all the states. It requires a president and a vice president to represent a political party. Bill needs someone... someone of your stature to stand with him until he can find someone else to actually be his running mate. Everyone will understand when we tell them that is what you are doing. No one will expect you to actually be a politician or make speeches. We're just asking for you to lend us your name. We'll switch you out with the real political candidate as soon as we find them."

"I'm just worried that it will make me look silly. I'm one of the leaders of the Vietnam POW group and that is something I hold in the greatest honor. It's something I do with a sense of duty to those who came back and those who didn't. I can't do anything to dishonor those men. This seems to be risky to me and something that could get out of hand."

"That's why we have brought people into the campaign like Mark here. He was over there too." Lewis pointed over to Mark, who sat quietly, with a slight chill up his back. "Our campaign is full of young officers back from Desert Storm. We've got professionals to run the nuts and bolts and, with your help to start us off, that will give us the time to find a good person to run as Bill's number two so then you can drop out. We can make it a smooth transition and do it overnight." Lewis looked down to gather his courage and then back up at Duncan. "Jeff, no matter what you decide to do, he'll continue to be a big source of funding for your organization. Bill Bartow has never asked you, nor any of the other veterans, for anything. He's just always been there when you needed him, and he always will be."

Mark thought, *My God! He's playing that card, NOW? Bartow must be feeling more than a little desperate to press a war hero into what feels almost like blackmail.* Then he thought, *Bartow must be the kind of guy who will always push as hard as he can to get what he wants.* He had met a lot of people like that in politics, but until now, he had thought that Bartow was different.

Admiral Duncan looked down at the floor and frowned. He lightly slapped his hands on the arms of his chair and then looked back up at Lewis. "Tell you what I'll do. I understand you are in a bind and need to get on the ballot within a certain time limit in some states. You can use my name for three months, but after that I'm coming off. You've got till then to find someone else, and the sooner the better. I don't want to get into any campaign things like speeches and press stuff. I'm not cut out for that."

Lewis closed his eyes and sighed in relief. "Jeff, thank you. It will make Bill so glad, and we will follow your lead on how you... on what you are asked to do."

Duncan looked puzzled at how Lewis had characterized his acceptance. He looked like he was starting to speak.

Lewis quickly continued, pointing to Mark, "Mark here will keep in touch with you and be a liaison with you and the campaign. You have done us a great honor to be on board, for a while. Don't worry about a thing. We will take care of everything for you. There will be some papers to sign, but it is just a formality."

Mark, who had still not participated in the conversation, felt he was watching a smooth lawyer close a deal like he had probably been doing for Bartow for many years. He looked over at the Admiral, who seemed to have deflated since the start of the discussion. If there was this kind of killer instinct in Bartow and his people, perhaps he had a chance of succeeding in politics after all.

Roger Stone

Roger Stone leaned into the phone. "Get some of your folks to start calling the press. Push them to vet this Duncan guy. I'm told he's half senile. It's the first significant decision Bartow has made. If his idea of presidential leadership is to put a mumbly-bumbly old doofus one heartbeat away from the Oval Office, that's got to hurt him."

Stone listened to one of his dirty-tricks operators explain why he thought that was a bad idea.

He leaned into the phone again. "I don't care what he did in the military 20 or 30 years ago; this story is about Bartow and the way he thinks. Hell, have your guys call Duncan and act like they are the media. Ask him hard questions and push him with follow-ups. Put him in a box."

Stone listened again.

Stone pulled the handset away and looked at it, then held it to his ear again. "Fuck him. This is our war and if you want to be in my army, you will do what I tell you. Keep those calls coming at him as long as Bartow's in the race. I'm not paying you to argue with me."

Three days after Duncan was announced as Bartow's running mate, Mark got a distress call from Duncan's wife that people were calling his home day and night with harassing messages. An hour later, he got another call that now they were beginning to get calls from the press on his private number, and there were cameras in the street in front of their house.

Field Operations

Mark entered the field operations office to find Ben Menendez. Ben came to the Bartow campaign because of his friendship with Mark and did not know much about Bartow. Mark found his old friend looking over a list of state coordinator candidates for the national campaign.

Ben's mother had run the local courthouse in Corrales, New Mexico, and she taught him everything about small government and local campaigns. His father was a handsome musician who taught him how to get along with anyone. Ben combined his parents' mastery of problem solving and managing people's egos into a career in election management. His modest size put people at ease and his penetrating, intelligent eyes and straightforward manner kept them fixated on him while he explained how politics worked.

When Mark walked into the office, Ben rolled in his chair away from his computer and began speaking to Mark as though they were continuing a previous conversation. "Hi. Take a look over there in the big open area. Those people you see are about 25 former military officers who have volunteered here. Most were in Desert Storm. Combat. They've got communication and management skills, plus a sense of order. I'm organizing them into a desk system to monitor and manage the state organizations. Maybe a couple of states for each one. They've already got a bond with each other, like most campaigns do after the campaign is over. These folks have already been to war. They're gonna be great." He rocked back in his char. "So, tell me all about our candidate."

"Well, I sent you the articles and the material on his life. I've only been in a few meetings and actually have not spent that much time with him. I have spent a good bit of time with George Lewis and a group from Bartow Industries and they are all first-class people. This place is the most efficient campaign operation you'll ever see. Nice office space too."

Ben smirked. "Well, I've never been in a campaign of a guy worth $4 billion. Actually, I've never seen anyone worth four billion. Hell, they ought to be efficient. Do they know what they are doing?"

"Not exactly. That's why I'm glad you've joined us. They have this incredible field organization potential with all these volunteers running around, but it's not organized. They are getting almost 200,000 calls a day from people who want to help. There are already some state campaigns up and running which are financing themselves through T-shirt and bumper sticker sales."

"Well, I still only have a vague idea why this guy is running and what he stands for, although from what you tell me and with what he is offering to pay, and with college tuition for my kids coming up, I guess I can finesse some of my idealism."

"Ben, you've seen this evolve just like everyone else. No one has a book on his positions. No one knows them. Hell, he probably doesn't know where he stands on half the stuff. You know Vicki's heading up the issues department and she has group of young lawyers that have been sorting through his positions for the past two weeks."

Ben nodded. "She's great. We're lucky to have her, and this is one campaign where the political hacks and the issue nerds might be able to define the positions together. Our desk system people over there are making notes on ideas the so-called state organizers are sending us. Oh, what about Collins and his crowd?"

Mark thought for a moment. "Well, we'll have to see how it works out. We're on the same side for this one, and we've divided the turf, so hopefully we won't run over each other. You know how to use these card swipe things?"

Ben laughed. "Yeah, they showed me. It's like we're going to work for the CIA or something."

Mark blanched but covered his expression. "Ben, I'm really glad you're going to be doing this with me. I think it's going to be interesting, and I'll take you to meet the Collins group tomorrow."

Blending In

The next morning, Mark introduced Ben Menendez to the Republican consultants Don Rizzo and Benny Weinstein as they arrived at the same time and parked their new loaner cars next to the campaign office. As they entered, Ben was half kidding back and forth with the Republicans he had come across in campaigns before.

Rizzo smiled at Ben. "So you're not going to hold Kansas against us?"

Menendez shook his head and said jovially, "Hey. I know when I've been beat, but if we'd had half your money, it might have been different."

Weinstein jumped into the conversation. "That's what you guys always say."

Now Mark joined in. "That's because you always have two to three times the money we do."

Rizzo countered. "That shouldn't be a problem this time."

Menendez pointed at Rizzo. "You got that right. I won't know what to do with a real budget."

Rizzo laughed. "Come ask me anytime."

Menendez said, "You got it, bro."

Rizzo and Weinstein split to head to their section of offices. "See you guys later."

Mark said, "Okay, have a good day."

Weinstein shouted back from about 50 feet away, "I bet that's the first time you ever said that to a Republican."

Next, Mark went to see his old friend Missy Winston, whom he intended to hire to help with the media and recruit press secretaries in all the states. He found her in one of the smaller conference rooms, where the Bartow staff had brought her earlier and given her coffee.

Mark gave her a peck on the cheek. He knew she had not had a job in the past three months even though she had an open and accepting nature, a strong work ethic, and a lockdown understanding of how media worked. Her upbeat disposition, eagerness, and ability to get along had always made Mark feel she was like human arnica for a difficult workplace. Unfortunately, even though she was an attractive Jewish brunette, her personal life had recently been a mess. He gave her a smile. "How are you doing?"

"I'm okay. Bored, actually. So, what is it with this guy?"

"Well, he's got $4 billion and wants to be president. But the bigger thing is that there is a real movement out there for a third party. There's a chance here to make history and, whether or not we win it, we've got a chance to shake things up and get Democrats and Republicans to pull their heads out of their asses."

Missy sighed and leaned forward. "But what do you know about Bartow? I've read the stuff you sent, but does he have what it takes. Is he smart?"

"Smart compared to Reagan, who had to read meeting notes off three-by-five cards, or smart like half the guys who've had the job? Does he have the same stuff as half the U.S. Senate who think they should be ordained as president? He's better than that. Is he perfect? Obviously not. Is he committed? I think so. He has a great story to tell. He's got a log-cabin-to-billions backstory, the charities, the patriotism. You can sell this guy. He comes across like an unrefined Reagan and talks in the same aw-shucks way. He's not strong on understanding how government works. Will he blow up? Who knows. Can we stick it to the deadheads in the Democratic and Republican parties? Hell, yes."

"So I'd be working under this woman, Safta Kleg, who works for Bartow himself."

"Yes. Direct access."

"Well, the pay sounded really good. How long do you think before the press turn on him?"

"He's almost to within 10 points of both the other guys. So, soon. The media will let him get close enough to scare the hell out of the political establishment and money people and then begin to cut him up."

"I get the sense he likes the attention. Does he have the skill to avoid shooting himself in the foot?"

"I don't know. He's done okay so far but he is a loose cannon, and he doesn't know what he's getting into. I don't know if his instincts will be good enough once the press start to home in on him. He may stand up and be counted, or run away, or turtle."

"Well, if it was easy, I wouldn't have a job. Who do I see to get signed up?"

"Start with Peter Newnan, he's the comptroller, get on the payroll, and the rest will take care of itself. I'll take you over to meet Safta after that."

"I suppose the very young lady who showed me in here wearing the very short skirt with the very... interesting walk can show me the way?" She got up and moved to the door.

"I'm not sure which one you're talking about, but one is the niece of the candidate and the other is your boss' daughter."

"Well, it's nice to know some things about ANY campaign never change. See you later."

"Wait. Here are some things that need to start happening right away. They have a news-clipping service, but when you are kosher, ask Ben to have our volunteers in every state send articles from local papers from local columnists, commentators, and letters to the editor. Put the more interesting articles into a daily news summary of not more than 30 pages for all of us to read. We need to know what's happening out in the hinterlands. Get your staff to Xerox about 30 copies each morning and distribute them by 8 a.m. to all the main offices and senior staff.

"Tape all news broadcasts and edit them into a cassette reel every evening containing any campaign news. Give copies to

Mr. Bartow, George, Ralph, Benny, Vicki, Ben, and me within about an hour or two after the news is over. Train your staff to become proficient at video editing."

"Got it."

Later, Mark entered the reception area by the volunteer office just to feel the energy in the room. As he was staring across at the ringing phones and frantic volunteers, Sally Crockett, the director of volunteers, grabbed him by the elbow. "Hi, Mark. They are looking for you over at security. You need to meet John Burchmeyer. He's been handling Mr. Bartow's security for years now. He or one of his lieutenants travels with Mr. Bartow all the time."

"Great! Yes. I have heard his name. Where can I find him?"

"They've taken some offices over on the other side of the field operations area. Just ask any of the Bartow people you see over there. They've got the green-colored name tags."

"Thanks, Sally, see you later."

Mark card-swiped the door, entered the field area, and waved at Ben Menendez, who was in a huddle with some of the former military officers by maps on the wall. He overheard Ben explaining some of the finer points of organizing a presidential campaign with the officers and went through a second door.

He was shown by one of the Bartow Industries people still setting up the phone systems to the exterior of a windowless wall with a coded, locked door. Standing near the door was a young man with a military bearing, wearing a dark suit, white shirt, and dark tie. After he introduced himself, the young man looked at a chart with names and photos on it. He made a call on his phone, listened, then nodded and opened the door for Mark.

As he entered the door, John Burchmeyer was escorting three muscular young men in suits out of the office. He looked at Mark with an open and friendly face. "Well, hello. Mark, is it?

I'm John Burchmeyer and I've been looking forward to getting acquainted." He gestured for Mark to enter and be seated at a small conference table with chairs. The office also had a desk containing several phones, partially surrounded by several extra chairs in a half-moon configuration.

"It's nice to meet you, John. I hear you've been with Mr. Bartow for several years."

"Yes. I joined his staff just after I got my 20 with the Rangers. We go back before the days he sponsored the homecoming parades for our soldiers after Desert Storm."

"I'm sure the guys appreciated that since one of the many lingering problems from Vietnam was the homecomings for our soldiers."

"Yes. Well, I saw your resume. Looks like you've been around a few political battles, as well as your time in 'Nam."

Mark nodded. "With scars to prove it, at least from the political wars. This is going to be a new experience for you and the other staff for Mr. Bartow."

"Oh, I think we'll be okay."

"Well, political campaigns can sometimes seem like combat, in a way."

Burchmeyer scratched his chin. "At least they're not shooting at us."

"Not with bullets. By the way, have you talked with the candidate or George Lewis about getting Secret Service?"

"We'll set up a liaison with them, but I doubt we'll need them for protection."

"Well, that's certainly your call, but they do have good communications with every security outfit, medical staffing, and are very experienced with the logistics of moving a candidate. It can become quite a chore."

"We've got some people who can help with that also." He leaned back further in his chair. "Look, before you and the other outside guys start to think us Bartow people are some pack of country rubes, we've been dealing with corporate espionage, counter surveillance, and all kinds of things here for years. Stuff you might imagine only our nation's spooks handle. Most of the surveillance hardware is commercial and most of the trainers and consultants in corporate security come from our CIA and other intel services, but we pay them more money to be with us, so we've got the cream of the crop. There is an international business security network that pulls data and people from the best around the world. So, I think we're tight." Burchmeyer rocked back and forth in his chair and gave Mark a look that dared him to challenge what he had just said.

Mark smiled. "Glad to hear it. Sounds like you've got that wired. No pun intended. Any concerns?"

Burchmeyer picked up a large pile of open letters on his desk and waved them. "You know any of these people in the anti-abortion or anti-gun control groups in Washington? We're getting nasty letters from members all over the country. Mr. Bartow has never said anything about that stuff. It seems to be organized and not random.

Mark thumbed through the pile of paper. The messages were very similar, some with identical language. "This stuff is likely coming from Richard Viguerie or one of his associates. It's what they do, and they are good at it."

Burchmeyer was surprised. "I heard that guy speak at a conference I attended. He's a Republican. A pro-business guy. Why would he sic these people on us?"

"You're in his way and he was likely paid by some of the Bush people to do it."

Burchmeyer frowned. "Well, what do you think we can do about the press?"

"From what I've seen, you are already doing a good job in roping them off at rallies and giving them good camera angles."

"No, I mean, apart from security. We'll check the bags, and do background checks on individuals, but I guess I'm thinking about a trust issue."

"I don't quite follow you."

"I mean trust! Will they or can they be trusted not to say some things or write something if they are told not to?"

Mark tapped the arm of the chair. "There are certain media

ground rules and I'm sure Safta and her staff can handle that, and the candidate has had some experience with it, but we are fair game for them, so, no. Bartow's on a free ride right now. There'll come a time when they will begin to get a lot more critical. That's the way they do things. And there is nothing you or Safta or anyone can do to change that. You can keep them away from him, but my guess is that he won't like that. He needs them to get in the news. He's got to sell himself."

"They can't be influenced somehow?"

"No. And if you or anyone tries, they'll burn Mr. Bartow. They are competitive, but they do talk to each other about what they don't like in a candidate. You guys are going to be attacked from all sides before this is over. They'll examine everything in everyone's past. The other candidates will accuse him of whatever they can think of, and they won't really care if it's true or not. They'll probably have people working inside this campaign if they don't already."

John Burchmeyer's eyes lit up. Mark continued, "We're going on a fast, bumpy ride that you can't control or even steer. Now, do you have enough people on your staff to protect the candidate, control the crowds and events, and stay ahead of the game?"

"Yes."

Mark leaned back, trying to imagine the size of a security army Bartow must employ._"You should make plans to sweep the main offices every week or so."

"We do it daily."

Mark nodded and pointed at the door. "There's a guy in the office area outside, Ben Menendez." Burchmeyer nodded. "He's been through as many of these things as me or anyone. He is honest and will shoot straight with you. Get to know him and he can help you, as will I. Call on me anytime."

"Thank you."

Mark started to get up when Burchmeyer leaned forward. "What about Collins and his guys?"

"Well, we've worked on opposite sides of the street before. I don't know them well personally, but they're professional.

They were hired on to help Mr. Bartow just like I was, and I've got to assume they'll do their best and will be as helpful to you as they can be."

Burchmeyer pursed his lips. "I'll tell you one thing, now that I've met almost all of you, on both sides: I've never met a more cynical bunch."

Mark laughed. "Nice to know you have a sense of humor. We do get that way. Just discount most of it as locker-room talk."

Burchmeyer tapped the desk with his knuckle. "Thanks again. Well, no offense, but at least they're Republicans. Let me know if I can help you too."

"Good. I will. Great to meet you." Mark started to the door, then stopped and turned. "Oh, and by the way, since you've seen the resumes. Any of those Collins guys ever serve in uniform?"

Burchmeyer looked down at his desk and back up at Mark. "Mmmmm. No. Point taken."

"See you later."

On leaving Burchmeyer, Mark Young re-entered the enlarged volunteer room and walked past over a hundred people manning the constantly ringing phones. He stopped by a group of people who seemed to have taken up residence there. He had asked them earlier to join him in a short meeting. Gradually, each of them finished their calls. They were wearing the name tags Bill, Paul, Jenny, and Pauline. "Glad you could stop for a moment and meet with me. Let's go over to this small office and talk for a few minutes."

As they assembled, Mark nodded at each of them and said he wanted to know what they were hearing from people on the phone. "Give it to me straight and unvarnished. What are people saying out there?"

Bill, the most dominant personality of the group, said,

"They're sayin we're gonna whip some fanny. I had a call from a woman in Oklahoma yesterday who told me they had more support for Bartow than their own governor who's running for re-election."

Then Jenny jumped in. "That's nothin'. I talked to a teenager in Oregon that told me her entire school was going to make Bartow signs and put them up all over town. They're getting organized on the school computers and sending out notices on the internet, whatever that is."

Paul spread his arms. "Well, all you have to do is look at this place. We're getting a quarter of a million calls a day. Not all here, of course, but they've got a way to kick some of them out to the states where we've got offices. The other day I handled almost a hundred calls myself right here."

Mark crossed his arms and looked from left to right across the group. "That's great. What are they asking for?"

Pauline finally got to speak. "Well, just where they can help, mostly."

Bill jumped back in. "I had a guy this morning wondered where we stood on veteran's benefits. I told him we were for them 110%."

Paul pointed and shook his head back and forth. "Bill, you don't know what Bartow thinks about that."

Bill spoke with conviction. "Yeah I do. I saw him on TV at that rally in Mississippi the other day and he told some veterans there they were the backbone of the country and he was behind them and always had been. I told the caller Bartow was even going to get them more of that first-line military equipment, like tanks and stuff."

Back in his office, Mark picked up his phone without looking at the display to see where the call was from. He heard a familiar voice coming on like an old friend. "Hello, old buddy! Been missing you."

"Bruce? I told you I'd be out of pocket for several months and off the payroll. What's so important that you're calling me?"

"Oh, nothing much. Just the future of our country and the free world. You know, no matter how many nukes we have, the power of the United States is largely dependent on what foreign leaders, and even their opposition, think about the abilities of our president. We have had some questionable intellects there before, but the main thing is that P.O.T.U.S. has to be emotionally stable and will listen to advice so we can at least continue the status quo."

"Bruce, we cannot be having this discussion. Your agency is directed to work offshore and not be interested in who's running for office here unless they are hooked up with some of our enemies. The way we vet candidates here, that will never happen."

"Sure. Sure. I know that. It's just there is a lot riding on our relationships with our allies and how we posture ourselves toward our adversaries. Balance is important. It's just as bad to have a liberal wimp as it is to have a sword-rattling right-winger. However, the real issue comes with the unknown, a candidate who has no positions and has not been vetted. The potential of a loose cannon scares people and scares nations. Scared people and nations can overreact in dangerous ways."

Mark rolled his eyes. "Right! I know that. Whatever this pep talk is, I cannot share inside information about this campaign. You should know me well enough by now to know I would resign if this campaign were moving in a dangerous or un-American direction."

Bruce did not respond.

Mark took a deep breath. "This call is not about your threatening me or threatening to do… something, is it?"

Bruce gave a controlled laugh. "'Course not. I know you'd be on CNN in a heartbeat. I just want you to know you still have friends and associates out here at Langley who care for you and this country and wish you both the best."

"I'm choking up."

"It's just that if something about the candidates in the election were to start to go wrong, or if strange things are about to happen… well, they usually can be fixed if we know about them before. Surprises are what can hurt."

"Bruce, I think this conversation has gone on long enough."

"Okay. Just friendly advice."

"Like the sound of a rattler before it strikes?"

"Just friendly advice. You, Vicki, Olivia, and Letty take care now. Bye."

Mark made himself a note to have Burchmeyer sweep their house for bugs at least once a week.

Part 2 - Just Another Day at the Office

Issues

Finally, the campaign leadership had a substantive meeting with Bartow. Seated around the small, fidgeting man were the campaign manager, George Lewis, the Republican deputy, Ralph Collins, the Democratic deputy, Mark Young, and the issues director, Vicki DuVall.

Vicki began, "As you know, Mr. Bartow, our government has been operating for the past few years like there is no limit to the money it has to spend." She pointed to one of the illustrative charts she was using in her presentation. "See here, for the 200 years before 1980, if you add all our debt including the Civil War, World War I, World War II, Korea, Vietnam, the Great Depression, and everything we borrowed to fund all that, it was less than $1 trillion. During the administrations of Presidents Reagan and Bush, that number has jumped during the last 12 years till now it's over four trillion. And let me remind everyone, we have not been in a war or in a depression. We did this to ourselves. We created a giant credit card and spent money we did not have on things we did not need.

"What we did in the 200-plus years before that was to prioritize our desires and pay for them by raising taxes or cutting other expenses to cover costs. Our debt has begun to skyrocket. We have not managed our impulse to spend money, and that is the major problem we face in the future."

Collins, relishing a role that gave him free shots to trash the government, said, "What about having Mr. Bartow talk about reckless spending in Congress and getting the excesses of government off everyone's back?"

Vicki spoke softly. "Ralph, that may be good political rhetoric and I know both sides have been using it, but it is insignificant compared to this..." She held up another simplified pie chart. "Look, entitlements... which are basically Medicaid and Medicare and Social Security, are by far the biggest chunk of what we spend as a government... almost half. National defense is about a quarter. What it takes to run the rest of the government—post office, highways, agriculture, all that other stuff—is just about equal to what it takes to pay the interest on the national debt. We're looking at almost 15% of our tax dollars going to pay the interest on the debt."

Bartow had never really studied how the government was funded or spent its money and leaned forward, looking at the pie chart. "Jesus!"

Vicki continued carefully, trying not to play too much to Bartow. "And while the rest of the government has been going down as a percentage of the budget for the past few years, only entitlements have been going up due to the built-in annual increases. Also going up are the interest payments on the debt because we've been adding more debt each year. It's like increasing a loan without more collateral."

Lewis leaned forward and said, "I didn't realize it was this bad. I've heard economists on TV say using deficits helps the economy by putting money where it is needed."

Mark said, "The positions of almost all the economists put together can be summarized that government is balancing political demands by spending from both ends—helping the rich and the poor. Over time, that will bankrupt our nation and put our future on a credit card. The talking heads on TV don't have to face the consequences. They just want to sound smart to their audience."

Collins growled, "That's not really fair."

Lewis frowned. "I've heard that deficit financing is the way to get us going again."

Vicki tried to keep the momentum of her presentation. "Yes, but that's only true if you are in a real crisis. It's irresponsible if you are being excessive at both ends of the spectrum to get brownie points with the public. Deficit financing is paid for with treasury notes that are bonds sold to institutions and governments. The interest on those bonds must be paid back with real money. Again, let me emphasize that we have mandated spending increases or budget costs set by Congress for Medicare, Medicaid, and Social Security. Those are things a president cannot control. For the defense and the rest of running the government, spending costs are a function of executive recommendations that are negotiated with Congress. The cost for those things are cooked into the budget years in advance and take longer to change.

"For the rest of the federal budget, the most rapidly increasing item is related to our debt, which is money we have borrowed and are not paying off... at all. What we must pay, however, or we will default, is the interest on the debt. And that, gentlemen, is the fastest-rising part of our federal budget. We're not yet spending the same amount to pay our interest on the debt as we do to defend this country, but those arrows on the chart are moving to intersect. That's an increasing expense we can and should do something about or it will eat into the military and everything else. It's a cancer."

Bartow, a strong supporter of the military, looked at the chart that showed the interest on the debt was moving to intersect defense spending and commented again. "Jesus."

Encouraged by Bartow's attention, Vicki continued, "So, Mr. Bartow, the only way to find the money to reduce the interest on the debt is to cut the entitlements or raise taxes. Plus, we need to means test all benefits. The only way to cut into the debt is to do it all. We must learn to live within our means."

Collins shifted his considerable weight. "But that could be suicide. You can't take things back from people that they are used to getting. You're going against the senior lobby, the retired federal employees lobby, insurance companies, retired military, indigent sick people. It's an age war." He was acutely aware of the entrenched lobbying and many decades of continued business-as-usual which had created the budget impasse. Some of those companies were his clients.

Vicki didn't comment, but instead pulled up another chart. "The numbers are so big and they're spiraling out of control so fast, that if we don't take this on now, there is not going to be a way to save us later. We're on the edge now. Politicians don't like being responsible and giving any bad news. A big government credit card lets them off the hook. Can you image what would happen to our country if we let the debt we owe climb to 10 or 20 trillion?"

Bartow, shifting in his chair, was getting increasingly uncomfortable as he began to realize the complexity of the problem. "But what about waste, fraud, and abuse? I thought that was the real problem."

Vicki kept herself professional in her answers, although inside she was astounded at his ignorance of how government worked. "Whatever that is, it's miniscule compared to the increasing debt. The offices of Inspector General were created late in the 1970s to take on those problems, but the financial awards are not that significant."

Mark now moved to make the point he wanted to in this discussion. "I think we should make this the main issue of the campaign. It must be explained simply, like talking about credit cards or some other metaphor, but it is consistent with all the frustration about a do-nothing government, the unease about our future, and the undercurrent of anger out there. Those charts we put together help to explain it. It's about having the courage to tell the truth. If we continue to let the deficit spending grow, the debt will kill our country. We should bake that concern into every position we take."

Lewis turned to Bartow. "Bill, if he's right, it is a good point. And it's also scary as hell."

William Bartow crossed his arms and sank deeper into the cushions of the sofa. "I like it in general, but I need to see more and know more. You guys need to do your research and give me more information. I want to know how this will affect anything I have said in the past or should say in the future, and I want to know how it will affect all aspects of government, business, the stock market, the international area, and all that. People are going to expect me to understand and be able to explain the economy. This stuff is a hell of a lot different than specking out an office building. Mostly I want to know what this debt and deficit stuff will do to business and the regular commerce in this country. That's your area. You do the work. I don't know a lot about the details of all this, but it sounds right to me." He looked at Vicki. "I just can't afford to go out on a limb and then saw it off."

"We'll do it," said Vicki.

Collins, realizing he was not going to control this decision, acquiesced. "We'll do some research and polling to test it for negatives and began to figure out how to sell it."

Bartow slapped his knee. "Good meeting. George, if you could stay, I've got some other things I need to go over with you." The others left as Lewis and Bartow huddled on the sofa.

Mark and Vicki walked together down the corridor back to their respective offices. Mark whispered to Vicki, "Great job in there. We need to revisit a way to tell them that to have any real impact, we're going to have to both cut spending and raise taxes. Can't lay that on them too heavily until they have a better understanding how bad the increasing debt really is."

Vicki bumped into Mark playfully. "Unfortunately, you're right. But given that you're the sort of 'go-to' guy around here, I'm going to let you be the one to tell them about that one."

Mark looked over at her. "So if I do that, does that it mean I won't have to take out the garbage for the rest of my life?"

She grabbed and hugged his arm while leaning into him. "But, honey, you're so good with the trash!"

Bruce

Bruce held the phone a few inches from his ear as the impatient voice reamed him out. "We can't risk it! Just look at what happened to George Bush in less than three years. He looked like a leader who could handle crisis management, like when Iraq invaded Kuwait. He had to deal with the Chinese military at Tiananmen Square. We invaded Panama and tossed out Noriega. All that stuff."

"Yeah... Boss, but..."

"No one know what is gonna hit them in the face when they walk into that office, and Bush was the best prepared SOB ever."

"Well, that's why we..."

"Could this Bartow idiot build a coalition to oppose Iraq? Could he negotiate an arms control deal with the Soviets like Bush? Could he handle whatever is going on in Somalia with all those kids starving on TV, or Yugoslavia, which is falling apart more every minute? We can't count on the E.U. to handle anything, even in their own backyard. Not gonna happen.

"Bruce, Bush has people around him like Baker, Scrowcroft, and others who we know. He's got people who know how to find the toilet here and at over at the Pentagon and at State. These other two are novices. Compared to them, Bush looks like an international hero in foreign policy. At least Clinton has decent advisors. Your Bartow guy doesn't even have anyone near him who knows how to find Sarajevo on a map."

"I'm working on it. You need to give me a chance."

"Chance! They've got fucking whackos at every street corner, in every mall, selling his T-shirts. We can't afford to be playing a game of *Who Can be the Most Popular on TV?* or *Who's More Handsome or Quotable?*"

"Well, boss, in a way, that's kinda how it is."

"Bruce, I know enough about politics to see that Bartow's lack of a campaign message is actually beneficial to him. Bartow has become the recipient of all the things people don't like about Clinton and Bush. Nobody knows how to handle this folksy populist with lots of money who never really says anything but the words 'freedom and patriotism.' What people are remembering about Bill Clinton is his marijuana and women scandals and President Bush for his 'no new taxes' quote and generally seeming to be out of touch."

"You're right, but..."

"Get me some answers."

"I did hear about one thing you may want to know."

"Go ahead."

"Last week there was a call into Bartow... through his people from Europe. Eastern Europe. It was an offer to do some business like a joint venture over there. Bartow would manage the real estate development and expand what he's doing here for partners in Europe to do the land deals and manage the government's property."

"Good. That would get him out of the race here."

"Yeah, but I found out that the guy who sometimes works for me and is over at the Bartow campaign stopped it. He told them it smelled funny. He told 'em he's either got to run for president or do business—not both. He said there are too many ways some of these European partners could be sleazebags and get Bartow into trouble that would wreck the campaign."

"Too bad."

"It was set up by some of the people who work for Bush... to screw Bartow over. They told me about it. So, I'm inside enough to find out what he's going to be doing. Give me some time."

"All right. Stay on it. Look, Bartow is an ego in search of a resume. Anyone can get lucky in real estate. Just because he has done well in business... well, too often there is no parallel between wealth and intellect. Get me some people I know and can trust inside and connected to that rich bastard. That analyst you had writing papers on politics and who stopped the Europe deal is not enough. I need to be sure."

"Right. Working on it."

"Results, Bruce. Not excuses." The phone made a ringing noise as it was slammed down at the other end of the call.

Trouble Brewing

The campaign field manager, Ben Menendez, was in his cubicle talking on the phone while rocking back and forth in his chair. He saw two young women from the Bartow staff walk past. Mark had given him a heads-up about them because they did not want their family backgrounds widely known. The young women also said that they did not want to get any special favors, even though there were obvious warning signs if they were not treated with respect.

Both came from privileged lives and treated the campaign as a fun social outing. Julie Kleg was the daughter of the press secretary, Safta, and Carmen Renolds was the niece of William Bartow. Both waved to him with smiles on their cute faces. They puffed their hair and managed to shake their very short skirts. The young women slyly glanced over at the team of young military officers in the field office who managed to eyeball them back while maintaining a controlled roar, all of them talking on their phones at once.

It looked as though they had stopped by the campaign dressed to go to an afternoon cocktail party. In most campaigns, there were extraneous staff, family, and others who were plugged in because the candidate or his family allowed it. Ben decided just to let them alone as long as they did not get in the way of the actual nuts and bolts of the campaign. Both women giggled as they passed his desk.

Menendez looked back down at his phone. "I think you guys in Michigan can put it together in a week or so and then I'll come out to give you some help with those problems."

He held one hand over the phone receiver and the other to his ear, covering both to hear better. "What? I did not hear..."

There was a scratchy noise on the other end of the phone as three people were shouting over each other all at once on a speakerphone from the Michigan office. Menendez stopped his rocking and leaned into the phone. "What? Look, I gotta go to a meeting. I'll call you folks back later to set it up."

Media

After Mark left the issues meeting, he walked down the hall to the media area to meet a reporter for lunch. He and his friend Ben Menendez arrived at the same time to welcome the *New York Times* reporter, Sandy Jennings. They both had known her from their time in Washington and previous campaigns.

As soon as they sat down, Sandy cut to the chase, "Okay, guys. What's with these polls? Is Bartow for real?"

Ben shrugged and said, "Ask him."

Sandy frowned. "He can't see me. They say he's too busy. I think he only likes TV news and softball questions about his parades for veterans and what's wrong with the other political parties. How are we to get a sense of what he's like if he won't see us?"

Mark shrugged. "Well, did you call for an appointment?"

Another frown. "Yeah. I talked to the junior leaguer, nice lady, by the way, but totally clueless. What's her name? Sofa, Safta. What kind of a name is that? It sounds like a black woman, but I don't think she has ever seen a black woman who was not serving hors d'oeuvres or cleaning toilets. Anyway, she kept talking about scheduling and finally blew me off."

Ben laughed and kidded Sandy as he had been doing for years. "Whoa, Sandy—sexist and racist in one sentence. It's hard to believe anyone would choose any other activity than spending time with you pulling arrows out of their backs."

Sandy leaned over to him. "Yeah. Screw you too. Now, what's happening? I'm going to see Collins this afternoon and I know he'll have a story for me with him flying around in a cape responsible for your poll numbers. So, this is your shot."

Mark looked at her evenly. "Have you spent time with any Bartow volunteers?"

Sandy pouted now. "Yeah, right."

"No. I know it's unlike you to actually talk to real people, Sandy, but so far, that's the story."

Sandy now looked disbelieving and puzzled.

Mark continued, "Normally I would not insult you by suggesting that you talk to the troops, but this is their fight. There is a political revolution going on all over America to change things in politics and the way we run the government, and these folks are way ahead of us political hacks or you folks in the media. They've got the passion and the drive here. You need to remember, we all got on this train after it had left the station. We're playing catch-up now."

Sandy smirked. "Right. So, you are not going to do any TV and not going to take any positions on abortion, gun control, environment, racism, city decay, erosion of the tax base, or gridlock on the hill, and instead run a campaign on nothing but some T-shirt salesmen on the street corner. That's your strategy?"

Ben leaned over to her. "God! You're so quick."

Mark, knowing the competitive nature of the major newspapers, added, "Well, that's what the *Washington Post* thinks."

Now Sandy had her back up. "Who? Blanche was here? Did she get to see Bartow? Did you give her this run-around? Do I have to write a piece on, 'candidate sequestered, staff disarray, volunteers running the campaign?' Who's gonna do the paid media? Jesus! Guys, give me something to write about. Not giving me any information on how this campaign is going to unfold is bullshit."

Both Mark and Ben were smiling at Sandy's harangue as she continued, "A guy with $4 billion and all you can come up with is this… is some populist insurrection? Give me a break. You know what these 'volunteers' look like in New York? It's a mixture of guys with sideburns, white socks, and tattoos; Wall Street types; housewives from Westchester county; and freaks from Tribeca. That's a carnival show. What kind of a story is that?"

Mark leaned back. "The truth? Plus, what you just described

is a cross-section of New York. What other candidate has a coalition like that?"

Sandy continued her pouting. "Okay. Well, at least Ralph Collins will give me a good quote and a lead. No wonder you guys haven't won an election in years."

Ben leaned over to her again and whispered softly, "Sandy?"

"Yeah, what?"

"Do I have your current address for my Christmas card list?"

Street Vendors

After his talk with the *New York Times* reporter, Mark decided he needed to follow his own advice and reconnect with the grassroots supporters, so he drove to the large, sprawling Lennox Mall in the ritzy Buckhead neighborhood. He parked in the massive lot and walked over to a busy corner outside the mall on the sidewalk next to Peachtree Street. There, several Bartow volunteers had set up a booth and were waving at cars and selling baseball hats, T-shirts, and other items. They also had American flag materials and a big sign that read, "If you can't stop, wave." He stood back about 30 feet to observe. He could feel their enthusiasm, but he had some concern about the financial transactions and potential for fraud or having the candidate blamed for what was clearly an unsanctioned and spontaneous activity.

One vendor waved a T-shirt at the traffic. A car honked, and the driver waved back. "Hell, don't just wave, stop and get one," he shouted at the car. "They're only 20 bucks."

The woman next to him said, "We're doing all right. How much we got so far today?"

The third vendor looked into a box. "I dunno, about $700. I'll take it over to the campaign office this afternoon and give it to them folks in the volunteer office. Or, maybe we need to pay the T-shirt lady back for printing them."

The second vendor was looking down the street toward a far corner of the mall. "I wonder how the others are doing."

The first man who had spoken and who seemed the alpha of the street-corner group said, "Well, those folks over where the Marta train lets out by Lennox Road and East Paces Ferry got the best corner, and those others at the back end by the parking are getting resupplied two or three times a day. Hey, you see the *USA Today*?"

"No. What did they say?"

"We're coming up in the polls close with those other two."

"Awesome. We're gonna win this thing. Damn. Won't those snobs in Washington be surprised?"

"Well, we're all gonna be in this together after it's all done. The problem we've been having in this country is that we've stopped pulling together like we did in World War II."

"Bartow's gonna straighten all that out. There ain't nothin' we can't do if we stick together."

A car pulled up and the person inside asked to purchase three ball caps.

"You bet. That'll be $60, and the money goes right to pay for our campaign office."

The car passenger paid and said, "Well, keep up the good work."

"We will. Drive safely now, and send us some more business."

Mark walked back to his car, head down, now mulling over a new set of concerns.

Campaign Budget

After the visit to Lennox Mall and hearing the conversation of the street vendors, Mark went back to the campaign office to find Benny Weinstein and discuss campaign finances. He was stopped by the secretary outside his door, who told him he had to wait and be announced and buzzed in. When they divided the responsibilities in the campaign, budgets and finance was part of the turf that Collins wanted, and Benny was the guy in charge.

As the door opened, a flustered Julie Kleg rushed out quickly, looking down at the floor while carrying a folder close to her chest.

Weinstein's secretary then said, "Mr. Weinstein will see you now."

As Mark entered, he saw that Benny's desk was filled with papers. Weinstein was mopping up a spilled drink of what looked like water with paper towels and looked up with some concern on his face, but he swallowed and said to Mark, "So, how's it been? Are you guys going strong?"

Mark looked back at the door where Julie had exited. "Yeah. It's been okay. Actually, considering the campaigns I'm used to, this one has been fairly luxurious."

Benny laughed. "Yeah. I know what you mean."

Mark gestured to the desk. "Ralph says you are the nuts-and-bolts guy who's working on an overall budget."

"That's right. That's one of the things I'm in charge of… and,"—he tossed the paper towels in the trash and looked up,—"it's amazing. You know, usually we spend so much time in a campaign worrying about money. I've been doing some math. The guy's worth four billion. If we can spend the annual interest of his net worth on this campaign, that's 200 million. And that's at a shitty rate. We can out-spend the other guys with the money they're getting from the government two to one COMBINED."

Mark nodded, impressed at the spending disparity because Bartow was using his own money and both Bush and Clinton were taking the money from federal matching funds to run their campaign. "How would you cut it up in a budget?"

"I figure half to 60% on media, 15-20% on phones, mail and print, 5 on polling, 10 in the field, and the rest as a safety. I'm assuming the Bartow business is covering the office space."

"You may want to check on how much they can give as an in-kind donation before we need to start to reimburse them."

"I'll look into that."

"What does George Lewis think of your budget?"

"How the hell do I know? We're running this show. Those guys are window dressing."

Mark was taken aback, remembering an earlier conversation in Collins' office where everyone seemed to agree that they needed to cooperate with the Bartow staff. "Well, the candidate thinks highly of them. Don't you think they could help sell this to Bartow?"

"Yeah. But that's Ralph's job. My job's to make the numbers work."

"Why so much for mail and phones? It looks like that could be handled by the volunteers in the field, at least the phone part."

Benny leaned his head to one side as he looked at Mark. "Mark, we've both been doing this for a long time. We're pros. I've been successful with targeted mail and paid phone banks for years. I know how to work them. When it comes down to it, we aren't gonna get much help out of these Bartow bozos here or those whackos on the street corner. Let 'em do whatever nit-shit things they are gonna do. We've got to run this thing with what we know will work, and, unlike any other presidential campaign in history, we have the money to saturate the voters in a way they've never been hit before. We're gonna use paid phone banks of professionals and paid mail houses who know how to churn out letters. Bam. Bam. Bam. We're gonna use the printing houses we have used before and know they will do it right. That decision has been made."

"When are you gonna show this to Bartow or get approval to start?"

"I dunno. It's taking the Bartow folks forever to make decisions. I've got to fine-tune this budget and get some contracts settled with vendors and then we'll take it in. We're ready to go now, but Ralph will have to be the closer."

"Well, keep me in the loop as it evolves."

"You bet."

War Room

Next, Mark met with Rollie Atkinson, a volunteer vetted by the Bartow organization and declared fit to hire who had shown he was bright, devoted, and unemployed. Rollie, carrying a pad and pen, followed Mark into a large, empty, windowless, square-shaped room in the center of the office complex.

Mark spun around, looking at the empty room. "Rollie, since you know everyone here and all the Bartow staff, I want you to be in charge of this war room."

"Sounds like fun."

"Depending on how things turn out, it could become the nerve center of the campaign. We'll need to have it fitted with some special equipment and gear, so take notes. Afterwards, call Reid Field and he can get the equipment and help with the install. Burchmeyer's guys may need to put in some security stuff. Over on that wall, set up a bank of TVs. We need to be able to watch the three networks, PBS, and CNN at the same time.

"We'll need a conference table and a speakerphone with a mute button and volume control. Set up two easels with flip-chart paper and magic markers or one of those new electronic marking boards that give you a printout. We'll need a computer tied into the internet.

"Over on that wall, set up filing cabinets for each congressional district and senate seat in the country. Put into each district, lists of all elected officials, maps, voter lists, election results from the past three elections, population trends, and general demographic information. Vicki DuVall in the research department can help you get all that stuff. Ask Ben Menendez in the field office what else he needs and he can give you the names of companies who do demographic research.

"Have our security block the room from any outside listening devices and set up sweeping mechanisms. I want this room secure internally from all four sides and from the floor above and below. We want cameras and sound covering the entry. Find a couple of trusted people that you know, give their names to Burchmeyer from security to check out, and then bring them on to help you. Key this room so that no one can enter except for you and the people you pick to help you and a list I'll give you.

"Got all that?"

"Gosh! It's almost like preparing for war or like spy stuff."

"Pretty close. There has to be a secure vault to keep information and plans and where the campaign is conducted. This is where we'll keep the secrets. In most presidential campaigns, there is a room like this. We won't have many secrets that we can keep, but when we do, this place will allow us to keep them for a little while longer." Mark walked to the door and started to leave, then turned back to Rollie. "Isn't Peter Newman's office down this way somewhere? I need to see him about some things."

He gave Mark the directions. "You do know that in addition to being the campaign comptroller, he's Mr. Bartow's son-in-law, right?"

"Actually, I had not made that connection. Thanks. I'm glad you told me. I'd be embarrassed if I had made some off-color joke about Bartow."

"He's a good guy. He'd probably like it and tell you one back. You know they just had their second child."

Campaign Finances

Peter Newman was in his office, and over the next hour and a half as they discussed the campaign finances, Mark got to know that, in addition to having a collegial innocence, he was smart and efficient.

Newman was explaining, "We've just about worked out contracts with all of you consultants... and we've taken care of our campaign space. Since we are self-financed, I don't anticipate any FEC problems, but I wonder if you anticipate anything we need in this shop."

Mark pointed to the stack of papers on Newman's desk. "Couple of things. One is that there are a lot of people sending this campaign cash in the mail or dropping it at various Bartow campaign offices. From what I can tell, there are thousands of letters containing money and hundreds of pop-up booths around the country selling hats, T-shirts and bumper stickers."

Newman smiled. "Isn't that great?! Mr. Bartow thought we should keep any money we get from them as a contingency."

"Yeah. But, you need to keep accurate records on who is sending the money in here, and we need the names and contact information on who sent it. We need the documentation on them, and we must screen corporate money which is banned by the FEC."

Newman wrinkled his brow. "Oh, really. I thought if we were not taking matching funds..."

Mark realized Peter needed some education on campaign accounting. "Peter, all this is very political. We don't know what the Federal Election Commission will do, but keep your options open. You must have good records. Whoever these people are, we need to have lists of them for the field operation, including addresses and phones. They are likely to be potential organizers or helpers. Just because you aren't soliciting their money, it doesn't mean the campaign won't be required to file reports."

Newman's face dropped. "Okay, we'll get on that, but we're way behind the curve. What else?"

"That's the easy part. The more difficult area is all the volunteers out there." Mark pointed out the window.

"What do you mean?"

Mark leaned forward. "There are tens of thousands of people in local communities collecting money, spending money, and making obligations on behalf of Mr. Bartow."

Newman protested, "But, we have no control over them. We don't even know who they are."

Mark put his hand on Newman's desk. "But we need to know who they are. They come to rallies. They call in here. They send us mail. They are appointing themselves to jobs and giving themselves titles. People believe they represent Mr. Bartow and the campaign. They are your ground troops. We need to know them and know what they are saying. We need to be able to get in touch with them and, more importantly, to direct them. They need to be organized, and to do that, we need the data and so does Ben Menendez over in field operations.

"It's like we're building a national organization with retail outlets and employees in every town. We need to know who is being contracted to make all those T-shirts, bumper stickers, and other stuff and what happens to the money. They are doing it in the name of Mr. Bartow."

Newman shook his head. "But, we can't possibly get control over that situation before the election."

Mark nodded. "Yes. And, you probably won't be hit with lawsuits or financial claims until after the election."

Newman leaned back in his chair. "Like?"

"Like some of the people selling T-shirts and promising the money to vendors are going to put that money in their pockets and walk away. The rent on the offices will still be due. There could be all kinds of obligations being made in Mr. Bartow's name and some may be illegal. The press and our opposition would love to create a story that Bartow is incapable of handling money.

"You will have self-proclaimed state campaign managers signing contracts on Mr. Bartow's behalf without anyone's knowledge here. Who are the collectors going to come after? Who's going to get sued?"

Newman's face blanched. "Oh, this could not only be about FEC legalities, it could be a civil and legal pain in the ass."

"Sure. And to avoid the potential bad publicity, you'll probably pay or settle. Either way, you are getting screwed without the pleasure."

"How can we avoid all that?"

"Write some standards for financial compliance. Put it into a disclaimer in nice, non-lawyer language, then send it to all those field operatives we do know about. If nothing else, it will show the FEC we tried. You need to work with the field operation to get someone responsible in every state to be in charge of all finances and recordkeeping. In the past, we've used accountants who donate their time in a sort of 'in kind' contribution."

"Good. We'll work on that. What other good news do you have for me today?"

"Well, I'm a little worried that we could have some bad actors among these thousands of volunteers that are making claims to represent the campaign. We need personnel files so the field organization can vet them, and also give us another defense against potential lawsuits. I'm guessing that Mr. Burchmeyer over in security would like to know that as well."

"Okaaaay." Newman made more notes. "You've given me a lot to think about. Anything else?"

Mark crossed his arms. "Well, we don't have a budget as yet, so we don't know what we will be spending. Remember, both Clinton and Bush are taking federal matching funds from checking to donate on the income tax form when we send in our taxes. The government will use that to pay for both of their campaigns in the general election. They both will have about $50 million each to spend, and by law they cannot go out and raise more money for their campaigns.

"If Mr. Bartow decided to spend more than that, he could

swamp them on television. He could use just the interest on his money for a year and outspend them both by twice what they have to work with. That will help make up for not having a national political party behind him. So, it's something to think about when you are considering the budget and how much you all want to win. My guess is that this election will be the last year major candidates take matching funds, so it's a rare opportunity to crush them moneywise. Kinda like in the Napoleonic Wars if one side suddenly had a bunch of 105 mm howitzers instead of old-fashioned black powder cannons."

"Mmmm. I had not thought about it like that. Something to consider. You're just full of ideas. Anything else?"

"Nope, but I hear you've got a relatively new baby."

"Five months, but I don't see too much of her just now."

"Well, get to her every chance you get. They change every day and almost every hour at that age. She won't stay this way long and whatever happens here, you'll regret missing her all of this time. Take some work home. I've got a six-year-old and she still amazes me, and I'm hurting at what I'm missing of her just by being here. Fortunately, I get to see her every night."

"You're right. Thanks for the advice. I'll try." He smiled.

Mark put his hand on the desk to push himself up to leave. "I've seen what campaigns can do to marriages, and I know personally from past experience what they can do to relationships." Mark headed to the door. "Hope my professional and personal concerns haven't been too contradictory."

Newman, still smiling, responded, "They are diametrically opposed, but thank you for them both."

"Night."

Balancing the Budget

A few days later, Mark stopped by the office of Ralph Collins as he was finishing a call, and his voice was softer than normal. "Yes. Of course, I will. *Today Show*. No need to shout. Honey, you can count on me…" He looked up to see Mark at the door. "Oh, look, I gotta go. Late to a meeting. I'll call tonight." Collins hung up and shrugged. "Girlfriend."

They joined George Lewis in Vicki's office, where she handed each a thick briefing book. Vicki began the discussion. "Guys. Take a seat. These folders are individually numbered and tagged to you on each page, but even so, please hold them in the strictest confidence. No Xeroxes.

"This meeting flows from the one with Mr. Bartow about how interest payments on the federal debt are eating into the budget more each year. If Mr. Bartow gives us the go ahead, this will become the main focus of the campaign. These books contain suggestions on how to address that problem. We all know we're not going to win unless we shake up the election, and the job's not worth winning unless we can make a change."

She then put a chart up on an easel. "Let's cut to the chase. Our position is supported by Mr. Bartow's statements, that… because of the upward trend in the annual deficits, balancing the budget overrides all other concerns."

Collins smiled. "Absolutely."

Vicki looked back at her chart. "We can't really trust Congress to be responsible enough to do anything that actually makes a significant difference.

"Today the federal government spends almost $4 for every three they collect in revenue. So, we are strangling ourselves in the increasing debt and the interest costs to carry that debt. It is eating into every other aspect of the federal budget and growing like a cancer that will consume our ability to function.

We could eventually have annual shortfalls of a trillion dollars! That doesn't even factor in crisis situations like wars, financial reversals, health crises, and other problems that can add to the annual deficit and feed into the debt. For the past 12 years, we have both sides pulling at the purse strings and trying to answer every request, fill every need—real or imagined. The federal government cannot afford to take care of every whim anyone has. Problems have to be prioritized, negotiated, and means-tested. We can't keep finding excuses to give money back to taxpayers just to make them like us, when we need it to pay our debts.

"The main message of our campaign is about running the government like a business. We should meet bottom-line expectations, and government managers need to control their portfolios. We have to dispel the idea that government will solve all problems, particularly those that business should be able to solve for itself without a government handout."

George Lewis mused, "Why won't Congress be more responsible?"

Vicki pouted. "The reason Congress is irresponsible is uninformed voters never call them on anything. Polling can tell politicians what to say to appease their constituents, and voters don't do any research to ask the hard questions. We've got to shock the system into facing reality. If the public understands our message, they will support it.

"We want to start by cutting down the budget deficit. However, because budgets are decided so far in advance, it is too confusing and politically impossible to find consensus on where to cut. Plus, the special interests will corrupt any process that takes place over an extended period of time. So, our starting position will be to freeze the existing and projected federal budget at a point in time one year after the election."

Collins challenged, "Most people don't know the difference between the deficit and the debt."

Vicki grudgingly gave him credit. "You're right, but both are killing us, and Bartow needs a reason to define himself." She sniffed. "Here's the deal. We would propose a simple, clean bill that rewrites all previous deals and agreements that would cut 2% a year across the board for everything in the government until the budget is balanced. This includes all entitlements, military, Medicare, Medicaid, Social Security, all salaries for the legislative, judicial, and executive branches, all retirement, civilian and military. Everything is on the table, including widows and orphans, and it all gets cut equally.

"Plus, we reduce by 2% all tax cuts and write-offs, grants, subsidies, loans... whatever the government is giving out in the way of tax breaks. Cuts on these tax breaks will include business loans and grants, home mortgage, gas and oil exploration, military, everything. That will give us revenue both by stopping the spending, as well as government giveaways. It will require a large SWAT team of accountants a year to go through all the OMB files and the tax codes to find all the stuff."

Collins, thinking of his corporate clients and friends, now frowned. "Everyone will raise holy hell. All the liberals will be screaming that we are abandoning the social programs."

Vicki said in response, "And the conservatives will scream that we are taxing people to death and not supporting commerce."

Collins shook his head. "But that would wreck the economy. Everything would come to a grinding halt and we would go into a recession."

Vicki nodded. "It would certainly affect things for the short term. It would be incredibly difficult just to assemble the budget parts and authorization statutes to be cut. The goal is to stop Congress from spending money we do not have and putting us further in the hole through tax breaks. It's to change the philosophy of how government functions. We take some licks now and avoid a total meltdown later. If people get used to that, then the economy will adjust and we will pick back up, minus the false benefits of deficit spending."

Collins growled, "It would be hard to explain that to everyone. It will be popular in general and very unpopular in any specifics."

Vicki nodded. "First, we've got to balance the budget. Take

a breath, and after that then start to whittle down the debt."

Collins shook his head. "It'll be very unpopular."

Vicki retorted, "Leadership for change usually is."

Lewis asked, "What if it were to fail?"

Vicki smiled at him. "Then at least we would have defined the problem. Everyone would understand how it is decimating our future. They can always turn the faucet back on."

Mark interjected, "Right now, we are blithely heading for the cliff. Everyone's enjoying the ride and looking at the nice scenery. Somebody has to shout out the danger and pull the steering wheel in a safe direction. This proposal plans to shake up everyone the car. The new road has bumps, mud, and gravel. If everyone insists on continuing to drive off the cliff, at least they will know what to expect. Now they are just lemmings. Voters love to believe the fantasy that it is all going to be alright and someone will take care of it for them. They don't want parenting. Yeah. It could fail."

Lewis, who had been listening, then said, "I'll have to think about how this affects not only Bartow's reputation, but how it will affect his business and everything."

Vicki answered him, "It's strong medicine."

Collins smirked. "Those liberals wouldn't be able to give it all away then."

Vicki took him on. "Not just liberals. It's true they are not as subtle in asking for what they want, but outside of healthcare, they are on the fringes. Republicans under Reagan used it for the tax breaks and Reagan's 600-ship navy. That's where the big money went. They should have paid the government bills with the money we had on hand, not give it back to their friends and business associates. It made them popular, but if it continues, eventually it will break the United States. Deficits mainly fund the rich, not the poor. They are the ones who won't like this proposal."

Mark stepped in to moderate. "We passed the crisis point a few years ago when everyone took their hands off the wheel. People will always find plausible justifications to spend the government's money. By trying to please some people in the short run, we've hurt everyone for the long haul."

Lewis said, "Although I still need to think it over and talk to Bartow about it, I liked this when we broached it with him the other day; now I love it. We treat everyone equally." He thought some more. "But, wouldn't that run the risk of decimating some programs that really do help people? We could get a lot of criticism from everyone."

Vicki replied, "Yes, and to handle some of the social outcries, we've increased the tax advantages for charitable donations to where there really is an incentive for corporate America to give a damn and give more to support those in need. We've got to get all the departments and agencies to set financial priorities. It may hurt for the short term, but they need to readjust their spending. For the plan to work, we've got to gore everyone's ox."

Mark saw that Collins was about to speak and quickly said, "We've put together the draft of a short bill, which will be released to the media at the same time. Remember, George, it's a proposal designed to appeal to voters. It needs to be explained and defended in simple and understandable terms, but it's not a done deal."

Vicki nodded. "Right. Everyone is either going to have to buy into the bill or reject it with no amendments, but it will be the key to our platform."

Collins mused, "We'd get incredible pushback from Congress and the lobbyists. Two percent cuts could really wreck the economy."

Vicki paused and smiled at Collins. "Well, just between us girls here, we figured they'd negotiate us down to about 1%. The main thing is a change in mindset. One percent would take much longer to correct the direction we've been headed, and that could also hurt the economy, but not as much. Anyway, we've got to start somewhere. Plus, remember we'll save some money by cutting the tax breaks. I don't think we can ever assume Congress will find the backbone to do what is needed to stop the bleeding. They're getting paid by the people who finance their campaigns to keep on shoveling taxpayer benefits to the same folks year after year."

Collins, seeing the direction the conversation was headed, decided to make his arguments another day and acquiesced. "Bold. Anyone that does not like it we can call a tool of the special interests."

Lewis leaned forward. "So how long under this formula to get to a balanced budget… What? Six or seven years?

Vicki nodded. "Maybe. Until we have a balanced budget, we've built in a national security emergency fund and other fail-safes in sort of escrow accounts. Those funds would be padded and would draw interest each year like a national savings account. To access each one of those funds, Congress has to vote on a clean bill with any resources specifically targeted to whatever the critical need is and no money for anything else. George, the point is to change the way we do business in Washington. We need to cut up the credit card."

Mark again pointed out the political benefits. "The point is that this will force priorities in spending and tax revenue. That is not happening today because both sides are gaming the system and Congress uses the appropriations clause and other tricks to spend imaginary money we don't have on the promise we will get it later. Today, no one is making hard decisions on what we can afford. The position Vicki just laid out forces that to happen."

Collins still growled. "It'll raise holy hell with all the institutions of Washington."

Mark chimed in, "Exactly. That's the point. Families and businesses have a rainy-day fund. Average people will get it. This plan cuts through the muddle of government to something that the average person can understand."

Collins wanted to get out of this meeting and let his colleagues know what Vicki DuVall had cooked up and how it would hurt their income once their clients learned they were a part of this proposal. He held up the briefing book. "This book contains the details?"

"Yes." She began to hand out more documents. "That and we also have here summary positions within this budget framework on the environment, trade, international affairs, health, whatever. But, everybody, let me remind you, we've tagged each book here with a large number specific to that book imprinted under the type on each page. Any copying is forbidden, or it will show up and identify the person who leaked."

Mark said, "Good work."

Lewis agreed, "Yes. This is very good."

Collins needed to seem like a team player. "Mark, I like your idea about rolling out one issue a week. Let's you and I talk about that some more. We need to plan on that after Bartow has approved all of this." He turned to Vicki. "Now, has Mr. Bartow seen it?"

To answer Collins' question, Vicki turned to look at Lewis and began, "Not really. Only in bits and pieces, like the other night. We have six other numbered books here and a presentation for you to take to him, George, when you think it's time."

Lewis nodded. "Before we do that, I'm going to warm him up. I've found over the years, it helps to prep an idea with him. It needs to become his idea."

As everyone was breaking up and leaving when they all had their backs turned and were walking out the door, Mark, who had hung behind, touched Vicki's back to get her attention, let his hand slide up, and leaned to put his head on her shoulder next to her neck. With her free hand, she reached up and touched the side of his arm lightly as he moved by her to return to his office.

Republican Consultant Meeting

Two days later, Collins, Benny Weinstein, Don Rizzo, and the recently arrived scheduler, Blane Harper, were meeting in Collins' office. Weinstein began the meeting for Collins. "Okay, guys, we don't have all day. We've got Press and Chappy coming in next week to work on the commercials. Don, you ready for them?"

Rizzo nodded. "Yep."

Weinstein continued, "I'm gonna cover direct mail myself through a firm in California."

Rizzo chimed in, "Yeah. But we don't have a fuckin' budget."

Collins said in his wise-man voice, "We'll get one soon. The little son-of-a-bitch is taking forever to make any decisions, but he's getting there. Is everybody all taken care of here and in your apartments and stuff? Got all the outside stuff set up?"

There were several yeses.

Rizzo said more calmly, "Quite frankly, for some things, this is the best campaign I've ever been in. I've never seen such an efficient administrative staff."

Weinstein responded in his sarcastic voice, "Don, these guys made $4 billion for Bartow being good at administrative shit. You'd think if they can do IBM's stuff, they could do a campaign."

Collins looked around at his subordinates. "Any problems with any of the Bartow staff? Be careful of that guy Burchmeyer. He's a spook or some kind of mercenary. The rest are robots. Just be polite and careful what you say around them and don't spend much time with them. We've got to get Bartow to finish turning this thing over to us."

Don asked, "What about Young and Menendez and the others he brought in?"

Collins shrugged. "They're okay as long as they keep doing what we agreed for them to do. But they're not in our club. Just deal with them as much as you have to. In the short run, having Republicans and Democrats together here was a good media story. As long as they don't get in our way, they're fine."

Weinstein mused, "Because of the matching funds limit for both Bush and Clinton, I'm guessing there will be a lot of money raised on the outside for Bush to put together negative ads. That's where the money will be in his campaign and it will go to other Republican consultants. Too bad we didn't get into that."

Collins came back quickly. "Benny, keep those thoughts to yourself. If there is something wrong with your employment contract and compensation here, let me know. Now!"

"No. It's just… I was thinking out loud and wondering what the Bush and Clinton people are saying. We've got to be driving them crazy. Bartow has everyone's attention and I just wonder if—"

Collins cut him off. "Benny and the rest of you, we don't need to be creating problems by someone overhearing disloyal bullshit, but if you hear what the Bush or Clinton campaigns are going to do through the outside groups, particularly about us, let me know right away. We all are going to do alright once this guy decides to start spending money." He shook his head. "So far the biggest problem I see is that he might want to make the deficit and debt a big issue."

Rizzo scoffed. "Everybody does that."

Collins made a disgusted face. "Don, everybody doesn't mean it. Our democratic friends over in the other offices are trying to make it serious. That could be a problem." He sighed. "However, I think we'd all like to show those smug bastards over at the Bush campaign that we can kick their blue-blood asses."

Morning News

On the *CBS Morning News* show, Bartow was bantering with the host in his usual folksy way. After a commercial break, the red light came on and the host looked at Bartow with concern. "Now, Mr. Bartow, what do you have to say about these rumors that are popping up about your history?"

"What rumors?"

"Well, several people have suggested that, in the past, some of your views imply that you had Nazi sympathies."

"What?! That's the craziest thing I've ever heard. Who the h— Who said that?"

"I don't have that information here, but your opponents have said that they do not have any similar sentiments."

"Listen here! You can stack my support of our country and our military against anyone, including those two. What you said is a bunch of bull."

"I'm just trying to get your side of these public rumors. You know, to give you a chance to clear them up. Another thing being discussed is that you have not treated your employees fairly. There are rumors that you have not them paid well and have been excessively demanding. So far you have not refuted those rumors."

"I have no idea what you are talking about. That is not true. Who said that? I can't answer that crazy crap without knowing who is making those charges. It's not true."

"Let me remind you, Mr. Bartow, this is a morning program, and we have younger listeners who may not appreciate such... colorful language."

"I'm just trying to find who is saying this crazy stuff. You people in the media just repeat wild-ass rumors and this is no way to run a television program or interview a presidential candidate."

As Bartow left the building, a throng of media on the sidewalk shouted for him to answer the questions he was asked on the program, and he flinched as his security detail hustled him into the limo.

In the den of a lavishly decorated home outside of Washington, D.C., Paul Manafort and Roger Stone smiled and clicked their bone china coffee cups together in a toast. "That worked well. Send that gift certificate to our friend in the CBS script research department. Bartow seems to rattle easily. Let's remember that for next time," said Manafort. They were starting to earn their money from the Bush campaign to mess with Bartow.

Bartow Media

Later that morning, Mark huddled with Safta Kleg and Missy Winston. Safta was saying, "I did talk to him and he does not like for us to accompany him on these out-of-town trips."

Mark leaned into her. "That's exactly why they are needed. He needs a buffer to interact with the media. Bartow is not just introducing a new shopping center development. The campaign press office is like having an ambassador in a foreign country. They can be a liaison between two principal powers. The media works best if they like you or understand what you are trying to accomplish. That's what a traveling press officer can bring to the table."

Safta jerked back. "I know that!"

Mark, in a calmer vice, said, "He should not be the one to debate with them. Let the media handler do that. He keeps repeating the bromides against the press as though they were part of his stump speech."

Safta, now calmer herself, said, "He just thinks they ask such snarky questions. He just wants to discuss what he wants to do to help this county."

"Sorry, Safta, but that's not an excuse. His constant attacks on the media make him look petty. He needs someone to be there with him to remind him not to do it. He needs someone to smooth the linkage."

Missy now joined the conversation using her soft, meek voice. "The media think their role is to press him... to find out if he is knowledgeable and if he can handle the unexpected. Presidents need to be able to do that, and they are testing him. A press assistant can help to smooth over that conversation and give the media more complete answers afterwards."

Safta expelled a breath. "Okay. I'll go back to him."

Restaurant

Mark's CIA training was still there, scanning the restaurant as he entered with his colleagues. Over dinner he wanted to get a better feel for Ben Menendez's state-by-state field operation and Missy Winston's progress finding press secretaries in each state. They settled in a booth at the busy Houston's restaurant on Peachtree Street.

They kept the conversation low-key and about the state jobs until after the meals were served and they were eating and enjoying a glass of wine. There was a blackened redfish special, and every few minutes the smell of garlic and cayenne pepper sizzled past the table.

Mark started his probe with a smile at Ben. "You know, Ben, it's true about what you have always said about Republicans."

"What's that?"

"They're like entitled Ivy Leaguers without the manners."

Missy sat her glass down with a clunk on the table. "So, you met Weinstein?"

Mark looked over at her. "I've met 'em all, so has Ben. Or, almost all; they've brought in Blane Harper to schedule."

Ben smirked. "It's like they are just sitting around waiting for Bartow to turn on the faucet. They only picked the jobs that involved cashing checks and punching the clock. They are not doing anything creative, just areas of the campaign that involve spending money and taking credit. We got the part where you need to get your hands dirty and interact and think."

Mark nodded and took a sip of his wine. "Well, there is no point in starting out the campaign fussing and fighting. If it works, there will be enough credit to go around and if not, it won't matter."

Ben scratched his beard. "I've only spent significant time with Rizzo, but I get the feeling they think they're running everything."

Mark nodded. "Yeah. For some people, it's that Washington thing of grabbing onto turf and intimidating everyone you can."

Missy smirked. "Well, they are probably finding justification in saying the same thing about us right now. How are we are going to arbitrate disagreements?" She turned to look directly at Mark. "I don't want to come whining to you about everything."

Mark laughed. "What? You're gonna change at this late date?"

Missy looked down. "Don't get smart." She continued, "It's just that… Collins' little buddy Weinstein… That guy has active hands. I saw Safta's daughter the other day when she came back from doing some errands for him. She was upset. The other day, I passed him in the hall and he sort of playfully slapped me on the butt."

Mark flinched. "What? What did you do?"

"I smiled and told him to keep his slimy hands to himself. But I'm not sure if the young women around here have developed thick skin as yet. The guy's an asshole."

Ben nodded. "What I said."

Mark said, "If he does it again, slap him. Tell me if you see anything again with any other women. I'll get Burchmeyer over at security involved."

Ben moderated. "We've all got to do our jobs and stay friendly with everybody. The Bartow people are fast learners, but they probably see no difference between us and the Republicans. That being said, we can't have Weinstein abusing women."

Mark nodded in agreement. "Another problem is the Collins group are ignoring the Bartow people."

Missy was perplexed. "What do they have to be arrogant about?"

Ben said, "I think it is that Washington power trip Mark was talking about. They think they're God's gift because they know how to read a poll."

Mark sighed. "Whatever it is, we gotta live with them. And,

we gotta make up for their attitude with the Bartow people."

Missy frowned. "Campaigns aren't fun anymore." She looked over at Ben. "I remember you telling me about letting the air out of the tires of the Moral Majority busses in North Carolina the night before the election so they couldn't haul all those people to go vote." Then she turned to Mark and said, "And I remember you getting the phone bank numbers of the GOTV for Reagan and getting the unemployed steel workers to call them from those pay phones in the country crossroads and then leave the phone dangling off the hook to tie up the lines."

Mark smiled, remembering. "Well, we used to be able to get away with some things at a certain level of the campaign, but now that we've become so sophisticated and mature..."

Missy snorted. "Right! At least we're getting well paid."

Mark moved to another subject he wanted to discuss. "Okay, looks like after that CBS morning interview, the media romance with Bartow is over. He did not look good, but the anchor pushed the questioning and looked too aggressive. Missy, continue to work on Safta to get him to have a press assistant go with him and to let us brief him before he goes on these programs. She started to come around in our discussion the other day."

Mark nodded at Missy. "Did you check with your CBS friends on who did the research for the *Morning News* interview like we discussed?"

"Yes. Working on it. I told you I'd get it done."

"Just checking."

"You're annoyingly persistent."

"Isn't the nature of persistence to be annoying?"

"Yes, and you've mastered it."

Ben laughed. "Okay, kids. Don't fight in the sandbox."

Mark nodded at Ben. "It's just the CBS research people... it was a setup. However, that kind of an ambush is exactly why we need his approval on the issues." He tapped the table. "Ben, we need to get a system of faxing information to the state coordinators and media people in the states when this kind of thing happens. We've got to build backfires and give our field people talking points before Bartow goes on the air or makes a speech. Send out a daily message fax blast, no more than a page."

Been said, "Good. Missy, let's meet each evening about 7:30 after the national news and come up with those talking points for the next day."

Benny Weinstein's Trouble

Julie entered Benny Weinstein's office flustered and worried. "Benny, ah, Mr. Weinstein, I think you had better come take a look and see what you can do."

Benny frowned, looking down at the papers on his desk as he spoke. "Julie, hon… Sweetie, I'm busy here. Can't you get someone else to help you?"

Julie, now more worried, said, "But it's the security; they've arrested the guy that was with you earlier."

Now Benny looked up with a surprised expression on his face. "Who?! You mean Chappy Knight?" Not waiting for an answer, he quickly got up and moved, hobbling to the door where Julie was standing. "Arrested? Where?"

As he left the entry office, he shouted over at his secretary, "Hold my calls. Find Burchmeyer, tell him I want to see him." He looked at Julie and nodded for her to lead the way." Then, on second thought, he shouted back at his secretary as Julie swiped the door for them to move out into another security-block area. "No. Just find out where Burchmeyer is. I may need to talk to him later."

He exited the Collins office complex and followed Julie with his congenital limp down hallways through several offices, where a security man in a blue blazer and gray pants had Chappy Knight pinned against the wall with one hand while talking on his walkie-talkie radio with the other. The young man was no taller than 5'10" but his arms tightly filled the sleeves of the sport coat, and his buzz-cut hair and thick neck made him look like a drill sergeant. He was carrying a foot-long heavy silver metal flashlight sticking out from under his jacket through his belt that looked like a billy club.

The fireplug spoke into the walkie-talkie. "Yeah. That's right, he's a real smart one. Said he was from the Republican Party.

No. He didn't have any campaign ID. Has no visitor's pass, nothing!" He pushed Chappy Knight harder against the wall as he was struggling to get his breath.

"I said, 'KEEP STILL'."

He then spoke again into the walkie-talkie. "Yeah. Send over Rudy, and tell Mr. Burchmeyer."

In the long corridor, Benny Weinstein ran a hand along the wall to keep his balance on his uneven legs as he rushed forward with Julie trailing behind. "Hold it! Hold just a Goddamn minute! What the hell do you think you're doing?"

The security man gave Benny a glance and then spoke again into his walkie-talkie. "Hold on, someone just came up." Then, to Benny he spoke evenly, in a calm, official voice. "Can I help you, sir?"

Benny, now red-faced from moving quickly through the maze of offices and seeing one of the top Republican media men in the nation being manhandled by one of Burchmeyer's goons, said, "Yes, you can. Let go of this man. He's with me."

Again, politely he said, "And who are you, sir?"

"I'm Benny Weinstein, the deputy campaign manager of this Goddamn campaign and whoever you are, you work for me. "

"I'm sorry sir, but I've never seen you before and I work for Mr. Burchmeyer. Do you have some identification?"

Benny took off the swipe pass clipped to his jacket that was needed to access the various levels of security through the building and slammed it to the floor. "Yeah. I've got this chickenshit, fucking pass and an office back there in the inner sanctum. And... I work for this campaign 14 hours a day, that's why you haven't seen me. The man you are trying to kill over there is the guy who is going to make the TV commercials for Mr. Bartow that will hopefully get him elected. Now, will you BACK OFF, you fucking Nazi?"

The security man eased up slightly on Knight but kept him facing the wall with his hands cuffed. In the distance, a door down the hall opened and John Burchmeyer entered with two other men and walked briskly toward the group.

The security man, still talking in an even voice, said, "Mr.

Weinberg. My job is to protect the security of this campaign. When I stopped this man because he did not have a pass, he got smart with me and would not identify himself. I have specific orders to detain individuals under those circumstances. And I don't appreciate your addressing me with derogatory comments."

"It's Weinstein, you fucking idiot."

The noise of Weinstein's shouting had attracted other people, whose heads were sticking out of doors from nearby offices to see what the commotion was about. Burchmeyer had now reached the gathering in the hallway.

Chappy coughed and held up his hand as though he wanted to speak.

Benny, with his blood still up at the guard, looked over to him, said, "What?"

Chappy, in a meek but calm voice, said, "It's okay, just let me go. I've got a plane to catch, and I just want to get out of this place."

By this time, Burchmeyer was taking charge. "Hold it. Hold everything," he said to Chappy Knight. "Mister, who are you?"

Benny said, "He's Chappy Knight. His firm has been hired to make the commercials for the campaign. He's the best Republican advertising man there is. And this... this guy here has been mudwrestling with him."

Burchmeyer, in the same calm voice as the guard, said, "Mr. Weinstein, I can appreciate the stress you must be feeling. But I hope you can understand that our job is to prevent surreptitious entry into this campaign, as well as guarding of all personnel and information in this building." He turned to Knight. "Mr. Knight, were you not given a pass when you entered this building?"

Knight, catching his breath now that the guard was not pressing him into the wall, whispered, "I came up the elevator with Mr. Weinstein. We walked past the desk and came on in here. Benny got busy with something, and I was on a walkabout to see what the rest of the campaign looked like, when this guy grabbed me."

Burchmeyer now turned to Benny. "Mr. Weinstein, don't you know that ALL personnel in this building, particularly in the red-code restricted areas, must have a pass and be accompanied by someone with proper authorization?"

Benny threw up his hands. "Look, this is a campaign. It's not a boot camp. It's not the Pentagon. The Russians aren't going to invade."

Burchmeyer squinted at Benny. "Weinstein? That's Jewish, right?"

Benny nodded.

"I thought all Jews were Liberals and Democrats."

"Not the smart ones."

Bruchmeyer smiled and nodded and continued with the same calm voice. "Mr. Weinstein, we had good reasons to make these rules. We enforce them without prejudice. No matter what job they are doing, if anyone does something unauthorized, we in security will adhere to our simple and fair restrictions. You need a credential to move around." He bent and picked up Benny's pass and studied it. "If you don't agree to that rule, you can't stay in the building. I've been handling Mr. Bartow's security for eight years now, and I know he concurs with what I have just stated."

Benny, realizing he should not have thrown down the pass, fumbled. "But..."

Burchmeyer turned to Chappy. "Mr. Knight, we regret any inconvenience this has caused you; please remember our restrictions in the future. Mr. Weinstein, if you have guests who wish to see other areas of the campaign, and you are too busy to take them, please call our office. We would be happy to provide an escort as you require."

He turned to the security guard and nodded. "You did your job." He then handed Benny his pass. "If you gentlemen will excuse us, we also have work to do. If you don't need someone to show Mr. Knight out, we'll be going now. Good day." Burchmeyer turned and retraced his steps back down the hall with all three security men in tow.

Manafort and Stone

As the slightly overweight woman with very red lipstick waited for her meeting, she nervously patted her hair, which was piled in a large bun on the top of her head. Roger Stone and Paul Manafort watched through the one-way glass as she re-adjusted herself on the sofa. Manafort shook his head. "Not sleazy enough. Where'd you get her?"

Stone cocked his head to the side and studied the woman. "I'm told she's a regular at the hotel bar where he hangs out in Little Rock. We looked at a couple of the others, but she may be the most… well, not articulate, but once you get her going, she blabbers on and on forever."

"So, she had sex with…"

"Said she did."

"Any photos or recordings, or anything like that?"

"Unfortunately not."

"Did she take the money?"

"Yep."

"Mmmm. Whoever we trot out for the first time has to be believable. We can't risk some wannabe to get discredited right out the box. The press and Carville will jump all over her to cut her story apart."

The woman flexed her shoulders and picked at her nose as she looked around the room with some impatience.

Manafort nodded. "That was a nice touch."

Stone, now getting impatient himself, threw up his hands. "Look, if she's not right, we can—"

Manafort cut him off. "No. Let's get some photos of her. Get a statement. Not a deposition and all legal-like, just a one-page account of her side of what happened. Make it juicy. They've got to know that this story is coming. Let's just spook them for now. I'll get one of our friends over at Tyson Foods to sneak it to the Little Rock media like he's doing them a favor. Let the Clinton folks spend time defusing her story and hiding her. She'll get paid from both ends. It'll get their team all riled up and worried and then give us time to see what we can do to old Bartow."

Stone smiled. "I like it."

"Yeah. Get her to make a lot of demands for money when they come to shut her up. Drag it out and distract them before she caves."

Stone laughed. "They'll realize what's coming at them and be looking over their shoulders for the rest of the campaign."

Bernice Bartow - Charity

Mark reread an article in the society section of the *Washington Times* newspaper with an interview speculating that all of the Bartow family donations were only for tax write-offs and they cared nothing for any of the charities they had supported. He knew it was a plant from one of their opponents and went to ask Missy to build a backfire. He knocked on her door and then entered. She was pacing the floor and talking to Bartow's wife on the speakerphone. He hesitated as Missy held up her hand. Then she held a finger to her lips, and he heard what he later found out was the voice of Bernice Bartow on the speakerphone.

"I just don't know why those people have to call me and ask about what we have been doing with our charity donations. That's private information. Bill and I have not been helping out for publicity."

Missy answered in her polite child's voice, "Yes, ma'am."

"I'm not going to let everyone come in and pry into our private lives."

Missy rolled her eyes at Mark. "Yes, ma'am. We don't want that either."

"Well, good! I thought you people were supposed to protect us from that kind of intrusion."

Missy shrugged at Mark. "Yes, we are, and we do. However, it is well known that you and your husband have been very generous to the city of Atlanta and to many national charities, and the media are going to be making inquiries into your charitable giving."

"Well, that's our business."

"Yes, ma'am. When we are called by the media with questions, it would be helpful to be able to tell them more about why you have supported those charities. That's the material we sent over to you. We suggested some things we can say to the media about your generosity. That's information that will help people relate to you and Mr. Bartow better."

"Well, Bill tells me you folks at the campaign are trying to tell him everything to do. He won't stand for that, I can tell you."

"Yes, ma'am."

Mark waved, made a face, and slowly and quietly closed the door.

Bernice Bartow continued, "Why would they want to know that? It's snooping into other people's lives."

"Ma'am, it's been reported that you and your husband, who is trying to become the President of the United States, have given over $200 million to charity over the past 10 years. If that's true, it helps to define you and your husband as generous and kind people, and that should help the public like you and Mr. Bartow. They don't know much about you, and they are asking questions to find out more."

"Well, I'll see what I can do. Ask Safta to call me this afternoon. I'm on my way to get my hair done and it's getting late. What did you say your name was?"

The Today Show

Three days later, Collins' girlfriend, who was one of the producers at NBC and aware what an audience draw he was, arranged for Bartow to be interviewed yet again on the *Today Show*.

As Mark watched from his office, Bartow was holding forth. "No, you've got that wrong, I don't have any pollsters and professional politicians working for me. We do have some folks helping to organize the national campaign, but this is still very much dependent on the volunteers and grassroots. I don't have any handlers or gurus or spin doctors and never will have."

He leaned back. "Now, to answer your other question—"

The host leaned into Bartow. "On the White House statement about the deficit."

Bartow smirked. Because he had been ambushed the previous time on CBS, this setup question was the agreement with the NBC program's producer to get him back on their program. "So, it's like this, and hold on to your hats, folks, 'cause this is coming straight from the horse's mouth." He laughed. "Our president's chief of staff—now, not one of these nameless sources you hear about, but the real thing—said just the other day that they were growing down the deficit."

Bartow smiled and raised both hands, palms up. Then he slapped them down on the counter. "Now if that doesn't tell you what is wrong with this government, I don't know what will."

The host reading from a script, who had not been informed of the deal to ask Bartow the debt question, was now feeling he was losing some control quickly, said, "But, Mr. Bartow, you must agree that..."

Bartow turned and looked at the host with effrontery. "Now, wait just a minute. You asked me about this, now just let me finish answering the question."

Bartow now looked directly into the camera, which was just behind the host's shoulder. "Here we are, folks, in the ninth inning of a losing game and the home team, which is way behind, sends out another pitcher in the hopes that if they just stop giving up so many runs, then the game will turn around."

Bartow shook his head. "I don't know how stupid these people think our fellow American voters are, but we know the deficit is running out of control. We know that interest in the debt is eating up our children's futures. We know that the interest, just the interest on the debt our country owes ALONE, is almost equal to… to what we pay annually to our elderly in Social Security or to maintain our national defense. Washington is running our government on a giant credit card. They are not paying for what they spend and that debt is piling up, and after they have been paid by lobbyists to run up the debt, they expect our children and grandchildren to take care of the bill.

"Folks, the alarm bells should be going off all over this country. We are in big trouble, big-time, and this guy comes out and says they are going to GROW DOWN the problem." He then smiled into the camera and shook his head side to side.

The host was trying to get the interview back under control. "But, Mr. Bartow, what I asked you was—"

Bartow, who was becoming irritated, turned to the host. "Would you PLEASE just let me finish? You asked me the question, now have the common decency your mama taught you to let me answer it before you interrupt with another question."

He turned back to the camera. "Folks, if your company was losing money like a bucket with a big hole in it, and your boss came out and said that they were going to stop the leak by pouring less water into the bucket, you would think they were crazy. You'd start looking for another job, 'cause you'd know that company was not long for this world." He smiled.

The host started to speak, but Bartow rolled on.

"Just look a here." He pulled out one of the charts Vicki had been using in her briefings and held it with one hand. He waved his other hand across the studio. "Bring in that camera you got over there to see this." Then he tapped the poster. "See here where we're spending $200 billion—that's with a 'B'—dollars MORE each year than we are taking in. You can't run a business like that, and we should not be running our government like that. Just look a here." He tapped the chart and waved it toward the camera.

The host looked down at his notes and then back to Bartow. "Mr. Bartow, we're running out of time."

Now calming down so as not to look ungracious with the host, Bartow quickly searched and then turned to the camera with the red light on it so he would be talking directly to the audience. "So, my point is this, don't let these Washington big shots try to put one over on you. You're smarter than that, and come November we're gonna let them know we're tired of the same old promises and do-nothing ways."

"Mr. Bartow, we've only got about 30 seconds left, but tell three things you would do to balance the budget."

Bartow leaned back like the host was speaking in another language. "Well, you can't explain how to balance the budget in 30 seconds. It took us 200 years to get in this mess and we're gonna have to all roll up our sleeves together to solve it. But I'll tell you one thing, I'd cut all the perks and freebies in Congress and the agencies. You don't need cabinet officers with their own personal chefs and physical trainers paid for with borrowed money that the taxpayers are gonna have to be paying back for the next generation."

The frustrated host, now trying to wrap up, said, "Mr. Bartow, I'm afraid..."

Bartow continued, "For starters, you don't need a fleet of airplanes standing by to take the Congress and administration officials to golf vacations to Tahiti and safaris in Africa." He turned to look into the camera. "Folks, it's time to cut up the credit card, and I'm just the man to do it."

The host, turning back to look directly into the camera, said, "I'm sorry, we're out of time. Thank you for coming on our program today, Mr. William Bartow, independent candidate for president, whose recent surge in the polls has him running almost neck and neck with both the current president and his Democratic challenger. Next, on *Today*, we've got our friend and wildlife naturalist, Jim Fowler, with some baby egrets."

Lunch

Mark was having sandwiches in the war room with Benny Weinstein, Ralph Collins and Vicki DuVall, and they began by reviewing Bartow's *Today Show* interview.

Vicki laughed. "I find it interesting to be having lunch with people who don't exist."

The ever-aggressive Benny responded, "Well, at least you're on the staff roster! We've had to list our polling team onto the org chart as speech researchers. We're afraid if the old man sees a line item for polling, he'll fire the lot of them. By the way, it's kind of a weird nepotism having you two married and in key positions on this campaign. Never seen that before."

Vicki popped back, "Well, Benny, I'm guessing there are a lot of thigs in this campaign that are unconventional, like us working on the same side. So, I hear Bartow actually looks at his budgets. What you are doing with the money?"

Benny shrugged. "Dunno. It's his money. They tell me he wants to know how his money is being spent. The richer the guy, the tighter they are with their money."

Collins grimaced and cut into the conversation. "Okay, enough of that. DuVall, we've got to take some positions on some issues. The press is picking us apart. The *Times* this morning did a piece about how we don't stand for anything. Mark, you must have really pissed Sandy off when you had lunch. She whined to me all afternoon."

Vicki said, "Yes, however, based on your meeting with Bartow, at least now we have the green light to define his positions. We're going to send him two to three ideas at a time so it won't be too much for him to… learn. The worm is starting to turn, as you macho boys would say. So, did you actually see our boy on the *Today Show*?"

Collins sighed. "He was all over the place. Still not being nice enough to the media. He didn't do what your girl Missy told him to do. They'll hold a grudge. Just you watch."

Vicki smiled. "I'm talking about the graphics."

Collins nodded. "Yeah. Your chart was the best thing he did on the show."

Mark now smiled as well. "It looked unplanned." He nodded to Collins "Good job, Ralph, with your lady friend there."

Collins nodded back and smiled.

Mark continued, "He was definitely not very smooth in his delivery, but we did fire a shot across the bow. His unconventional style plays well. He must have liked the charts to carry one to the interview and use it. He may not be reading everything we are sending in to him, but at least he's looking at the pictures. Let's include graphics with all our descriptions of the issues. Charts may help articulate our positions and... strangely, it makes him look smarter."

Weinstein frowned. "Yeah, but until he agrees to the positions and our budget gets sorted out, nobody knows what Bartow stands for. I was scared to death he'd actually try to answer the question about what he'd do about the deficit. He doesn't have a clue and neither do we, although we seem to have staked our future on that turf. We NEED to be on television."

Weinstein turned to Mark with a slightly accusatory tone in his voice, which was how he approached many conversations. "Mark, our guy is saying the same thing over and over again about what is wrong with the country and all that crap. When are you gonna give them reasons why they should really like him?"

Vicki continued to speak as if Benny's remarks had been directed at her and not her husband. "Benny, I know the problem. We've cracked the wall and got the major positions identified, but we need him actually to BELIEVE in some of them. We need to work deficit and debt language into each issue position. George is taking them in to him, and we will get some results soon. We're ready to roll out the 'issue a week idea,' once he blesses them. If we do this right, each position will reinforce the others and all be part of his big economic message. But we need his okay. Hang tight."

Mark joined in. "If we use charts with everything, it will help him understand and decide."

Collins smirked, as he often did, to show he knew better. "Tell you what. Give me the top 10 issues. No more than a page on each one. A paragraph or bullet points would be better. I'll get with George and we'll go sit on him till we have some of it done. We can't make commercials or send out direct mail or write good speeches until we define what he stands for."

Mark skipped over Collins, assuming that he was the one to decide these things, and cut him out. It was a task they had agreed to do together. He also believed that, because of the collegial nature of most of the Bartow staff, nothing would come of Collins' aggressive demeanor, and he said, "I've been trying to read this guy and he's not easy. He seems almost scared to define what he stands for because it's likely he does not really know. Most politicians are more afraid of making mistakes than having good ideas. I think it's better to let him take one bite at the time—like you and George and I agreed."

Weinstein immediately said, "What d'ya mean? We don't have the time to dance around. We've got to start paid media and we've got to get going on mail and phone banks and stuff. Ralph is right. The press is killing us."

Collins, now taking the good-cop approach, and turning to Mark patiently, said, "Benny, let him finish. What do you mean?" He stopped talking and looked over as the door opened.

George Lewis joined them. "Sorry, folks. I got tied up. What did I miss?"

Collins looked at Lewis as he sat. "Glad you could join us. We're discussing,"—he gave Mark a look—"how to speed up the process of getting Bill Bartow to decide his positions so we can get on television and define him. We need to get this campaign running on all cylinders now. It's time to start that 'issue of the week' thing, and it will take several weeks to fully roll out."

Lewis looked at Collins. "I'm meeting with him tonight and will sit with him until I have at least one or two agreements on his positions, and I'll get the rest as soon as possible. But what were you talking about with a rollout of one issue a week?"

Collins pointed over to Mark. "Tell Lewis how it would work."

Mark smiled at the campaign manager. "The good side of no one knowing what Mr. Bartow stands for, and that he has a ton of money, is that we can define him. We can use the media and public interest in his beliefs to create demand. We'd start with television spots saying, for instance, 'Listen on Wednesday for Bartow's speech on education.' Then he'd give the speech and we'd cut commercials from the speech and play them all through the weekend. Then we'd start over on Monday with, 'Listen to what Bartow is saying about jobs.' He can go on the television talk shows and repeat the message of the speech and then promote the next week's speech.

"We'd dominate the campaign dynamic, build a huge television audience for the speech, and have a week to hammer home the message. He's got the money to dominate the airwaves with our paid advertising. The best part would be that the news media would be asking our opponents what they thought of Bartow's message and positions. They'd be reacting to us rather than defining themselves. I figure, once we start, we can ride it for about 10 weeks timed to happen just before our convention and theirs. The Bartow campaign would control the summer."

Now Vicki was joining in enthusiastically. "We could produce position papers which would be compared the other candidates' positions and point out problems in their areas. Plus, come up with more charts for him to use in the explanation."

Lewis laughed. "Damn. Where'd you come up with all that?"

Mark continued, "I've been thinking about it for some time, but never had a candidate with the mystery or the money to make it happen."

Not to be left out, Collins said, "Yes. We've been discussing this here among ourselves." He looked at Lewis as is if to explain. "Now, this idea is only effective because no one knows anything about him and there is all this curiosity. We can use the media interest in Bartow and make it a theme for the week. That's an idea we've been kicking around."

Weinstein added redundantly, "We'd have the press going to the other candidates and asking them what they thought about Bartow's positions."

Mark now jumped back in to get George Lewis' attention before they could completely run away with his idea. "Question is, will Bartow do it? Let's take the budget deficit, which he spoke about on the *Today Show*. What if Ralph gets his media people to write some spots, quickly and simply, on budget deficits. Use some of the language or cut some of the lines directly from his *Today Show* interview. Get them to George here to take to Bartow FAST before he forgets what he said.

"George, you can explain to him that he is leading the charge and we need to push what he has started. Let's make it his idea. We can find another issue next week for him. It is not perfect or cohesive like we would want, but if we can get him started to define himself, then maybe we can get ahead of him and coordinate ideas one at a time in subsequent weeks. Ronald Reagan connected with voters using a rebellious tone and underlying humor. We're recommending the tag line: 'Balance the damn budget,' even if we have to blank a couple of letters in the word damn."

Lewis smiled. "He might just like that."

Collins reassumed his 'I'm the boss' posture. "He's got to do something. Christ! He's running neck and neck with the other two candidates. He's a player. He's got to start acting like a candidate. Certain things are expected of a campaign I run. Frank Press and Chappy Knight are coming in here next week with the material they've been shooting and they said the film looks good. We've got to get a media budget approved and get some spots on the air. And, I like this idea we've come up with for an issue a week. That might work. I'll get them to do a rough cut of a spot based on the *Today Show* interview on the deficit. Be interested to see what Frank and Chappy think about it."

Vicki, making her 'to do' list from this meeting, looked at George Lewis. "Well, in the meantime, I'll try to have those position paper summaries on your desk tomorrow with a comparison showing our position compared to the other guys."

Acting as though the remark had been directed at him instead of Lewis, Collins nodded and said, "Good."

Benny, not to be left out of the emerging plan, said, "I'll run some numbers on the issue-a-week roll out and look at media buys, events, and backdrops for each issue, print materials, media mailings, all that."

Mark, ever cautious and keeping in mind that all of them were the hired help in the campaign in what was an otherwise tight group of old associates from Bartow Industries, said, "George, what do you think? Will he go along with this idea?"

"It will go over better with Bartow if it's his idea."

Collins, realizing the logic of Mark's thoughts, said, "Good idea. I'll talk to him."

Mark, feeling the edge of Collins' aggressiveness, but still trying to keep it friendly, suggested, "Maybe on this new concept, we should let George here have the first shot." Mark suddenly froze and, wrinkling his brow, he looked down, mulling something over.

Collins looked at Lewis. "Want me to come with you?"

Lewis shook his head. "No. You go on and do what you're doing. Think about how we would put in the advertising. Put cost figures with it. I can handle this." He turned to Mark. "How is the war room coming?"

Mark said absentmindedly, "Another day or so."

Collins smiled. "Good. We need to start having our daily meetings in there. That way we can have a better chance of keeping what we are doing a secret."

Mark then slapped the table, which made everyone flinch. "No. Collins is right. We can't keep playing this campaign on the margins. We need to fish or cut bait. George, get us a meeting with him as soon as possible. Tell him the campaign is at a crisis point."

Come to Jesus

George Lewis, Ralph Collins, and Mark Young had gathered earlier to discuss how they would present their arguments to Mr. Bartow and who would do the talking. Lewis had implied to Bartow that this meeting represented a critical time in the campaign. He told Mark and Collins that Bartow was irritable and in a bad mood. Collins surprisingly had backed off and suggested that Mark be the main speaker. Mark wondered if his reticence gave him cover to say later that any problems from the meeting were not his idea, or if Bartow got really upset, he could fire Mark and keep Collins to run the entire show.

As they settled into the plush leather, Mark could feel that Bartow was nervous and defensive. The nuances of a campaign were foreign to Bartow, and he still did not understand that a candidate needed to understand the facts to sway public opinion. Mark whispered to Collins, "Last chance, do you want to make the pitch?"

He whispered back, "You go ahead, and I'll back you up."

Bartow scowled around the room and said, "George here tells me you all,"—nodding at Mark and Collins—"have something to tell me." He emphasized the word "tell" as though the imposition of unpleasantness had brought them together. He opened his hands wider to indicate they needed to get on with it. "Well, go ahead."

Mark sat up taller and cleared his throat to indicate to Bartow he was the one to deliver the bad news. "Mr. Bartow, we've been planning how to help you win this presidential election. We have a good team of experience and knowledge coming from both directions of politics, and you have the money to sell yourself. Let me play the devil's advocate for a minute."

Mark paused. "Mr. Bartow, I am going to be very frank here. People don't know why you are running or what you want to do if you are elected. We can give you suggestions on what we believe will be good for this country and what people will like to hear, but you must and let me repeat this… you MUST tell us what you want us to do to help you, and also what you stand for. We've sent you positions on a number of issues, as well as campaign budget information and you have not responded.

"By looking at what you have said in the past, and recently on TV, we think a focus on the deficit is a good basis for your candidacy. It reinforces your businessman persona. We can make everything spin off that to build your case. However, the public must believe you mean it, and we have no reason to be here unless you can make us believe it.

"Presidential campaigns are wars. There are skirmishes and battles, air raids and ground attacks. They involve strategy and tactics. None of it means anything without passion. It takes a leader who can convey their passion to the troops to give them the courage to run into combat. With you, the passion comes FROM the troops. You don't show it. You are treating this presidential campaign with only casual interest.

"Even so, you are doing remarkably well, due to the passion of your supporters. However, you've been skating along because people assume that you agree with them. Now that idea is getting old, and they are starting to wonder if you stand for anything. You have to give them something. If you don't, then they will make another choice, and frankly they should.

"Unless you start to run a real campaign, you will become a target and take incoming fire that will destroy the reputation that you have built over many years. Right now, you are wrapped in the Velcro of public attention. All the negative stuff that your opponents and the media will throw at you will stick. It will not only make you look bad, it will make your family look bad. Think of all the soldiers you have supported over the years who fought for their country. How is it going to look to them if you will not put up a fight?

"If you were selling a building and your staff told you in order to make the sale you needed to paint the lobby, replace the carpet, put flowers outside, and then put ads on TV and send out brochures, you'd do it. This campaign is a much more complicated version of that. You are not marketing yourself and you are not going to make the sale unless you do. But this is not a real estate deal. This is selling you and your ideas, concepts and messages to the public. You have never had do that. We have.

"Ralph Collins and I are good at what we do. You have a good staff and team at the campaign. We have a plan that will make you win. You need to let us do our work, and part of that is for you to listen to what we have to say. You don't have to do all we ask, but so far you have done virtually none of what we have requested. Ask yourself, why do you have us here? If you are not going to listen to us and get engaged in this campaign, which you can win, by the way, then we might as well go home and leave you to do whatever you want.

"You are out of time. Give us the green light to tell you how to run for president and how to win. Give us a budget to work with. We need to go on TV. We need to control your campaign schedule. We need to define what you stand for. We need to tell you what to say to get the reporters off your back. And you need to let us. We need decisions from you now."

"If you do that, you will have a tremendous advantage over the Democrats and the Republicans as candidates." Mark took in a breath and leaned back.

Bartow broke his frown to ask, "What advantage is that?"

"They are both trying to become something they are not; you just have to decide who you are."

Bill Bartow stared at Mark and let his chair rock back and forth a few times. Then he looked over at Lewis and Collins. When he spoke, his head rotated back and forth between them all, but mostly it was focused on Mark.

"This campaign thing has grown into more than I thought it would. When I was on Larry King, I was just speculating, and I think he was leading me on. Next thing I know I'm actually running for president. People are expecting me to lead them and this country that I love." He waved his hand around in the air. "All this stuff has come as a shock to me and my family. All of a sudden, we are the center of everybody's attention. I'm not used to this level of scrutiny." He tapped on his desk with a knuckle. "I'm also worried that the budget and deficit position could wreck the economy. But the horse is out of the barn. I don't want to embarrass my family, myself, and mostly all those soldiers who have believed in me and who I've supported all these years."

Mark answered quietly, "There is a risk. With the deficit thing, we'd be dealing with a controlled crash now rather than a catastrophic highway multi-vehicle pileup later. You are the one who has to decide if you want to shake things up."

Bartow sighed. "Yeah. I haven't done more than scan all those papers you have been sending me. Maybe I thought it would sort itself out. But that's not going to happen. I'm kinda trapped in this thing." He stared at Mark. "I heard what you just said. I didn't like to hear it, but I get it. If I gotta do this, I'm going to do it to win. I've got three stipulations. If the campaign gets to my family and upsets them or hurts them, I'm out. If this effort makes me risk the business I've built up over the years and rely on, I'm out. If I find out your guys,"—his finger pointed and waved back and forth between Mark and Collins—"are screwing me or lying to me, I'm out and,"—he looked over at Lewis—"I'll fire you for not managing these guys and watching my back. I'm trusting you to take care of me on this."

George Lewis immediately said, "That's not going to happen."

Bartow nodded. "Okay, then you three have a job to do. George, bring back to me in a priority order the decisions I need to make. Give me pros and cons like we do when we're working on deals and put budget numbers by each decision and I'll settle on the first three tomorrow so I can get these press people off my back for not being specific. Let me make this crystal clear: I'm not going to be micromanaged. If I feel like doing something, I'm damn well going to do it."

George nodded. "Absolutely."

"Okay, set me up to approve what you call the issues and then I'll promote them. Now, I'm not just going to open my wallet for you guys to run TV ads night and day willy-nilly. I want to see operational plans and budgets for every month and every week. George…"

"Yes."

"Let's set up a briefing every morning, starting Monday."

"Will do."

"Okay, boys, let's go to work."

As they were leaving, Lewis was in a very upbeat mood and was fist-pumping when Collins leaned over to Mark and whispered, "You should have said something more about making a big media buy."

Mark answered, "In case you didn't notice, we only got a start there. Maybe not even half a loaf. I don't know if it's your experience, but in most campaigns, there is time when the candidates realize they can't just keep running their business or taking family vacations. There is a time when it gets real, and they realize it's a seven-day-a-week commitment they have to make or they should fold. Most of them are too far gone by that time and it would be too embarrassing to quit, so they buckle down and really become candidates. I hope that is what will happen here, but he's not fully on board yet."

Mail Room

Six volunteers were busy sorting mail by hand in the mail room. Missy Winston and Reid Field were walking along among them as they dumped money, dog tags, checks, letters, and resumes out of the envelopes. The task of sorting all of this into cohesive piles looked enormous.

Missy shook her head. "My God! Look at all this stuff."

The conservative Reid Field considered this deluge of mail falling out of the envelopes as a technical problem that needed to be solved. "Yes." He explained to Missy, "We get about 25,000 letters and packages a day now and over 200,000 calls."

Missy waved her arm. "How do you deal with all this? Who handles all this stuff?"

"Well, security gets it from the post office and scans it. Bartow Industries set up the operation, and when it comes in, we sort it by campaign department, then open and code for priority of response, and—"

Missy nervously asked, "WHO is making all these judgment calls?"

Reid, not fully understanding the question or why it was asked, said, "Well, we're using our volunteers to actually run the functions of the operation. They're supervised of course, and—"

Missy muttered to herself, "Mmmmm. Good. I don't know if the national media are ready to see what's in here."

Reid, overhearing her, jumped in. "What?! Media? No. We don't want any press. Mr. Bartow has not authorized—"

Missy sighed at him and folded her arms. "Reid, we are contenders to be the President of the United States. The press has to report on SOMETHING. We are still deciding our positions on issues and, so far, the candidate will only talk to a select few people in the media, like those on the *Today Show* or Larry

King, who are not real journalists. Real reporters only want to talk to him. They don't really care about talking to anyone else. We're not giving them anything to report."

She stopped walking, put her hands on her hips, looked Reid directly in the eye, and said sarcastically, "You do realize there is a good and positive story here in how the public is responding to Bartow's candidacy." Now back to a normal voice. "This place here is the graphic representation of Bartow's support from all over this country. It shows the volunteers … the people, making decisions. However, TV people can't say that; they've got to show it. This place helps. It's graphic, but it might not be exactly right." She imagined a picture with the tables and workers set up differently for a better camera shot. She visualized the television news with a camera rolling by the piles of mail one table after the other with volunteers dumping out dollars, cookies, letters to Bartow….

Reid shook his head and made a nervous grimace. "I think they just need to report on something else. Let them film the volunteer phone bank."

Missy, half listening to him, responded, "They've done that 10 times already. Until we get the issue stuff ready, which may take a week or two, we need... some... variety or they will start looking for trouble spots, reporting bad rumors, anticipating problems, or interviewing our opponents about our campaign."

Reid drew back, somewhat shocked. "Our opponents?! Why in the world would they do that?"

Missy, now realizing Reid's incomprehension, looked at him in disbelief. "That's how they work, Reid. That shows conflict. It shows tension. It shows animosity. It shows trouble in River City. It gets people's attention. People's attention gets ratings. That's how they earn their money."

Reid, still trying to comprehend, said, "But, why? That's cheating somehow."

Missy smiled slightly. "Yeah, somehow it doesn't seem fair, but, Reid, that's the deep pond we are in and we need to start swimming. I'll talk to Mark about it."

After she finished with Reid and was walking back to her

office, Missy was thinking how she'd pitch this mail room media opportunity to Mark. Suddenly she remembered an earlier campaign when Mark had rescued her from an uncomfortable situation with the brother-in-law of the candidate. He was an arrogant, clueless guy who would not back off on harassing her. She had tried to talk to him about his advances in polite terms, but he kept coming on to her. Sometimes it took a big guy like Mark intimidating them to make the point. Mark got in his face and threatened him with bodily injury, and the man backed off immediately and never even spoke to Missy again.

Roger Stone and the Volunteer

The young woman finished her shift in the Bartow volunteer office, squared up her desk for the next day, waved at her coworkers, and walked to her 1986 red Miata. Following her instructions, she drove to the pay phone at a strip center where she often grabbed her supper to go at the Schlotzsky's restaurant. She dialed the number and the familiar voice answered.

"Is this Mr. Stone?"

"Yeah. Who else would answer this line?"

"Sorry. I just wanted to make sure I had the right person."

"What you got for me?"

"It was another very busy day. Phones kept ringing, but I did notice the managers looking worried one time when they were gathered over at the side, talking together, like in a huddle."

"Could you hear what they said?"

"No. I was too far away. They have me in the volunteer area in the middle of this row of tables, but I did take a picture with my Instamatic. I kinda made it look like I was just taking pictures of the office and shot several all around, but really concentrated on them, but my camera does not have a zoom."

"Well, send the pictures to me anyway and get a better camera. You got the address?"

"Yeah."

"What about other places over there?"

"They've got all the doors coded on swipe cards so we can't get into the other parts of the campaign, but I did manage to get inside briefly. They almost caught me before I found out anything important."

"Keep at it. Try to get another job that will get you back into the inner sanctum. You're good-looking enough. Play up to another one of the guys who work back there. Sugarcoat him to move you back into his area. You know how to do that, don't you?"

"I know what you mean, but that's riskier than just spying. I almost got caught last time when I went to see the army captain. I did get you the layout and photos of their operation."

"Keep at it. I put you there to get me something I can use. You got to do better. You can be replaced. Earn your money!"

Celebrities

Sally Crockett, the director of volunteers, Safta Kleg, the press secretary, and Missy Winston, her deputy, entered the office of George Lewis.

Sally, who had known George the longest, started with, "George, we have a concern that I hope you can help us with."

"Glad to help if I can, Sally, what's the problem?"

Sally hesitated. "Well...It's about the celebrities."

"Who or what do you mean?"

Safta could not hold herself back any longer. "We've tried to keep as many of the calls from you and Mr. Bartow as possible, but we have quite a following of well-known people who want to help."

Sally added, "They're from show business, you know, music, television, and film."

Safta nervously added unnecessarily, "And artists. We know they're a sensitive resource and we don't want to offend any of them, and we can't just tell them to go to the local volunteer office."

Sally mused, "Some of them are quite enthusiastic. They normally are just asked to give money or host events. But, under our situation, we—"

Missy now interceded. "'Scuse me. But, why don't we invite them to a party?"

Sally turned, surprised. "Pardon?"

Missy continued, "The media love celebrities. If we had an event, a lunch or dinner with Mr. Bartow and celebrities, it would make great pictures. It would not need to be substantive, and it could be held here, so it should be easy to schedule."

George now leaned forward in his chair for the first time. "Yeah. That would be a lot of glitter and would give the celebrities something to look forward to and should not be too much trouble for us to arrange."

Safta, following Lewis's lead, said, "We could get some of the women from the Atlanta social clubs to do most of the work. Several have been asking me what they can do."

Missy, happy to give the idea over to the older women who had the social connections in Atlanta, added, "We just need someone to manage the egos and organize seating and recognition and such so as to keep everyone happy."

George, now warming to this more, said, "We ought to get some of the articulate people to say something to the group once they are assembled, and to the media. We just don't want someone going off half-cocked in some kind of tirade."

Sally replied, "Good idea, George. I knew you would be able to help us. I'll call the clubs and see about a place, maybe Cherokee or Piedmont."

Safta added, "I'll talk to Mr. and Mrs. Bartow and find a day that fits their schedules, and I'll talk to Bernice directly to get her ideas."

Missy, with her mind on how this could help the campaign, said, "If we can pick a day that gives us time to prepare hand-out materials on positions and information about the campaign, and get it to the celebrities in advance, it would prepare them to talk about the campaign when they are with the press or go back to Hollywood or New York or wherever. We may need to think about not doing something at a private club."

Sally, nodding as if that had been her idea, exclaimed, "Certainly!"

George, now leaning back in his chair again, said, "Well, it seems like you ladies have this well in hand. You've got a good idea here."

Field Office

Ben Menendez and Julio, one of the regional coordinators, scanned some papers quietly while talking with the state coordinator of Michigan. From the speaker, they heard the voice of an exasperated former volunteer and now self-appointed state campaign manager named Mitch Karbonsky. "So, this Miriam bitch comes in and tells me she is going to be the campaign manager. I ask her, 'Where were you when all this started?' I was watching fucking Larry King fer Christ sake on that first night when Mr. Bartow announced. You don't know what a problem you are going to have here in Detroit and all over Michigan if this bitch gets involved. She's a nut case."

Ben Menendez, with a calm voice, answered, "Do you know if there is a role for her in one of the other cities?" He looked down again at the paperwork he was holding. "Her records show that she has some experience, and her group of volunteers sent in over 30,000 signatures. They must have some ability."

From the speaker, a gruff-voiced Karbonsky answered, "Listen, you don't know what she did. She may have had some housewives to get signatures at the mall and shit. That ain't the same as running a state. Believe me, I ran the election for our union. I know what it takes and she ain't got it."

Ben asked, "How's the money holding out?"

He reached over and held down the speaker mute button so Karbonsky couldn't hear their side of the discussion as Karbonsky continued to talk over the speaker. He looked down at the papers Julio had just brought them. "Julio, did you get this memo from Burchmeyer?"

Karbonsky continued to rant. "Well, the T-shirt sales and other shit is going on okay. We're using about half the money here to run our shop and plan to send the other half to you guys there in the home office."

Julio answered Ben in a soft voice, not fully trusting the speaker mute button. "Yes." He looked down at the memo. "It looks like Mr. Karbonsky got thrown out of the union for pilfering funds. He was tried and acquitted when they couldn't prove anything."

Karbonsky, now pitching his voice with self-assurance, continued, "We're getting enough to cover some of the expenses like phones and the office and stuff, but it won't be long the way we're growing before we're gonna need some real support out here."

Menendez released the mute button to ask, "What's your budget look like?" He then pressed the mute again. He said to Julio, "Get one of Burchmeyer's men to go with me to Detroit next week. I can't go before that. And, get someone from accounting to go to check the books and bank accounts for Michigan. Also, make sure we've checked the background on that Miriam woman. We don't need to go from one bad situation into another."

Karbonsky continued from the speaker, "We're looking at about 250 to 300,000. Most of it is scheduled for get-out-the-vote efforts. I guess you guys are going to do the TV."

Menendez continued to hold the mute down. "Talk to Miriam and get her prepped to take over. If she got all those signatures for us to put Bartow on the ballot, she's got to have some organizational skills. We'll need a statement for the press if this gets out. Talk to Missy Winston over in the press office. She can help draft something."

Karbonsky droned on, "We're getting a lot of requests for yard signs. I know some guys here that can do 'em cheap. I'm thinking that we'd sell them to the homeowners and make up a couple hundred thousand of those and some brochures also. We're already making the bumper stickers and selling them."

Menendez continued to direct his attention to Julio. "I want paperwork on the union firing and the trial. Get a copy to Missy. Find someone at the union that will support us in public with a statement to the press on dumping this asshole. Do it quietly."

Then he lifted the mute button and spoke back to Karbonsky. "That sounds good. I would appreciate it if you could send me your budget plans and any lists of vendors and their phones and addresses you have put together to carry out the plan this week."

Karbonsky replied, "I'll try to do that."

Menendez spoke casually to Karbonsky. "The reason I'm asking, Mitch, is that I may have to take a trip in the next couple of weeks and I would like to drop by there and have all this approved and have some money for you, but we gotta get things approved here first."

Karbonsky quickly answered, "Oh. I see. Well, I'll make a special effort then. It will be great to meet you."

"We're looking forward to it too. You got my fax number. Send me the budget stuff and all the information on your vendors."

"You bet. See you then."

Ben said to Karbonsky, "Ah, don't do anything with that Miriam woman until I get there. We can meet with her together and just maybe find a peaceful solution to your problem. Also, if you have some of those vendors that you can get cheaply, I'd like to have one of our people meet with them. Maybe they can help us elsewhere. Remember to send me that list of their names and phone numbers."

"Yeah. That sounds great! I'll tell them. They'll be looking forward to it." Karbonsky shuffled some papers that could be heard over the speaker.

"Me too. Goodbye."

He disconnected the phone and turned to Julio. "How many other states do we have these kinds of problems… where we need to make a change?"

Julio said, "Near as I can figure, about four to maybe six. Some are better than others. Some are working out, but there's a lot of fighting over who's in charge. John Burchmeyer found three state directors with criminal records, but we've managed to bump one out already. There are some with a lot of debt and bad credit. And some other legal odds and ends."

Menendez looked at his calendar. "Make me a list of the four worst. I'll figure out how to handle them on my road trip." He got up to stretch. "Good work. Welcome to the reality of a presidential campaign."

Issues

The next night, Vicki, Ralph Collins, and Mark were sitting in the lobby outside Mr. Bartow's office. Inside the office, Bartow, George Lewis, and Susan Kaufman were meeting to review the issues DuVall and Susan Kaufman had devised and also Mark's plan to roll them out. Although the walls were thick, they could hear loud voices occasionally from inside. DuVall, Collins, and Young took turns looking at each other and occasionally raised their eyebrows or made faces, but they were quiet.

The door opened, and Susan walked out and looked sheepishly at the three of them. As she exited, they could hear more clearly Bartow's angry voice in the distance. "I'm not signing off on all this crap I didn't say. What the hell are you and Kaufman doing over there? I hired you to run this campaign. I don't know these other guys." Kaufman closed the door, cutting off the more distinct voices.

Mark smiled at her. "Sounds kinda bad in there."

Susan demurred, "Mmmm. Not necessarily. It's a vetting process. It may take more than tonight to complete. He does not like surprises. He likes to be the one doing the surprising. The briefing book was new to him. He needs assimilation time."

Collins had a disappointed look on his face. "Susan, I don't know if our sitting out here and having him shouting at you and George in there is the best use of all our time. I thought we all had already agreed to the plan and the train was roaring down the tracks. We're running out of time for him to... assimilate. Are we just waiting our turn here or what do you think we should be doing?"

Susan shrugged. "I'm not sure, Ralph. He's always nervous when making a big decision. But I've not seen him this worked up for quite a while. Good news is he did agree on the first three areas. We can get started with the speeches and TV follow-up. He needs more time on foreign policy and some of the finer points on the environment, but he will come around. These first on education, economics, and civil rights he checked off on. So, we're good to go on those. I think you guys have been doing a great job."

The door to Bartow's office opened and a red-faced George Lewis called to Kaufman, "Susan, you may want to come on back in here."

Now they could hear more clearly from the room again Bartow's voice. "Look at what's here. I never said that about the Russians and Bosnia. Hell, I've never been to that part of the world."

Susan walked to the door that Lewis had just re-entered. "You guys might as well go home; we'll fill you in in the morning."

Mark leaned forward. "Susan, we probably should bring in some foreign policy experts to get him up to speed on that area. It's important."

She nodded. "One step at the time. Let's get him comfortable with what we're doing now. I don't think it would work to bring in fresh faces just yet." She walked through the door, and as she slowly closed it, they could hear, "Who made that up? Susan, get on in here."

The three looked at each other, then slowly got up and departed.

Mark said, "Well, at least we've got a start. Let's give it some time and give George another shot. I think the three of us should get together first thing in the morning and plan out the next few weeks of issue rollout with speeches and television."

Collins nodded. "Absolutely. It's about time we got on television."

Mark looked over at his wife, who had circles under her eyes. "Vicki, even though we are in a time crunch, you and your staff should figure out how to take some time off. All of you have been working past midnight, and it may be a day or two before it heats up again. This may be the last chance you get." He looked back at the door. "Susan deserves a Purple Heart for getting shouted at so much."

Vikki said, "I think she is used to it. I'll let half the staff off tomorrow and the rest can go home early, and I'm heading home to see our child before bedtime."

Mark turned. "I'm going to talk to Missy. We need a story to cover the office so any snooping media or anyone else can't figure out that you are taking time off." He looked back at the door. "Hopefully they can't hear through that wall."

Collins headed toward his office. "See you all tomorrow. Somewhere there is a beer with my name on it. Mark, see you in the morning."

Planning the Announcement

Vicki and Mark entered DuVall's office where Susan Kaufman, Blane Harper, and Missy Winston were waiting for them. Vicki sank into a chair. "Everything changes starting now. Our job here is to get the three issues he has agreed to support ready for public consumption. We've got fairly good papers on education, economics, and civil rights. Now we need to find several anecdotes of Bartow's support with specifics on how much money he has given, how much personal time, and people in each of these areas who will say good things about him. Plus, we need to include criticism of the budget deficit in everything.

"Education will roll out next week. We need handout brochures or briefing papers for the public rally. We need banners that tie Bartow to supporting good education... slogans, photos, whatever we have to plaster that plaza where he will be making the speech."

Blane Harper, the scheduler and lead advance person, said, "I've got plans to bus in thousands of school kids and their parents. Bands will be playing. We need Bartow signs for them to be waving." Harper, short and overweight, had a reputation for being tremendously efficient. He was neatly dressed, stayed focused on details, and always carried a briefcase with him since his days as an assistant to pollster Bob Teeter.

Mark added, "American Flags."

Blane nodded to Mark. "Exactly."

Missy added, "In the press office, we will be preparing media handouts that include the basic positions, anecdotes, people they can contact to interview about his speech, photos of him, and whatever educational cutesies we can find. It's high time for this stuff."

As he got up and headed for the door, Harper said, "Well,

sounds like I need to get cracking on the layout, staging, and TV angles for the speech. I'm going back to my office. Sorry to break up the party."

Mark added, "That's great, Blane. George is going back to talk to him this evening, so you are likely to have many more of these to do."

"It's what I'm good at. Love the details."

Vicki coughed out a dry laugh. "Now, Blane, I never figured you for a masochist. How does such a nice man end up sweating all those tiny details?"

Blane smiled as he left the door. "Pretty lady, in my mind, you are the one with the tough job. See you kids later."

Vicky looked over at Mark. "Of all our Republican friends on this gig, I like him the best."

"That's just because he pays you compliments. Deserving, but still…"

"You hush."

Mark said, "George told me he hoped to catch Bill on a good day and he thinks he will come around when he has time to consider what we've done to make him become a better candidate. Unfortunately, we don't have enough time to make the TV commercials and air them to bracket the speech. He's just going to have to see the effect through free media coverage." Mark, thinking about damage control, said, "Everyone, just a reminder, we need to keep all of our plans in this room. Don't give your staff something to talk about that gets in the newspapers or on television."

Susan frowned. "But—"

Mark, more emphatic, now, said, "Excuse me, Susan, but the book we're ghosting for him is going well and will be ready soon. It illustrates all our positions. Bartow has no alternatives. We all know how long it takes him to move on anything. Let's assume this is a done deal, but we don't want it to leak out and be killed by our opponents or ambitious reporters. Missy, figure out a way to stall the press. Get talking points on our education program plans to George, Safta, and Collins. Give Bartow another day or two on the rest of the stuff. I'll get George to work on him. Let's continue to do one or two of these at a time rather than flood him with everything at once."

Vicki sat up. "You're right. He's given this campaign an opening and we're gonna take it. Education coming up."

Don Rizzo

Don Rizzo walked to a pay phone near the Bartow campaign and dialed the number he had been given.

"Hello," said a mechanical voice with a thick European accent.

"Oh, I'm glad it's you. It's been a while. How are—"

"Don, can the small talk and tell me what's going on there."

"Okay. The campaign is very well-organized, and they have put lots of money into structure."

He could tell the tough-guy voice was being run through a manipulator. "Rizzo, get to the point."

"The guy is very insular. We rarely have any communication with him directly and it all goes through his people, who have worked with him for many years. Security is like our CIA only maybe tighter. They've got a lot of ex-military running around. There're different sections of the office that are keyed to little plastic credit cards, so when you swipe them, they will only let you into places where you have clearance."

"Is the guy sane and balanced?"

"Can't tell yet. They are holding the budget cards close to the vest and have not green-lighted any big spending, so we are not doing many of the things we should at this stage. He's not using the money advantage he has."

"When is he coming out with any positions… foreign policy stuff?"

"That's in the Democrat's area. This guy Mark Young's got some interesting ideas about taking a dozen issues and then rolling them out at one per week. Because no one knows anything about Bartow, the media are craving some substance. Hell, he could dominate the conversation over the summer and right up to the election, but we don't have the green light to do anything. He's gonna start on education soon, but we haven't heard anything about a media buy. We've got Frank Press and Chappy Knight lined up to make spots but can't get the go ahead. You remember what a good job they did for Reagan."

The remote voice mused, "Yeah. They're the best. Why he is such a turtle?"

"None of us know. It's like he's scared to succeed." Rizzo wondered why the European accented voice used a term like 'turtle' to describe Bartow.

"Does he have any foreign policy people there; you know, people with experience from State or Defense?"

"No. It's just us chickens from other campaigns. No expert advisors. That guy Mark Young's wife is handling the issues area. She was on the Hill, but no experience in any specific area. There is this one thing they keep talking about. It's like making balancing the budget and holding down the debt a really serious part of the campaign."

"Everybody says that, but they'd never be able to keep everyone happy if they balanced the budget."

"Yeah. Right. But it keeps coming up. I think these guys are serious about it."

"Well, keep your eyes open over there. Call the number you have if anything changes. I'll check back in a couple of weeks. And don't be so stupid as to share with anyone that we are having these little talks."

Rizzo quickly said, "You can count on me." The hairs were up on the back of Rizzo's neck when he hung up the phone. This strange voice had menace in it, like it could come through the wires and hurt him if it wished. Rizzo wiped the sweat off his forehead and remembered the mantra he had repeated so many times over the past three years. "Hello, I'm Don Rizzo and I'm an alcoholic."

Pressuring Bartow

As Mark entered Bartow's expansive office with George Lewis, he noticed an original 800-year-old Magna Carta, only one of 17 copies in existence. Bartow set aside what he had been working on and interlaced his fingers to look at Mark and George.

"Okay, what is it?"

George took the lead. "Bill, we need you to finish approving the list of issue positions for the speeches and rallies and the budgets for the television advertising. That's the concept we discussed earlier. We need a full game plan to execute. You're moving up in the polls steadily. We've got hundreds of things to do, and it takes lead time to set all this stuff up."

Mark chipped in. "We also need to bring in some advisors in specific areas. We need to be able to call on experts in finance, foreign policy, and other areas. You need bench strength to give advice, people who are known for being smart and experienced. They can go on TV to speak on your behalf.

Bartow looked back and forth. "Seems like every time we meet, it's about spending more of my money."

Mark nodded. "We won't waste any, but it costs a lot to run for president. If that bothers you, we need to set up an office to start raising money, but we are late in the game for that."

Lewis now rejoined the conversation. "Bill, perhaps you should consider letting go of the reigns. We've hired these experts and you have me to run this campaign. We have a job to do and so do you. I give you my word on our friendship that I will make sure we do what is right for you. Let's sit down this afternoon and agree on the issues and the budgets to promote them. Then let's look at the next three months of plans and budgets and get agreement on that. You need more to say about specifics when you are on TV. We need to roll out these positions and promote them on television. We are about even with those other two and you are poised to take over this race. You can do it, but not if you micromanage."

Bartow slapped his hands down on his desk. "Okay, come back this afternoon and we'll go through all this stuff and make decisions. But If I have ideas and things I want to do, I'm gonna do them no matter what you say. I will not be controlled." He gave Mark a determined look.

Mark smiled back at Bartow. "I get that. I will get a list of specialty advisors to George to vet and then share them with you. We need to get them here quickly."

Bartow made a sour face. "I don't want people who have screwed up things in the past. I don't want a lot of college professors who think they are smarter than everybody else. What I do want are people who have been in uniform to help on the foreign policy. I like people who have practical success on their resume, and not some eggheads."

Mark nodded. "Makes sense. I'll work on that and get the names and their specialties to you as soon as possible. Understand they don't have to be here all the time sitting around. We just need them to be available to help and for advice. They will add gravitas and confidence to the positions we will be taking. Your positions."

Friends and Family Commercial

Unexpectedly, Collins and Rizzo were invited by George Lewis to view campaign commercials made by a local filmmaker, Geoffrey Bentley, who was friends with the Bartow children. As they settled into his office, an almost apologetic Lewis explained, "Geoff has been experimenting with some commercials for Mr. Bartow to show his generosity. You know, to show his softer side like we've discussed."

The young, lean Bentley interjected, "That's right. For over 20 years, Mr. Bartow and his family have been doing things for people here that no one knows about. If people could see that side of him, it would make him look more acceptable to the press and the public."

Collins looked out of the window for a moment, rolled his eyes, wiped his face with one hand, and sniffed as he patronized Bentley. "That sounds right to me."

"Yes. And since I know about many of the things he's done, I thought I'd take a shot at some TV spots to show that side of him. You know, I think he should be on TV now anyway."

Collins nodded and gripped his chair tighter. "Yes. I agree. He needs to be on TV."

Lewis said, "Mr. Bartow authorized some funds for Geoff to make these spots and he wanted you to see them."

Collins, forcing a smile at Bentley, said, "That's great."

Rizzo, realizing his role was to ask the harder questions now, entered the discussion. "So, Mr. Bentley, you have already made these commercials?"

Now Bentley broke out in a wide beam. "Absolutely. That's what I want to show you today. I'd like to invite you and Mr. Collins to come to the shoot on Friday where I've got two more planned."

Rizzo swallowed. "Well, I can't wait to see them."

Lewis, now realizing this was a fruitless exercise, but also needing to protect the Bartow family friend, added, "In the past, Mr. Bentley has made some training movies for Bartow Industries. He filmed his son's wedding, and he feels he has a working knowledge of what Mr. Bartow likes."

Collins forced himself to say, "That's a... a valuable asset."

Mark Young knocked on Lewis' door and entered. "Oh, hi. I didn't know you had a meeting going; I thought you wanted to see me."

Lewis leaned forward. "Yes. Come on in, Mark. I thought you might want to see the video." He motioned with one hand. "I'd like you to meet Geoff Bentley, a friend of the Bartow family who has made some commercials he wants us to see."

Mark, understanding the situation immediately, sat on the edge of a couch near the door. "Oh. Good. I'm just gonna hang back here."

Collins looked at his watch and nodded at Geoffrey Bentley. "Well, let's see 'em. I'm anxious to learn something more about Mr. Bartow's charitable donations."

Bentley said, "Yes. Okay." He moved over to the wall, where there was a built-in TV, VCR, and other equipment. He fiddled with the dials and inserted a tape.

George Lewis took the opportunity to say in a very even voice to the others, "Mr. Bartow's office called me this morning to tell me that Geoff was coming over to show us this material. He told me he met with Geoff a couple of weeks ago and asked Geoff to create the spots we're about to see."

Collins, just as evenhandedly, said, "Yes. I see."

Bentley turned back to the group after setting up the tape and smiled. "Okay, folks, here goes." Bentley hit the start button, sat in a chair, then leaned forward with his hands on his chin, looking intently at the screen.

The video opened on a montage of gruesome close-up shots of people in misery... children with no legs, burn victims, a man in an iron lung, starving people, veterans' hospitals with people staring off into a void... In the background, slowly the music of *America the Beautiful* began and built over the images. Then they heard Mr. Bentley's voice used as the narrator…

"Yes, America! The land of opportunity and no one knows it better than…" On the screen as he talked, still photos flickered in a progressive sequence of Bartow from 15 years ago to the present day. Various clothing and hairstyles of Bartow began to merge through the montage of victims.

"…Bill Bartow. Bill Bartow, who gives generously to help those less fortunate. Bill Bartow, who funded hospitals, playgrounds, skin grafts, artificial limbs, and…"

The images dissolved into a motion video shot of the front of a beautiful civic center building lit at night. The camera tilted down from the building to reveal people exiting the building in tuxedos and evening dresses, then continued to tilt down to limousines in the foreground, where the stream of people got in and drove away as other limos arrived .

"…and Atlanta's new civic center, where cultural events enrich the sprit and soul of our community."

This scene dissolved into a waving American flag flapping full screen and slowly a still photo image of Bartow rose from below to fill the screen in front of the flag. "Bill Bartow, a man who cares, a man who acts, a man who leads." The video then dissolved and ended with a 'Bartow for President' tag.

Mark looked over at the faces of Collins, Rizzo, and Lewis. Bentley was beaming proudly. Lewis was ashen. Collins was poker-faced. Rizzo, whose mouth was agape, spoke. "My God."

Collins quickly covered for Rizzo. "Yes. That's powerful stuff. Are they all that quality?"

Bentley leaned back. "Oh, yes. Thank you. You see, this is the cover spot. The other six or eight go back and tell the story of the individuals you saw at the beginning. We show each life story and how Mr. Bartow helped each one. It's told in their own voices. I think it's more powerful that way. Actually, the man in the iron lung even narrates his own story. It's compelling the way he has to struggle to get his breath to say what a wonderful man Mr. Bartow is and how much he has helped him."

Lewis, now finding his voice, said, "Well. Well…"

Collins, trying to get out of seeing them all, said, "Would

you have copies of this whole reel?"

Bentley, now fishing in a briefcase, pulled out a cassette tape. "Yes. As a matter of fact, I made copies for all of you. Or at least I have four more."

Collins nodded, reaching for the tape. "I think we need to study these commercials. Let me have a copy and perhaps you could leave another with Mr. Lewis? We'll take the time to fully appreciate… these." He waved the cassette.

Lewis, also now wanting this meeting to end, said, "That's a great idea."

Bentley was still enthusiastic. "Well, while I'm here, I thought I would go over each one with you and you could ask questions."

Mark took this opportunity to make an exit and said as he walked out the door, "I'm sorry, folks, but I didn't know about this meeting and I have a group of people waiting for me in my office. I hope you'll excuse me."

Collins almost jumped out of his seat. "Yeah. Me too." He shook Bentley's hand. "Powerful work. Powerful. I'll be talking to Mr. Lewis once we have had the chance to review these carefully."

Rizzo took his cue and also got up. "Yes. Yes. We have to go now, but we'll be in touch."

They left Bentley sitting quietly with Lewis in his office.

Michigan

The Bartow campaign's Michigan headquarters bustled with activity. There were over 30 tired but busy people packed into the cramped campaign office with phones ringing, fax machines buzzing, copying being done. There was a section of people stuffing envelopes, and elsewhere phone banks were making calls to voters. By the Coke machine, a well-dressed woman was sitting quietly in a folding chair. The woman could see through a large plate-glass window into a spacious office nearby but could not hear what was going on inside.

Behind the soundproof window of the largest office in the area, Mitch Karbonsky sat behind the big desk he had brought in especially for him. There were photos of him on the walls meeting with elected officials and two framed certificates he had received from his union.

In front of Karbonsky sat Ben Menendez, a large man from Burchmeyer's office, and an accountant, who was paging through a portfolio of documents on his lap. They were talking with Karbonsky, whose face was beginning to show worry, although the men were still early in the conversation.

Karbonsky stood and began to make what appeared to be protests and he waved his hands, and his indistinct shouting could be heard through the glass. The accountant and Ben Menendez continued to talk. Gradually, Karbonsky stopped waving his arms, sat, and slumped deeper down in his chair. As his head slowly dropped, Ben Menendez and the accountant continued to place documents in front of him. Finally, Karbonsky got up and grabbed his coat, and the large Burchmeyer security man led him out.

Menendez then came to the door and opened it, and said in a pleasant voice to the well-dressed woman sitting in the chair by the Coke machine, "Hello, Miriam, would you please come in?"

TIME Magazine

Mark closed his files and clicked his computer until nothing was showing on the screen as Missy Winston and Clint Jennings entered. Clint was the *TIME* magazine political reporter Mark had known from earlier campaigns.

"Hello, Mark. How's the campaign going?"

"What did Ralph tell you just now?"

"He said that if it weren't for him, you'd be in the low teens and nobody listens to him enough."

Mark smiled at how predictable Collins was with his outsized ego. "Clint, you've been talking to Ralph long enough to write that story in your sleep. You could have saved yourself a trip to Atlanta. What are you hearing?"

"I hear you guys are a balloon floating on thin air, and there are a lot of sharp pins out there."

"I've also read that story from you before."

Clint leaned back in his chair now that the initial banter was over. "When are you going to let people know what you stand for?"

Mark looked over at Missy. "Have you set up any ground rules yet?"

"No. Ralph wanted to meet with Clint alone and after that we came straight here."

Mark looked Clint straight in the eye and held the look for several seconds. "Deep background. No quotes. No allusions to my name or position."

Clint sneered, "Make my day, Mark. Don't you guys want any coverage? Do you just want the stories to be what the other candidates have to say about you?"

Mark was not buying the reporter's argument for a more open discussion and he looked Clint in the eye again. "Do we have a deal on the ground rules?"

Clint smirked. "Okay."

"As you know, we've not had a lot of time to get this campaign ready for you guys. I think in a couple of weeks we'll have some positions for you on many of the issues out there."

"Two weeks?! Jesus. It's springtime. Don't you know what you stand for?"

"Collins may have told you already, but next week Mr. Bartow will be making a major speech that gives his full position on education. I think you will see that it is more complete than anything that Bush or Clinton have said."

"What is he going to say? Education is just a sideline thing. That's not why someone runs for president. Why doesn't he talk about foreign policy or the economy? When are you going to get real?"

Missy jumped in to be the disciplinarian and protect Mark. "Clint! Your editor is not here to watch you show off. Chill. We're not going to give you material to cut us up with because it has not been thoroughly edited."

"Well, then who are your advisors? You guys don't know it all. Don't you have some people we can check with on your philosophy of the economy, fiscal policy, on being a hawk or a dove on foreign positions? We've got the Balkans heating up. They're killing people right and left. Every half-ass agreement they cobble together comes apart in a few days. Our military people are worried. Where are you on all that? What would a President Bartow do? Give me something." Clint shrugged. "Look. I've got to write a column each week. What else have you got? Who are those storm troopers out there, and why doesn't Bartow have Secret Service?"

Mark spoke slowly and calmly to Clint. "First, we will be announcing some of our advisors soon so you will have the opportunity to pester them to death. When you can see what we stand for, then you can dissect the policy with them. Second, those security people have been with Bartow for years. The guy is worth $4 billion. He needs security and these guys are good. Many of them are ex-Secret Service and military... etcetera. They are in touch with the Secret Service and they coordinate activities with them. We're saving the taxpayers money."

Clint rolled his eyes and tried another approach. "Right. Okay then, what's your peak? The undecideds nationally on this election are down in the twenties. Your negatives are starting to climb, partly I think because no one knows what the hell Bartow stands for and they are getting frustrated. Your guy has done nothing except go to those flag-waving rallies where he says the same innocuous things. When are you going to go on TV?"

"We're not going to be able to give you our strategy to-day."

"What strategy? I hear Press and Knight haven't even shot anything yet with the candidate. They're doing man-on-the-street stuff. What kind of a strategy is that? You've got more money than God and you're sitting on it? Some people I talk to are saying that's kinda dumb."

"Good thing that 'some people' aren't running this campaign."

Black, Manafort, Stone

Charlie Black slammed his briefcase down on his desk. "Boys, Bush is in trouble."

Surprised, Manafort and Stone both leaned forward in their chairs. Charlie Black was never this demonstrative.

Black continued, "The latest polls and focus groups show the 'no new taxes' thing he said is kicking him in the ass with conservatives and now the fallout from the Savings and Loan crisis is heating up. The costs of the S & L failures to the government are skyrocketing. People are worried about their mortgages and savings. At the same time, Jeb defaulted on a $4.5 million loan in Florida and that dumbass, Neal, had all kinds of stupid deals with Silverado in Denver. The government, including their daddy, had to bail out both of them. If all that gets out, moderates are worried Bush will look incompetent, if not corrupt."

Stone shouted, "None of that is his fault."

Manafort looked over his more impulsive buddy. "Doesn't matter. He's sitting there, so he gets the blame."

Black nodded. "Paul's right. We need to build some backfires." He turned to Stone. "Roger, get your people to scour the bars in Little Rock and turn up the heat. Find some sex stories and the women to back them up. Get it out now. Make up something. Dangle some leg at him. Paul, go to your guy in the Collins group. Get him digging deeper. That squirrely little son-of-a-bitch has to have some dirt. The Bushies are looking to us to save them."

Manafort frowned. "Crap. The main guy I have in there is a doofus and should have 'modest competence in limited areas' written on his business card."

Stone chirped, "Too bad you couldn't have found someone more reliable."

Manafort gave him a sharp look. "I already have them in the Clinton campaign."

Black raised his voice. "Cut it out. Get it done."

Manafort and Stone looked at each other. Manafort said, "We're on it.

Scheduling

Blane Harper, the campaign scheduler, and Safta Kleg, press secretary, were sitting on the couch outside Mr. Bartow's office. The door opened, and George Lewis came out, looking tired. He walked over and sat down in a chair near Blane and Safta.

An anxious Blane asked, "So, how'd it go? What'd he say? Did you get approval for all of it?"

George stretched and moaned. "Ohhhh, God. Blane. I don't know how to say this, but he still wants to have a lot of control over his time, and he is not willing to turn over his schedule to you, me, or anyone else. He's been doing it his way for 30 years, and he… he needs more time to see how we can help him. For now, he won't budge."

Blane's face blanched. "But, George. He said he would turn it over to us. We're trying to run a national presidential campaign here. We can't do that and have him doing whatever he wants at the spur of the moment. It's just crazy. You know that."

George turned to Safta. "Safta, you've been with him for 10 years; you know what we're up against."

Her shoulders dropped. "Blane, I'm sorry. I was afraid something like this was going to happen."

"But, Jesus!"

George was feeling sorry for the outside consultants and offered, "So far, we have three full days a week we control. I'm sure he'll let go of the rest soon. I'll tell you what we'll try. When you have scheduling items, make out a wish list, give them to me, and I'll take them in for our morning meeting. I'll try to get him to put them on his calendar, I'll get his secretary to copy and send his daily schedule to us, and we'll get his agenda as far ahead as possible so we can see what's open.

Safta nodded. "Yes. That might work."

Lewis continued, "I've got to work on getting some military

and foreign policy advisors here. He has to meet them to approve them, and I've been trying to get that on his schedule. Mark Young has been pestering me about that for two weeks now."

George now leaned closer to the dejected Blane. "We'll try to influence the calendar and we'll get more control over it."

Blane shook his head. "But we're running a national campaign here."

George spoke softly. "This has all happened suddenly. He's never been exposed to the intricacies of a campaign before. He does not know what's going on over at the campaign office. We've got to bring him along so he understands how important it is to schedule him."

Blane slapped his hands down in his lap. "Christ! I scheduled George Bush during the fucking war. I know what I'm doing. I feel so insignificant."

Safta, now being motherly, said, "I'm sorry, Blane, it's not your fault. It's not anybody's fault. It's just how things are, at least for now."

Blane leaned over and shook his head over his lap. "Okay. I'll have my wish list to you this afternoon and bring another every evening. I'll check with you after the education speech. I'd really like to show you what I'm capable of doing."

Education

The next day on the UGA campus, Bartow knocked his education speech out of the park. He even included some of the talking points Vicki had woven into the speech that related to moving toward a balanced budget, a more responsible government, and a more stable long-term economy.

Mark and Missy watched the replay.

"If a student with financial needs maintains a B average in high school, we're going to offer them a no-interest college loan. They'll have to pay it back but won't get eaten up with interest, and they'll also have to maintain a B average in college to keep it.

"We've got similar deals for nursing schools, trade schools, and other places where the high school graduates can get help to find a good-paying job. We're also going to provide standardized adult education courses for those who want them.

"We're also going to work with businesses to hold retraining programs for workers in threatened industries.

"We're going to ramp up remedial education in high school to get guidance to those who need it to help them get up to that B-level student loan.

"We're going to set up mentoring programs with retired people to help tutor in special categories like science and math.

"We've had our heads in the sand for too long, and it's time we all rolled up our sleeves and helped others. You've never too young or too old to learn. Education should be a lifetime experience. That's what our businesses need to make our nation strong and steady. That's going to give us internal economic security. That's going to give us a new generation of leadership."

Mark leaned over to Missy. "Do we have all the people,

including education experts, ready to go to the television and newspapers to say how much they agree with Bartow?"

"Yes."

"Do we have the op-eds ready to roll tomorrow?"

"Yes."

"Do Rizzo and the others have the video editors ready to cut spots from this speech to flood the networks with the highlights?"

"Yes."

"Okay. We need to show Bartow how this has worked for him. He needs reassurance. Get Rizzo to make three minute reels from the best of the local television comments sampled from all over the country, and get favorable testimonials to show him. We need him to be able to see how this can work when he cooperates."

"That should help."

"He's not there yet, but he's learning."

"I sure hope so."

Mark looked over at Missy. She was an exceptional woman and he hoped she could find a man deserving of her. She had been a bad picker and this last man was the worst so far. In addition to being unfaithful, he had stolen money from her.

She looked at him and noticed his distraction from Bartow. "What is it?"

He came out of his reverie about her. "Nothing. Just wondering... if we are ready for the civil rights and economics messages?"

Missy leaned forward. "Vicki has that all set up. I'm working on the specialty economic press, as well as the regulars."

Mark nodded. "You and whoever... just need to get him ready. He doesn't look like he fully understands the nuances of economics enough to explain what we are proposing. Keep the charts near him. He can talk off them. We don't need him going off script."

"Yeah," she said. "Thanks for the reminder."

The Today Show

The next morning, Missy gave the position papers to the NBC producers. She had briefed the gaggle of press on the street in front of Thirty Rock and answered preliminary questions so they could be ready to get a Bartow quote to use in their reporting. Then she went into the studio to make sure Bartow had his talking points and charts and found a place on the side to watch the show.

Bartow sat with his hands folded on the *Today Show* set with its anchor, Brent Sagan. The crew checked his mic and the stage manager counted down and pointed to cue Sagan, who, to show his independence, decided to prod Bartow before getting into the questions on education. "Well, we're back from the break and still talking with independent presidential candidate, William Bartow. Mr. Bartow, let me try a different tack. When and how are you going to distinguish yourself from the other two candidates by taking a stand on the issues? Do you plan to run television commercials?"

Bartow forced a smile on his face that looked contrived. "I just love it. You see, that's what I love about you folks in the media. You can't stand it if everyone is not playing by the rules you set down. You're only happy when everyone is engaged in mud wrestling because that's what sells newspapers and gets you the high ratings on the TV."

Missy closed her eyes.

"Mr. Bartow, with all due respect, how are the people going to know what you stand for and make an advised judgment before casting their vote if you won't take any positions or tell them what you believe in?"

Bartow waved his hand in the air. "Hold on to your hat and watch your wallet, folks, he's doin' it again."

"But, Mr. Bartow—"

Bartow talked over the host, "Stand by! If you folks in the media would just come to one of my rallies, you'd see what is going on in America. We've got hundreds and thousands of great American people out there who want change, not status quo. Are you ready for this?" He shook his head. "The American people, or at least 99% of them outside Washington know we need engineers to build up this economy. What we've had for the last dozen years are demolition experts."

"But, Mr. Bartow—"

Bartow kept going. "No ifs, ands, or buts. It's simple. We don't need a trainload of Harvard professors to tell us what's wrong with this country. And, we don't need me and the other two guys dressed up like professional wrestlers Hulk Hogan and Haystacks Calhoon jumping at each other off the top rope. This country has had the sleeper hold put on it long enough. I'm here to tell you, they are waking up, and now they're not gonna play by your rules."

"But, Mr. Bartow..."

"I'll tell you and your listeners our there watching the TV and eating breakfast who need to hear this... just yesterday I talked about what was wrong about the educational system in this country, kindergarten through grade twelve, and what I propose to do to fix it. I've also talked about college and postgraduate education. I was over at the UGA Colosseum where they play basketball, and I made some three pointers. If you had listened to it, you would know about that part."

"But—"

"I'm gonna give it to you straight, and we're gonna get our kids educated once and for all. I'm going to give it to you and your media friends straight and unfiltered. But most of all, I want to tell the American public what I think. I've been listening to the people and they have good ideas. It's time we used the common sense of the American people to show what we can do."

"So... you're going to finally tell us what you think about why..."

"I'm going to be rolling out more things like that in the coming weeks."

"Can't you tell us something now..."

Bartow froze and smiled calmly at the interviewer. "You know, that would not be ethical and would scoop all your other competitors. One thing I've always tried to be is fair."

"Mr. Bartow, the last time you were here you had a chart about the debt and deficit. You implied that you had a plan to balance the budget and you were very critical of the current administration and your other opponent. You chart showed a $200 billion imbalance in the U.S. budget. The current administration said that money is needed to support our military, to secure peace in the Balkans, to provide healthcare for the poor and needy. How can you balance the budget with all those pressing needs?"

Bartow pinched his nose and squinted his eyes elaborately before looking back at the anchor. "Management. This government needs management. We haven't been making tough decisions. We've been letting the special interests have their way... on both sides of the aisle."

"But management! That's not going to balance the budget. How will you—"

Bartow stopped him. "We're gonna cut it all, and in about three weeks I'll come back here to tell you exactly how. But I'm here today to tell you about education."

Later, coming out of the NBC facilities at 30 Rockefeller Center in New York, the security guards had roped off an area where a crowd of about 40 people, including the local press, waited for Bartow to appear following the program. Some had Bartow T-shirts or hats on, but most were just curious street people gawking. Missy trailed them as Burchmeyer led Bartow from the door toward the waiting limousine. The crowds pushed the rope line towards security as they moved forward, cheering and shouting at him. He turned to wave when someone in the second row threw the contents of a bucket at him. Bartow winced and moved back toward Burchmeyer, who lunged to protect his boss. A shower of small-sized paper confetti rained down on Bartow. The man who had handled the bucket turned and ran with considerable speed down the street.

Issues

The next afternoon on the way to a meeting, Mark walked through the volunteer room and saw that the place had filled out even further with more people, phones, and tables. Workers were putting up campaign banners and "We're Gonna Win" signs on the walls. There were some volunteers taking school kids on tours of the room packed with people working the phones.

At the meeting, Mark, Vicki, and Benny Weinstein sat in Vicki's office with the ghost writer hired to produce the book to cover issues related to William Bartow. There were galley proofs of the book laid out all over the desks and table surfaces in the office, and the television was turned to a program on CNN called *ON POLITICS*, as the CNN announcer was cutting around to different campaigns for reporters' comments.

Benny thumbed through the layout of the book. "Let me tell ya. I was skeptical of this at first, but I think it's gonna come out okay."

Mark complimented his wife. "You've done a good job with a difficult subject. It even reads well to me and I hate reading about issues."

"Watch it there. We're gonna save your ass in this campaign."

Benny mused through several documents and stopped at one. "What about this thing on the environment..."

At that time, the CNN program cut to a Bartow rally.

Mark held up his hand. "Whoa. There's our guy; let's watch this."

Vicki turned up the volume as they all gathered in front of the television...

...just as the CNN studio anchor was saying, "William Bartow showed us once again that he's not afraid of criticizing the media. Let's take you to his rally earlier today in South Dakota."

Benny stepped toward the television. "What the fuck's he doing in South Dakota? Nobody lives there."

Mark shushed Benny.

On the television screen, they could see Bartow at a podium with flags and banners waving behind him. In front of him, there were well over a hundred people cheering. Bartow was walking around on the stage, waving to the crowd. There was a group of veterans in worn camouflage uniforms in the front row. On the side, a riser had been erected to hold the television cameras, and the reporters were roped off in another area nearby.

Bartow grabbed the microphone and waved an arm across the crowd. "So, my friends, you are why this country is the greatest nation on earth. We don't need think tanks and K-street lobbyists and million-dollar staffers to tell us what we need to do in this country. We just need to get rid of all that special influence and this country would work a lot better. That's what has got us in the debt and the mess we're in today."

From the crowd, there were whoops and shouts of "You tell 'em, Bill."

"And we don't need all these Monday morning media quarterbacks that have never held a real job trying to tell us anything either. If those people who think they can tell you what to believe would just come out here and work an honest job for one month, they'd sing a different tune on the television."

Bartow walked over to the side of the stage and stood above the area roped off for the media.

"Well, there they are. I'll tell you what, folks, before you leave today, come by here and give these folks a good look. Those are the people who want to tell us all what to think. There's not a one of 'em got socks to match."

On the screen, the camera cut to an attractive female reporter standing in the crowd. "This is Summer Storm outside of Buffalo Hunting Lodge in South Dakota, often frequented by the candidate, where today, William Bartow sharpened his attack on the media to go along with his criticism of the other political parties." Bartow droned on in the background as she gave her report.

Mark made an unhappy face. "Please turn that down."

Vicki reached over and muted the TV as the reporter was saying, "He has criticized everyone in Washington, D.C., intellectuals, college professors..."

Weinstein got up. "Christ! Sorry, guys." He walked to the door and stopped. "The book looks good. I hope we're alive long enough to publish it. I'm gonna go see Ralph with this... news." Then he left.

Vicki, still looking at the images on the TV, said, "What's going on here, Mark?" She nodded to the television. "We finally got our spots approved and funded follow-up on the education speech and they are flooding the airwaves. Missy told me they are swamped with media requests. Now... maybe they will just be talking about this silly outrage instead of his positions on education. He's stepping on his message. It's so frustrating."

Mark lifted his head from the desk and looked at Vicki. "I dunno. Politicians love to take cheap shots at the media. Everybody wants to have a villain to rail against. Maybe he thinks what he is saying is democracy in action? Free spirits in the air? He looks like a guy searching for a self-destruct button." He leaned back and looked over at the images on the screen and shook his head. "He walks so close to the edge. That's his attraction and his weakness. As to what's going on in his head when he talks, I don't think he even knows. What's he doing on a trip to fucking South Dakota?"

Roger Stone and the Volunteer

Roger Stone listened to the familiar voice of a young woman he had inside the Bartow campaign. "I just wanted to give you an update on what happened in New York day before yesterday. Whoever it was that threw stuff at Mr. Bartow really freaked him out. I've gotten kinda friendly with one of his security guys, and he told me that Bartow was shaking and really scared. He said the security detail had to postpone his next meeting and it took like a couple of hours for him to calm down. And the guys on the security detail were really freaked out also. That man, Burchmeyer, gave all of them hell for allowing it to happen. I mean, he was there and he still blamed the other security guys. He's a real control freak."

Stone smiled. So, there was an Achilles heel. Bartow was not used to getting jostled in public and he could be scared. Good stuff to know. Whiny little boy. Had to be protected by that Nazi Burchmeyer. That was probably why he tucked himself away in Nowhere South Dakota the next day. Stone rocked back and forth in his chair. Okay, Mr. I'm a billionaire, Mr. I'm a patriot, Mr. I support the troops. You are a quivering little bitch when someone pours some cut-up paper on you. Well, Mr. Bartow, there is more where that came from.

Mark and Bruce

Mark sat in the main-floor central lobby of the National Gallery of Art in Washington, waiting for Bruce. Bruce had called him to come to D.C. for what he said was an important meeting, and grudgingly Mark left the campaign to fly up for the day. He looked around the circular room, starting with the fountain in the middle, while throngs of people passed by the curved stone benches lining the sides.

He marveled at the room's perfection. The homage to a circle. The columns tapered as they rose from the floor to the ceiling. Patterns circled in various colored marble along the ceiling and the walls down to the floor. The tiles leading to the fountain. The rings round the fountain. The graceful figure. The sound of water. During his days working in the Carter Administration almost 15 years before, he often came here to decompress. This place took him away from the daily grind and unpleasantness of a political campaign. He had recommended that the meeting be here just so he could have this time to unwind from the campaign in the peaceful serenity of the enormous round room.

Bruce approached and, sticking to his tradecraft, sat at the other end of the stone bench. He looked like a bored husband waiting for his wife and kids and carrying a large bag of rolled-up posters and a stuffed toy from the gift shop. He looked at his watch, crossed his legs—the sign it was all clear—and rocked back and forth. The crowds crossed in front of them coming in all directions, but no one else was nearby.

Mark spoke softly, still looking at the fountain. "I've always loved this room as much as any room I've ever been in."

Bruce sniffed strongly. "Must be all those phallic columns and gushing water and all the Freudian aspects of the design."

Mark had to laugh. He looked over at Bruce and replied,

"You spooks say Freudian like you actually know what it means."

Bruce shrugged. "Freud was the guy that was always horny. Jung was the guy that was always looking for God."

Mark nodded. "Right. Always simple and reduced to CliffsNotes on a three by five card. Mmmm. Why am I here?"

Bruce now turned to Mark as though they were two strangers who had struck up a conversation waiting for others. "I got to know if we can be all right with the guy you are working for. I can't tell if he's a whacko or if he's shrewd. I need to know where he is on foreign policy."

"You know me well enough, and I've already told you what I can. I will not tell you insider campaign stuff, that is, if I actually knew it. Which I don't."

Bruce shuffled his foot. "It's just that with the other two and the advisors who are around them, we know what to expect, and it's about the same thing. We're worried your guy is a chest beater, and usually those people just want to whup up on someone and don't understand the subtleties of diplomacy. Your guy is a blank slate. He does not have any foreign policy or military advisors. That makes a lot of people nervous.

"National security involves getting into other nations through soft power—foreign aid, food distribution, relief to rebuild after a natural disaster, education exchanges, culture stuff. We send rock bands, scientists, and scholars to trade culture with people. All of that opens doors. All of it comes from funds hidden in budgets all over the government—places where isolationist idiots can't find it and cut it. You can't just rely on muscle to influence places where we need to have a voice. To some people, your boss looks like the guys who wear camouflage clothing everywhere and strut around like they have been in combat.

"Mark, we've got to counter the rumors by Russia and China that we sponsor poisonous vaccinations or kill babies. They want to create wedges between us and other governments to give them economic and military leverage. A novice may not understand that, could cut out things that have taken years through many administrations on both sides to build. A loose cannon could cause damage, and that's why he needs people around him that know what to do and how to give good advice. Good national security advisors understand the alliances we have with nations in Europe, Asia and Africa, and South America that help to protect us from Russia, China, and whoever else is a threat. Ignorance of and abrogation of those contracts is strategic suicide. Remember Ronald Reagan wanted to abolish the Department of Energy until he found out that was where the nukes were stored.

"You've been around long enough to understand the complexity of our geopolitical systems. Bush and Clinton have those guys. It does not matter so much if they are liberal or conservative, but they've got to know how the game works. There are layers of procedure and knowledge in foreign policy and our national security constructed over many decades. The president who does not know the international players or the lessons of history can hurt our nation badly. You can't get that kind of knowledge in on-the-job training.

"We need to know that people close to Bartow are ready to give him advice to avoid mistakes in the first weeks and months of the presidency until he gets up to speed. Understand me, this is very real."

"I think we've sorta had this conversation before. I can't help you."

"You've been there a while and something has got to have jelled by now. What's he like?"

Mark waited as a group of school kids in a packed crowd walked by near the bench, looking at the massive columns and walls, and then moved on with their teacher and guide. "THIS conversation is why I'm here? Bruce, when we have positions that are vetted, we will make them public. We will be getting foreign policy advisors on board… eventually. Hopefully soon. There is not any consensus on policies right now. Be patient. Now, that is more than I should be saying and that is all I have to say." Mark made a move to get up.

Bruce reached out and touched Mark on his arm. "In other circumstances, we are colleagues. You need to know, however, that I have associates who are worried about this guy. Uncertainty makes us nervous. He's becoming too viable to win to remain unknown to us. We need to trust his foreign policy instincts or advisors. Understand… I'm saying this for all of us out of friend-ship or… anyway, our past relations."

Mark sighed. "He's always had a reverence for the military. He put up money for their benefit. He's honored veterans."

Bruce was back looking at the floor as he spoke. "Yes. All that. But it's sorta like he's a college alumnus who pays to come into the locker room after the game to see the damp showers, towels all over the floor, jerseys, and uniforms scattered about. People, and I'm talking about important people, are worried that he is a jock sniffer. We need someone who knows the rules of the game, not just an overzealous fan."

Mark stood and looked down at Bruce. "Honoring those same past bonds, if I have any evidence you or your buddies try to screw with this situation, like that attack after the *Today Show* recently, I'm on CNN faster than you can say Wolf Blitzer. Do not mess with our presidential election system." Mark walked away and headed to the airport to get the first flight back to Atlanta.

Carville

James Carville stared at the result of the focus group as he thought, *How could this Bartow guy be gaining on us? He was a rich peckerwood who spouted platitudes and essentially had no campaign message or marketing!*

Clinton was doing everything he could, using every card he had, including playing the saxophone on late-night TV, and still seemed stuck. This Bartow nut was getting the good-ole-boy vote that should be theirs. Their guy was supposed to be the anti-blue-blood everyman. Clinton was the accessible, charming guy who loved people. He'd talk to anyone forever, for Christ sake. His guy jogged, wore jeans, liked women. On paper, they were the ones positioned to get those angry, upset, disaffected voters. They were the anti-establishment candidate. But here was this squeaky-voiced gnome sucking them up like a Hoover. The unconventional billionaire had stolen their turf. At least the past was catching up to that nerd, Bush. His numbers had stalled and were now starting to sink.

He sat the report aside and scratched his bald head. Bartow's amorphous image had become the empty vessel where disaffected voters poured their dreams and anger. When would these people wake up and see that no one was in there? Voters were so stupid. To top it off, the unconventional bastard was getting there not even spending the endless supply of money he had.

Once people found out the guy had no positions and knew nothing about being a president, Bartow's empty shell would implode, but WHEN would that finally happen? What the hell was going on in the Bartow campaign and how could he attack him? Was this a genius move on the part of the consultants Bartow had hired or something else? He felt his wife, Mary Matalin, was just as frustrated over at the Bush campaign. Bartow was taking away what the press had called the Reagan Democrats and the small business people, even some of the soccer moms. This guy should have been pulling more from the Republicans than from the Democrats. What could he do? He looked again at the focus group results and thought, *What's the world coming to? People were supposed to want security and predictability. Status quo. This little squeaky-voiced twit was offering to wreck all that, and the dumbass people liked it. The rich, quirky upstart could actually win.*

Manafort and Rizzo

Paul Manafort was dressed down in a beige-colored windbreaker and without a tie for his meeting at the Hilton near the Atlanta airport. He had zipped down here for the meeting and would be back in D.C. this afternoon in time for his workout. He held the *TIME* magazine up to cover most of his face as he watched for the weasel, Don Rizzo, to arrive. Finally, he saw him at the door. He dropped the magazine and nodded his presence.

Rizzo hurried over and folded himself into the nearby chair and held out his hand. "Good to see you. I think I saw you last at that Chamber meeting. I remember you were working on that—"

Manafort held up his palm to halt Rizzo and did not shake his hand. "Tell me about Bartow."

Rizzo froze temporarily and his hand dropped to the arm on his chair. "Ah, so you can still do what we talked about. We've got a deal? No repercussions?"

Manafort leaned forward. "When this guy craters, I'm your lifeline. Now, tell me about Bartow."

Rizzo's shoulders slumped as he relaxed. "Because we don't have budgets approved and hardly ever see the guy, we're not sure. You know, we sit around and speculate and try to get some ideas about him from the Bartow Industries people and—"

"Enough. I'm interested in results, not how you got them. Tell me the fuck about Bartow, now."

Rizzo dropped his head and began to wring his hands. He began to speak as though it was a message he had memorized and practiced. "Okay. He's a business guy who is good at plodding along in incremental improvements. He's got these ass-kissers around him always giving him good news. Does not have a clue about how to answer questions when he does not know the answer. He's not used to surprises. He's a control freak with a thin skin. Like a lot of rich people, he's tight with his money. Seems to be a straight arrow, no women or booze that I've heard about."

"I could have gotten most of that from reading *Business-week*. Prove your worth."

"Well, he's really tight with his family. Like they are sacred or something. Protective. Real security conscious. Freaky. Got these access controls and protectors all around him. Got a good security team, but they have never had to deal with a campaign. I think he's worried about getting kidnapped or held up for ransom, or something like that. Nervous. Insecure like. He's real intent on having things go his way. I haven't gotten close enough to him or been around him enough to know more for now." Rizzo hesitated and made a strained expression.

Manafort opened his hands. "What?"

"Well, they keep talking about balancing the budget and cutting deficits as a big part of his platform."

"Hell. Everybody says that."

"Yeah, but they talk like they mean it. You know, really cutting both spending and tax breaks, as well as government loans and stuff like that."

"Nobody could do business like that. For the past few years, both Democrats and Republicans use budget deficits to finance things. They use that to fund whatever they really want to do. Nobody expects a budget to be real or to actually be paid for with taxes. There is not enough real money to buy all the stuff everybody wants anymore. It would wreck the economy."

"I'm just telling you what they're talking about."

"Nah. That would kill the golden goose. Not gonna happen."

"Just sayin'."

Manafort tapped his thumbnail against his teeth several times while looking down, then nodded. "Call me at the number you have when there is something to report. You've got to keep me informed and also help me get some special people into the building."

"Wait a minute. I can't do that; it is too risky. Those people are security freaks. They'll catch me for sure."

"Donnie, Donnie, Donnie, you'll do what I ask, or not only will I forget about holding the door open for you in the party, I'll shut it forever and you'll never get another political gig anywhere. You'll starve. Now, are we going to work together on this thing or not?"

"Yeah... yeah sure."

Manafort leaned forward. "Find stuff or make it up. We need to put this guy off his stride. Now."

Rizzo swallowed. "Yes. Will do."

Manafort tapped his knuckles on the edge of his chair, indicating the meeting was almost over. "When it's ready, I want to know the media buy. Now, I'm off, back to D.C. Go to the café here, relax, and have a coffee before you leave."

Part 3 – Crunch Time

Celebrity Reception

Streatch limos were dropping off the familiar faces of celebrities for the luncheon with Bartow at Atlanta's Ritz Carlton, Buckhead. The media gathered outside the building were shouting at the well-dressed stars as they entered the gathering. A red carpet could be seen by the television cameras and it looked much like the Academy Awards gauntlet.

In a corner of the reception, Missy and Mark were watching as the celebrities crowded around Bartow and his family in the center group of tables. They talked in low voices while smiling and nodding at the crowd. Bartow worked the room nearer to them, smiling and laughing and shaking hands, slapping backs. The people seemed to love him. Small flash cameras were going off as the celebrities asked him to pose with them for a photo.

Missy whispered, "This is a grade A zoo. You know it was his idea to keep the media out of here! He told Safta he did not want them bothering his supporters. That's a huge risk. Huge. We're missing a golden opportunity to get these people saying the right things to wow the press, and he would not even look at talking points. At least he let us prepare material to give out to the people attending. And then… he keeps the press out! This is a *People Magazine* puff story and he keeps them out!"

Mark murmured, "He still doesn't get it. Did Safta make a

pass at him getting him to do it?"

Missy held her hand near her mouth. "Yes. He trashed her. This guy is making it hard on everyone."

Mark leaned nearer to her. "Well, he'll probably just say the same old thing. Having these people talking to the media is also risky. Even if they tried to repeat the talking points, there is no telling how it might come out or that the press would use them, but I get what you mean."

"How can we run a campaign like this?"

They moved further from Bartow as he worked, shaking hands, moving from the center toward the corners of the room.

Mark, now in a more normal voice, said, "I dunno. We are slowly making progress. He's on board with the issue rollout and did an okay job setting it up on the *Today Show*. It's just a slow process. We do seem to have enthusiastic people though. You can't manufacture that."

"Does anyone know what he is really like?"

Mark shook his head. "Not I."

War Room

Inside the war room, Weinstein and Rizzo were meeting with Vicki about the timetable and budget to have all the issue positions completed and ready to be printed into handouts. Ben Menendez, who would be helping with the distribution, was also there, but had not been saying much. They had been there for about 15 minutes when the rhetoric and temperature had begun to climb. Rizzo's voice rose an octave as he stood and walked around the table behind Vicki's chair. "I don't care! It's your job to get us some issues we can use to make commercials and brochures and shit. If we had a real person here and not a junior hill staffer, we'd have this done by now."

Menendez now chimed in. "That's unfair and uncalled for. You know we have just gotten to the point where the candidate is making decisions. We can't just go off and say anything we want in our paid media."

Rizzo replied, "Bullshit. I bet if we just had the balls,"—he looked over at Vicki—"we'd put something out there, and the guy would have to go along with it. I've done that before plenty of times."

Vicki reasserted herself. "Boys!" She looked at Weinstein and Rizzo. "I don't care what you two have done in your jackleg, gerrymandered congressional districts with razor-cut marionettes who never had an original thought in their programmed lives. This is a presidential campaign with a man who needs our HELP. This is not about our egos or our imaginary timetable to do our assigned jobs. Yes. This is tough stuff, but we've got to grow up and deal with it. You two need to stop thinking of yourselves as superheroes."

Rizzo sneered. "Oh, listen to the cheerleader. Well, little junior miss, I've been doing this since you were in grammar school and, unlike some people in this room, I know what I'm doing. If we don't get this fucking campaign into the next gear soon, we're all dead. I didn't leave my party to come here to die without a fight. You need to get your office off its cute little ass and get the papers done and approved so we can do our jobs. Otherwise we're all just going go home in embarrassment and shame."

Vicki leaned back in her chair so she could look up directly up at Rizzo, who had been standing behind her. "Got some experience with that, Mr. Rizzo?" She let her chair down, then she spoke across the table to Weinstein. "We have started a program of one issue a week. Our COLLECTIVE plans are to use media to promote those one-issue-a-week rollouts. You may remember your boss, Ralph Collins, agreed to the plan and to the budget that YOU put together." She got up to leave the room and stopped at the door. "I trust you boys will not get your undies in a twist until we have time to get the candidate's approval on all the issues." She glanced down at their crotches and then back up quickly. "Not sure your equipment could handle the stain."

A few moments later, Vicki and Menendez returned to their separate offices after they all had vented their frustration to each other and calmed down. Ben Menendez, as calmly as he could, gave Mark a much-toned-down version of what happened and what had been said.

Mark smiled at Ben and, after he left, slowly got up and went to find Rizzo and Weinstein, who had remained in the war room still working on their budgets. They looked up when he entered with some guilt on their faces, then back down at the papers on the table. Mark said, "So, guys, I understand you had some words with my wife earlier."

Rizzo shrugged. "Yeah. I think we're all a little frustrated with the way things are going and we got into it for a few minutes. We've all had a long day. No big deal."

Mark forced a smile, standing at the edge of the table across from the two. "Just so you both know it, I don't like you not being respectful to my wife or to any of our other colleagues here in this campaign."

Both Rizzo and Weinstein looked at him with surprise and more than a touch of irritation. Rizzo said, "Tough shit. This is a campaign. People get pissed off at each other. Get over it."

Mark said evenly, "I just came here to tell you both never to speak to my wife that way again."

Now Weinstein spoke. "I don't know who you think you are, but you can't talk to us like that. We're gonna do what we need to do and we're gonna speak to whoever we want in whatever way we want in order to get the job done. If you don't like it, what are you gonna do?"

Mark leaned, placed his hands on the surface of the table, and leveled a serious stare down at both of them. "I'm all about peace and polite decorum in politics and in life, but you see, Mr. Rizzo and Mr. Weinstein, this is about your taking advantage in a public forum and being offensive to my wife... actually, or any other woman in this campaign. So, despite all the wonderful bonding we've had here and the many kumbaya moments, if I find you have done anything else to disrespect her in any way, I'm going to take you out on the loading dock behind this building and beat the shit out of you. I'll take you on one at the time or both together. Don't care which."

Both men now were shocked and a little intimidated. Rizzo exclaimed, "But you're so much bigger than we both are... that's unfair. It would be the end of your career."

"That's the part I'm going to like the most. You are not much of a threat to hurt me back. Easy peasy. Do that again and I kick your ass. Karma. Clean up your act and bottle up your bullshit or I will come calling. This is more important than your or my reputation or the jobs we have in this campaign. I know what matters to me and I know what I'll do about it. I kind of don't care if you believe me or not. But you will get hurt in some permanent ways if you have not been listening to me." He gave both of them separate hard looks and said as he walked out the door, "Now let's leave our little conversation in this room and not let it affect how we work together or the jobs ahead of us. Like you said earlier, get over it. Have a good evening."

Pushing Bartow

Mark and George settled into Bartow's plush office, acutely aware he was only giving them 15 minutes before leaving. Mark started. "Mr. Bartow, things have been improving and we are having success with the rollout of our issue-a-week plan. We will have new polling results about your education speech in a couple of days. However, sir, we need you to finish approving the rest of the issues and we need to block off a good bit of your time staring Monday for the commercials, interviews, and talks with experts who will need to brief you before you have press interviews."

Mark pulled several pages from his breast pocket and handed them to George Lewis. "These are about 20 names with their bios who were involved in the Ford, Carter, and Reagan administrations in national security. Please look them over. We need to pick several of them to get involved with us. Sooner the better. I've marked two or three that I think would be good to lead the group. You need to start briefings in the next day or so on foreign policy."

Bartow made a grumpy face. "Why all that? I've got other things to do, and I've already given the campaign lots of time as it is. I decided to wait to see how the fallout from the education speech thing worked before I did the next one."

George squirmed uncomfortably. "Bill, we have a plan here and it will not work as well if we interrupt the flow of what we need to do. There is a strategy and order to all this stuff. You are doing really well, but there is so much more that we... that must be done..."

Bartow huffed. "I don't know. I didn't like that guy breaking through my security detail and throwing that confetti. There is a lot of this stuff that I do not like. I thought it would be..."

Mark, raising his voice, burst out, "Why are you doing this?

Why are you running for President of the United States? It's the toughest job in the world."

Bartow looked at his desk and tapped a pen on the wood.

Mark continued, "Sir, this thing we are in is serious. The polls say you've got between 20-25% of the people in this country including the military, all these volunteers, your family and all these others believing in you. It's time to decide if you believe in yourself.

"The spots we've run on your education plans, and the free press you got before and after the speech, were a big success. Both Clinton and Bush have been peppered with questions from the media about what they were going to do for education... compared TO YOU. You've become a temporary landing zone for the undecideds and disaffected. Even though you are just starting to define your message, your campaign has legs.

"We need to clear all this other stuff from your schedule and decide to put all your energy and that brilliant mind of yours on this campaign. It's time to fish or cut bait."

Bartow looked up with anger on his face. "I told you before, I'm not used to anyone talking to me like that."

"It's not only me. It's all those other people. You gave all of us your commitment to get down to work. You can win this thing, but you need to deserve to win it."

Bartow reached over and clicked on the intercom to his assistant, Lucine. "Clear my schedule for the rest of the day. Call Bernice and get all the kids over at the house. I need to meet with them in one hour. Also, don't take any meetings that George doesn't bring to you until I say different."

He looked from Mark to George. "I'm going to talk to my family tonight and if I decide, you'll see a different commitment tomorrow, but I'm telling you, I will not give up my life or have other people telling me what I MUST do. Postpone next week's speech on the economy till I'm better prepared to go."

George smiled and nodded. "Remember, we're in crunch time here."

War Room

Inside the war room, Collins, Weinstein, Young, Lewis, Menendez, and Burchmeyer were meeting to go over the campaign structure in the states.

Menendez said, "We've got most of the state leadership settled. There are still one or two where the self-proclaimed leaders are certifiable. John, tell them."

Burchmeyer looked at his notes. "We've done background checks on some of the problems that Ben pointed out and still have two claiming to be the manager." He flipped over some pages. "One was convicted of fraud and the other has been bankrupt in the last two years."

Collins frowned. "Jesus. The press will kill us. They're just waiting for a story like that to beat over our heads."

Menendez, who had been making the changes, said, "Most of these people just showed up and proclaimed themselves to be the state coordinators. It happened overnight as Bartow's candidacy boomed. Everybody thinks they're a general. He smiled at Collins. "We'll make the other changes quietly so it will not be a media story."

Glad to see Ben Menendez taking charge, Lewis said, "How are you going to manage it?"

Menendez smiled at Lewis. "We're using the field staff of the young officers who recently left the military. Gave each of them a state or two to coordinate. They are used to handling personnel issues and are focused. They've found out who's telling the truth and who needs to be replaced." He turned to Lewis. "George, I recommend you delay returning calls from the two problem children on this list until we can brief you." He slid a piece of paper across the table.

Lewis shook his head. "Any other good news from the field office?"

Menendez nodded at Burchmeyer. "John and I have a good working relationship, and with his help, we are developing the nucleus of a good field operation."

Lewis turned to Burchmeyer. "How about you, John?"

Burchmeyer glanced over at Weinstein as he spoke to Lewis. "Everything is a little crazy, but I've got no complaints."

Mark then said, "While we are all here, I want to throw out an idea Ben Menendez and I have been working on. We don't have a budget, all the issues approved, or an approved media strategy… but the one thing we do have is the enthusiasm of hundreds of thousands of volunteers. Let's use our main strength to our advantage. Our massive volunteer organization got us on the ballot. Now we have several million frustrated people full of energy out there that need something to do. Let's train them and turn them into local campaigns.

"I propose we have a convention. An unorthodox convention on television." He could see Collins start to say something and held up his hand to stop him from speaking.

"Here is how it would work. We would actually have 50 conventions, one in each state. We'd start by renting a convention facility, likely in each state capitol over the same weekend. We'd invite all the volunteers in that state to come. They would be organized to drive in several motorcades starting at the border extremities of each state and head to wherever we hold the conventions. These motorcades would be timed to pick up more vehicles as they passed through towns on the way to the convention site to create several long strings of vehicles in caravans all decorated like they were going to a high school football game, with Bartow posters on the cars and flying banners. They'd attract a lot of attention.

"The motorcades would stop at every media outlet: radio station, newspaper, television station, and county courthouse. We'd give all of them talking points about the Bartow campaign."

Weinstein started to say something when Mark again held up his hand.

"Let me finish this and then we can discuss it. The motorcades would start on Friday. They'd arrive in the evening and we'd try to get them all to stay at the same hotels or several near each other in the capitol or wherever. On Saturday morning, we'd have campaign classes in the ballrooms of each hotel. These would be simple classes on how to do neighborhood canvasing, how to use voter lists, how to distribute yard signs, write letters to the editors, and get speakers for civic clubs. This would be basic instruction on running small county campaigns. At the end of the day, we'd supply them, with voter lists, yard signs, bumper stickers, brochures, and whatever campaign supplies we could provide for each of them to take home and pass out.

"Now, on Saturday night, we'd have the convention speech. It would require Mr. Bartow to be ready to announce some of what he stood for, but until the end he could mostly give his regular speech. We would, however, need to throw down the gauntlet on some of the details and cuts on balancing the budget and dealing with the deficit. The speech would be the first time we gave a good description of what we want to do and the potential impact will shock almost everyone. At the end, I want to have the line, "If anyone out there thinks they have not been asked to play a role in what we need to do to fix our broken government, call me."

"After the speech, we'd have the roll call of the states, like most national conventions in the past. There would be coverage at each state convention feeding into the national convention TV program. But the difference would be that the state coordinator, or whoever was on camera pledging to support and work for Bartow's election, would be in the foreground and we'd have the entire arena of 30,000 to 50,000 volunteers behind them showing up in a wide-angle TV lens cheering as the camera panned back and forth. By the end, as the state countdown went along, you know, Alabama, Alaska, Arizona, and so on… we'd have shown over one million people on television all raring to go home and kick ass for Bartow. The national media would be overwhelmed. Each state convention would dominate the local media in that state and the national media would have our made-for-TV speech and roll call as their show.

"The next morning, everyone would go home in the reverse order they came, flags flying and material ready to distribute. That would be our campaign."

Lewis beamed. "Wow. An incredible kickass idea."

Collins shook his head. "Really creative. We can cut TV spots from the coverage."

Benny also was smiling and enthusiastic. "That would take tons of material to be produced and distributed and lots of organizing, but, man, what a hit."

Mark looked over at George Lewis. "It would also require the approval of Mr. Bartow and the expenditure of the funds to cover the weekend."

Lewis beamed back at Mark. "You've come up with a way to get him off the dime and make some decisions that do not actually seem like commitments. This convention idea would put a move on the issues, campaign materials, and other things that have been stuck."

Mark smiled back. "We've got to do something, and this might just combine everything into one ball of action that does not involve Mr. Bartow so much. Might be easier for him to see this as an activity rather than a theory.

"I've done some preliminary math and with a million or so volunteers, we should be able to give out Bartow brochures and knock on at least 50 million households. A hundred million if we work on it. That is about the total number of households in the U.S. If this is a big-turnout election, we might expect a hundred million votes to be cast. This plan is how we overcome the existing parties."

Handyman

Vicki got a call from her sister Letty, who had stress in her voice. "Did you call for someone to come to fix the cable TV?"

"No. Nothing's wrong with the cable that I know of."

"That's what I thought. Well, this man came to the door and said he had a work order that our cable was shorting out or something. He was some kind of a technician. Anyway, just as you and Mark said, I told him to wait, and I started to call you to check. Then I heard a noise and he had gone and shut the door. He didn't say anything, just left. I got scared."

A slight chill came over Vicki. "Is Livy all right?"

"Yes. She's watching cartoons. I did not let on that I was worried."

"You did the right thing. In the future, don't open the door to anyone unless you are absolutely sure we sent them. It was probably nothing. Maybe a wrong address. Don't you worry. I'll try to get home early this afternoon and you can take off and go to that movie, *Basic Instinct*, you've been wanting to see.

Vice President Search

The campaign board room was decked out with a large, long table, comfortable stuffed leather chairs, chalkboards, flipchart stands, and a media wall with a rear-projection video screen. Mark Young and Don Rizzo joined Safta Kleg and Reid Field in a meeting already in progress, introduced themselves, and took a seat.

Reid set the stage. "Mark and Don, thank you for coming. I want you to meet the management of the Anderson Firm, located here in Atlanta. He pointed as he called their names, although it was apparent that the older man of about 50 was the lead, and the young woman in her late twenties looked a lot like her father. "Frank Anderson, who heads the firm, Charles Walker, who is his right hand, and Susan Anderson have been the primary head-hunting firm for Bartow industries for what, about 10 years now?"

Reid turned to the Anderson group. "Mark and Don have a great deal of political experience in both the Democratic and Republican Parties, respectively, and will be invaluable to this discussion. George Lewis has been asked by Mr. Bartow to find an appropriate running mate. As we all know, Admiral Jeff Duncan was kind enough to stand in for us so we could get on the ballot earlier. Now it's time to change his name for a person who will be the real running mate. As the administrative officer, I'm to develop a process for the search and wanted Safta to work with us since it will no doubt be an issue of interest to the press." Nodding at Mark and Don, he continued, "He wanted you two here because of your political experience. Mr. Anderson and his firm have worked with Bartow Industries in the past on similar matters, so we naturally thought their input would be useful."

The older Anderson, impeccably dressed, sat in his chair

almost to the edge. "Actually, Reid, we've been working closely with you almost 12 years, but who's counting, ha ha."

Reid continued, "I spoke to Mr. Anderson about two weeks ago, when Geo… ah, Mr. Lewis asked me to look into this. He is here today to talk about the procedure his firm uses in their searches and give us some preliminary ideas about this particular project."

Rizzo leaned forward. "Excuse me. But," he said, nodding to Anderson, "you're a head-hunting firm. Is that right?"

Anderson inched up even further in his seat, and now he seemed precariously balanced on the front edge. "We like to think of ourselves as executive problem solvers and we work closely with all levels of management—"

Rizzo jumped back in. "Yes. 'Scuse me, and you've done some work for Bartow Industries like finding executives, and such…" He gave Mark a sly "what the hell?" look.

Reid, being protective, said, "They've done an excellent job for us."

Rizzo, with that slight admonishment, leaned back to see where this was headed. "Thank you. Sorry for the interruption."

Reid turned to the senior Anderson. "Well, perhaps Mr. Anderson can tell us what his firm has been up to."

"Thank you, Reid. Actually, we have only included the members of the firm in this little secret who absolutely would not divulge the classified nature of this activity." He paused for a look around the table. "But we have had significant resources planning and devising the WHO and the HOW for this most important assignment." He moved to get up from his chair and looked over at Reid for permission. "May I?"

"Certainly." Reid smiled and leaned back in his chair.

Anderson walked over to a chalkboard, picked up a piece of chalk, and wrote in large letters WHO and HOW in two side-by-side columns. He put down the chalk, turned to the room, and dusted his hands slightly.

"Before the 'who,' let me go over what we have learned about the 'how,' and how, ha, ha, it might apply in this case. When we find the right person for a job, we don't just take a chance they might turn it down." He held out his hands like he was guarding someone in basketball and bent over slightly. "We've learned over the years to use what we call a 'full court press'." He shook his head confidently. "Yes. We go after what we call the influencers." With this, he turned and wrote INFLU-ENCERS under the HOW column and turned back to the table.

"We learn who might be able to encourage, subtly of course, the intended executive to make a positive decision that will enhance their career and meet our client's needs." He leaned toward the table and as he reeled off the potential people involved, he patted the palm of one hand with the other held steady as a baseball mitt. "It might be the wife, the broth-er, the pastor, or a friend at the country club, a golfing buddy. We have ways of letting these people know that their friend or relative has a choice to make that can change their life."

He then leaned back as he now held his hands wide apart. "And, buddy, let me tell you it works. COUPLED with…" He turned and wrote under INFLUENCERS the word INTERVIEW then turned back to the table. "…the interview. We don't just interview, we surround. We cajole. We show the person WHY it is in their interest to make the right decision. We just don't give them a chance to say no. Isn't that right, Reid?"

"We've had very good luck working with Mr. Anderson's firm."

Anderson preened. "And that's because we don't leave one stone unturned. We close the deal with…"—he turned and wrote under INTERVIEW the word PACKAGE—"the package! We know that particular person so well, that we know how to construct a benefits package that we call 'the GODFATHER'." As he said 'the godfather,' his hands flew apart and he raised up on his toes for a moment. He then turned and stood by the chalkboard and wrote GODFATHER.

"So, we know what they NEED, what they HAVE TO HAVE, and we construct a benefits package they can't turn down." His hand slapped the word PACKAGE on the board and chalk dust flew.

"We cajole, we flatter, we tell them what they NEED to

hear. We know them so well that we become their best friend THAT's…"—now his hand slapped the word INTERVIEW. Dust puffed again. "That's how to talk to 'em that's how to get 'em to trust you. That's an interview." Now his finger was pointing into the air. "AND, when you combine that with reinforcement from all quarters, and the godfather benefits package, they can't say no. They have to take the job. It's almost like they have already made their decision and to turn it down would be disappointing all their friends, their wife, their children."

With determined purpose, he tapped his finger once, twice, then a third time on INFLUENCERS. "That's the kind of attention to detail that has made us probably the leading executive recruitment firm in Atlanta." He now walked back over to the table and leaned over it. "And let me tell you we know, we feel the responsibility of this task. We are not taking this lightly. This is to be by far our firm's biggest challenge and we are up to it." He straightened up and took a step back.

"We believe that for Mr. Bartow, only the best will do. That's why in our concept for this search, we established as our benchmark criteria to only look for the great minds in America. Susie, honey, could you hand out those lists?" His daughter pulled out several folders and passed them around. "We began in the past two weeks to build a database of the great minds in America and grouped them into categories which seemed to be a good place to start, and they are…"

He turned and again wrote on the blackboard four names and said each name after writing it.

"Government!"

"Business!"

"Civic/Cultural! Those are people who are in public service but perhaps not in government."

"Miscellaneous. Some names came up that didn't quite fit any category but which we thought deserved the merit of consideration."

Mark looked down on the paper to see hundreds of names on the lists. He thought he heard a break in Anderson's monologue and jumped into the conversation. "This is quite impressive work. I know in your haste to prepare all this, you probably have not had the time to screen or review some of these names…"

Susan Anderson quickly said, "Only that they meet the great minds criteria, which admittedly is somewhat subjective."

Mark quickly said, "No. It's not that, it's just under the, ah government area I see two that are dead. And I believe Senator Bob Packwood, though he has a good mind… but it is my understanding that there are behind-the-scenes sexual abuse charges. If it's okay, we can clean this up, although it's a very good start."

Reid quickly covered for the Anderson people. "Yes. Thank you for this excellent work."

Rizzo chimed in as he stood, "Thanks, we'll be seeing you soon."

As Mark walked out, he remembered meeting the frail Admiral Duncan and hoped they could find a real vice-presidential running mate soon to get the admiral off the hook. Duncan never should have been subjected to the bizarre experiences of a campaign. Mark thought the honor the broken Admiral had shown in his life was so much greater than the collective intentions of everyone else in the campaign.

Carville and Manafort

Paul Manafort wrinkled his nose at the smell coming from the coffee shop at the Deluxe Inn in Landover Hills, MD. He was glad he had dressed down for the meeting. This place looked like the pits. In the small cubical space that was really just a counter and some scattered tables, he immediately spotted the bowling ball head belonging to James Carville hunched over in one of the corner booths along the window. Other than an old couple at the counter, they were the only customers there at 10:30 in the morning. Carville nodded acknowledgement and Manafort wiped down the seat with several napkins before sliding into the booth across from his nemesis.

Manafort opened with, "Even for you, James, this place!"

"On purpose. I doubt we'll be seen in here by one of your Bulgarian or Lithuanian clients asking for their money back or some snoop from the *Washington Post*."

"I'd have to agree with you on that."

Carville wrinkled his brow. "Okay, let's get this over with. I don't necessarily enjoy being with you, and it would be a juicy a story if someone spotted us. Both our faces are becoming too familiar."

Manafort looked serious. "So, what's going on with this nut bag from Georgia?"

"Dunno. Polls show he's hurting both of us almost equally. Logic would argue one more than the other. He's a balloon that will pop, but when?"

"We can't find much on him. Straight arrow."

"Yeah," Carville answered. "What about your Republican buddies working in the campaign? They got anything to say?"

"Not really. Just another quirky rich guy. How about your guy, Mark Young, working in the campaign?"

"Not my guy and I doubt he'd talk to me."

Manafort leaned across the table. "You hearing the same thing I am about them making the budget and deficit a big deal?"

"That's a loser. It'll put everyone to sleep. Voters still want to hear about controversy or stuff they want to get. They don't want their toys taken away."

Manafort rubbed his chin. "I can't understand why he's not spending more of his money. He could kill us on TV."

"Like you said… nut bag."

Manafort shook his head. "So, this meeting was kind of a bust. Let's at least agree to share notes on him if it gets to a debate. We can hit him from both sides on a couple of things and throw him off, maybe."

"Makes sense." Carville tapped the table. "Look, I know you guys are going to keep coming at us with the rumors and stuff."

"Rumors?"

"All right. But let me tell you. You need to turn it down or we'll come back at your guy. I know where Jennifer Fitzgerald is stashed in France and about the sleazy deals that have been pulled by all three of the Bush boys."

Manafort smirked. "The difference is that no one will believe it about the president, or his family. Your guy, on the other hand…"

Carville leaned in. "Consider this a friendly warning. Lay off. How's my wife doing over there, by the way?"

"She's tougher than you are. Sort of found her role with the media."

"I bet it takes a big room to fit in all you guys for a staff meeting. I'm outta here. Sorry you didn't have more to tell me about this Bartow guy. To be safe, give it a couple of minutes after I leave before you go."

Consultants Meeting

A few days after Mark had confronted Rizzo and Weinstein over their treatment of Vicki, Collins called a secret meeting of all the main consultants in the morning before the campaign office opened. He began by standing in front of the group settled at the table with their coffee, biscuits, and sticky buns. "We've all experienced the insanity of this campaign and, in particular, the candidate. There was a dustup the other day with some of us in this room, and we all need to put that behind us and see that it does not happen again." He gave Rizzo and Weinstein a look. "I thought we should have this little conference to see if we have any ideas how to get this campaign on solid footing. Our reputations are tied into the success or failure of this guy. He spent a little on the education spots, but then stopped and did not go forward with what we had planned, so it was not sustained. If it were a senate or governor's race, I'd just walk, but this is high profile. So, who's got any ideas?"

Rizzo started in. "We've still got all the elements here to have a good if not successful effort. If the guy would just decide to spend some of his money... The other thing for me is that they are paying us fairly good money to be here and I don't have another campaign to move onto."

Weinstein said, "So you are suggesting we just ride this out and maybe prepare the media so when the campaign falls apart, we don't get blamed?"

Rizzo shrugged. "The other campaigns will soon cut into him. It's getting too obvious that he doesn't know what he is doing and is not listening to us."

Ben Menendez added, "We do have the start of a fairly good field operation. If we did that convention idea and got good press off it and Bartow got inspired, that might turn all this around. He's starting to agree on issues, and let's hope he will continue spending on the issue-a-week media blitz. I don't see this time as being as bad as you do."

Rizzo quickly came back. "Right. But, Ben, you can't win an election on grassroots door stuffers and this issue media stuff. We need a budget, and we need to be on TV big-time."

Weinstein said, "If we are going to dump this guy, we need to do it in a way that we don't look disloyal. We'd never get another job if we look like the bad guys."

Mark leaned forward. "I agree with all of you that this guy is difficult and uncooperative, but all of us should try to think of how this looks from his side. He blindly jumped into the race and does not know the rules or how to act. He's scared. Our job is to use his idiosyncrasies to help this campaign. If we don't want to do that, we should not have signed up, and now that we are here, we could really hurt the potential good we could do by leaving. We can't make him into something he's not. He's not going to suddenly become an ideal candidate. We've got to adapt to him.

"While… as we are hanging out here anyway, we need to try to see if our efforts have a chance of moving the Democrats and Republicans into a position of talking about real consequences for once and not just the emotional bullshit they normally use in campaigns. We've all been shoveling the same shit for years using platitudes and carefully groomed candidates. This may be the last chance to take a real person and tell the truth in an election. For that chance, I think it's worth sucking up a little of our egos. If Bartow loses, it may not matter as much if we can get honest discussions on the stage.

"For the past few years, our government has been operating like there is no limit to the money it has to spend. It's everybody's fault, not just Reagan's and Bush's. However, if Bartow will make the economy and the growing deficit and lack of balanced budgets his centerpiece, it will force a discussion with all the candidates on setting priorities about what's important. That will drive federal spending, tax breaks, all of it. Everything else is on the fringes.

"We've gotten into this mess and we need to use this time

and the attention we can get from the media to do some good. We have what Teddy Roosevelt called a bully pulpit. Let's lay it on the public and make Bush and Clinton react to it."

Benny Weinstein pointed to Mark. "Our liberal friend here makes a little sense, but we've still got to watch out for our careers. The clock is ticking on this campaign. It won't do us any favors if the guy becomes a good candidate by election day, but the voters remember the doofus from television six months before. I don't think we have more than a couple of weeks to get this place in line, or it will be too late. It's already going to cost him more money to correct for his earlier foot-dragging."

Collins slapped his hands together. "Okay, let's try for a little while longer and keep getting paid. There has never been anyone who has the potential to spend what this guy can and that can cover up a lot of warts. We can keep one eye out for where we all go next, but we still have a very good chance to win here."

As they were leaving, Collins asked Mark to stay. "Just wanted to let you know that I am sorry that thing happened. My guys are wrapped too tight sometimes."

"I appreciate your gesture. I sure hope it does not happen again."

"Me too. It shouldn't. We're too close to winning this thing. Why do you think Bartow is being like he is? I mean, Mark, if Bartow would let us run the commercials, do the issue-a-week thing, and have the convention you suggested, he could be President of the U.S. It's that simple. He just has to write a check and let us do our jobs. What do you think is going on with him?"

"I agree with you. We're right there, and he could win. It feels almost like Bartow is scared of it."

Burchmeyer

John Burchmeyer got a call. "They've gotten another one." He returned quickly to his office to see several envelopes on his small conference table and one of his staff wearing thin plastic gloves and going carefully through them with tweezers. He leaned over, looking at the line of identical envelopes and the way they had all been addressed to the residences of Bill Bartow and to all of his children. Inside each was a standard hand-out press photo of Bartow with a banned symbol over his face and his eyes rubbed out with what looked like violent scratches by a pencil. Each photo had different scratches, so each was done separately, although the frightening message was the same.

The man sifting through the envelopes spoke while still inspecting the pile of paper. "We're just about to send these over to the fingerprint lab, but it's likely they're not going to find anything. These look like the others."

Burchmeyer raised his head from close to the paper. "Yeah. That'd be my guess. Send them to the Secret Service after the lab gets the results. How many does this make?"

"This is the fourth batch. These all seem to have been dropped at the same time at the same post office. Just like before, they use a different post office drop box each time. The Bartow kids recognize the envelopes now and don't open them, so we don't have their contamination when we do the fingerprint tests."

Burchmeyer frowned. "Yeah. It still bothers them though. My guess is that they talk about it among themselves and with their mom and dad. Did they say the phone calls are still happening?"

"Yes, sir. No pattern there either. Daytime, nighttime, whenever. Different calls, to different kids or the main house. We've set up a screening process to vet the calls before they are put through to the houses now, but they don't like it because it interferes with their friends calling and other stuff that has nothing to do with the campaign or Mr. Bartow. It's starting to grate on them to have us in between them as a filter, and they're starting to complain. Mrs. Bartow is the most upset. She just doesn't get it why people would do this. She's kind of a refined and old-school lady who has had a protected life."

Burchmeyer pinched his nose between his eyes and squeezed them in a pronounced blink before shaking his head to clear the weariness he was feeling. "Yes. The boss is feeling it too. He doesn't let on. Keeps this shit to himself, but I can tell it bothers him, particularly when his family is upset. Poor bastard. Do the nighttime patrols have anything more to report?"

"Just the occasional cars driving past and playing loud music. Usually they only do it two or three times before leaving for the rest of the night. We've only been able to catch that one of them a week ago. It was just some kid who said he had been paid to do it and had no idea who lived there or who had paid him. These bastards are irritating, but they are good at what they do and do it just enough to bother everyone but not be criminal."

"Do the Secret Service folks have any ideas?"

"Nah. They are sympathetic and have looked over all of our reports and whatever you could call evidence, but there is nothing there."

Burchmeyer tapped the tabletop. "Okay. Well, clear this off as soon as you can and let's hope we can catch a break. Let's keep this to ourselves. We don't need another rumor around the campaign."

Dumbarton Oaks

Mark meandered off a street in the upper section of Georgetown into the beautifully manicured grounds of Dumbarton Oaks. Years before, the property was a land grant made by Queen Anne of Great Britain and had been a showplace for over 200 years. The early home was residence to industrial and political powers and gradually evolved until the property became a library and museum. In the fall of 1944, it was the site of an international conference that led to the League of Nations, the precursor to the United Nations.

He was dressed as requested, with a fat vest worn under his shirt that added 25 pounds to his appearance and the rinse used on his hair made it a medium shade of gray. The additional moustache and clear-lens glasses with the thick frames made him look at least 20 years older. The greatest indignity, however, was the clothes—ugly, muted, plaid, and mismatched shirt and jacket, an outfit a blind man would not have chosen. It reminded him of the disguise he'd been given when he met with Bruce in Frankfurt, Germany, during the Greek campaign. With this costume, he added an unsteady gate to his walk as he moved into the back area containing the formal gardens. It was likely he could pass an old neighbor and not be recognized. Kind of the point.

As he moved through the extensive space, the lack of tourists this morning made it easy to see that he had not been followed. With that confirmation, he walked down two levels to a quiet rectangular garden with a string of gazebos shading benches along one side. There he found Bruce dressed as a homeless street person in old clothes with a grocery cart near him which was stuffed with plastic bags and extra clothes. He was holding a bag of seeds, which attracted several pigeons watching him while pawing the ground nearby.

Mark sat toward the other end of the bench a few feet to the side of Bruce, glanced at the pigeons, and then scanned the beautiful garden. He laughed and said, "Your disguise is a big improvement over your normal look. Didn't take you for a bird lover."

"I'm not, but I found that most people are not likely to crash a party containing a dozen hungry birds." He broadcast another small handful of seeds in a sweeping gesture, which scattered and animated the birds, bobbing their heads while stepping quickly back to peck at the grain. "Also, we hired someone like you who did a study and found that if you want to have a private conversation in an urban environment, dress like a homeless person." Bruce shook his head. "Anyway, I've gotten to be too well-known in some circles in this town and can't afford to be seen with you. So, this ridiculous outfit is what I had to do."

Mark sniffed. "Do you have to smell that way?"

"Gotta sell it."

Mark continued to look at the garden instead of Bruce. Then he looked down at his own ridiculous outfit. "Well, I feel like we are two old guys dressed up for Halloween. Anyway, we're here now and I want to know if you are hearing anything about the election."

Bruce leaned back toward the bench from his bird-feeing posture and looked out at the flowers in the garden instead of at Mark. "I thought you didn't want anything to do with me or the organization that has been paying you for the past several years. Thought you were in your ivory tower of integrity, all wrapped up in the noble campaign mode."

"I'm still loyal to the campaign, but some things have been going on in Atlanta and elsewhere that don't seem like random coincidences. I thought you, in your role as the political ear-to-the-ground of the agency, might have heard something."

Bruce rolled up the top of the paper bag and sat it on the bench next to him. "I have concern about your guy's stability. However, you'd know more about that than I would."

Mark shook his head. "Maybe not."

Bruce blew out a breath in a rush. "Look, I told you about

my national security concerns, but you said the agency can't have a dog in this fight." He looked around the garden. "Mark, this is your meeting, but… do you know why I picked this spot?"

"Enlighten me."

Bruce looked around slowly. "This is one of the most historic places in D.C. Over beyond that wall is the Oak Hill Cemetery, with people in it from before the Civil War, a war that saved America. This house behind us is where we started the UN, which some people think helped to save the world. Think of all the changes that happened during the Civil War, including weapons, communications, tactics. The next big evolutionary change of all those things took place in World War I. It's just gone on from there.

"Since the Civil War and World War I and World War II and on and on, the technological differences have only gotten greater by factors of hundreds and thousands. Everybody moved on forward, changing—that is, except politicians. You political guys are still making speeches off the back of flatbed trucks and counting ballots by hand.

"Your profession is only now beginning to catch up with computers, fax machines, teleprompters, phone blasts, and such. Business is kind of like that too. There is a very wide gap between what you do and what we and the military do."

"Never thought about it like that, but you're right."

"You have been around us long enough to understand that the federal government is in the process of creating the capacity to analyze and develop communications technology far beyond anything previously imagined. It will be the key component in our national defense strategy for the future. Think about it. A hundred years ago we were still throwing cannonballs at each other.

"Our increased communications capacity will give us information to make the U.S. dominant worldwide in finances, military, security, and intelligence. All we need is the cooperation of elected officials to provide the money and not jeopardize operations. Bartow has no knowledge and no competent advisors in that area. He is a threat to our future.

"The reason we hire guys like you is because the American electorate is an ill-informed bunch of gullible sheep. They don't read. They don't study. They only want to escape into some childcare version of fantasy. They can see one 30-second commercial or hear an entertaining segment of a speech by a candidate waving their arms around and decide immediately how to vote.

"The American people are dumb as bricks. They can be led around by a good conman to follow their most basic instincts and believe any simple explanation. Look at Hitler. There was a reason he was successful and could be again today. That's why we need the stability in our military and intelligence services and we need people on the inside who know the score to advise our politicians. We realize we can't control the politicians, but we do need for them to listen to advisors who can help them make decisions that are within the boundaries of what is good for our nation. Work with us here."

Mark now understood Bruce's point. "I understand you are worried about a third-party guy you don't know who has a chance to win the election."

"You are not such a dumbass, after all. My point is that foreign policy, foreign affairs, military, defense, security... all that is light-years ahead of you. You political guys are playing catch up and you don't have the skills or resources to do it well. To understand today's national security and military, you need people who already understand the systems."

Mark protested, "Bartow's got former military people—"

Bruce interrupted, "You are not hearing me. Mark, somebody that is in love with the military does not understand all the ways the Defense Department budget is bloated and wasteful. There are programs there solely to support certain Congressional districts, not protect the borders of the USA. What has changed about defense is the information and communications technology. The military hardware is only about 10% of national security and defense. To be a viable and effective president, you need people who understand how things work.

Mark looked around the garden. "Message received. I'll push harder on the advisors." Mark scuffed his feet on the ground. "Something else. I thought you might have heard from your vast circle of friends about someone or some organization trying to stir up problems for my guy by creating unsettling situations. Like that attack outside NBC in New York or some of the drive-by things at his house, or planting stories or questions in the media. You know—PSYOP stuff."

Bruce took on a long breath and let it out. "None of the campaigns need us for that. Everyone does it. The thing that makes it noticeable is that the other two candidates roll with it and your guy gets his back up. All those false trails and sneaky shit are to throw people and the media off. Mostly it does not work, but there are some successes. The trick in politics is not to react to it publicly. The fact that your guy does shows what a novice he is and that he is thin-skinned. I thought it was your job to prevent that."

Mark looked at the ground. "There is truth in all you say, but there is a line being crossed that is more than just dirty tricks or fuck-your-buddy stuff. There is a calculated menace to the events that is slowly escalating in a way that argues an intelligent and planned approach. In the past, those kinds of dirty tricks have been done by arm's-length campaign supporters that had deniability. This stuff smells better organized. That is why I came to you."

Bruce leaned back and crossed one leg over the other, still looking out at the garden as he spoke. "If this was coming from offshore, your guy is exactly the kind of candidate they would want to have in their pocket, but Russia just after their fall is too much in disarray to make it happen. If it's planned, it must be from your opponents."

Mark now looked over at Bruce for the first time. "I know all that. That is the obvious stuff. The reason I came to you is your concern that my guy would be dangerous to our national security. You seem to be afraid he'd say or do something stupid to harm our posture in the world. I want to know… did you act on that?"

Bruce continued to look at the grounds and stayed silent.

Mark continued, "You know we've started this issue-a-week stuff. We were holding off on national security because it's so important. We wanted to cap this rollout with that. I can tell you that I think you and your buddies will like what you will hear. I think it also bothers you that we are serious about balancing the budget and not adding to the national debt."

"Everybody says that."

"But we believe it. I think your bosses are afraid that we'll find those pockets of money you have hidden. All that communications stuff you just talked about costs lots of money."

Bruce forced out a breath in a silent laugh and then looked over at Mark with a steady gaze. "I'll share this with my superiors and I'm sure all of us will look forward to Bartow's little talk on national security. But... in the meantime, the clock is still running and we think your guy is a loose cannon and either of the other two would be better. The more viable he gets in the polls without a clear foreign policy or advisors that we know, the more worried we get. We're out of time. It would be scary for this country to have a guy with no offshore vision get elected. However, like I said, we don't have a dog in this fight."

Mark nodded. "I know, and I'd be very disappointed to find out you were doing anything differently."

Bruce looked at him. "You don't need to be worrying about me. Your job and your attention should be focused on getting your guy under control. He's his own worst enemy. If enough of us feel that he's a security risk... well, that shit is your line of work, not mine. Your time would be better spent coaching the guy to behave like a normal person than flying up here to sit in this garden with me."

Mark felt suspicious of Bruce's denial of any knowledge of the events that had spooked Bartow. Still, he didn't want to challenge him directly because he knew it would only cause him to redouble his efforts. So, he smiled and nodded his head. "Okay. Thanks for seeing me. I may be too close to this whole thing and looking for scapegoats."

Bruce nodded back. "Well, you're moving toward a critical

time in the contest." He opened the bag of seeds and dumped the rest on the ground, which caused a flurry among the birds. After that extra activity, he continued, "Best to check all these things out. The world's getting crazy again. This stuff in the Balkans between Bosnia, Serbia, and Croatia is going to get very nasty. The Russians are stirring it up and we're likely to get sucked into it, and not in a good way. That's where I'm spending most of my time. You stay healthy. Have a safe flight back and say hello to Vicki and the kid."

Mormons

Early the next morning, Mark bumped into Blane Harper when the scheduler rushed out of the boardroom. In the background, Mark could see that the room was filled with over a dozen very old white men dressed in black suits.

Blane said urgently to Mark, "Mark, thank God. Do you know where Bartow is?"

"No idea. Did you check with George?"

"No. He wasn't in when we all got here."

Blane pulled Mark away from the boardroom and closed the door behind him.

Mark nodded at the room. "Did somebody die? It looks like a mortician's convention. Who you got in there, anyway?"

Blane looked surprised. "You didn't see the schedule? I've got the elders of the Mormon Church in there. They are thinking of endorsing Bartow. This could be huge. I've been working on this for two weeks through back channels. I sent all this in a memo to Bartow. It was on his schedule. He should have been here to greet them."

Mark told Blane, "I was out of town yesterday and did not see the schedule. If they'll be okay for a few minutes, you ought to get George to call over to Bartow's office and see what's up. You want me to do it?"

"No. No. I'd better go. I know all the details. Thanks." Blane looked back toward the door to the boardroom and then hurried off to George Lewis' office.

Lewis looked up from his desk as the door opened and Blane entered. "Morning. Sorry to barge in, but do you know what's keeping Mr. Bartow?"

George looked surprised. "What? Ahhh, no I don't. Oh, that's right, we had him down to meet with the Mormon group this morning."

Blane nodded. "Well, if you don't mind, could you call over there and see when he'll be coming? I don't want to keep them waiting too long. It's very hard to get this group together outside of Salt Lake."

"Sure." George picked up the phone and dialed. "Good morning to you, can I please speak to Mr. Bartow? Yes. What?" He looked up at Blane with a worried face. "When did that happen? Why did no one call me? Great! Janice, in the future, please contact me directly on any changes no matter what time, okay?" George hung up and rubbed his face.

"What's wrong? Where is he?"

"Evidently, last night sometime, Mr. Bartow got a call from a producer on the *Today Show*. They invited him to come on this morning. He called his plane and got up and left early to fly up to New York to be on the program."

"But. But. We have all these guys in there. He agreed to meet with them. What are we going to do? Do you know how hard it is to get the fucking Mormon Church to have a political meeting with a third-party candidate?"

George got up slowly from behind his desk, looking very tired. "Blane, I'll go in there with you, and I'll tell them something."

Blane, looking a little more relieved that he would not have to deliver the bad news himself, said, "But, you didn't do anything. It's him…"

"I've been his lawyer for over 20 years and I'm the campaign manager. I'll do it."

Don Rizzo was watching the drama unfold from the Collins staff area. He had smiled when he saw his old friend Blane Harper rushing to George Lewis' office. It would only upset Blane to tell him that he was the one who had called the *Today Show* producer to encourage her to call Bartow to appear on the program. He had discussed it with Manafort before to make sure that he got credit for screwing up Blane's efforts to get the Mormon Church endorsement. This would be one more thing to Rizzo's credit when he returned to the Republican Party's fold after Bartow collapsed.

One day down the road, after all the scars from this debacle had healed, he'd buy Blane Harper several drinks and then let him know what he had done and how smoothly it had worked. Rizzo figured he'd saved Blane's relationship with the Mormons, because in the long run, if they had endorsed Bartow, his eventual collapse would have made them look that much more foolish than this aborted trip to Atlanta. Yeah, Blane would thank him down the road, even though today, he was very upset.

Commercials

The media meeting was held in the secure war room with the famous Republican media advisors Frank Press and Chappy Knight. When Mark and George Lewis entered, the conversation was already in full swing and Press was saying, "So, until we have the go-ahead to work on the bio and the other issue spots, we can show the enthusiasm of the volunteers in the spots we have here today. It will reinforce what people see on the TV news." He looked at Mark and Lewis as they were seating themselves.

Collins said, "This meeting is to discuss getting on the air with whatever we can. We've got to get in the game. We've got to use our ability to dominate the airwaves and put pressure on the other guys to spend their money in reacting to us. They are limited by taking government matching funds, and if we can bleed them now, they won't have money left for the final push."

Then Chappy Knight spoke to the campaign manager. "We've got to take this opportunity and identify Bartow. Once we do the establishment spots, we'll need to start the issue-a-week run. The key here is reach and frequency. However, if we don't do it soon, our opponents or the media are going to trash us badly."

Press tag-teamed in again, this time looking at Lewis. "That's absolutely right. And it will be critical to get several days of his time blocked off for our shoot as soon as possible. Plus, we need to know when the budget is approved so we can get on the air."

Collins asked no one in particular, "How fast can we be on the air?"

Knight answered quickly, "With a good buy, less than a week. We want to do some blocking buyouts at some key prime time spots and some evening news adjacencies. That may take a little longer."

Lewis confirmed to himself, "That's like buying everything at the same time?"

Knight replied, "Right. Like we'll buy all the nets and CNN at, let's say, the spot just before 9:00 p.m. Eastern time. That way, no matter what channel they're watching on television, they are seeing our spot."

Collins sensed they were finally getting to the point of spending some serious money. "Benny, what's the budget look like?"

Weinstein checked his notes. "We've got to bust out with a thousand points a week everywhere. We hold that for three weeks, drop back to 750 during sweeps, then kick it back up to a thousand, maybe even 1,500 a week for the next three weeks. This first flight has us in their face for eight weeks with significant saturation."

"What's it cost?"

Benny checked his spreadsheets again. "About $18 million, maybe $20 million. It should be $25 million. We may get a better break with some of the cable people, but those numbers aren't significant. We may save $500,000-600,000 from that or we could bump it up 50 to a hundred points with what we save."

Chappy Knight spoke again. "But... the problem has been getting time on his schedule to get some footage with him and we've got to have an approved budget so we can make the commitments to the networks to secure the air space and get the good time slots."

Collins now moved to the soul of the meeting to put the pressure on George Lewis. "George, when do you think we can see Bill on this?"

Lewis checked the schedule he had on Bartow. "Let's try for... not tomorrow, day after tomorrow. I'll see what we can set up. This may take some selling."

Collins nodded. "Good. We need to see him as soon as possible." Collins now added more pressure. "If we don't do this now, we're going to get in real trouble. I mean, this is what running a presidential campaign is all about. Today we're gonna see the rough cuts on some of the volunteer spots."

Mark was getting nervous about these plans when no one, especially Bartow, had approved the budget. He had seen this kind of 'hot-boxing' before and wanted to slow things down to take some pressure off Lewis. "So, you want to spend $18-25 million on man-in-the-street testimonials and Bartow speech excerpts?"

Collins, who was used to being able to throw money at the television, was impatient. "Hell, Mark, you make it sound like we're wasting our money. We've got no choice but to get on TV and make an impact. We'll push the other guys into reacting to us while we're laying out the good-guy claim. Then we can go negative. We've got to set the narrative of who Bartow is before we get into the cycle of the new issue-a-week commercial run. We need to roll these spots out and keep them coming for the eight to ten weeks we planned so Bartow's issues will dominate the campaign messaging of everyone. That was your idea. We've got to go with it now, and once we start, we've got to keep it up. That is the campaign."

Trying to balance being congenial with all the various consultants and the Bartow staff with what was an optimistic timetable, Mark said, "Would it help if you could show Bartow the spots?"

Lewis was looking for all the help he could get when he went to see Bartow. "That's not a bad idea."

Collins, in his gruff voice, countered, "Yeah. But, guys, we're in the big leagues now. If he doesn't like the spots, it's too late to recut them. We need to commit to be on the air to get this campaign going. He does not need to see TV spots for that. It would be nice, but I don't think it's important enough to wait on getting a commitment from him to pull the trigger."

Lewis said, "Okay, then, I'll set it up."

Collins nodded over at the filmmakers. "Okay, let's see the volunteer spots. Frank, you want to set this up?"

The veteran media man, Frank Press, stood. "Research shows that the volunteers have made a great impact. Everyone knows about them in general. Many people know someone personally who is a volunteer, but the public needs an emotional connection to them. Since we can't get the candidate's time as yet, we shot volunteers telling who they are, why they are involved, what their hopes and dreams are for this country, why they like Bartow. It personalizes the people we see on the street corner selling T-shirts and stuff. Research showed some women are intimidated by the volunteers, and we aren't doing as well with women in general, so we focused on them. These spots make the volunteers seem real and seem safe. By the choices we made in what they are saying, we're introducing some biographical information on Mr. Bartow to lay down at least something of a base until we can get him on camera."

Collins gushed. "That's genius stuff." Collins motioned to the side. "Don, you want to turn down those lights?"

As Rizzo turned off the overhead lights, Frank Press picked up a remote and turned on the large-screen TV. Images began to appear and the leader counted down the seconds until the start of the commercial. As the numbers rolled from 10 to 2 before the commercial, there was a brief flicker of text at the beginning of the countdown from the lab which processed the film which read, "A Rizzo-Weinstein Production."

As the commercials began, it was apparent the filmmakers had used a handheld camera, which made the spots almost abstract in harsh lighting. In some shots, only half of the faces were seen or the shoes of the people talking were all that were on the screen. The audio was noisy with static, like it was coming over a phone or in the middle of all the other street and household noise. The shots did not flow interconnectedly, but they jumped from one place to the other. Interspersed in the images, there was some talk about Bartow and his business background and support of the military.

Mark, who had seen this technique used before, assumed this was to cut through regular commercial TV clutter and grab the viewer with an overall impression of the volunteers on the street corners as though they had observed them. This technique was sometimes used in product advertising, but to leave a substantial impression, it required the viewer to see many separate commercials. Usually this method needed several weeks of intense and very expensive advertising exposure, such as the rollout of the new Infinity automobile.

On the screen, volunteers were talking in random sound bites. "We all felt we had to do something."

"Yeah, it's hot out there and sometimes people bring us drinks."

"I picked my kid up from school and he said to me, 'Momma, when are we going to sell some more T-shirts?'"

"It's gotten out of hand. None of them up in Washington know what they are doing anymore."

"Yeah, but Bill Bartow is a successful businessman, and he knows how to get things done."

Collins commented to Lewis as the commercial ran, "This is great stuff. No one's ever done anything like it."

The volunteers on the screen continued to talk, one person after the other. "We sat down and talked to them. And, they said, let's go for it."

"Some days, when it's raining, it's hard to put in my two hours."

"All the people seem to thank us for doing it. That's the nice part."

"Remember when Bill Bartow had that parade for the veterans? It was a day like this."

In the background, Rizzo whispered to Collins, "These are like what they did for those AT&T spots. It's cutting-edge."

On the screen, the people continued to talk in disjointed phrases. "We're gonna get every signature it takes to get him on the ballot."

"Yes, honey, it's over there. I'm talking to this man right now."

"I think we'll get twice as many as we need."

"We gotta do this for the country."

"We gotta do this for ourselves."

"We gotta do it for,"—the man nodded to the child standing nearby—"him."

Rizzo turned the lights back on.

Collins said to George Lewis, "Pretty good stuff, don't you think? If he won't give us the money to run these, he is crazy."

Mark said, "Frank?"

Frank Press turned to Mark. "Yes, Mark?"

Mark shifted in his seat. "I agree with everyone that these are very different and will stand out and do what you intended to define the volunteers."

Press leaned closer to Mark. "I hear a 'BUT' in there."

Mark, frowning, said, "Well, it's just… do you have any material that helps to define Bartow?"

Collins, sounding defensive, said, "What do you mean, Mark?"

Mark made another face. "I just felt that in addition to what's here, it would be good to give more information about Bartow. A lot of people don't know about his charitable donations, his business career, or his involvement in good causes. I think we need to define the candidate. He's getting hammered by others and sometimes sticks his own foot in it. Do we have anything that helps with that?"

Collins, now more defensive, said, "For a start, that was not the purpose of these commercials, and if the candidate would give us some of his precious time, we could tell his story. I don't think you fully appreciate the quality or the power of these spots."

George Lewis now acted as mediator. "Ralph, there is no need to get defensive. We all appreciate these spots. But, I do agree with Mark that defining Bartow with or without his help is needed. I'm not sure Bill will fully appreciate the moving camera and some of the artsy parts of these spots, but he'll like it that they are about the volunteers. Let's show them to him as soon as possible."

Frank Press stood. "We'd like to do a little tightening on a couple of them, and let me have a couple of days to do that. We'll get you guys a cassette over here later in the week in time for your meeting with him. I understand and appreciate your comments. We'll go back through our material for more informative material on Bartow and we'll plan some more traditional bio spots."

In a grumpy voice, Collins said, "Well, I think they were great, just great." He then looked over at Don Rizzo. "Don, you need to clean up those intro tags."

George Lewis stood. "Look, folks, we can tweak the spots, we can make new ones, we can do lots of things, but not without a budget. I realize we are at the point, as you gentlemen in this room have said more than once, that we need to make the go or no-go decision. I thank all of you for what you have done, but now I've got to get the green light to make all this happen. I'm going to see Mr. Bartow tonight."

As the meeting was breaking up, Mark grabbed George Lewis by the arm. "Can I speak to you a minute?" Lewis nodded and then stepped back into the now-empty room. "George, I've mentioned this before, but we need to get the foreign policy advisors signed up. We're going to be criticized that we are weak on foreign policy and defense intellect around here. What happened to the list I gave you of the names and bios?"

"Yes. We haven't had time to think about that."

"It's time."

"What about Admiral Duncan?"

"George, everyone knows his days are past it."

"Okay, I'll talk to the boss. It may take a few days to get this done."

Mark was upset. "We're... we're past due on this. Things need to start happening here."

"I'll... I'll get to it. I can't make everything happen at once."

On the way back to his office, Mark bumped into Missy. "Did you see all the commotion?"

"No. I've been in a meeting. What happened?"

"The Burchmeyer people caught a woman volunteer back

in one of the protected areas. She had some files with her that were about the issue rollout and the plans to budget the TV spots around it. Stuff she shouldn't have had with her. They took her to Burchmeyer's office and are holding her there."

"Wow. Thanks. I'll look into it."

In the security area, Mark could see the attractive woman through one-way glass seated in a small room that looked a lot like the interrogation rooms in police movies. He pulled Burchmeyer aside. "What did you find out?"

He glanced through the glass at the woman. "She's holding out so far, but we'll get through to her."

"John, even if she is a spy, she's got rights and we are not the police or government. You can't keep her prisoner. We don't need a media story out of this. Better to ban her from the building and maybe even put a private eye following her to make sure she doesn't try to get back in, than to play hardball and have her go to the press."

Burchmeyer frowned. "She's likely connected to the other stuff that has been happening and—"

"John, hold it. Whatever involvement she has, the damage is done. Don't make it worse by giving her a story to take to the media. They'll give her the sympathy. This kind of thing happens in campaigns like it happens in business. Warn her and get her the hell out of here."

Burchmeyer's shoulders slumped. "Shit. You're right. I'm looking for a scalp because of the confetti and other stuff. She's not the answer." He gave an affirmative nod. "I'll scare the hell out of her and cut her loose. Thanks."

Ralph Collins

Ralph Collins sat in his office talking with Blanche Fieldman of the *Washington Post* and John Reynolds of the *Wall Street Journal*. "I appreciate you both meeting with me. What I have to say is deep background. You can call for quotes when this story hits. And I'll give both of you a heads-up call in plenty of time." He paused thoughtfully. Collins enjoyed playing coy with the media even though the reporters knew how he worked and just wanted him to get to the point. "It's not earth-shattering yet, but it could be."

John Reynolds tapped his pen against the notepad. "As you can tell, we're both breathless with anticipation."

Collins was sensing that he needed to move on and stop with his normal games. "Well, I think I've finally got these guys around here understanding how important it is to have a strong media strategy."

Blanche, in a frustrated tone, said, "Cut to the chase. So, when are you going on TV?"

Collins, who had no authorization to be having this conversation, wanted the reporters to speculate that Bartow was preparing to go on television. In Collins' experience, news speculation often forced the candidate to commit to the spending he wanted. "Soon. There are a few details to clear up. But I've got them convinced that's the way to go."

John, sensing it was his turn, asked, "What's the nature of the spots?"

"You know that Press and Knight are the best at this. You remember what they did in the last California governor's race. And everyone knows the 'Morning in America' they did for President Reagan. A classic. Anyway, we're going to start with the volunteers."

Jaded from many years hearing political consultants shovel

bullshit, Blanche expelled a sigh. "Spare me. T-shirt vendors and computer nerds. Ralph, you'll put all the viewers to sleep. All anyone's seen on TV for the past several months are those whackos."

Collins was now more defensive than he had anticipated needing to be. "You're right, but these will be the stories behind the volunteers, who they are, how they and Bartow have made this connection with America."

"Oh then, bullshit."

John, playing the good cop in this interview, said, "Okay, then you're doing testimonials. Then what? When are you going to tell anyone what this guy stands for? When are you going to give people a reason to vote for him?"

"That's coming, and I have a great strategy on rolling that out. You heard the education speech. It was powerful stuff, cutting edge. But, we've gotta start with some background on why he's in this and who he is, you know."

Blanche continued her cynicism. "Well, this is exciting, Ralph. You got us here to tell us you're going to air testimonials from whackos and puff shots of the candidate, and you guys are not ready to let anyone in on your positions on abortion, the economy, Bosnia, the environment, or any of the things which are really important. Boy, I'm really glad I agreed to sit with you. My editors will be so pleased."

Collins was enjoying the give and take now. "Hey, I've known you too long for you to pull that shit on me. There's nothing happening in this election. By our taking the offensive, it gives you a race. It gives you competition and conflict. That sells your fuckin papers. I've given you and John a head start because you've done me a few favors in the past. I want you to be ahead of your competition. No, we're not announcing a cure for cancer, but in this election, a summer TV offensive is news. If we put $150 million into this, we will swamp the Bush and Clinton campaigns."

"Your guy can spend as much as he wants to. You're saying he is ready to spend three times as much as either of the other guys?" John asked calmly.

"Off the record, yes."

John looked at his notes. "Democrats and Republicans are taking federal matching funds and have about $50 million each. That's all they can spend unless they have some unaffiliated ads, which they're not supposed to know anything about."

Collins leaned forward. "Yes. And here's the kicker, off the record and you can't say anything about this till we start, but once we lay down some basic bio stuff, we're gonna roll out one issue a week. Like the education, we'll do a new one every week. We're gonna crush the numbers with ads and dominate the message. Bush and Clinton aren't gonna know what hit them. I'll call both of you when we're ready to go. I've given you both the exclusive so you can fight over how you tell it."

Blanche looked over at her competition, then back to Collins. "So, if you start a pissing contest early... and they have to react, then you'll bleed 'em out of money for the fall."

John smiled, slightly anticipating a rowdy campaign and lots of reader interest.

Collins smirked. "Yes."

John closed his notepad and put his pen in his pocket. "This is the political equivalent of the Germans trying to take Russia."

Blanche smirked. "John, he's trying to buy the election; let's not try to get too noble here. Besides, it's more like the V-1's hitting Britain when they couldn't fight back with comparable weapons."

Collins, now trying to suppress his pleasure and how he was being perceived by these two national correspondents, said, "We're operating under the law just like everyone else."

Blanche closed her notepad. "Yes, but everyone else doesn't have $4 billion."

Bug

Mark Young and Benny Weinstein were surprised when they were called to the war room to find John Burchmeyer and Reid Field already seated in the room. The table was clear of any objects except for a small metallic disc. Weinstein spoke as he and Mark took seats opposite Burchmeyer and Field. "Guys, I'm sitting in for Ralph Collins."

Mark looked at his watch. "So, it's 8:00 p.m. What are we meeting about?"

Burchmeyer reached out and twirled the small disc around a couple of times with one finger, which made no noise on the smooth surface. He then softly shoved it across the table. "As you know, we sweep the whole building at random several times a week. With the security measures and access restrictions we have on this area, it should be the most secure place in the campaign." He sighed. "However, this afternoon we found this thing here." He pointed at the disc.

Benny picked up the small object, squinted, and frowned. "So, you're telling us this is some king of a bug?"

Burchmeyer nodded. "Our team found this device here in your so-called war room. I thought this was the place where our sensitive material could be kept safe. So, what the hell is it doing there?" He nodded at the bug. "We've got to close this place down, and because we've restricted the room to only key personnel, and have fairly sophisticated ways to monitor entry and exits, it had to be an inside job."

Benny smirked. "Must have been those college kids Mark has hired to man this place. They are the ones who have been spending the most time here."

Burchmeyer nodded. "Normally I'd agree, but we vetted them well before they were hired and this afternoon after we found that,"—he pointed to the disc—"we did a polygraph on all of them. They passed with flying colors."

Benny pushed the disc back across the table. "So, what are you saying?" He looked at Mark and then back at Burchmeyer. "One of us did it?"

Burchmeyer opened his hands palms up on the table.

Benny then sat up taller in his chair. "Look, guy. We're here to run a campaign. However, this a campaign unlike any of us have ever been in before. The candidate can't decide on anything. You guys are like stormtroopers with your security, and we are not given permission to run a campaign like it needs to be run to get your guy elected President of the United States. I don't know anything about that bug thing over there, but ask yourself, 'Why would anyone want to hear that we have to say?' We're not doing anything like a campaign. We don't have any secrets. Now, maybe you like doing this at,"—he looked at his watch—"eight fifteen at night, but I've got other things to do that may actually be a benefit to this campaign and to your boss. My advice is to check the kids again." Weinstein got up and left.

Reid Field looked at Mark. "You're being rather quiet."

Mark looked back and forth at the two men and then stopped at Burchmeyer. "I didn't want to interrupt the drama. Sounds like you don't have any idea who did this. First of all, it is not MY war room. It belongs to Mr. Bartow's campaign, where you are the security guy. Second, the reason you found it is that we all requested and agreed to have the room swept frequently and at random. So, kudos to your team. They did their job well. Third, I assume it was not there the last time they did the sweep, so we have a baseline to check for when it was placed and who did it. I assume you are checking the security cameras and interviewing everyone who had access to the room for the time in question. Fourth, I don't know anything about it or how it got there, and you don't need to be so defensive or hostile in the way you are asking questions of me. Fifth, when I had this room set up, I wanted to protect what happened in here from outside interference, and I did not think of putting cameras to cover security inside the room. That was my bad. However, neither did you. We're in this together."

He nodded at the bug. "If you haven't put up hidden cameras in here and other sensitive choke points, do so now. I don't think any of the young people we have working in this space would do this."

Burchmeyer nodded. "Any ideas?"

"Nope. I kind of agree with Benny. Does not make any sense. Yet... here it is."

"We may need to poly everyone with access." Burchmeyer tapped the table.

"I understand, but that's a time-consuming and disruptive thing to do and that lack of trust will hurt the morale and dampen the motivation of everyone who gets strapped into the machine. You need to think if the poly, which may not prove anything, is worth it. Is it worth damaging the campaign or is there another way to catch the person, like cameras, or putting out a trail of false bread crumbs? But that's your job, not mine."

Burchmeyer squinted. "Sounds like you've had to deal with security before."

"You've got my file and know about the military and international stuff. It's not my call, but I'd think twice about frog-walking your consultants to take a polygraph that may not show any results."

"We'll think about it. But it's unsettling to think there is a traitor in our midst."

"John, I agree, but I'm also guessing this is not your first rodeo. You caught that woman the other day. Mr. Bartow must have had to deal with industrial espionage and other security stuff before, or you would not be here."

Mark pointed at the small bug, which Burchmeyer had left on the table. "If we have a mole, let's find the son-of-a-bitch and prosecute. You've got a job to do."

"You also need to re-examine your logic about the secure space. This war room has narrowed down the target area for whoever put it here, or you'd be looking all over this building for bugs. Add cameras or whatever makes sense about increasing the security in the room, but the room stays. If they got a bug in here, you might want to look closer in other places as well. However, don't bother Bartow with this. He needs to concentrate on the campaign and not worry about things he cannot affect. When you solve the mystery, then you can tell him and get the credit."

Burchmeyer picked up the bug again and rolled it in his fingers. "This is the latest in new technology. Some bozo did not just go get this at a Radio Shack. There is some sophisticated stuff going on here. I'm thinking government."

Mark nodded at Burchmeyer. "All the more reason to make your investigation thorough. Maybe it is time to call in the Secret Service. Maybe just to consult on this one thing. They have experience examining this kind of stuff. Whatever you do, this is not the time to go into a shell. You've got a real target here to find. Time to earn your pay."

Burchmeyer leaned back, smiling. "You're liking this, you S.O.B."

Mark walked to the door and then turned back. "John, we've all got jobs to do here. I believe you are very good at what you do. Now is the time to prove it. I'll help in any way I can. Just ask. Find who did this and crush them. Keep it from happening again. Trying to bust my balls is not going to help." He left Burchmeyer spinning the bug on the table.

Rizzo and Manafort

The mechanical accent disguising the voice on the speakerphone growled, "So, what happened with the bug? It went silent."

Rizzo fidgeted in his chair. "Burchmeyer's stormtroopers found it. Now they are snooping around everywhere and interviewing people like the gestapo."

In an icy tone, the voice said, "Did you put it in the place I told you and set it up like I said?"

"Yeah. Right about there. I couldn't get behind all that wiring shit, cause I was afraid I'd electrocute my ass, so I just put it just under some other stuff."

The voice was now more aggressive. "So, you did not put it where I said and how I said. How dumb can you be not to understand that putting it in the middle of the other electronics would mask the bug. When people look for bugs, it is easy to find if you just have the thing sitting there by itself. It was a very sophisticated piece of electronics and it was designed... I said it was DESIGNED, to be hidden inside a mass of other technology, hooked to other wires and electronics. You stupid, incompetent, fucking twit."

Manafort, tanned and groomed, sitting across from Rizzo and wanting to stay in favor with the voice, jumped on the abuse bandwagon. "So, Rizzo, you are telling us that not only did we lose the bug, but now his security guys are running all over the place interviewing everyone, looking for more bugs? We wanted to put them to sleep and now you've got them jazzed up on a fire alarm!"

Rizzo squirmed. There were chills going up and down his back. "Guys, you can't put all this on me. I'm not trained to be some kind of spy. If you wanted that bug surgically placed, you should have gotten someone else to do it or trained me and let me practice it. I've got lots of other things to do there. This spy shit with you guys is a sideline for me."

The voice, now even more serious and calm, asked, "Are they using lie detectors on the staff in the search?"

"Not so far. It's been mostly the young interns and people who staff and run the room. They've just been bringing us in and asking questions." Rizzo twisted his hands.

"You know how to beat the lie detector?"

Rizzo had begun to sweat. "No. Of course not. I'm a political consultant."

Now more nurturing, but still demanding, the voice said, "Well, if they start to use them, delay your session and tell Manafort to contact me immediately."

Manafort frowned now with his nerves more on edge. "We've got to work on spooking Bartow more. He's squirrely and we need to use that. We need to make him come apart in public and embarrass him to his supporters. I can't figure what all these people see in him. He's just a blowhard showman. This guy's polling numbers are bulletproof."

Rizzo thought to himself, *Man, I could use a drink.*

The next evening, Missy called Mark to watch something she'd spotted on the evening news. "There's something in the program you need to see. Here's the clip." She pushed a button and turned up the sound on a videotape machine. There were a few seconds at the end of a commercial and then the story came on the screen. There was a woman reporter who had been standing outside their campaign office building that same afternoon.

"This is Summer Storm in Atlanta outside the Bartow for President National Headquarters Office, where rumor has it the campaign is getting ready to go into high gear. My sources say a big media buy is in the works and with the money Bartow has to spend, he could virtually blanket the airwaves. I asked Campaign Chairman George Lewis about these rumors as he was leaving the building earlier today."

On the screen there was a picture of Lewis coming out of the building and Storm going up to him with microphone in hand as the camera followed close behind her, shooting the pictures over her shoulder. "We're with George Lewis, longtime business associate and confidant of Presidential Candidate William Bartow. Mr. Lewis, anything to the rumors we're hearing that a fairly substantial medial buy is in the works?"

Lewis looked surprised by her question. "No. I don't know anything about that, but when we do complete our plans, we'll be pleased to let you know."

He turned to leave, and Storm touched his arm. The camera zoomed in closer to Lewis' face as she continued to speak off camera. Lewis looked increasingly confused and put off by her insistence. Storm now added a sense of urgency to her voice. "But you did have a big meeting with your media consultants, Frank Press and Chappy Knight, here in the last few days, and they are known as THE hotshot media team in the country. Did you come to any conclusions in those meetings about the timing of the first series of commercials?"

Lewis shook his head no. "Miss, I told you there have been no decisions. Any discussions we have held are preliminary and have not involved Mr. Bartow. Now if you will excuse me, I've got to get home to my family."

Lewis gently pulled his arm away and the camera followed him and stopped when Storm was in the center of the frame. "In Atlanta, where the rumors are flying, the Bartow campaign is not yet ready to admit their plans for a big media buy. This is Summer Storm in Atlanta reporting."

Mark muttered to himself, "God. He just can't let it alone."

Missy leaned forward. "Are you talking about Ralph Collins?"

"Yeah, he's got a media jones. See you later."

Restaurant

Later that same night, after work at Houston's bar and restaurant, the drinks continued to be ordered and dinner turned into some snacks on the side. Mark, Ben Menendez, Missy Winston, and Susan Kaufman were now into their third round. As Missy and Susan were having an intense conversation on one side of the table, Ben and Mark were having a more intimate and quiet talk on the other. Mark took a long sip of his drink and clanked the glass down while looking at Menendez. "Ever ask yourself, why do we still do this?"

Ben thought about it for a minute. "I'm not sure anymore. The first time it was because I believed in the candidate and that he could actually change things. Then I think it was for the rush and the glory and the power of attention. Remember Angus used to say this was as close as you could come today to the Napoleonic Wars? I think now it's because we are a part of a handful of people who can actually do this stuff, maybe make things better, and this here son-of-a-bitch pays well."

Mark laughed. "Tell the truth!"

Ben Menendez leaned forward. "It's like we've learned to do something really big, really well, and now someone's actually giving us the chance. There is no other job in the world where we could have the opportunity to influence everyone's mind, everyone's opinion. We could make a difference in this country, and really the whole world."

Mark looked away across the restaurant in the dim light at the bobbing heads and filtered flashing lights coming from cars passing the curve on Peachtree Street nearby. "Yeah. It's all that, and you've also got the faces of the people you see in the volunteer room each day. They still have that faith, which we got beat out of us a long time ago. But we both want the same thing. We both want the best choice and the best future, without all the bullshit and flag-waving, but with some of the hope left."

Menendez thought for a moment. "Bartow is far from perfect, but at least he's not some manufactured, assembly-line cut-out like some of them."

Mark nodded and let out a sigh. "Well, there are plusses and minuses to all of the choices."

Menendez looked intent as he leaned closer to Mark. "So, you think Collins is trying to sandbag the campaign?"

"I think that's too strong. He just can't stay away from the media. He talks to them all the time and I'll bet that's where Summer Storm got it. Collins and his guys are used to working the press that way, but it could come back on him."

"Then why take that risk?"

"Ben, for Collins, talking to the press is his life. He's got to feed them something all the time to stay viable."

Ben said, "He doesn't really give a shit about the campaign. This is about him."

Mark looked down. "It is in the long run. Collins and his group are conventional campaign managers. They've always had plenty of money to work with. They muscle the opposition. They take all the credit. They go on to the next one."

Missy leaned over to the two men in a huddle. "Okay. Enough of that. I want to hear something fun that happened today. Campaigns are supposed to be places where there are good stories. I want to hear one."

Menendez said, "Yeah. What was that stuff you started to tell me about the vice president search thing?"

Mark leaned back and finished his drink and then signaled the waitress to come over for another round. "Well, our friends from Bartow Industries brought in a search firm to find the VP."

Missy, in mid swallow, spat her drink back in the glass. "No. Are they that CRAZY?!"

Menendez was incredulous. "What? These guys think the Vice President of the United States is like some vice president of sales or production? The press would kill us. What did those people say?"

"They said they plan to ask someone else to run with Bartow instead of Admiral Duncan and surround them with like cheerleaders to ask them to take the job. It's like Senator Nunn going in to pick up his laundry and someone behind the counter saying, 'You know, you should think about being Bill Bartow's running mate.' Or their accountant calls them and says the same thing. It was absolutely crazy. And, they were SERIOUS."

Susan shook her head. "That's so like them to do that. What did you do?"

"We said it was great work and we needed to study it."

Missy interrupted, in an aside to Ben, "That always works."

Mark smiled more broadly as he remembered the conversation. "And they had all these groups of names already made up with half the executives of Atlanta on the list and people like the president of the Birmingham Rotary Club."

"What?!"

"Yes. It was hard to keep a straight face. Anyway, we told them it was a big job and that we needed to narrow it down to a handful of names."

Missy said, "Would the media kill for this, or not!"

"We gave the search firm and the Bartow folks the business list and the civic leaders and all that. Rizzo and I ended up with the elected officials and anyone else that would be realistic. We're a meeting or two away from having them out the door."

Menendez asked, "Did they realize that?"

"I don't think so. I think all they kept seeing was their letterhead with a slogan, 'We Placed the Vice President' across the top."

Menendez held his drink up for a toast. "To the campaign having more distractions."

Mark raised his glass and said, "Right. It's crazy we're spending time on the vice president, and we don't have approval on all the issues or a media budget." He took a sip and then stood. "Sorry, but I've got to get home or Vicki will have my clothes out by the curb."

Meet the Press

Sunday morning on *Meet the Press*, the producers had moved the program from the NBC studios to the top-floor dining area of the exclusive Hay Adams Hotel. In the background through the window, the White House could be seen in the distance across Lafayette Park. The host Werner Sanderhagen finished whispering to an older white man and a young black woman and looked up as the stage manager gave him the countdown.

Sanderhagen began the program. "We're here today on *Meet the Press* with William Bartow, third-party candidate for president, who has taken this election year by storm. In the past three months, he has qualified to be on the ballot in all 50 states and has legions of volunteers on almost every street corner. He has also magically risen to the top of the national polls.

"Right now, however, people are asking, 'What does William Bartow stand for? What are his values? What are his positions on the issues?' We're here to find out today on *Meet the Press*.

"And joining me on our panel is Chess Sturdivant, *Washington Post* senior political correspondent and Leslie Tower, White House reporter for NBC News.

"Mr. Bartow, I'll start by asking, when are you going to release some sort of platform on the issues?"

The camera cut to a closeup of Bill Bartow. "Well, it's always amusing to me that you folks in the media spend more time reading the rule book than watching the game. If you'd just watch what's going on in America, you'd see the people of this great country are ready to take back their government from the professional politicians and career bureaucrats that have got us in the sad state we're in."

Sanderhagen tried again. "But, surely, Mr. Bartow, you realize that the public wants to know where you stand on issues.

What, specifically, for instance, would you do to reduce the deficit? Give me three concrete areas where you would cut the budget."

Bartow smiled and shook his head. "Well, you see, that's my point. You want me to give you ammunition on your program so that you can go to those other fellows and ask them to top it. You want to say, 'Bartow told me he will cut $50 billion, so how much will you cut?' Folks, the government of the United States is not a game show. I'll be specific when and where it will be taken seriously and to an audience of people, not paid media entertainers masquerading as journalists."

Sanderhagen leaned forward slightly. "Forgive me, Mr. Bartow, but you are sounding like every career politician in history who will not give a straight answer. We all thought you were distinct somehow, but it seems like you are just like the rest of them. I'm disappointed. I thought you were different." He turned to hand over the interview to another panelist, when Bartow stopped him.

"Wait just a minute. I was going to tell you all this in a couple of weeks from now, but I can't let you imply that I'm just an empty suit. We're gonna propose to balance the budget and we're gonna propose to bring down the deficit and maybe even take a whack at the national debt. Now, I'm not gonna say more till I'm ready to lay it all out. If all you people on the TV news looked like me, you'd be in the back room typing up wire copy. I'll discuss my plans with real Americans."

The veteran dean of the Washington press corps, Chess Sturdivant, now took a shot. "Well, Mr. Bartow, in 35 years as a journalist, including time as a war correspondent, I've never been accused of being just another pretty face. Although, my wife and children would probably appreciate your remarks and take them as a compliment. We'll all look forward to the specifics of your budget-balancing act. For now, let me now ask you about the rumors that your campaign is run like a military camp. We hear stories of armed guards and strong-arm tactics against your own staff. Is any of that is true, and if it is, is that how you would run the government?"

Bartow stiffened. "I don't know what you are talking about. But, no. My campaign is run by business associates of long standing and some so-called professional political operators to organize things in the office. We do have security there just like the other campaigns. We do not have Secret Service like the other campaigns, but we have a private security service."

"Are you afraid of your opponents or the American people?"

Bartow squared his shoulders. "As you know, from the days of Watergate and even before, there are unscrupulous people in politics who would break in or do dirty tricks or worse for their political party. In fact, the other two parties have departments to train their staffs to conduct such operations. We're trying to change all that, and it makes the other parties nervous. We have taken obvious precautions to prevent these dirty-trick squads and Watergate plumber types from breaking into our headquarters, because we realize campaigns are vulnerable to sneaky ambushes."

Sturdivant, sensing an opening for news, asked, "Are you saying that the Democrats and Republicans have training camps for dirty tricks, and that they are planning to sabotage your campaign?"

Bartow threw up his hands. "Both operations hire expensive consultants to do the training, and all this is well known."

Sturdivant tried again. "I still don't get why you are so afraid. Surely you don't mean that—"

Bartow cut him off. "Listen, this is not that difficult. It's like professional wrestling. You know what you see on TV when the guys pound the canvas or put their foot over the ring, or when the manager with the cane reaches in and bops the guy when the referee is not looking? It's like that with politics. Everyone knows these guys are doing all these things. They call up and cancel the meetings of their opponents. They make up these fake polls where you call up voters and tell them the candidate is pond scum and then ask if they'll vote for him. We've all seen it. Well, where do you think they learn these things? We want to stop all that and it's got the other two parties scared."

Sturdivant jumped in. "What? You think they are scared? Why are they afraid of you?"

Bartow leaned forward. "Let me tell you what has really got them scared. What if we decided to cut all the government by one or two percent across the board? I mean everything. What if we also cut all the tax relief and special government funding or studies and research and all that stuff the government does that keeps our tax dollars from balancing the budget and cutting the debt? What if I sent in a swarm of accountants to look under every rock into every special pocket of money the government has squirreled away to pay for all that stuff we don't really need and they don't tell us about? What if we cut all that out? What if my whole reason to become president was to make the government pay for itself? What would all those lobbyists and fat-cat corporations and Wall Street big shots do if I cleaned all the sand in the sandbox? I'm not gonna say more today, but I'm gonna announce all this in a few weeks in great detail.

"That's why they're are all afraid of me. I've run a business that has to meet the bottom line. I've had to meet a payroll based on how much money was left over after we paid the bills. What if government had to live on what it made? We have got to stop wrecking our future by printing money. We've got to live within our means. We have got to stop all those backdoor side deals by the insiders who cheat the rest of us hard-working Americans who want to see an honest return on their tax dollars.

"We've got to stop all the fancy know-it-alls. We have got to get government back on a paying basis. If you don't think they have a pile of dirty-tricks people out there to trying to stop me from doing that, you're crazy. Yeah. I need protection from all that. Wouldn't you?"

The set got uncharacteristically quiet after Bartow's outburst until Sanderhagen, with an attempt to put the discussion on a more even keel, asked, "Well, Mr. Bartow, we look forward to your announcement on government finances, but what do you have to say about the reports that you conducted unauthorized, private, and illegal surveillance on the Bush family a little over five years ago?"

Bartow rose higher in his chair and leaned forward. "You see, that is what I'm talking about. That is the kind of stuff that a Republican research team has claimed. It's a lie plain and simple. I've got a clean record."

Sanderhagen shook his head, frustrated. "Leslie, you want to give this a shot?"

Leslie Tower calmly and slowly smiled at Bartow before asking her question. "Mr. Bartow, many people in the minority community are wondering about your positions on race, affirmative action, and other issues which concern them. Given your record as a businessman, what can you do to reach out to the minority community and encourage their consideration of your candidacy?"

Bartow nodded at her. "Well, if you look at my record and look at my life, you'd see that I grew up relatively poor. My parents did the best they could and we did not want for the basics. There was plenty of love in our house, but we lived on what you could call the wrong side of the tracks. There were black families in our neighborhood. I played with black kids growing up."

Tower, looking for policy, said, "Yes. But Mr. Bartow, just because you played with black children, that doesn't mean we know your positions on ideas relating to black adults."

Bartow shifted in his seat. "I'm tryin' to get to that. In my business, we consistently have rewarded people for what they could do rather than the color of their skin. I don't care what a person looks like. If they can do the job better than the next person, they get promoted. And any businessman who doesn't think like that is not being competitive."

Tower, homing in on the answer, asked, "So, does that mean that you do not support affirmative action?"

Bartow, now with his finger in the air, exclaimed, "Listen to what I say. I don't believe a person's skin color should affect how they are considered in the workplace. The most affirmative thing a businessman can do is to hire, train, promote, and reward excellence. If you check, you'll find that I had black and

Hispanic foremen before anyone else. I paid better wages than anyone to them before it was popular or required. I promoted and paid everyone equally. No regulations can match action. And, when you look at my record, you'll find I'm very supportive of minorities."

Tower, still trying to get a policy answer, said, "Mr. Bartow, what you have said sounds good. But, do you believe in and promise to support the existing federal regulations relating to affirmative action if you are elected president?"

Bartow, still waving his finger as he answered, said, "Miss Tower, I have said repeatedly that everything is on the table. When you take on a new job, you've got to look at everything about the job, how it was done in the past, look at the good and the bad, and determine how you will do that job. Now, I can't be fair to that promise if I start exempting things, even very worthwhile things, from some sort of review."

Tower, now leaning into the table, asked, "So, you're saying that if you are elected, you will review all the duties of the president, even the legislatively and judicially mandated responsibilities, and then decide which ones you will enforce?"

Bartow leaned back now. "Well, there you see, you're trying to twist and turn anything I say into something that sounds bad. I don't know what's wrong with taking a fresh look at things. If we all didn't do that once in a while, we'd never go forward. We'd always be stuck in the same place. If folks hadn't taken a fresh look at slavery, you might not be here today. What's wrong with seeing where you need to place your emphasis? What's wrong with setting priorities?"

Tower sat up straighter. "There is nothing wrong with all that. However, the founding fathers set up a government with some traditions and laws to govern its operation. Slavery was opposed because it was morally wrong. It was not a business school exercise. I believe it would be useful for the voters to know that you planned to uphold SOME of the laws while you're conducting your own review of all of them. Also, usually in presidential elections, voters have the ability to take a look at the priorities of the candidates BEFORE the election. It's what we call the 'pig in a poke' syndrome."

"Well, that's what's wrong with the way our country is governed now. We know what the other guys will do, and they've been doing it to us for Lord knows how many years. We are ready to take back our government from these professional lawyers and liars and politicians. We believe electing honest people will be GOOD for the country."

Bartow tapped on the desk with his index finger. "So what if we don't have all the answers for running the country neatly laid out? All you get when you ask for that are promises, and those of us that work for a living in the real world know that those promises have not been kept by ANYONE who has ever held that office. The Democrats and Republicans have been making promises all their lives. And they have not kept a one of them. That's what change is about. That's what the volunteers are about, and because you people in the news are so used to listening to the same bull from career politicians, you are not comfortable with hearing anything else. All you can do is ask the same questions and look for the same predictable answers as you always have. Well, we're different. We're here to change things, and if that includes how you folks in the media have to make a living, that's all right with me."

After *Meet the Press*, William Bartow's limo pulled up to the curb outside the hotel on 16th street. A group of gawkers flanked both sides of the exit, hoping for a glimpse of him. As they watched, a gaggle of bodies approached the door, and one of Burchmeyer's security men emerged first to lead the way and open the car door.

This motion alerted the photographers looking to document the visit, as well as hoping for an awkward photo of Bartow making a strange face they could sell to various newspapers. There were also two television cameras perched there and waiting.

Another security man passed, followed a few seconds later by several bodies in a group with Bartow in the center. They cleared the building and were moving purposefully toward the limo when a middle-aged man with hair askew in a worn trench coat pushed past the rest of the gawkers and shouted at Bartow, "War-mongering baby killer." He produced a pint-sized container of red paint from inside his overcoat and threw it. The paint fanned over a wide area and splattered on some of the other onlookers and Bartow's security detail, but most of it fell on him.

Quickly the well-trained detail moved Bartow to the car while one of the men grabbed the wild-eyed man in the trench coat and pushed him to the ground. He continued to shout as the car sped off. NBC security and a local policeman rushed in to help, and soon the paint thrower was in cuffs and on the way to the police station for questioning.

Fifty yards away across "H" street and near the entrance to Lafayette Park, Roger Stone, wearing a muted suit, dark hat, and sunglasses, patted the man on the back he had hired to engineer the paint incident. A man with mental health problems had been located, encouraged, paid, and primed to be outside the NBC building. He had a history of supporting radical liberal causes and had been arrested several times for protesting and demonstrating in the never-ending circus of Washington politics. There were no fingerprints on this for Stone. He felt the incident would feed into Bartow's penchant for paranoia and bolster his growing image as being a little kooky. He would check later with their friends in the Bartow campaign about how effective this bit of theater had been. Stone felt certain the video of the paint all over Bartow would dominate the news for the evening and the next day. He patted the man again on the back and walked north on 17th street to find some brunch.

Later the same day in Atlanta, Rizzo left the consulting office and walked a few blocks from the low-rent warehouse he and Weinstein leased to process orders for the TV commercials. He headed to meet Paul Manafort at a small bar nearby.

Manafort wiped down the bench seat with two napkins from the bar before he sat at the table. He disliked seedy environments and had done his best to avoid places like this as his career and income had moved up the scale in the past few years.

He was confident, however, that none of the blue-blood Bush family entourage or his corporate clients would spot him in this rundown pile of bricks talking to someone as sleazy as Don Rizzo. Manafort wanted to get the meeting over as soon as he could and get back to the Ritz Carlton Hotel for a shower. Rizzo joined him, sliding smoothly into the seat across the table like there was grease on his butt.

With a half frown, he nodded at Rizzo and began to bring him up to date. "The NBC thing went well up in Washington. Makes Bartow look foolish and like he was a target of the crazies on the left. How are things going here in Atlanta?"

Rizzo smiled. "We've got some more guys to ride around his estate late at night and make noise. Different times. Different cars and trucks. Just enough to spook the security guys. They've put more lights on the edges of the property. Bartow has to notice that even if they're not telling him." Rizzo hunched his shoulders. "One of his daughters has a wedding coming up, and we had someone call from out of state with a kinda threat to disrupt it. Made it sound like an obsessed former boyfriend."

"Good. Hit that again to keep them off balance. Maybe get the guy to say he has naked pictures or something so it will get everyone's attention." Manafort then leaned forward towards Rizzo. "There is no way the guy making the calls can be tracked back to us, is there?"

"No. I ran it through two filters of people I trust who don't know each other. The caller is some S.O.B. who just got outta prison and needs the money. He'll keep his mouth shut on the promise of a job if he does what he's asked. If they catch him, he doesn't know enough to get back to us."

"Okay. Just keep everything at arm's length."

Rizzo looked over his shoulder at the mostly empty bar and back at Manafort with a gleam in his eye. "I got another idea to screw with them, but you gotta promise me a cut of the money."

"What the hell are you talking about?"

"Well… all of us on Collins' staff have spread out the potential to make a little on the side from the campaign. Weinstein and me are gonna take a cut to place the TV ads and the print stuff. Now the big percentage money from the placement will go to Press and Knight, and I'm guessing Collins will get a taste of that. We'll only get a little to do the mechanics of the buy."

"So what?"

"Well, as you know, the TV people want their money up front. So, when we make a buy for the final push just before the election, we'll have $15-20 million in an escrow account pledged to the buy. Maybe more."

"So?"

Rizzo smiled. "What if we don't make the buy? You know how hectic the last week is before the vote. What if we switch that money to some offshore account and then turn in the bogus paperwork to the campaign showing that it was spent on the ad buy?"

Manafort leaned back and looked at Rizzo with new appreciation. "I like it. Spread the ad buys through third-party shell firms. I can set some up myself so we both can get sweet on this. These campaigns never look closely at spending after the campaign is over and they have lost. They are too broken up to have good due diligence. They just want to get drunk and sit on a beach somewhere.

"We can set it up so there are lots of management fees and carrying charges in addition to the fake media buy. We can do all right on this. I know where to send the money, wash it through a couple of banks offshore, and then get it back through consulting contracts. They'll take a small haircut, but it will be clean and untraceable. No questions. Good stuff."

Admiral Duncan

The next day, George Lewis grabbed Mark. "Come with me; we're going on a short trip."

"Where?"

"Admiral Duncan's wife called and said we need to come there today. She sounded very insistent. We've got the old man's plane." A car took them to DeKalb-Peachtree airport, where the Bartow Industries private jet waited. Lewis looked troubled and spoke little during the flight.

Mrs. Duncan let them into the modest living room where they had met with Admiral Duncan before. He did not rise to greet them but sat stiffly in a chair and waved one hand, motioning to chairs opposite his. As Lewis and Mark offered greetings, he nodded and looked over at his wife.

She folded her hands in her lap and looked at them. "Only a handful of people outside the doctors know this, but Jeff's had a mild stroke."

They both turned to look at Duncan, who averted his eyes and directed his attention to his wife.

She continued, "As I say, it was a mild... ah... event and we have begun therapy. We expect an almost complete recovery over time, but obviously you... you need to move on with naming someone else to work with Mr. Bartow."

Lewis turned to Duncan. "Admiral, we are so sorry this has happened. Is there anything we can do... to help... any medical—"

Mrs. Duncan interrupted, "If you name someone soon, the media will stop calling here and won't find out about our... situation."

Lewis stammered, "Of course... it's just that... is there any chance... is there any way..."

Duncan now shook one hand slowly side to side. "Gggg.

Naaa."

Lewis blanched at hearing the admiral. He turned to Mrs. Duncan. "Of course. Just anything we can do? Any treatment or medical needs you may have?"

She looked at her husband and back to Lewis. "Get the press away. Let us have our privacy."

Back on the jet, Lewis moved into damage-control mode. "Say nothing to anyone, not even your wife." He leaned back and breathed deeply. "Oh God! The press would kill us. I'll set up a meeting with Bartow to go ahead and pick someone else. Damn."

Mark, looking out the small window of the jet at the clouds zipping past, remembered the image of the war veteran trying to regain his life after being abused for so many years now slumped in his chair looking away from them.

Livy and the Bad Man

That afternoon, not long after he had returned to Atlanta, Mark got a call from Vicki. "Something's happened. Drop whatever you are doing and get home."

When he rushed through the door, Vicki was in the living room with Livy and Letty. Livy's eyes were red and swollen from crying and Letty was flushed. Vicki was hugging Livy and rocking her back and forth while crooning, "It's all gonna be all right. Mommy's here. You're going to be all right. I'm here." While Vicki continued to console Livy, Mark motioned for Letty to join him in the kitchen.

Mark did his best to remain calm and not frighten Letty more than she already appeared to be as he led her away from them. "Letty, what happened? Why are you and Livy so upset?"

When they entered the kitchen, she could not meet Mark's eyes. Instead, she walked directly to the sink to get some water. She moved with the glass shaking in her hand and collapsed onto a chair. Mark sat to join her. She began to speak while looking down at the table. Her hands were still shaking, and Mark touched one and held it. "We were having a good day. We'd been to a puppet show and then went to Piedmont Park to walk around. We were on the back side past the lakes and a man came up holding a little puppy. It all happened so fast. The man squatted down with the dog, holding it out by one hand wrapped around the middle under its tummy, and Livy ran from me over to pet it. I followed to where I was just behind Livy.

"He was about eye level with Livy and looked at her and then up to me, smiling. By this time, Livy was on her knees and rubbing the head of the little dog, who was licking her hand. Then the man started talking about the campaign and Mr. Bartow in a regular voice. Not loud. I didn't get all of it, but he was saying how he didn't like Mr. Bartow and how bad it was that he was in the race, something like that."

Letty started to breathe faster and rubbed her hands together as she continued. Her face flushed again as she talked. "While he talked, he started to squeeze the little dog. It all happened so fast. The dog began to make crying sounds and wiggle at the same time Livy was petting him. Livy did not understand and thought maybe it was whining because of something she had done, and she continued to try to pet the dog even more. The man's hands were strong, and I watched in horror as the muscles tightened. I could tell he could crush the animal at any moment. I reached for her and the man looked at me with this menacing face and said in a loud voice, 'Don't.'

"That shocked me, and I froze for a few seconds. I was scared. I could see over Livy's shoulder the panic in the eyes of the puppy. Livy must have seen it too because her shoulders and back tensed. She started to cry.

"The man laughed and squeezed harder. The dog was really struggling now, and making little high-pitched whining sounds, but he held it firm in both hands, which were as big as the dog. The man looked directly into her face that was not more than a foot away and said..." Letty was crying and fighting for breath to speak as she remembered. "He said, 'What I'm doing to this dog we're gonna do to your mommy and daddy.' I grabbed Livy back toward me and he stood up and jerked the puppy from Livy's hand.

"I came to my senses and pulled her to me and hugged her. I backed away from him. He was so scary. She was so scared too. Livy seemed like she was in a trance, still looking at the little dog. She did not fully understand his words, but she definitely caught the menace in his voice about you and Vicki."

Letty wiped the tears from her face, then shook her head and started to cry all over again. "As I pulled her back, he said to Livy, 'You'll never see this mutt again." He left, holding the dog under its stomach like a loaf of bread. I was still behind Livy, pulling her backwards away from him and then I lost my balance and fell down. That's when I heard the first sound coming from Livy. Small crying at first, then full-throated screams.

Really loud screams.

"Oh my God, Mark, I've never seen anything so hateful in my life. There was nothing I could have done. The whole thing was over in a few seconds. He just walked off, leaving us there. Livy just kept crying. We came home as fast as we could and called Vicki.

"That man must have known we were going to be there and was waiting with the puppy. What kind of people would do such a thing? If he would do that in the park in broad daylight, he could come back here and hurt us when you're at work. I'm afraid, Mark."

Mark was boiling with anger and fear. He felt helpless but also that if he could get his hands on the man, who had destroyed the innocence of his little daughter, he would kill him right then. He realized there was nothing he could say to his daughter so she could get over that experience and not remember it for the rest of her life. Then he thought how vulnerable they all were in a strange city with him and Vicki at work almost all the time.

He gave Letty a long, deep hug and smelled the stale sweat of fear. "I'm so sorry that happened to you and Livy. It was to scare me and Vicki, but they went through you two to do it. Let's try to be as calm as we can tonight for Livy. I'll make some arrangements for us and then we all need to think this through going forward. You should go and lie down for a while, and I'll take care of making supper."

Mark immediately called John Burchmeyer and told him what had happened and demanded personal security around the clock for his family and the house. Thirty minutes later, there were men outside.

That night, Livy stayed in the bed with Mark and Vicki. The next morning, Livy was somewhat better, and they worked to take her mind off the incident. Vicki was taking the day off from work to be with their daughter, and Mark left their house as soon as he could.

He had called John Burchmeyer again earlier that morning and went directly to see him. He had also called George Lewis to make sure he had his support. As he sat in Burchmeyer's office, he gave him a serious stare. "John, I know you have no way to fix what happened to my daughter yesterday. I'm here about what happens next. Thanks for sending the guys last night, and someone else was still there this morning. I'm making a formal request for 24-hour security for my family. I've already cleared it with George Lewis, and for me this is a non-negotiable requirement for me to continue to be here. That was a very crude effort to scare me and Vicki off the campaign and it is in danger of being successful. My daughter is six and I'll not have anything like this happen to her again."

Burchmeyer nodded. "George called me earlier. I've got kids and understand. I'll have someone on your daughter as a driver and bodyguard and can arrange for security and drivers for you and Vicki and to escort you to meetings outside this building. We'll have a car outside your house at night. We can put more electronic surveillance in and around the house if you wish. Any idea who did it?"

Mark was listening and nodding at what Burchmeyer was saying about the security. "That sounds good, but I also want some kind of alarm button, or pager thing… like a panic button that calls your guys and the local police and makes noise. We will need three of them."

"Done. Now do you have any idea—"

"Got to be someone organized… like one of the other campaigns, or maybe someone who has a personal grudge against Bartow and wants to hurt the campaign. The Piedmont Park action was, however… extreme. To go after and frighten my daughter says they know who we are. This was not just some crazy guy who showed up. This was professional. We are leading in the polls and likely are becoming a big worry to the Bush and Clinton folks. I just don't see them doing something like this thing in the park. It was so violent and uncivilized."

"Me neither. No one saw anything. I've talked to the local cops. They will be in the loop about our protective detail of your family and know to look out for your safety, but I don't have much faith in them. My bet is that it is the Clinton people. I can't believe my fellow Republicans would do something like that. Sounds more like Democrats. You think they may try something else?"

"John, I just don't know who was behind it, but it was designed to rattle me and the campaign and in that it was successful. Actually, doing harm to me or my family does not make much sense, but scaring us again does."

Burchmeyer nodded. "I know about your military experience. You want a piece?"

Mark thought. "No. I think that me carrying a gun might just complicate things. Let's just stay on top of this. I'm trusting you with the safety of my family." Mark did not tell Burchmeyer that he had his own weapon in the house that he had brought with him from D.C.

Burchmeyer nodded. "I understand. We'll do all we can to honor that and keep them safe."

"Thanks. Also, let's not make a big deal about it here. We don't need the distraction."

By that night, at least on the surface, the incident had passed. When he got home, Livy was excited to tell him what they had done that day at the Atlanta Zoo and about the nice man who had driven them around and walked with them everywhere they went. She was helping Letty prepare dinner while sitting on a small step stool by the sink, washing the vegetables and looking serious about her work. Afterwards, she returned to a large puzzle she was working on at the far end of the long dining table, head down, quiet and with a determined look on her face.

Mark could tell, however, that there was a sadness in his daughter that had not been there two days before. What had happened was the first wound to her young heart, and it had happened because of his job. He made a promise to himself that after this one ended, he would never be involved in campaigns again.

Ben and Missy

As Mark sat with Ben Menendez and Missy Winston at a nearby restaurant, Ben posed, "Who would have the most to gain by Mark's dropping out?"

Missy quickly responded, "Ben, with Bartow frozen in making any decisions, Mark's ideas are the campaign. You've put together the field organization to carry out whatever we do, but there is no move to run any television. Nothing's happening. All we've got are Mark's ideas about the convention and picking an issue of the week and dominating the media. That's it!"

Ben mused, "Even though we are a little bit ahead in the polls, why go to all that trouble for a candidate that is moribund? The Bush and Clinton people should be worried that Bartow will write a big check. This thing creates a risk that Bartow might get pissed and retaliate by getting off his ass and behaving more like a candidate. Don't they understand that?" Ben then tapped the table a few times, shaking the glasses of beer. "Maybe, however, Missy has finally said something that makes sense."

Both Mark and Missy looked at him, puzzled.

He continued, "Mark has been coming up with the ideas. All the Collins people have done is to hire some expensive media guys and keep on harping about spending tons of money running TV spots. If the three of us were gone, our Republican friends would be the only game in play for Bartow."

Mark shook his head in the negative. "But the Collins guys are right about our need to make and run the ads. What we've been doing are stopgap measures. I'm with Collins and his guys on what they want to do."

Ben nodded back. "You may be making Missy's point. I repeat, who would have the most to gain by your leaving? I think it's the TV guys, our TV guys. Bartow would have to give in to their demands to get on TV or withdraw."

Missy screwed up her face. "Did I say that?"

Ben laughed at her. "No, but we all know you talk around in circles and on every loop, you may hit on some truth in passing. Even a broken clock is right twice a day."

Missy frowned and poked him on the arm. "That's about the worst compliment I've ever gotten."

Mark looked at one and then the other. "Although crazy, what you both said needs to be considered. Collins' guys are not the friendliest people in the world, but they signed on to do a job here and we should consider them our colleagues until we find out otherwise. Even though Bartow is stuck in neutral, they do have something to gain if they were the only consultants in this campaign. I had not looked at it that way."

Missy nodded. "You're welcome."

It was getting late, and Mark wadded up his napkin and put it on the table. "Well, in addition to all the other things we have to do, let's watch the other consultants in case anything pops up that shows them to be disloyal. In the meantime, we are here to try to help Bartow the best we can. Harmony among the staff should be a top priority."

Ben whispered, "Sorry about what happened to Livy. That's off the charts shitty."

Missy stood. "Yeah. Me too. Let me know if I can help in any way."

As Mark walked to his car, a strange feeling occurred to him that this was a kind of a dirty trick that Bruce and his friends in the spy business might pull.

Green Light

George Lewis called Mark and Vicki into his office. "First, let me say how terribly sorry I was to learn of what happened to your daughter. I want both of you to know Bartow said you can have any resources you need to protect her and yourselves from whatever is going on.

"Second, I wanted to tell you both together at the same time, because you two are the most responsible, and well, Mr. Bartow has agreed to everything. The issues, the ghost-written book, the TV commercials, the convention with all the states training, and being on television. All of it. He may still have some hesitations, but he's in it all the way. We'll have the money to blast the other two out of the water. He'll get whatever advisors on board we need. I realize it is late in the game, but we're here because you two kept pressing on and coming up with good ideas. We're gonna win this thing."

As Mark and Vicki left Lewis' office, he wondered if it had been swept for bugs by Burchmeyer.

Part 4 – Told ya So

Mark and Carville

Mark entered one of the most prestigious Democratic law offices in Atlanta and was quickly shown to an office normally used for visiting attorneys. In the spare office sat James Carville, Bill Clinton's chief advisor.

"Hello, James."

"Oh hi, Mark, isn't it?"

"Yes, we met a few years ago pitching that governor's race in Florida. As I remember, neither of us got the business."

Carville leaned back. "Yeah. Probably just as well. That guy blew up and went down in flames. I heard he never paid everybody off."

"So?"

Carville now leaned forward. His bald head and angular, aggressive face always made him seem angry. "So, you're with a guy now who won't have any problems paying the bills. I thought we might have an off-the-record little chitchat. Tell me,"—he rapped on the desk twice with his ink pen—"you think you've got a shot?"

"Good. Right to the point. You know anything can happen in politics, and I'm sure you guys are polling every five minutes. So, you know for certain we've got a shot, particularly because Bush is weak and your guy seems to have some baggage."

Carville leaned back and tossed the pen he was holding on

the desk. Mark could almost see the switch thrown as Carville moved into his marketing mode. "Not really. Well, nothing serious. Bill Clinton's really good on the stump and on TV. He has more natural political gifts than anyone I've ever met."

"So, James, why are we here?"

"I thought we might meet in this out-of-the-way place and consider, just supposin', what might happen if for some reason your guy falters. I know you won't admit that's possible, but we both know it is.

"You've got all these people on the street who would be crushed if Bartow falls. I see that energy as a political asset that should not be wasted. I think my guy could pick up that banner and re-energize those folks to stay involved in politics, to keep up their dreams. I don't think we are that far apart on the substance. I was just wondering if you felt some obligation to those two or three million people who are charged up now and should stay involved to use that energy to help our country."

Mark smiled. "Well, that was smooth. Duty, honor, country. Also, it shows a little panic on the edges, you know, between the words. You want us as a backstop for your guy's problems."

Carville started to talk. "I—"

Mark raised his hand. "Hold on and let me finish. You know you can't transfer loyalty like that, and you know after a loss there is a period of mourning and reconsideration. Perhaps we should be discussing your supporters who could vote for an independent instead of a Democrat."

"Perhaps, my skinny ass. What happened to your loyalty to the party… to your beliefs in what we stand for?"

"James, please. You don't have to put on a show like that for me. Despite the campaign rhetoric, there aren't many differences in the issue positions between any of the candidates in this race. This is about winning. We've both been hired to help our candidate do that."

"Yeah, but you've got all those Republicans helping you. All those Reagan guys who supported Iran-Contra and fucked up the environment and the economy. No. We are not the same. You strut around like you are too much of a Boy Scout for this business. I think it it's an act."

Mark smiled. "Running a presidential campaign has always been the gold standard, the brass ring of political consulting. Why don't YOU stop acting? You're not in this for purely altruistic reasons. You're a very competent consultant, but you're not noble. I don't think that Bush has been a bad president. He's got good people around him and hasn't done a bad job. That being said… after my guy, Clinton is my second choice. However, I've still got a job that involves doing my best to kick your ass. The volunteers our campaign represents are for real and are a huge mass of pissed-off voters who don't like the way standard politics has been going. If we don't make it, I'm not sure they will be easy to pull into supporting you with some standard Democratic Party rhetoric.

"Most of our supporters are moderate and practical and are looking for something that is genuine and not some predictable, focus-group-tested bullshit. If we lose and they are trying to decide what to do with their votes, I doubt they would care or listen to what I or Bartow has to say any more than listening to you. Just looking at all this from the outside, your wife having a key role in the Bush campaigns is so bizarre, it makes us average people out there wonder how either of you can be genuine. I'm not being critical of your beliefs, just saying how it looks. Can't you see how it would be hard for you or your wife to convince our volunteers, who are suspicious of all government motives, that you are true believers and agents of change?

"My guess is these people on the streets will stay angry and look for the next messenger who does not represent the status quo. I don't think they will transfer to your guy or Bush. You both are too predictable and cookie-cutter for them."

Carville smiled. "Whatever. You need to remember that this third-party bullshit is a one-time thing. After this is over and you cash your check, you may need help to get back as a consultant with Democrats, which is where you live. The governor and I can help with that. If you work with us now, we can be your lifeline."

"I suspect that is true. It's also why I got involved in a third-party movement. I am so tired of the backroom deals. I wanted to believe in something real and that felt true. That is what those volunteers on the street corners selling T-shirts represent. That idealism, even if it is misplaced, is what attracted me to politics in the first place. To do a deal that would violate that trust would feel corrupt and would make any lifeline you could throw at me not worth catching. If we don't win, I hope you do, but I'm not able to bring anyone else along."

Carville forced a smile. "Clinton is brilliant. He's studied this thing and has the best ideas for governing of any candidate in decades."

"Yeah. He reminds me of the kid in class who always had his hand up."

"Fuck you. We're still gonna win."

"That may be, but just so you know, Bartow has decided to open his checkbook. We're getting ready to rock and roll."

Peter Newman

Peter Newman, the campaign comptroller and Bartow's son-in-law, entered the office of Reid Field, the campaign administrative director, carrying a stack of documents. "Excuse me, Reid, but a couple of days ago I got an anonymous phone call with a weird, altered voice that sounded metallic. It encouraged me to review some of our contracts, and in my research, I've come across something which puzzles me. Since I got the word we're going to start to spend a lot of money on television and other things, I thought you could help."

"Sure thing. What do you have?"

"Well, it's these bills for some video production and the setting up of the campaign printing and mailing systems." He put the ledger books with spreadsheets down in front of Reid.

"Err, I don't know much about that sort of thing, but if I can help... Looks okay to me." He continued to glace over the expenses.

Newman pointed. "Well, you see there is the TV production billing address."

"Yes."

Newman continued, "And, here is the address of a business where Mr. Rizzo and Mr. Weinstein listed as their permanent office address."

"Mmmm. They are the same. But I thought we were contracting with those other two to produce our commercials... Press and Knight."

"Yes. And here is their business address. I looked it up and you can see it's different."

"Well, there must have been some kind of mix-up when the papers were filled out or the accounts were set up."

Newman laid out some more pages. "That's what I thought, but here." He pointed to a list of charges.

"What's this?"

"This is the information we were processing to establish credit with the direct mail firm... same with the firm to print materials. And you see..."

Reid Field's head turned from one document to the other. "Although it's made out to the direct mail firm, it's the same address as Mr. Weinstein's business. Their contracts stipulate that all these things were to be put out for bid and contracted out. They are supposed to get us the best price, or they would give us a reason why we should choose the more expensive firm. It would be a gross conflict of interest for them also to be making money from the vendors they recommend we hire." He looked up.

Newman nodded. "That's what I thought. Here's the real address of the mail firm. It could be some coincidence or mix-up." Newman took a deep breath. "Because he has so much experience in these things, I asked Ben Menendez what he thought... and he wondered if all the vendor contracts were similar."

Reid was now looking concerned. "Mmmm, I'll call Burchmeyer and have him send over a couple of his people to research this for you. Good work. This mistake, if that's what it is, might have gotten past us if you hadn't been so thorough. I'll call John. For the time being, let's keep this between us."

Reid Field picked up his phone and dialed security. "Hello, is John in, please? Tell him it's Reid Field calling from Admin." Slowly, a look of anger began to form around his lips.

Bartow's Daughter's Wedding

Bill Bartow and his wife were getting ready for his daughter's rehearsal dinner in their expansive bedroom's dressing area. Bernice was sitting at her dressing table as Bill came in, sat on the couch near her, and said, "I hope no one does anything to mess with the dinner or the wedding."

Bernice looked at him through the mirror. "Well, I don't know why they should. This is our private function and it's about your daughter, not you."

"Hope so. It's just… it's been hard these past few months with the election. I've been thinking I should never have gotten into it. They are all saying such bad things about me all the time. It's like no one in the press will just accept what I say as the truth. They're trying to make me into some kind of a nut. That, and these nasty things someone has been saying about our daughter. Whatever happens, this campaign thing is likely to damage all of our reputations."

She put down the lipstick she was holding for a final touchup. "Well, we started with nothing and we've done all right. We've got good kids and we have had a good life. So, if this president thing doesn't work out, I don't care and I don't think the kids will either."

"I just hate to get beat at something I start out to do. I've had to work so hard all my life. You don't know how hard it is. You've never had to run a business or make the kinds of decisions I've had to."

Bernice turned around now to look at him directly. "Like teaching our children what is right and what is wrong? Like telling them why they have to be extra careful when other kids tease them about their father being a rich big shot? Like why dating a certain child would be bad for your image? No. My decisions don't have to do with BUSINESS. My decisions have to do with life. Our lives. Our children's lives.

"And Bill, it's not that I mind. We all want what is best for you. We all see you as the light we follow, but don't think it hasn't come without sacrifice, or strain, or consequences. We know it's not all about propriety and publicity for you. We know when you come through that door at night, there is a part of you, maybe not all of you, but a part, I think the best part, that loves us just as much in return and sees us as something you live for too.

"Sometimes when you're talking on television, I can see that young man I married who did everything for his wife and kids and who had to develop the hard shell to cover the fear that someone would look inside and see that he was just like everyone else. I remember when we had nothing, and I sewed the curtains out of cast-off netting so we would have window coverings and be respectable in case your boss came over to visit.

"So you are right, I've never had to make those decisions you say are so hard to make and have caused you such stress and discomfort. Remember, we've all been at home waiting for you. We've all played our parts, and for us as well as you there have been consequences. I will ask you one thing... at the end of the day if all the stuff goes away, and it's just us left... your family... try not to let this thing embarrass us." She nodded at him and stood. "Finish zipping me up." She stepped back then reached up to him. "Here, your tie is crooked. Now give me a hug. We can't be late. We've got a daughter to get married."

He looked at her. "I don't deserve you. You make me feel I've done the right thing to tell George to go full force with the campaign. I've had reservations about that, but never about you."

"I'll ask you one question."

"Yes?"

"Do you think after we get our daughter married, these bad things will stop?"

Minority Address

Two days later, Safta Kleg, Bartow's press secretary, rushed down the hall to meet Missy Winston and Benny Weinstein. The three entered a boardroom, where a large television was showing a convention podium with signage for the National Coalition of African American Leaders in the background. Bartow was seated on a stage filled with several black middle-aged men and women. Bartow sat with his arms crossed and was not talking to the others on the podium, and only responding politely when spoken to. Then a distinguished man at the podium stood to introduce him.

The tall man, Coleman Stone, with grey hair brushed back on the sides, spoke in a slow preacher cadence with inflections sprinkled between almost in every other word. "Today, we are privileged to have with us a self-made man, a man who has brought himself up by the bootstraps, a man whose character was defined by his modest background, but a man who has defied the odds, a man who by any stretch of the imagination has made it, and made it big. This is a man who has been generous to others, a man who refused to be kept down, a man who has recently begun to look for higher pastures, a man who is standing up and saying to the establishment of this great nation, there is a place at this table for all our children, a man who even today is now slightly ahead of the leaders of the two traditional political parties in the race for president of these United States. Ladies and gentleman, it gives me great pleasure to welcome today, Mr. William Bartow, chairman of Bartow Industries and an independent candidate for President of the United States of America."

There was significant, if polite, applause. Bartow got up and shook hands with Stone, then went to the podium and waved at the crowd.

Safta Kleg, Missy Winston, and Benny Weinstein found chairs in the boardroom to join Mark and Vicki Young, Ben Menendez, George Lewis, and Ralph Collins. Approved budget plans and television placement schedules for the media campaign and other papers were spread around the table and the large-screen TV was following the speech on CNN.

Lewis beamed. "Vicki wrote a great speech for him."

Vicki bit her lip. "We'll see. If he only gives the main points even in his own words, I think it'll help."

Bartow squared his shoulders in front of the television screen. "I thank you very much for those kind words of introduction. I appreciate you having me here today. As I look around this room and see all of you here, it reminds me of my own childhood and how far we've all come in the past few decades."

Vicki was softly coaching him in a whisper, "Stay on the speech. Don't wander off."

On the screen, Bartow paused, slowly looking around the room, and was not looking down at his speech on the podium or the teleprompter when he continued, "All the campaign stuff has made me remember growing up in a rural part of the South. I have always been around you colored people. My mama used to take care of I don't know how many families that lived near us and even though we didn't have much, they had even less."

Lewis leaned forward. "Oh, shit, where's he going with this?"

Bartow continued in his squeaky voice, "The point is, growing up, I was around both blacks and whites. I've known people like you since I was a kid and I've always treated you with respect and kindness and just like anybody would want to be treated… decently, just like we'd treat anybody else."

Everyone in the boardroom was now staring quietly and grimly at the screen.

Bartow smiled confidently and continued, "And I've run my businesses just like that. I don't care what color a fella's skin is as long as he can do the job. I've always been fair and honest with you people, and I believe that's the way you would want to be treated. I know the hard times you have gone through, 'cause I had to go through my share of hard times to build a successful business."

Vicki now whispered louder, "I wonder if he ever even looked at the speech."

Bartow was warming up now. "I know you are tired of being pandered to by the U.S. government and the two main political parties. They've told you just about anything they could to get your vote and then not been there when you needed them. Well, I won't be like that, because I've always looked after you folks. We've come too far together for me to make up promises and not keep them. I don't want to see you and your families locked into endless cycles of poverty, drugs, prostitution, jail, failure, and illegitimacy."

Now the hand-held, secondary television cameras were roaming the crowd looking for reactions. They showed a group of people in the audience looking confused and angry. Some began whispering to each other and shaking their heads from side to side.

The screen cut back to Bartow. "So I'll always tell it like it is, not like it ought to be. You don't have to worry that I'll not be straight with you. We came up together. We've both seen how two-faced Democrats and Republicans can be when they want something. I will give you this one promise. If I'm elected president, when you come knocking on my door, it'll be as open to you as any fat cat on Wall Street. I'm the least racist man you'll ever meet."

In the meeting room, it was quiet. Finally, Collins stood slowly and moved to the door. "Even though some of what he is saying is the truth, people are not used to hearing it. He's so raw, it sounds racist to come out of his mouth. I think I've got some other things to attend to."

Vicki looked over at Mark and said quietly, "Can we climb out of this?"

"Gotta try, but I doubt it. All the promise, the people, the timing, the money, everything, and we've got a guy who won't listen to any advice."

"At least we have each other. Love you."

"That's what keeps me going. That and the knowledge that this will end someday, and when it does, we'll be together in some saner place."

Vicki leaned toward Mark and whispered, "Sooner than later, perhaps?"

"Perhaps."

Bartow rambled on and the audience sat listening, uncomfortably but politely.

The next morning on CNN, the host, Tosty Green, was talking to two of the black leaders who had been on the podium with Bartow. Green bubbled with enthusiasm and shrugged her shoulders up and down as she asked her first question. "Sooo, gee whiz. You had quite a conference yesterday. Everyone's talking about the speech by presidential candidate William Bartow. We've just seen a brief excerpt, but tell me, what did you think? I mean, what was the mood in the room?"

Coleman Stone, the moderator, said in a deep voice, "The conference was very polite to Mr. Bartow, as we are to all our guests. He had some things to say which were true, but some of our members took exception to the way he expressed himself."

The heavyset woman next to him in a colorful dress wearing a multicolored headband jumped into the conversation. "I believe my colleague here is being a bit too kind to Mr. Bartow. What we heard in that room was the voice of someone from the 1930s. That was a man who has no idea what has been going on in the world. He talked to the conference as if we were a bunch of his plantation workers in a cotton field and he was the massa passing by for a Sunday outing."

Green, now sensing this interview would make news, leaned in to the conversation. "Golly. That's certainly two different views of the speech. How have others around the country reacted?"

The man pursed his lips. "You mean other black people?"

Green, not wanting to appear insensitive, was careful. "Well, ah, not necessarily. Just what do you think the public mood is concerning what Mr. Bartow had to say?"

The woman was anxious to reply. "I don know about no other people, but let me tell you, black people are hot. I ain't heard anybody talk like that since… well, not even back in the days of George Wallace."

Green, loving this, cut to the chase of the discussion. "What do you think this does to his presidential chances?"

The black woman snooted, "Some of them rednecks may like that kind of talk. Maybe that's who his friends are. Me, I'm done with him."

George Lewis' Office

In George Lewis' office, Lewis, Collins, Mark and Vicki Young, and Safta Kleg watched with stone faces as the tape replayed earlier reviews following the conference speech.

The distinguished black leader, Coleman Stone, said, "I think this was a missed opportunity for Mr. Bartow. He did not help himself on Saturday."

Lewis burst out, "Turn that fucking thing off. God!"

Safta Kleg spoke reservedly, "Needless to say, we're getting swamped with calls."

Collins frowned. "He can't run away from this."

Mark Young nodded at Collins. "Ralph's right. We can't let this sit and we can't run away. Bartow's going to have to explain himself."

Safta Kleg, with many years of experience at seeing Bartow shirk from things he did not like to do, grimaced. "But couldn't someone else..."

Collins blew out a sigh. "Christ, Safta, for months now, he's done nothing but attack the media. I've been trying to explain that a time would come when we would need some credit with them. Now it's too late. They have been waiting for something like this. It's obvious our guy missed the vetting process in being a candidate. We're in the shit."

Lewis asked, "What do the overnight polls say?"

Vicki looked down at her notes. "We're holding our core, which was about 15% of the national polls. We've lost about half of our support from those people who were with us because they didn't like the other options. It's too early to tell if they are gone for good."

Lewis asked, "How do we get them back?"

Mark Young looked down with a sick expression on his face.

Collins said, "Mea culpa. Bartow's gotta say, 'I was wrong.

You misunderstood me. I'm not that way. Forgive me'."

Mark Young, listening to this, rubbed his face and nodded.

Safta looked over at her longtime friend George Lewis. "George, you know that's..." she said and dropped her head.

Lewis nodded at Safta and finished her sentence. "... not his style. He called me this morning early. He does not want to meet with any more groups or be in any situation like a public gathering with media in attendance that is not heavily made up of his supporters."

Mark looked over at Collins and then back to Lewis and added, "Having set piece gatherings of adoring followers will make him look weak. Leaders look like leaders when they are willing to confront the opposition or people who are not already their followers. He will not fix this problem or win back his supporters if the only people he's with are those who were already for him. We are dealing with expectations here. The press have been looking for him to stumble. If no one expects him to say, 'I'm sorry,' that's exactly what he should do. He needs to be unpredictable to correct for some of the damage the speech has caused."

Collins nodded. "Absolutely. And, the sooner the better."

Safta looked over at Lewis. "George, can you get him to do it?"

Lewis, with a long face, said, "I don't know. And I'm getting press calls from the media saying you consultants are telling them that you are becoming disillusioned with the campaign."

Collins quickly responded, "Well, it's not coming from me."

Larry King

Bartow and Larry King sat facing each other on the set of the popular talk show.

King leaned in toward Bartow. "So if you had it to do over, would you have said the same things?"

"'Course not. I was trying to say what I thought and do it in the spirit of friendship I was feeling. If I hurt anyone's feelings or if I could have said what I was trying to say better, of course I would say it differently."

King nodded sympathetically. "Well, I've known you for some time now, and I really believe you are sorry and that you are sincere."

"You know, Larry, sometimes I'm just too darn open. Maybe it's a problem, but I don't want to change who I am. I don't filter things like most politicians and nine times out of ten it works okay, but sometimes it doesn't."

"Well, aside from the speech, how is the campaign going? Is it as much fun as you thought it'd be?"

"Larry, I must be doing something right 'cause I've got all of them after me."

King furled his brow with confusion. "What do you mean?"

"Well, every time I turn around, there's a car behind me. They've got people trying to infiltrate my campaign. They're out following not only me but my wife and family. The other night my guards chased three people from my back lawn. They did not catch them, but they saw them running away."

King, now sensing a larger news story, looked even more troubled. "Well, this is unusual, to say the least. Who is doing all this?"

"I don't know. I don't know if it's the Democrats, the Republicans, our government, or some other entity here or abroad. All I know is that my being in the race has revved them up."

King, now leaning on one elbow toward Bartow, said earnestly, "But none of this has been reported. Why haven't you called in the police or the Secret Service? This is America. No one should be able to intimidate a presidential candidate."

"Well, that's just it. The press don't want to report the truth. They are only interested in 'gotcha' journalism. Besides, I've got very good security. But it's not me that gets bothered by all this. What I don't like is these people bothering my family. That's a low blow. Like, remember when that fellow threw paint at me.? I can take it. But when they go after my wife and family, that's beyond the limits of decency, and I'll have to admit that bothers me."

"Why hasn't anyone done anything to stop it?"

"I don't want a herd of local police or the Secret Service all over me; I couldn't get any work done. But we are going to keep a sharp lookout and one of these days we'll catch one of them and won't that be interesting? Won't it be interesting if it's one of the dirty tricksters from our opponents?"

King shifted in his seat. "There are also some rumors that you are planning on asking everyone in your campaign to sign a loyalty oath. Is that true?"

"I don't know where you heard that, Larry, but an employer does have some, you know, expectations of support by his employees. I think that is just standard in any job situation. Like a non-compete when someone leaves a job, or a confidentiality agreement. I think that is standard practice. Soldiers take an oath to support their nation. Where would we be without loyalty?"

"Indeed. We've got to take a break here and when we come back, we'll be taking your phone calls with William Bartow, independent candidate for President of the United States."

Collins' Office

Reid Field, Peter Newman, and John Burchmeyer entered the offices of Ralph Collins and the other consultants who had come to the campaign with him. Newman was carrying a batch of papers. Collins' secretary, ever officious, stopped what she was doing and politely welcomed the men.

Ralph Field spoke for the group. "Hello. We're here to see Ralph Collins."

"Oh! He's in a meeting just now. Was he expecting you?"

Field leaned into her desk. "I don't believe he was, but if you'll tell him we're here, I believe he will agree it is important enough to interrupt his meeting."

Trained to protect Collins from such interference, she gave herself a quiet harrumph. "Ah. Yes. Whom shall I say is calling?" They told her. Now recognizing the names, she said, "Oh! Of course. Excuse me, please." She went into Collins' office and was gone for a minute or so. Then she came back out, and Benny Weinstein followed her.

Weinstein nodded at the three Bartow administrative leaders. "Hi, guys." He gave Burchmeyer a more solemn look. "We're just in a budget meeting. Is there anything I can do to help you?"

Field, with a serious face, responded, "Not at the moment. However, we may wish to talk to you shortly. Will you be around?"

Weinstein pointed. "Right there in my office."

Collins' secretary then added, "Please, gentlemen, go right on in."

Weinstein slowly looked back at Collins' closed door, shrugged his shoulders, and said to his secretary, "I'll be in my office."

About 30 minutes later, there was a knock at Weinstein's

door. "Come in."

Peter Newman entered. "Mr. Weinstein?"

"Yes. Peter, isn't it? Please come in. What can I do for you?"

"Well, you know we've just had a visit with Mr. Collins. We are now visiting his staff individually. I know he'll want to speak with you as soon as we finish."

"Why? What's going on?"

"It came to our attention about two weeks ago that there were some potential irregularities in some of our campaign billing."

"Like what?"

"First, we did a good bit of checking and allowed a payment cycle to pass to confirm our suspicions."

"Peter, I'm busy. Could you cut to the chase?"

"Well, we found that you and most of the others on Mr. Collins staff seem to have organized shell companies under your control, which were listed as vendors to this campaign. In particular, you have authorized payments to a direct mail firm which carries the same address as your political consulting firm."

"So, what? You mean you've been snooping around here for weeks while we've been killing ourselves trying to get your boss elected president?"

"Mr. Weinstein, whatever you may think of us, we do know how to manage money and administer a company's business. Part of our job is an ability to detect fraud."

"What the hell are you trying to say?"

"Mr. Weinstein, I trust that we can discuss this in a calm and rational manner. I know what I am doing, and you needn't insult my intelligence or demean yourself further by denying the facts."

Weinstein frowned. "Mr. Newman, I don't care what you think you know. I will say that however you decide to run some stick-up-the-ass widget factory is not how you run a presidential campaign. It is an accepted practice to farm out work to good consulting firms for their expertise. That's how it's done in politics."

"Yes, but the fact that you are laundering funds from this campaign for a 10% haircut before you pay a vendor for some mailing lists to actually do the work is not considered usual or appropriate.

"You are being paid considerably above market rates for your time here. Your employment contract specifically states that you are not to charge other fees to the campaign. However, to make sure, we checked with four other sources in the political consulting business and our assumptions were correct. Your practice was not only unethical, but it is likely prosecutorial. Our legal team has been over the contracts and our judicial position is solid."

"You fucking clerk. Get the hell out of my office."

"I'll be happy to leave in a moment. First..." Peter Newman pulled out several pieces of paper and laid them on the desk. "I have several documents that you need to sign. I'm sure you will want some time to look them over. However, I will need them returned to me by five o'clock this afternoon."

Weinstein looked down at the papers and his tone was now softer and less indignant. "You listen to me."

Peter Newman leaned forward. "NO. You listen to me. You sign these papers and we won't prosecute you. Sign these papers and we will never talk about this again. Sign these papers and keep whatever you have already stolen from this campaign. Sign these papers, resign from this campaign as of five o'clock today, get the hell out of these offices, and don't come back. That's the deal. That's the deal we offered Collins and what is being offered to your other buddies. I personally don't care what you do. I would love to get you in a courtroom because, win or lose, your ability to work in the campaign business would be over. If you do take this deal, you still have the chance to go rob some other poor, unsuspecting candidate."

"But you can't be serious."

"You'll note there is a clause in these documents, that if you talk about this any time in the future, the deal is off and we will prosecute you. If somehow this gets out to the press, we will find you and prosecute your slimy ass." Peter then got up and walked to the door. "Now, I'm sure you will want to talk this over with your colleagues. Remember, sign the papers and get out of this building by five. Turn in any security cards, cars, pagers, apartment keys, and anything else related to the campaign." He opened the door. "Goodbye, Mr. Weinstein."

With his face now several shades lighter, Weinstein picked up his phone and began to dial, then he held it out and looked at the receiver. "My God! The phone's dead."

Ashen-faced, the team of consultants met in Collins' office. Weinstein spoke for the others. "Ralph, what are we gonna do? If this gets out, we're screwed."

Collins pointed at Don Rizzo. "Everybody would have been just fine if you hadn't put that tag on the commercials and pretended you were in the commercial production business." Rizzo started to speak. Collins held up his hand. "I don't want to hear it."

Weinstein blurted out, "But boss, what are we gonna do now?"

Collins let out a sigh. "Pack up your stuff and get out of here like the gestapo said. Don't talk to any media. Anyone at all! Fortunately, I have a friend over at NBC who's been thinking of starting a new news network, kind of like CNN but with a more conservative message. Like Rush Limbaugh on TV 24/7. This Aussie, Murdock, wants to expand the Fox Entertainment Network into news. They're putting something together and it may take a couple of years to get the pieces in place, but I'm gonna see if there is a place for some political talent over there. My friend Roger Ailes thinks something with a sharper edge and more personality-driven news coverage would work. In the meantime, lay low or get whatever gigs you can find. There's gonna be a lot of stuff happening with computers. Cover your asses and we can talk in a few months."

The End

The next morning Mark, Ben Menendez, and Missy Winston were called to George Lewis' office. As they were walking together, Menendez said, "This meeting must be about the bloodbath."

Missy had a look of concern on her face. "Yeah. We're getting press calls from everywhere. That story about differences of opinion on policy decisions ain't flying. The news guys have heard that once too often."

Menendez continued, "Where does this leave us? Are we in charge? Is anyone?"

Mark mused, "It's pretty bad. We've got a candidate who's in shock. It's late in the game, and we've only recently gotten approval for our issues and media budgets. We had the stupid comments by our candidate that made him look like a racist from the 1930s. We've got high-profile management leaving suddenly."

Missy mouthed the obvious, "So, we're in deep doo-doo?"

Mark nodded. "We've always been floundering, but all this stuff has been piling up, and I'm not sure the campaign can survive. It might be a good time for me if the campaign was ending. Vicki found that she's pregnant again… we need to move back to D.C. and make plans."

As they entered the office, Lewis politely nodded. "I've just come from seeing Mr. Bartow. He's decided to announce he's withdrawing from the race."

Missy spontaneously burst out, "Oh!" and put a hand to her face.

Mark asked, "Is that firm?"

"He's coming over here to make an announcement an hour from now."

Mark moved into damage control mode. "What reason is he

going to give?"

Lewis sighed. "Well, he told me it was a combination of things. The media, the harassment, the speech, Collins, and his group, the... I don't know." He leaned back and took a deep breath. "I don't know what he'll say to the press. I don't know if he does either."

Later, as they walked to the press conference, Lewis said to Mark, "Too bad. I was getting to like the deficits and debt idea."

Mark smiled sadly. "It represents our future. If you wanted to redo all the schools, take care of public health, fix rundown neighborhoods, or if you wanted more research for our businesses or finance more business investment by our government or give more tax breaks, you could do it all with the money we pay in interest on the debt. Every year it gets worse. We are slowly killing ourselves over short-term desires, entitled behavior, and greed. The only way to stop that is to reverse the deficits.

"Now, both Democrats and Republicans will continue to make the same mistakes, to get money to spend because it's the easy way to get what they want. There is no adult in the room in Washington. It's too late now, but this campaign was our one shot to stop it. Now it's gone."

Mark stopped at the volunteer room to see the efficient Sally Crockett moving chairs around and setting up more televisions to watch the Bartow press conference. There was a chill in Mark's stomach as he saw the volunteers who he had known for many weeks now excitedly moving to find their sets near the front.

As he entered the media offices, he reflected on the losing efforts and the shock, denial, and eventual crush that would be hard to take with this much idealism in the campaign. At 10:00 a.m. as he settled near the wall, Bartow, in his trademark thin-lapelled suit and black tie, walked up to the podium and all the television lights turned on.

Georgetown

Paul Manafort sat at the table in the back of the small restaurant in Georgetown when Don Rizzo arrived. "Sorry for the timing. Still getting readjusted after our fast exit from Atlanta."

Manafort nodded. "Not a problem. After we blew the whistle on you guys, things worked out as well as we could have hoped."

"Yes. We're a little embarrassed at how it happened, but we'll all survive. I've got some corporate stuff coming up, but with your help, the party will let me back in by the next election."

Manafort cocked his head. "Anyone suspect anything... about you?"

"No. It came off clean."

"I'll see that you get a contract next week from an Eastern bloc country to cover what we had agreed. You won't have to do any work, just sign some papers and bill them for consulting through our firm."

"Okay. Have you guys done any polling to see how Bartow's dropping out will help President Bush?"

Manafort shook his head. "It's too soon. We'll let the dust settle for a few days."

Rizzo leaned forward. "How did you know Bartow would panic and buckle?"

"We didn't, but from what you told us, and just looking at his indecision and quirky nature, it seemed he was looking for a way out. It was a calculated risk, but he didn't belong in the game anyway."

"You should have given me a heads-up before dropping a dime on us and getting us fired."

"Yeah. Right."

After the meeting with Rizzo, Manafort stopped at a pay phone and dialed a number.

"Yeah?" a voice said.

Manafort looked around. "It's done. You were right to use the voice manipulator with that weasel Rizzo. He never suspected who you were. Can't trust him, but you know, Bartow's campaign has shown that a very rich guy with a high outside profile can make a real run at the top job."

Bruce replied, "Look, you keep doing whatever it is you do to make money by conning those suckers. Bartow was as rough as a corncob in an outhouse. Whatever happens in the other two campaigns, we've managed to keep the job in the hands of someone who will be predictable and will have some idea of what it takes not to screw up the world. We don't need to talk again." The phone went dead.

The Bad Man

Mark sat with his head down across from Bruce in a coffee shop in Tyson's Corner, a Virginia mall across the Potomac River from Washington, D.C. Bruce had just finished saying that he was glad they could be seen together again in public.

Mark stirred the remainder of his eggs, looked down at the table, and said, "I need something from you."

Bruce raised his hands apart and then dropped them back on the table. "Okay, what?"

"This thing is about the incident in Piedmont Park back during the campaign."

"Look, I don't know—"

Still looking down at the table, Mark raised one hand with his palm toward Bruce, which was the first time he had ever stopped him from saying anything. Earlier, when Bruce denied knowing what had happened to Livy, Mark figured that he was in on it. However, now still looking down, he said, "I'm not saying you were involved. I am just saying, I want a name. I want an address and I want a phone number."

"You can't ask for something that might lead you to… there are laws that will be enforced. You are talking crazy."

Now Mark was as angry and determined as he had ever been in his life, as he looked up from the table and into Bruce's eyes. He held them, leaned forward, and could see what remained of Bruce's conscience squirming inside. "Get me that information by Monday." Mark stood and left Bruce with a concerned look on his face and the check.

The money for the simple job of intimidating someone's

business partner sounded like a great deal to the man. Too good to pass up, so he headed to the appointment to review the details, driving south from Lawrenceville on Georgia 124 toward Snellville. The closed strip mall was run down with weeds sprouting in the parking lot, yet he easily found the former ice cream store with the door unlocked, as the voice had said it would be. It was dark inside without any electricity and he was glad he had brought his gun secured to his hip and a knife taped to his calf. He would not be comfortable or relaxed until the business was settled and he was paid.

He blinked to adjust his vision as he entered the dim space and walked back toward the counter holding his small pen flashlight. There he saw from the light a short stack of bills sitting on top of a paper towel. Well, that was promising sign. As he shined the small flashlight in one hand and reached for the money with the other, he was hit in the kidney by a blow that buckled his legs. Then a powerful arm grabbed him and rammed him into the three-foot-tall countertop. A hand grabbed him by the hair, pulled his head back, and then hammered his face again onto the metal surface. His nose broke and blood splattered all over the counter. Pain exploded in his head. He could feel a numbness in his mouth where his teeth had lacerated his lips and he felt the blood gag his throat.

Then he felt a newer, greater pain as he was hit again in his kidneys, three, four, five full blows that made the whole middle part of his body feel as though it was made of burning soup. He clutched the counter to hold himself up and then vomited and lay with his face in it for a moment until a foot crashed down on the back of his knee, dislocating it and dragging him onto the floor. He was barely conscious now and his mind begged for the pain to stop.

He gurgled and tried to crawl as he lay on his stomach, and then whoever it was grabbed one hand and cracked the index and middle fingers back, breaking them and then the thumb. Both hands. He was barely conscious now. Pain was everywhere. Nothing had been said. No more than 30 seconds had passed. He knew he would never be the same. He felt himself urinating. The gun was still secured to his hip, and the knife to his leg.

La Fonda Restaurant

After the Bartow campaign imploded, Ben Menendez was grateful to get back to his friends and family in New Mexico. He loved driving those open spaces and hiking up in the mountains with his family to the natural hot springs. Almost immediately, he was contacted by several political campaigns and two commercial accounts and was soon immersed in that new work even before he had a chance to decompress from Bartow.

A few weeks later, he had to go to Washington to check on a congressional bill that would affect one of his new clients. He welcomed the change of pace and took two extra days to visit with old friends in D.C.

On his last afternoon there, he and Mark nursed Corona beers at La Fonda, a Mexican restaurant on the corner of 17th and R streets. It was the first time they had been together since Atlanta. They soon breezed through the chitchat and were mostly quiet as they watched the creeping traffic and the young Washington staffers bustling down the street.

Ben spoke as he looked at the rush hour. "I wonder if we could have pulled it off? Or... I wonder if anyone will in the future."

Mark looked at him. "I have no doubt someone will. They'll need some of the same ingredients and timing, but our world is crazy enough for that."

"Think they'll come to ask us what we did?"

"Nah. Egos won't allow that. What we did won't matter in the future." Mark fiddled with a straw.

Ben felt a distance between him and his old friend. Something had changed in Mark. There were things unsaid that he needed to approach. He expelled a loud breath. "Did you know they are still working over at the campaign office? Still taking the calls in a smaller volunteer room. The military officers are still talking to people out in the states. Crazy." Ben crunched on a tostada. "I heard from one of those guys back with the Bartow field organization that they found this guy someplace outside Atlanta who had done some dirty work. When the police got into who he was and went through his stuff, they found all these tie-ins to political and corporate intimidation. Stuff like that. Anyway, it got back to Burchmeyer and that's how my friend heard about it.

Mark was quiet and continued to look out the window. He absentmindedly swiped some guacamole off a tostada and ate it.

Ben sniffed and hunched up straighter in his chair. "We'll, seems like he had Rizzo's phone number with him, and the speculation is that he may have done some dirty tricks on us, or something like that." Ben turned and looked out at the traffic for a minute or two.

Still facing the traffic, he said, "My guy said this person had some fairly significant injuries, like he was really fucked-up. Now you are my friend and I'm with you no matter what happened; I mean, if anything happened that involved you." More time passed, and Ben took a swallow of his Corona.

He now turned to face Mark. "It's just that I can't imagine you being aggressive like that. You are the most peaceful guy I know. Whatever happened to that bad guy had nothing to do with us. It's just not in your character. I told this guy to forget it, and that whatever happened to Livy would never be resolved. The main thing is that she is doing well now. Right?"

Mark smiled as he looked down at his beer. "Vicki teases me about being too... sort of serious and analytical... not emotional enough. She says it makes me good at the job of politics." He shook his head, still looking down at the beer. "I grew up in the rural places where I learned early on the life cycle of the cows, chickens, pigs, and horses. Later, when I got my gun at Christmas and was told that it would make me a man, I hunted rabbits, squirrels, birds, and that sort of thing. Any remorse I felt in the killing was covered by the Band-Aid I got from pats on the back from my father and others. I found Band-Aids useful for other deaths—family, friends, or pets who passed into glory.

Later they were used for broken hearts, embarrassing losses in sports and jobs, or academic failures.

"When I went to war and there were the losses of those who did not return, there was the familiar comfort of Band-Aids, always there to comfort. They kept the blood in there safe. They kept the pain away. Problem is, Band-Aids have a habit of getting unstuck at awkward times and places when you don't have a spare handy."

Ben wrinkled his brow. "I'm not sure…"

Mark looked over at his old friend. "Thank you for caring about me and Livy… well, for all of us." He took another swallow of his beer.

Ben now smiled more and nodded. "Yeah. I know that could not have been you. You are not like that. Or…"

Mark looked back down at his beer and continued in a distracted tone. "I remember when I was about eight, or maybe it was nine years old. I was at summer camp in north Georgia and we were going to spend the night camping on this island in the middle of Lake Rabun. They had a whole bunch of us kids at a boat dock pavilion with all our camping gear waiting to be shuttled to the island on a ski boat that would only take four of five at a time, so they had to move us in staggered loads. Took over an hour. One of the workers there, an older kid, was playing the jukebox, and a song by Little Richard came on.

"Now, I had never heard Little Richard. I was from a church-going family and was taught to be straight, to mind my parents, work hard in school, and all of that. It's likely that was the first real rock and roll record I ever heard. But when I listened to the power and pace of the music, it just changed me. It opened a door to possibilities I never knew existed. There it was right in front of me: the drive, the compelling lack of permission, the sin. There was a beat that moved forward, driving and running over all the brakes that had been installed in me since my first day in Sunday School.

I'm ready, ready, ready teddy,
I'm ready, ready, ready to rock 'n' roll.

Gonna kick off my shoes, roll up my faded jeans,
Grab my rock 'n' roll baby, pour on the steam,
I shuffle to the left, I shuffle to the right,
Gonna rock 'n' roll to the early, early night.
I'm ready, ready, ready to rock 'n' roll.

Mark smiled and shook his head. "Obviously, the lyrics were shit, but it was the overall power of it. I could tell from the music that there was another side to life. It was the place my parents had kept from me. It was the place adults went in the night and, though I knew it was wrong and sinful and taboo, there was something that awakened in me. Sitting there on that boat dock, I found passion in Little Richard's music and felt the anticipation of moving past my childhood."

Mark took in a deep breath. "I may not be seeing you out on the campaign trail as much. I've been talking with Angus Whelan and decided to do some consulting work for the Duncan Rogers firm in New York. They have a fairly good list of corporate clients, and I'm going to be working with them sort of as a part-time advisor in long-term strategy relating to politics and other areas."

"Like what?"

"Well, I'll go in and talk to the executives, look at their clients, talk to some employees in focus groups, and make suggestions of political stands to take and to support candidates that will be in their interest. They all have governmental affairs people, but this is just another layer, an outside view of what's in their interest. I think these big companies have so much money that they want to cover all the possible bases so no one can accuse them of not anticipating problems later on down the road. Gives them someone else to blame for mistakes. I'm not sure they will follow any of my recommendations, but whether they do or not, I'm being paid to give them."

"That sounds incredibly boring."

"Boring is kind of what I'm looking for just now. And I can do the job with limited travel. With Vicki being pregnant again, I want to be at home more. This job lets me do that."

"But you may drop off the radar of political consulting. Out of sight, out of mind."

"That's okay with me. I'm not sure I have the energy to work those long hours and deal with the stress and uncertainty again. I care about the direction things are going but just don't know if I still want to be in the middle of it anymore. Maybe I'll move into teaching at some point. I've got friends over at Georgetown and American University. Maybe I'll try to help train the next generation of people to charge the windmills."

"You'll miss it."

"Maybe, but not for now. Anyway, I wanted you to know." Mark had never mentioned to Ben his part-time job writing memos for the CIA. As he discussed pulling back from politics, he planned to pull back from Bruce as well. He'd have to be more careful with Bruce, because his controlling instincts would not want to let Mark go. He could be vindictive and sabotage Mark's plans to withdraw into a more private life, and Mark wanted to avoid that, as well as a confrontation with the smart and capable CIA agent.

Ben shook his head. "I can't see you being satisfied with just doing that."

Mark smiled. "Well, also I've been talking to some people I met about helping government analysis folks and some computer nerds on the outside. Vicki introduced me to them. They've got this research thing developed by DARPA. Anyway, I got to know some of the people who were involved in modifying the tools that grew out of the Internet Configuration Control Board and has evolved into something called the Internet Architecture Board."

Ben coughed. "That sounds SOOO boring."

"Yeah. I'm not involved the technical details. Anyway, one thing led to another and now there are growing commercial uses. It's about access to data, and I mean all the data that's out there. It's called the World Wide Web. The people I've known for a few years on the Internet Architecture Board have invited me to join them to consider approving standards and practices."

Ben squinted. "You're putting me to sleep here. Besides, we already have encyclopedias for that."

"Well, anyway, this World Wide Web Consortium is headed by a British guy named Tim Berners-Lee, who sort of invented linking everything into one big network. I met him a few years ago through Vicki. So, I'm going to be kibitzing on something that I believe could have real promise not only for the research, but maybe someday it could be a really big thing for politics and business."

Ben sat down his beer. "With you involved, whatever it is, it could only get better, but I can't see anything that nerdy ever catching on."

Home

Wearing a colorful maternity blouse, Vicki threw several bags on the couch from their shopping trip as she, Mark, and Livy entered their Washington home. The new clothes had been a reward after her visit to the doctor to confirm that her pregnancy was progressing well. Livy did not fully understand what was happening, but she could tell her parents were suddenly very excited and happy. They kept talking about moving into a new house and that there would be a big room for Livy with all her toys. Livy picked up a book that she loved to read over and over, opened it, and soon was lost in the story.

Mark turned on the TV to CNN. Vicki took the shopping bags to the bedroom and talked to Mark from there. "You are going to freak when you meet some of my cousins, but it will be good to see them again."

Mark walked around the apartment tidying up loose papers, including a couple of books on child-rearing and some travel brochures mixed in with the *Washington Post* and other material. Mark was half watching TV while he cleaned up. He saw there was a message on the answering machine to call Bruce, but he ignored it.

On the television, the CNN announcer was saying, "And we're back in Atlanta, where the news today has sent the political world into another spin." The TV screen showed images of the Bartow Headquarters from the exterior of the building, then into the large room, where he saw some of the same old volunteers still working the phones.

The screen image cut to Bartow. "And the volunteers just kept coming to me and there was no way I could refuse. But I told them, whatever you want to do I'll help in any way I can. But it's your show."

Mark could see Vicki passing back and forth beyond the

door to the bedroom, speaking loudly so he could hear. "You know Phil and Allison want to throw us a baby shower? She called me yesterday. I told her I didn't know when we could work it in, but that was so nice of them."

Mark noticed the television announcer saying, "Polls have shown Mr. Bartow's approval ratings have dropped to the mid-teens since his withdrawal two months ago, but his reentering the race may give those ratings a boost." Mark stopped his cleaning and looked more closely at the television.

Barrow was now saying, "This is a campaign for the volunteers. They are in charge and if they want me as a candidate, I don't see how I can refuse them after all they have done. This new change is a 'for the people' campaign."

Vicki, now raising her voice above the television, asked, "Mark, do you want to meet Tim and Molly at the Biograph or get something to eat first? We can go to one of those places right there on M Street and walk to the movie. Letty will be here to take care of Livy at six. You know, with that new guy in her life, we can't just count on her to be available whenever we want her anymore."

The television announcer continued, "For reaction to all this, we take you to Democratic campaign headquarters and Summer Storm. Summer, what's the mood there at the Democratic..."

Mark looked out the window, where the fall weather after a cold spell last week had begun to turn some leaves in the distance red and yellow.

Vicki said in a louder voice from the bedroom, "Anything in the news?"

He reached over and turned off the television, put down the remote, and went into the bedroom. "Nope. Let's just walk around Georgetown and have a popcorn supper at the movies."

The End

Afterword

This book is a work of fiction, but it contains factual and historical elements. If there is no change in the polarization between Democrats and Republicans, another serious third-party run will be made for the presidency, which will be possible because the internet has shown new ways to finance campaigns and reach voters.

There are additional issues/problems to consider:

Truth has become a casualty of what passes for news information. The substance of campaign messaging, always fragile, has become more tenuous. There are no facts anymore.

The public longs for someone who is genuine, sincere, and capable, but the inefficient method of vetting and selecting candidates needs reform. There is no system to hold candidates accountable or require them to actually tell the voters what they plan to do.

The media and political parties have done a poor job of explaining what is important and instead focus on the superficial and sensational. Phony reality news programs and the overmanaged grooming of candidates have created a false impression of what is genuine about a potential leader.

Underlying substantive financial problem

There are countless ways to look at the U.S. debt. The one thing most economists do agree on is that it took off with President Ronald Reagan. The rising deficit and the debt were becoming a crisis in 1992. Neither party has taken it seriously. It is a cancer eating at the future of this country and we may have passed the tipping point of recovery.

Congress no longer functions as a deliberative body looking out for the interest of our country and only acts as a cheerleader or deterrent to the executive branch. Today, Congress passes something called a continuing resolution instead of a real budget paid for with real revenue (i.e., taxes). They kick the can down the road.

The executive branch functions through executive orders that can be rescinded by the next president, resulting in no long-term policy advancement by our nation. We have no collective priorities. The one thing both operational branches of government can agree to do is to spend more money.

By about 2030 (if not before), we will have annual deficit spending of close to $5 trillion a year. That almost equals the entire federal debt in 1992, as discussed in this book. This is a runaway train. There is nothing in the institutions of our government or the motivations of our leaders to change the disastrous path we have taken.

Take a look at the trend lines on the chart below. Outside of our defense costs, they cover increases of running the basic functions of government. Note the solid line **interest** (what we must pay on the debt we have already accumulated). It's the rocket ship. There is no way to pay for it and eventually it will force dramatic reductions in everything else having to do with our federal government for generations to come. The dollar and all the assets we own will be devalued.

Spending Increases

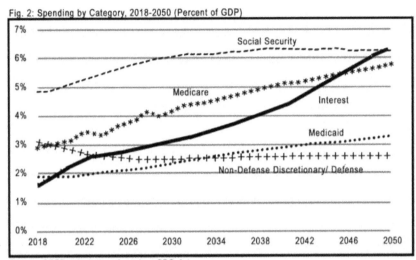

Fig. 2: Spending by Category, 2018-2050 (Percent of GDP)

Source: CRFB calculations based on CBO data

Other books by Jay Beck you may wish to read

The recent novel, *Island in the Storm*, reached # 1 on Amazon in the Disaster Recovery category

Reader comments on
Island in the Storm

"I bought this book to possibly enjoy some easy 'pandemic reading' for a few days. Little did I suspect that I would sit down in the early afternoon and not stop reading until I had finished the book that evening... This is a genuine 'page turner' story, masterfully told by an author who really knows his subject (or subjects)! A seemingly simple start to the book evolves into a complex and frightening plot, which is especially frightening because the author makes it all so believable. Well done, and thank you, Mr. Beck, for an enjoyable experience... Also, I've added Albany, Georgia, to my bucket list to visit... Sounds like a great and interesting place to enjoy."

"Jay Beck's skill in bringing the reader into the story is remarkable. The evolution of Henry, the conflict within himself, and the skills needed by the people who once shunned him showed an intense development of his character and inner strength. In addition, the detailed defense of the town, strategic negotiations, and planning draw the reader into the reality of what life could look like in this reality. It's more than unnerving to wonder could I survive? What would I bring to the table? It leaves the reader with much to ponder. Thank you."

"Jay presents an apocalyptic story with all of the elements that exist today: polarized government, pandemic, computer viruses and a failing power grid. His characters are flawed yet heroic as they face a world I hope we never see. Great book!"

"Jay Beck has written with great detail and imagery of a dystopian future in rural Georgia. It's eerie how the book evokes recent and real fears of authoritarian governments, isolation, and social disfunction. The story is compelling and the characters are well-developed. Congratulations to the author."

"Jay Beck is a visionary writing a very timely and thought-provoking post pandemic novel! "Island in the Storm" brilliantly imagines human survival living without the basic needs taken for granted in the 21st century. Beck tells an intriguing action-packed story of endurance against all odds. He brings together two different worlds of ingenious survivalists living off the grid along the swamp and their Albany, Georgia neighbors who collaborate to defend their city. The suspenseful visual plot is filled with a commanding knowledge of the military and crisis management. The story is creatively interwoven with love, loss, loyalty and trust. I would love to see "Island in the Storm" made into a movie screenplay."

"Island in the Storm is a unique tale. The Island is in the middle of a vast Georgia swamp, occupied by a reclusive band of survivalists. The Storm is the result of the breakdown of society, in the wake of a virus, a depression, the loss of the electrical grid and optimum health care, plus shortages of everything. Ultimate confrontation finally takes place between desperate assailants and town defenders, now including the swamp people. Vignettes of characters are colorful, reflecting a unique southern culture, both literal and fantasied. Sometimes, Beck makes you feel as though you're living 150 years ago."

Jay Beck's book, *Casting Stones*, was awarded the best historical fiction written in Georgia by an independent writer for 2019.

Reader comments on *Casting Stones*

"I found this book to be gripping both for its intrigue related to the Greek election but also for the understory of the ancient statues of the Greek gods. Jay's background inside of a presidential election comes through the pages as you feel the reality of what he writes. Heartily recommend the book!"

"This is an interesting, extremely well-written historical novel about a young American political consultant advising a presidential campaign in Greece in the 1980s. The story is filled with political espionage and intrigue, well-developed characters, and fascinating descriptions of both Ancient Greek history and modern-day Greece. It's also the story of the behind-the-scenes battle between the United States and the Soviet Union to influence the political and economic future of Greece before the fall of the Soviet Union in 1991. I highly recommend the book."

"The author takes his incredible gift of storytelling, adds wit, suspense, and political expertise, and the result is another good book. I'm impressed with the way he takes his extraordinary professional experiences and weaves them into a narrative that is both compelling fact and fiction. I recommend this book and can't wait until the author's next book is out."

"In reading this book, you become totally involved in the characters. The descriptions of them in their many circumstances make you keenly aware of the dangerous time it was during the 1985 election in Greece not only for Mark Young but for the author as well. Reading about the treasures of Greece, Maria Beckett, a truly brilliant, passionate patriot and especially the author's brilliant writing is a must-read for everyone."

"Wow – this was an amazing book!!! Jay Beck's writing keeps the reader totally engrossed in the story!!! This is a historical novel – so as well as being a good story, you might just learn a little history while you are at it!!!"

"The story is set in Greece during the 1985 elections. The story is written in the perspective of Mark Young – who is a political consultant. The story tells a lot of the battle between the United States and the Soviet Union – in regard to the Greek election. I don't write spoilers – BUT, I will warn you that once you get into this story, that you will have a hard time putting the book down until you reach the ending. (I would be awake all hours of the night reading!)"

"You can count the truly riveting novels on campaigns and politics on one hand. But John Beck, with his hands-on knowledge of American consultants abroad, has produced another great read, following a previous story on a campaign in Panama. This time the action is set in Greece in the mid-eighties and the U.S. and the U.S.S.R. are both 'meddling' in tough and devious ways. And, again, Beck has a 'femme fatale' as a key player in the action, a Greek woman who may be the most interesting character (in my view) In the book."

His prior book, *Panama's Rusty Lock*, reached # 2 on Amazon in the Central and South American category

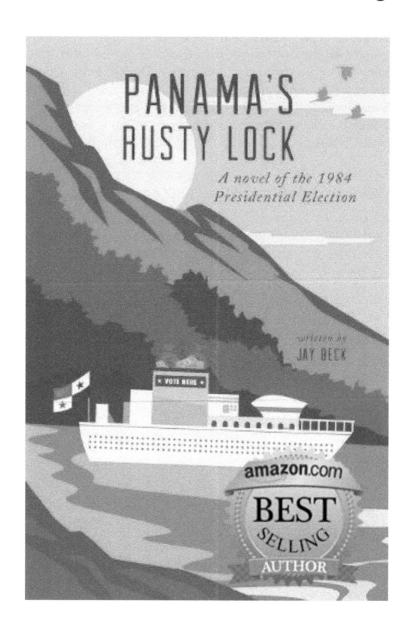

Reader comments on *Panama's Rusty Lock*

"Page-turning! Panama's Rusty Lock is interesting and intriguing. Jay Beck really is an insider that can communicate a story. Descriptions that are very vivid - a must read. Thank you, Jay, for showcasing the Panamanian story that has not been told in such a lively fashion. It is compelling to me and everyone else that I know that has read it. Modern history well written."

"As a history major in college, this book was impressive in its scope and the author's personal knowledge of actually being involved in the history as it was being made is an incredible read. Five stars seems inadequate. I give it 10."

"Best book I have read in many years. Don't miss it!"

"As someone who has never given Panama much thought at all, I didn't expect to be very engaged here. Jay Beck managed to yank me out of the comfort of my home and into a climate of political unrest and corruption. The unsettling accounts of the drug trade in the area was by far my favorite part, and I will be seeking out books on that subject in the future. Panama's Rusty Lock will appeal to those who love their drama mixed with politics."

"I absolutely love historical fiction and non-fiction books, and it seems like they have come together in Panama's Rusty Lock: A Novel."

"I would highly recommend it, especially to lovers of historical fiction."

"Panama's Rusty Lock is a fascinating backstory of the 1984 presidential election in Panama, the country's first free political election in 16 years. The author, Jay Beck, takes the reader on a deep dive into the machinations of multiple, and warring, political entities during the campaign and, in the process, reveals a land rife with corruption, drug trafficking, fraud, CIA sponsored wars, abuses of power, and endless spying. Jay Beck, who worked in Panama on this campaign, captures the essence and exposes the underbelly of this landmark political event. Highly recommend."

"I absolutely love historical fiction and non-fiction books and it seems like they have come together in Panama's Rusty Lock: A Novel. I learned quite a bit about Panama and the world around it - something I hadn't really read about before. Usually, when we think of historical fiction, we think of wartime novels, but that certainly isn't the case here. The unrest and corruption felt hauntingly real and I appreciate that, no sugarcoating, but no overdramatization as well. Certainly, a great read for anyone who wants to know more about Panama's history or anyone who just wants a great story. Note that there are some elements of drug culture for those that are sensitive to it."